1924 and
You Are There!

A fictionalized baseball replay

JEFF POLMAN

Grassy Gutter Press
Culver City, CA

Cover photo courtesy Library of Congress
Title page photo from Google Images
Page 9 photo courtesy Everett Collection
Page 27 photo courtesy Underwood & Underwood/Corbis
Page 75 photo from Google Images
Page 117 photo courtesy Library of Congress
Page 165 photo courtesy U.S. Postal Service
Page 227 photo courtesy Library of Congress
Page 265 photo from Google Images
Author page photo by Carmen Patti, 2004

BEFOREWORDS

Welcome to something different. *1924 And You Are There!* is a book for lovers of pure baseball, meaning baseball without steroids, without contract news and without wet, freezing World Series games past midnight. It is also for lovers of story and character, and for the fun of not knowing how either will turn out.

Back in the early 1960s, Hal Richman invented a fun, realistic baseball board game called Strat-O-Matic Baseball, and has developed it into a hard-earned success. With its uniquely crafted cards for every player, you have the ability to enter a baseball world from the past or present with the mere drop of three dice.

For a little over a year beginning in February, 2009, I replayed the 1924 season in Strat-O-Matic's super advanced format, and reported the daily events through the eyes and words of 17-year-old Phillie fan Vinny Spanelli and others, in the language of the time, on my Google Blogger Web site. I had no idea how the season and format would play out, because the schedule and game results basically dictated the direction of the plot, but I was more than happy with how the fictitious baseball world of 1924 unfolded, and especially how the characters blossomed as the months progressed.

Hopefully you will also enjoy your time spent with them.

—*J.P.*,
Culver City, CA

8. PHILADELPHIA. And then we have the Quakers, a sorry collection of what-nots, if-onlys, wish-they-coulds and why-bothers, who should emit foul athletic odors to every region of the latrine-like Baker Bowl. Do you doubt my words? Said Phillie "hurlers" allowed 1008 runs in 1923, which by my calculations is approximately two hundred more than any other club in base ball. My pity for the followers of this reeking outfit is bottomless; they should be allowed into their grandstands free of charge, much as witnesses would to an execution.

— Excerpted from "McGraw's Mashers Set to Reclaim
World's Title in National League"
by Calvin J. Butterworth,
Detroit Free-Enterprise, April 10, 1924

for Jake and Hooch

PART ONE
April

SOMEHOW I GOT A TICKET FOR OPENING DAY
April 12, 1924

Hi readers. I'm Vinny Spanelli, and I'm almost 18 so do not think for a second I ain't old enough to tell you about my Phillies. Plus my neighbor Mr. Rollo gave me this typewriter to use the night before he was shot and died in a bar fight on New Year's Eve, so I guess it's mine to write on forever as long as I don't keep Mama up at night with the clacking noise.

It's real hard to be a Phillies fan these days because the Giants have been league champs for three straight years and the Phils haven't won since 1915 when I was only eight and Pete Alexander wasn't a drunk yet. Papa was still alive then and he took me to one of the World Series games, but everyone in front of me had big coats and hats and I could mostly only see Bert Niehoff's legs while he played second base or a little bit of Gavvy Cravath out in right.

Like most of my friends do, I hate the Giants and especially their evil midget manager John McGraw. I plan to go to every Baker Bowl home game this year, but when the Giants come to town I will be there plenty early to find good seats for me and Benny. Benny Zepp is my best friend and he hates those Giants even more than me. Benny gets us in trouble sometimes, but he's also a real good friend. Once he almost got me an autograph from Cy Williams.

I sneak out of school all the time to go to the games but Benny doesn't go to school at all so he always gets me a ticket if he has enough money from selling newspapers that morning. Anyway, Benny made friends with lots of ushers and peanut guys and other people who work at Baker Bowl and he somehow got us third base tickets for the Opening Day game on Tuesday against the Braves, and I'm so excited I'm going to leave school before lunch instead of waiting for Mrs. Crackerbee to fall asleep at her desk.

Benny also reads the newspaper to me sometimes and said that a writer guy in Detroit named Buttercake or something said that the Phillies are probably the worst team in baseball this season. Oh yeah? When that dope comes here to watch his Tigers play the Athletics, which is a team that stinks worse than us, me and Benny are going to find him and punch a hole in his hat!

One of my next diary chapters will be after I get back from this opening game. Good night, reader people!

WHY THE PHILS WILL BE CHAMPS AGAIN SOON
April 14, 1924

I know it was nine years ago when the Phillies last won the league flag, but that means we had a lot of time to figure out what didn't work and fix it.

Our pitching last year stunk something awful, but now we just got Hal Carlson, a good ball-thrower in a trade with the Pirates, and he should help make the rest of the hurlers more stable. Jimmy Ring should throw many innings for us again, after supplying 304 of them last season. Whitey Glazner, Bill Hubbell and Clarence Mitchell weren't all that good, but I believe they will be better this time. Wait—my mama just yelled for me to come downstairs and brush the fleas out of the dog so I'll be right back...

Okay, I'm back. The captain of the hitters once more should be the incredible Cy Williams, who I think I told you I almost got an autograph from once. In 1923 Cy smashed 41 homers, most of them over the short fence in right field at Baker Bowl, and I saw most of them in front of my eyes so I know he did it. He also knocked in 114 runs, and I'll be surprised if enemy pitchers don't run for cover and hide every time he swings this year. Also in the outfield will be Johnny Mokan who hit .313 and maybe Curt Walker again except I'm not sure.

Manager Art Fletcher who seems real smart to me says that Walter Holke will play first base again. Walter used to be on the Braves and hit .311 for us last year with 31 doubles. We did have Cotton Tierney playing the second base, but I didn't like him much so I'm glad he's gone and that we got Hod Ford from the Braves to take his place. I guess we like old Braves or something. Heinie Sand plays at shortstop and has two big problems: He hits like a flea, and he calls himself Heinie even though his real name is John Henry. Seems to me there's too many of these players with Hun nicknames already. My papa didn't die on that French battlefield six years ago so we could watch these kraut-eaters every day.

I have to stop soon and get to bed so I can get up early for school and Opening Day, so I'll talk more about the Phillies team as I watch them. Also, don't forget there's no home games on Sundays because of the Church Day laws, so that will be a good time for me to put any of my new thoughts in order.

Tomorrow for the first game they will have extra streetcars running from here in South Philadelphia to the North neighborhood where Baker Bowl is, so I should have no problem getting to the field and finding Benny in time. I have never missed a first pitch in my life and don't expect to now.

THE BEST OPENING GAME I EVER SAW
April 15, 1924

So I snuck out the door behind the auditorium right before lunch, jumped on the Broadway streetcar and got to Baker Bowl 15 minutes before game time with the trolley only breaking down once. West Lehigh Avenue and 15th were real stuffed with people, especially kids, and it took a minute to get around them and find Benny, who was waiting for me with one of Mr. Brown's victory sausages. (We used to call them frankfurters before the War.)

Anyway, we found our seats, smack in the middle of a bunch of runaway businessmen in big coats and hats, which we didn't mind because it was awful cold and they made it all warmer. We were behind third base with a good view of the short, 60-foot right field wall, and we could see some kids sitting on top of it like crows. A band played and the guy with the big megaphone said the lineups and the season was here!

Jesse Barnes started for the Braves and reliable Jimmy Ring for our Phils. Ring got out of two early pickles with double play balls, and then some Braves dope named Ed Sperber dropped an easy fly by Ring for a 2-base botch to start the 3rd. Holke doubled after an out and we were up 1-0! After Russ Wrightstone hit a scoring fly in the 5th it was 2-0 and me and Jimmy hooted and hollered until the men around us gave us dirty looks.

There was a real exciting play in the 6th. That crazy man Stengel walked for the Braves, and manager Bancroft doubled into the corner with two outs. Casey ran all the way around but George Harper fired a cannon throw, Butch Henline blocked the plate and Stengel was out to end the inning! Boston got a run in the 7th, but then Holke doubled in another for us, and then Barnes gave up a single and doubles by Ford and Sand and it was suddenly 5-1! Ring looked like a champion. The game was over.

But I've been warned never to expect easy wins at Baker Bowl. Ring got no one out in the 9th, with singles by Gibson, Padgett and Smith and a pinch double by Powell that made it 5-3. Huck Betts took over for him but threw a home run ball to Sperber that cleared the wall in right and probably bounced on the train tracks. We were losing 6-5. Skinny Graham pitched now for Boston, but he was awful too. Holke hit his third double, Joe Schultz got a pinch single, and with two out Mokan doubled for the tie! Schultz raced around but Stengel unbelievably threw him out at home! Benny screamed and smashed his peanut bag with his shoe. Extra innings!

Graham and Betts quieted things down until the first two Braves walked in the 12th. Betts got two outs but Les Mann pinch doubled for two runs and it was 8-6 Boston. But Woehr doubled to start our 12th, Cy Williams who did nothing the whole day finally walked, and Mokan doubled to make it 8-7. Stryker came on to relieve and got Henline, Ford and that no good Heinie Sand to finish the game. Agony!

Riding the streetcar back afterwards I was still glad they fought so hard and almost won lots of times. At least we found out we can beat this team.

I stopped at Mort's Cigars before I went home to get the other National League finals and some details. I'll be doing this most every day. Mort has a betting parlor in the back with the latest baseball news and lets me in because he used to know my papa.

Anyway, tomorrow's another game, reader-people!

BOS 000 000 105 002 — 8 15 2
PHL 001 010 121 001 — 7 15 0

WE TAKE NO PRISONERS!
April 16, 1924

Me and Benny were plumb tired after yesterday's crazy first game, but we sure didn't expect anything this easy.

The crowd was a lot smaller, and we went to our usual place in the left field bleachers with a real good view of Johnny Mokan. If we yell at him between innings sometimes he fetches us a spare ball from the dugout and throws it our way, but today he must have been in a lousy mood because he didn't even turn around when Benny said "You're my dad's favorite Mr. Mokan!" Johnny didn't know that Benny doesn't have a father, so I guess he just was too busy concentrating.

And all the Phillies did! Cy Williams singled in a 1st inning run off Cooney, and then would you believe Johnny Mokan clubbed one high toward left the next inning, and it dropped a row behind us for a two-run home run! He decided to hit the ball to us instead of throw it, and Benny rolled around on the wood planks with two bigger guys trying to get it but got a scratched face instead.

Bill Hubbell gave up a few Braves hits but they couldn't score even once, while the Phillie bats went cuckoo. Cy smashed his first homer of the year in the 7th to make it 5-0, and after Holke's double knocked Cooney off the field in the 8th, this rube named Al Yeargin took the ball and Jimmie Wilson bonked a grand slam that went farther over our heads than Mokan's ball!

It was a fantastic first win, even though we heard from Gambling Gus on the way out that the dumb Giants had won, too. But Benny was still happy enough to come with me to Mort's Cigars later. Mort had a couple jugs of whiskey under the floor in the back and Benny had a few samples until he started singing negro songs and they threw us both out.

BOS 000 000 000 — 0 7 0
PHL 120 010 15x — 10 16 0

BAD DAY TO HAVE A SICK SISTER
April 17, 1924

Poor Benny! While he was home putting wet cloths on his little sister's forehead, I was in the Baker bleachers munching warm salted peanuts and watching our Phillies smack the crummy Braves around for the second straight day. Hal Carlson made his first start after coming over from Pittsburgh and he was pretty darn good, giving up only eight hits and a run. Meanwhile the Phils tore up Larry Benton for six runs in the 1st inning with Cy tripling for two runs and Sperber tripping over himself in right field on a ball that Sand hit. It was awful ugly.

The game got boring after that so I sat with Gambling Gus after the 5th. Gus always sits in the same spot, which is right over the heat from a sausage man underneath the bleachers, and he bets on everything you can possibly bet with anyone who will bet with him. Not just if the next pitch will be a ball or strike, but who will get the next double or walk, how many balls Casey Stengel will catch, even how many seconds the wooden bleachers will rumble for when the train goes under the outfield in right. I only had some nickels left so I bet just once whether someone would hit a homer, and guess what? Hod Ford poked one out in the 8th against his ex-team and I made a quarter on it! Good old goofy Gus.

BOS 000 100 000 — 1 8 1
PHL 600 020 02x — 10 11 0

WE BOMBARD BOSTON AGAIN!
April 18, 1924

Mr. Tuggerheinz saw me duck out the back door today just before lunch and he almost got me by the ankle but I was too quick. It's a good thing because if he did I probably would've missed or been late for the THIRD STRAIGHT Phillies win! We scored over ten runs in each of them and today the top of the lineup must have had rabies or something close. Mokan, Holke, Harper and Cy went 14-for-18 with five doubles and a Holke homer and boy do the Braves ever stink. Oeschger pitched for us and he's really no good but the weak Brave lineup was helpless all over.

Thank God Benny was back because he would've been real sore if he'd missed this. Hod Ford even homered again in the 8th with the game long gone and Benny tried to talk the kid who caught it into giving him the ball but the kid had rotten teeth and a dirty face and looked like he could've whipped him silly.

Now the Brooklyn Robins are coming for four games, except for Sunday when everyone's supposed to go to church instead, but forget about that for me. I'll be over at Mort's getting all the details of other games. As for tomorrow I have to try and find a new way to escape school without that creepy Tuggerheinz seeing me. I'll work on it.

BOS 000 220 021 — 7 13 1
PHL 201 305 12x — 14 18 0

LOOKS LIKE A CRAZY WEEKEND
April 19, 1924

Well, I found a better way to sneak out of school for today's game, a window that was open a crack in the boy's bathroom, but didn't know Mr. Tuggerheinz was hiding in a stall waiting for me. He grabbed me and hauled me to his office for a ruler whacking and half hour of lecture, and I told him I had a sick brother and had to take care of him every afternoon. I also promised to make up any time I missed and he said okay but I hope he never finds out I don't have a brother.

Anyway, I missed my streetcar and had to run over to a different street and hop another one. Somehow I ended up in some scary Irish neighborhood, so I found a guy who had a recent map and he got me configured the right way, but I ended up missing Whitey Glazner get butchered by Brooklyn for 11 hits and 8 runs in the first three innings. This was probably one of those disguised blessings. Benny was so bored by the time I got there he was gambling on foul balls with Gus.

The Robins got 19 hits altogether, and we only got eight off Tiny Osborne. Plus we hadn't made an error all year and threw three away in this one. Believe it when I say we were garbage-eaters.

But the big news is that the day off I thought we were getting tomorrow for Church Day is not a day off at all. The teams are taking the train up to Brooklyn for the opening Ebbets Field game and then coming back, meaning we won't get to see Dazzy Vance pitch on Monday like we were counting on! Benny really wants to find a way to travel up to Brooklyn but my mama will burn her muffins if she knows I did that.

So I guess I won't tell her. Benny's going to come wake me up first thing tomorrow with a plan for how we're going to get up there. He's crazy so I trust him to come up with one. If it happens it'll be my first time ever in New York!

BRK 062 002 011 — 12 19 1
PHL 000 001 100 — 2 8 3

ME AND BENNY AND DAZZY AND RACHEL
April 20, 1924

I was wrong about old Benny. He couldn't wait till daylight and climbed up the drainpipe to my window at 4 a.m., all excited. He knew this colored man named Collins at the train station who moved luggage, and because Benny saved him once from getting beat up, he owed Benny a favor. Collins would hide us in empty fruit crates and load us into the freight car of the 6:15 to New York City but we had to be down at the Broad Street station way before then. I borrowed some money from Mama's drawer, left her a note that I was going to an all-day church outing with some kid from school, and off we went.

The opener at Ebbets Field began at 2 p.m. so we'd be there plenty early, which was good because we still had to find tickets somehow. My empty crate smelled like grapefruit and Benny's like brussel sprouts, which was too bad for him. While the train was moving we stuck our heads out and talked, even played a little cards on top of a third crate. Collins had already talked to a porter friend of his on the train. I think his name was Oscar and when we got to New York he wheeled us off himself and helped us sneak up a back stairway. If we had any spare money we would have tipped the heck out of him.

Pennsylvania Station in Manhattan was the most beautiful building I'd ever been in, like a big church of traveling, but we had to keep moving and finally found the right elevated train that would take us across the Brooklyn Bridge.

Ebbets Field was another kind of church, and it was nice to be in a city where they weren't afraid to make God mad by playing ball on Sundays. The streets around the park were stuffed solid with men in bowlers and dark coats and even some fine ladies, like they all thought they were going to the opera. We had a couple of hot dogs that were most delicious, then watched a row of kids line up on their bellies to peek under an outfield fence. Benny would have none of that, and when he saw this real drunk fan pass out while waiting in line to get in, Benny picked his pocket clean—and got us two lower box tickets for his effort. He was a lowlife so we were sure he was just going to sell them for a much higher price. They should come up with a name for that kind of person.

It was a beautiful place inside—much nicer than Baker Bowl—with a bright green field, double deck stands, and smells of sausages and cigars everywhere. Left field was pretty deep at 419 feet, center field was a mile away at 450, but right field was an easy poke like in our park—292—so things looked good for Cy today. Our seats were right behind home plate, and we couldn't believe our good luck. Benny wore his Phillies cap and it was cold enough for me to wear my Phillies sweater, which I turned inside out to be safe.

We didn't have to worry about angry Brooklyn fans, though. Jimmy Ring walked three in the 1st and the Robins took a quick 2-0 lead. Zack Wheat singled in two the next inning, and Dazzy looked dazzling. Vance throws an incredible curve ball that we could hardly see, so we knew our hitters couldn't. We had no hits the first five innings and were behind 6-0 by the 6th. A young, pretty girl about four rows behind us kept standing up and screaming for her Robins, and Benny kept looking at her but I think he was more attracted than anything.

Then in the 6th we came alive. Ring singled, Mokan doubled, Harper doubled them in and when Cy Williams cracked a ball into a pasture beyond the right field fence, we jumped up and cheered crazy for the Phils. The girl gave us dirty looks from then on, but those turned out to be our only runs for the game.

After we lost 8-4, we were walking out and this same girl came up behind us. She had another girl with her who wasn't as cute, and I think she felt bad about the dirty looks or she was just happy Brooklyn won because she asked if we wanted to go drink some sodas with rum in them at their rooming house up the street.

Turns out this girl who was about 20 and whose name was Rachel had been a Brooklyn fan since she was seven and went to almost every game like me, even though it wasn't supposed to be right for a young lady to do that. We saw maybe ten other females there the whole day. Her friend's name was Dolores and she was awful shy, and because Benny was making moves on Rachel I kind of just sat there and sipped some of the illegal rum they had. After that we put on Rachel's Victrola and danced a little but I got sick pretty fast and we had to find our way back to Pennsylvania Station before long. Benny wanted to stay longer and go to a picture show with them or something but I just couldn't, so he told me to go on ahead and he would take a later train.

Sitting in the same fruit crate on the way back that night, all I could think about was Rachel's pretty face. She hated the Giants even more than I did, and I never thought that was possible. New York lost at the Polo Grounds that same afternoon, right across town, and I'm sure that made her want to have a party even more. Maybe I should have stayed in Brooklyn with them, but at least I was able to remember her address. I think she might even have been Italian...

Nope, Baker Bowl just won't feel the same tomorrow.

```
PHL 000 004 000 — 4 9 1
BRK 220 021 01x — 8 10 1
```

A NICE DAY TO RECOVER
April 21, 1924

I had no problem with Mama last night, even though I got home at almost eleven. See, there was a flower man at the station and I bought some daisies from him, then told her that I picked them special for her, right from the meadow we had our church picnic in, so that was that.

Mrs. Crackerbee gave me a pat on the head this morning in class because Mr. Tuggerheinz must have told her about my sick brother, so I think I'm free and clear to leave school early for games whenever I want. Except today I might have had more fun learning my division because Brooklyn bombarded our spirits again by an unholy 18-5 score, which included 24 safeties. Bill Hubbell, who pitched like a champ for us his first time against the Braves, got his rump waxed for 10 hits in a bit over two innings before Fletcher sent him on his way.

We were behind 13-2 in the 5th when Benny finally arrived in the bleachers. His eyes were all red and he was moving like he was still asleep or something, and he was sure glad he missed the first half of the game. He ended up sleeping in a Brooklyn alley all night because Rachel made him leave around ten at night when he tried to smooch her and she said she didn't like him that way. Benny said to heck with girls, especially Brooklyn ones, and I said yeah you're right even though I was secretly glad she didn't like him.

Anyway, Benny was in a foul mood the rest of the game and was really giving it to the Robins players, even Zack Wheat in left, who hit a homer in this one along with Jack Fournier their clean-up man. Clarence Mitchell came in for us to wipe up the mess, but he just added to it, allowing three in the 8th and two more in the 9th. By then most everyone had left Baker Bowl so me and Benny snuck down to the real good field seats to watch the bottom of the 9th.

It's incredible how much more you can see from up close. Burleigh Grimes was still pitching for Brooklyn, and the big blue "B" on his jersey was all smudged with red dirt from running the bases earlier. Hod Ford hadn't shaved in a few days and Heinie Sand was even dumber-looking than we thought. The Phillies got two walks with one out in the inning, and then they started hitting right in front of us. Harper lined a single to load the sacks, Holke singled into right for a run, and then Wrightstone, who Fletcher moved to the 3-spot and got four hits, singled in two more! We were going to watch a miracle comeback! Jolly fat Wilbert Robinson went to the hill and replaced Grimes with some guy named Ehrhardt and we stood up and shouted and didn't care what the few well-heeled types around us thought. The ushers had mostly gone home, too. Cy Williams was coming up, and in a ballgame, anything is always possible.

But then Cy grounded into an easy double play on the first pitch and *we* went home.

BRK 317 020 032 — 18 24 0
PHL 100 100 003 — 5 12 3

PHILS TAKE ROBINS DOWN WITH EXTRA BIRDSHOT
By Vincent Q. Spanelli the Third
April 22, 1924
It was nice to have Benny with me for a whole game, and for the weather to get a little warmer, because let me tell you, baseball isn't supposed to be played on tundras. And I was in such a good mood after today's thriller that I ate all of Mama's broccoli stew and gave myself a fancy reporter's name for the day.

Jimmy Johnson popped a cheap homer off the foul cage in left off Carlson to get Brooklyn's scoring going, but Andy High made a bad boot for them at second base to help us tie the game in the 3rd. Then the Robins got a real lucky run, when Wheat doubled with two outs in the 5th and ended up scoring on Carlson's wild pitch, which was basically a 1 out of 20 chance of getting past catcher Wilson.

Me and Benny were going bananas, though, because we must've had at least two guys on base every inning and couldn't move them an inch. Finally Sand hit a sac fly in the 8th, we were tied, all 9,000 or so of us were yelling, Benny was chucking peanuts at Zack Wheat, and we had a chance! Johnny Couch took over for Carlson and he started leaving Robins all over the bases.

Wrightstone started a third to catcher to first double play to get us out of the 9th, then walked to start our 10th. Cy Williams, who had not hit a lick in a pinch for days, then smoked a single into right to get Wrightstone to third. Our left field friend Mokan then bounced a single between Mitchell and High for the winner, and no hats were left on heads at the Baker Bowl.

We're back at .500 as we hit the trail again, this time to Braves Field in Boston and uh oh...the Polo Grounds. Think I've had enough travelling for a while, though, so I'll suffer through these games down at Mort's. He gets telegraph reports all day and serves a wicked cherry soda.

BRK 010 010 000 0 — 2 13 1
PHL 001 000 010 1 — 3 9 2

A ROUGH AFTERNOON AT MORT'S
April 23, 1924
When the Phils are out of town, I basically got two choices to follow

them: take a streetcar up to Broad Street News to watch the fake players move around on their diamond board, or head over to Mort's Cigars. And I already told you I was going there today so I guess it's no surprise.

Mort had the cherry soda fountain all ready to go, and poured me one the second I walked in. Benny didn't come because he decided to sneak into the Athletics home opener at Shibe Park instead. That idea didn't excite me, because I'm way too far gone for the Phillies to root for those second-division idiots.

Anyway, Mort had his telegraph cooking with news from Braves Field every few minutes, and I jumped off my stool when the first ticker for the top of the 2nd read MOKAN HOME RUN. The next one said SINGLES BY SAND, FORD AND OESCHGER. 2-0 PHILLIES and I put a nickel down for my second cherry fizzer.

Norbert the Naysayer was over at a table playing gin rummy, and every time I hooted or hollered he pounded his beverage glass on the table and yelled "Just you wait, sonny, just you wait!" I hate being called sonny. You'd think grownups would take a minute sometimes to learn your stupid name.

But either Norbert the Naysayer was right or he put a big whammy on us, because Mort's ticker for the last of the 5th read POWELL HOME RUN, 2-1 PHILLIES and in the 8th it was POWELL TRIPLE, CUNNING-HAM PINCH SINGLE, 2-2.

From then I was too nervous to drink any more soda and had two fresh hot pretzels instead. Mort's lucky because he's so busy selling drinks and cigars and making sure card games and betting is going on that he doesn't have time to get broken up when the Phillies blow games.

And he was sure glad when those three cops came in later to get their payoffs, because he missed Huck Betts throwing the game down the laundry chute in the 11th. McINNIS SINGLE...STENGEL WALK...GIBSON WALK...I let the ticker paper roll into my hand but kept my eyes closed, then finally opened them to read BANCROFT SINGLE, BRAVES WIN 3-2.

Supposedly they had a warm Indian spring day in Boston, so I'm sure the Braves fans were thrilled. It's easy to be when your team hasn't won a pennant in ten years. Hopefully Glazner will shut them up good tomorrow.

PHL 020 000 000 00 — 2 9 1
BOS 000 010 010 01 — 3 10 0

CHERRY FIZZERS COULDN'T HELP ME TODAY
April 24, 1924

This was going to be our rebounding day, and I knew that when SCHULTZ HOME RUN, 1-0 PHL came across Mort's ticker after the very first batter. Then the same Joe Schultz dropped a fly in the bottom of the 1st, the Braves tied the game, and I needed my first cherry soda to relax.

Benny was back, after enjoying watching the Athletics lose their home opener over at Shibe yesterday. Benny hates the Athletics much more than me for a reason I still can't figure out, and you'd think because their field is right down the street from ours they'd be some kind of shared home team for us, but they're just not. Sometimes I think people can't root for two clubs at once and create excuses to divide them in their heads.

Anyway, Benny was in such a good mood that when the Braves scored three in the 2nd off Glazner with the help of an error by Frank Parkinson at third that he just shrugged and went to a table in the back to squeeze into a poker game.

But the Phils fought back, scored one in the 4th and then a Heinie Sand double tied it in the 6th. Marquard was pitching for Boston and we thought he was going to fall apart but just didn't, and got even tougher. After Sand's double he didn't give up another hit, and after Parkinson hit into a double play to ruin a rally in the 7th, I knew we were in trouble. I don't like Parkinson. He fills in sometimes against lefty pitchers because Wrightstone has trouble with them, but he's so bad they could name a disease after him.

So in the bottom of the 10th, Mort's all filled with cigar smoke by now, McINNIS HOME RUN, BOS 5 PHL 4 FINAL came across the ticker, and I couldn't even finish my fizzer. I always said it's easier when your team loses on the road because it's not right in front of you, but it's never easy to lose by one run, even if the game is played on the Moon.

PHL 100 102 000 0 — 4 5 2
BOS 130 000 000 1 — 5 9 1

IF THIS KEEPS UP I'M STAYING IN SCHOOL
April 25, 1924

I was only down at Mort's for an hour and a half of one today, because Jesse "Nubby" Barnes of the Braves speed-threw a shutout masterpiece at my stinkin' Phils before I barely had taken my coat off.

This guy Barnes holds the record for pitching the fastest 9-inning game in 1919—against the Phillies of course—which was 51 minutes. This one felt like 45. Henline got a double in the 2nd, Ford got two singles and Sand got one and that was it for the day. Our top five lineup men went for no hits in 18 at bats. The 4-to-8 spots in the Boston lineup got all seven hits and four walks off Jimmy Ring, who hasn't caught one of those breaks yet.

Benny was there in a bad mood again because he stayed at Mort's till almost dark yesterday watching the Athletics beat the Senators in 18 innings on the ticker. His card games didn't go well either which might have been a bigger problem. Personally I think he's still mad at Rachel for not letting him kiss her. I still have her address in Brooklyn so I think I'll write her a letter soon.

One more of these games at Braves Field tomorrow and then we take Sunday off before the Polo Grounds. Spending all day in school doesn't seem such a bad idea at right now, and now that we're tied with the Cubs for last place, church doesn't either.

PHL 000 000 000 — 0 4 2
BOS 020 200 00x — 4 7 1

NATIONAL LEAGUE through Friday, April 25, 1924

Pittsburgh	7	3	.700	—
New York	6	4	.600	1
Boston	6	5	.545	1.5
Brooklyn	5	5	.500	2
Cincinnati	5	5	.500	2
St. Louis	5	6	.455	2.5
PHILLIES	4	7	.364	3.5
Chicago	4	7	.364	3.5

A BIG WIN BEFORE WE ENTER HELL
April 26, 1924

When the Braves wrecked our early 2-0 lead with three runs in the 3rd on a Casey Stengel double, I said oh boy here we go again, another lousy day at Mort's. But this time Bill Hubbell calmed way down, Steineder pitched three innings of relief without a hit, and we got two big hits late, a pinch triple by Schultz and 9th inning triple from Steineder himself to win this one 5-3.

We needed it bad because now after a day off we go to the Polo Grounds to start eleven straight games against the Giants and Robins. I'm not kidding. Whatever dope thought up this schedule must be a Phillies-hater. Hopefully those two mashers will play as average as they've been lately, otherwise we might be out of this race in no time. Cy Williams had a triple and single in this game but he's gotta do much more for us.

Mama wants me to go to church with her tomorrow, so I guess I will because she did let me get away with going up to New York the other day. I don't like our preacher much but that's okay because it's usually easy for me to slip baseball cigarette cards into my coat pocket and flip through them during the sermon. Benny has a couple of Yankees cards he promised me once for helping him change a tire on some guy's jalopy, but I'm still waiting for them and got stuck with a bunch of St. Louis Browns this year. Oh well, have to make the most of them.

PHL 101 000 201 - 5 6 0
BOS 003 000 000 - 3 5 0

A LETTER FROM CHURCH
April 27, 1924

Dear Rachel,

How are you doing? The Phillies are off today and the Athletics went up to Yankee Stadium, so here I am stuck in church with my mama. Lucky for me she's always so busy praying I'm able to read my little baseball magazines or do things like write letters inside my coat.

I just wanted to say that I had a real good time up in Brooklyn last weekend and liked meeting you an awful lot, so I hope you'll write me a letter back and we can be friends for the year. I heard you weren't all that happy with Benny. I understand because he's my best friend and I know he can be a little rough about certain things, but I hope you don't grudge him for it, or grudge me for being friends with him.

Anyway, I just found out that the newspaper job I do with Benny sometimes is talking about adding a whole bunch of more carriers, and they need someone to go up to New York and do research stuff with some of the big papers there so they know how to do that. I volunteered for this research right away, but they want me to come up alone to save them money, and they asked whether I had any friends to stay with to save them even more money. So that's why I'm writing you now.

If you're too busy to spend any time with me I understand, but I hoped you might have a space on your couch for me to sleep on. And guess what? As it turns out, the Phillies will be playing in New York and Brooklyn for eight straight games starting tomorrow, so if I finish my research stuff in the mornings, there's a good chance I'll be able to go watch to them play. Is it possible you have some extra tickets for the Brooklyn games or know where I can get some? You can go with me to the games if you want, but I didn't know how busy you were.

Anyway, I plan to tell Mama about this great opportunity as soon as I can, but in the meantime, write me back as soon as you can or send me a telegram. I didn't know your last name but figured I wrote down your address right.

Best sincerely, your Philadelphia friend,
Vinny

SURE GLAD I INVITED MYSELF
April 28, 1924

Well, I never got any quick telegram from Rachel so I thought what the heck, why not go up to New York anyway and surprise her after the Phillies-Giants game? Mama bought my story about the newspaper carrier research, actually she was overjoyed that I was thinking about a job even though I wasn't, so all that was left was to either invite Benny with me or not.

Seeing the Phillies play at the Polo Grounds was exciting to me, but maybe seeing Rachel by myself was even more, so I decided to do my own adventure this time and tell Benny about it later. His luggage friend at the train station luckily remembered me and put me in a potato crate this time, and I just had to put up with sneezing once in a while.

When I got to Pennsylvania Station it took me a while to find the right el train that went to the Polo Grounds. The thing rolled right by brand new Yankee Stadium and let me tell you, that place is so huge it's frightening. Seems that the Yanks are playing kind of lousy, though, so I don't figure other teams have been too scared of them lately.

The Polo Grounds got bigger and bigger as the train got closer, and when I saw all the crowds outside I knew it would be tough to find a ticket. I had taken all the extra money I was saving in my snow boot in the closet, but if I spent it all on baseball tickets all week I might be in trouble. So lucky for me I saw a cop chasing away some poor kids trying to sneak in an outfield gate, and took a chance and slipped inside when his back was turned.

Wow, what a beautiful palace of baseball! They were finishing construction on one part of the upper grandstand in left, but I found a bunch of empty seats on the upper first base side that was pretty far from the seat ushers. The big centerfield was way open and you could see for miles, including Yankee Stadium across the river. It was strange to be with all Giants fans, and it was a good thing I didn't wear any Phillies clothes because they were in a bad nervous mood for most of the game because they just finished a pretty poor series at Ebbets Field.

Carlson was pitching for us and Art Nehf for the Giants, and even though pitchers were giving up hits, not many scored. Frisch hit a sacrifice fly in the 5th for New York, and it seemed like the one run might be the only one. There was a close play at first base in the 6th where Holke was called safe, and I saw McGraw jump out of the dugout right below me and scream at the umpire, but the fans around me were yelling so much I couldn't hear any of his cusses.

Then in the 8th, Sand led us off with a single, and Holke doubled into the right corner. The stadium got real quiet, like they were waiting for a hangman noose. And they got one. Cy Williams knocked a high fly to right, which disappeared into cigar smoke for a few seconds, then dropped into the stands for a 3-run homer! I jumped and let out a yelp, then quickly sat back down when someone threw a peanut at the back of my head. Frisch flubbed a ball the next inning with Sand on third, and we had a fourth run we didn't even need. We outhit the Giants 15-6 and now have the same record as them!

Afterwards I found my way to Brooklyn and Rachel's rooming house, but believe it or not she had gone up to Boston to watch her team play the Braves! Plus her roomer-friend Dolores didn't even know when she was coming back so I left a note for her and walked up the street. I ended up in a seedy part of Brooklyn in the rain and slept in a doorway with a couple vagrant kids who spoke some language I couldn't figure out. Tomorrow I'll try this again and if I don't get a Phillies win maybe I'll at least get Rachel.

PHL 000 000 031 - 4 15 1
NYG 000 010 000 - 1 6 1

WHERE WILL I SLEEP TONIGHT?
April 29, 1924

I woke up in the Brooklyn doorway to find that the vagrant kids made off with all of my cash except for a five-dollar bill I stuffed in my sock. Not a great way to start a day in another city. After I checked to see if Rachel was home yet (she wasn't) I bought a buttery roll for breakfast and got myself back to the Polo Grounds.

I snuck into the park the same way I did yesterday, but took a seat down the right field line in a section that was less filled with Giants fans so I could enjoy myself more. And boy did I ever. Oeschger was throwing for us against Bentley, and for six innings we looked like world's champions. Schultz and Sand began the game with doubles and we scored three runs. Bentley was real terrible, giving up a double to Cy and a 2-run homer to Jimmie Wilson in the 3rd. Even Parkinson doubled in a run in the 6th to puts us up 6-0 and that was the showers for Bentley. Ryan, Baldwin and Jonnard calmed the Phils down, right when Oeschger began to get hit, but Huck Betts came on to pitch the last few innings and put us ahead of the Giants in the standings!

It was a warm sunny day but even though we won kind of easy, I started to get nervous around the 7th inning. I could see a lot of New York from up there, and all I could do was worry about where I was going to get dinner and end up sleeping that night. I actually began to root for extra innings, like 40 of them, because I knew if the game never ended I wouldn't have to leave and could just fall asleep in the grandstand. Of course I knew this would never happen until someone invented a bunch of spotlights that could let the teams play at night, but it was a nice dream to keep me going anyway.

I had about three dollars and fifty cents left, which bought me a sausage in Brooklyn and got me into a late-night nickelodeon, where I fell asleep to an organist serenading a small crowd while they watched a romantic story taking place in old England. Hopefully Rachel will be back tomorrow, because if not I'll probably have to go home.

PHL 302 001 000 - 6 11 1
NYG 000 000 121 - 4 9 0

A VERY GLORIOUS LOSS
April 30, 1924

So the creepy Nickelodeon manager rudely woke me up and threw me on the street around midnight, and when I spit on the sidewalk in front of his building he yelled for a cop who chased me three blocks, grabbed me by the collar and dragged me down to a local jail for the night. At least the cell was warm.

Me and some other lowlifes got fed watery oatmeal in the morning and then I started pleading to come out, which got me nowhere. Finally I of-fered this guard all the rest of my money and faked like I was crying and that worked, but it was one in the afternoon by the time I hit the Brooklyn street again. I ran past a ticket booth to get on the el train back to the Polo Grounds but stupidly took a connector train into Manhattan by accident, so there was no way I could get there for the start of the 2 o'clock game.

My mama always says that sometimes your best days are happy accidents, and this was sure one of those. I ended up in Times Square, the most crowded, exciting city place I'd ever seen, roadsters whizzing around everywhere and people all dressed up, and at one corner of it the *New York Times* had set up a giant electrical scoreboard that was showing the Giants and Phillies game, minutes after the action was happening at the Polo Grounds. What luck! A pretty large crowd of business men had skipped their lunches or afternoon work to stand in front of it, and I blended right in with a handful of kids who wanted no part of school like me.

The board had green lights for the balls, red ones for the strikes, and had these little mechanical men that moved around on the diamond. When Wrightstone hit a homer in the 3rd to put us up 2-1, I let out a cheer and got some low curses from the people around me, who I'm sure were mostly all Giants fans. New York has truly been playing bad so far, and their fans can't stop complaining about it. George Kelly their first baseman has been real rotten with men on base, something he never is, and I heard two different people say he shouldn't be making anywhere near his $7,000 a year.

Anyway, the 3-1 Phillie lead grew to 5-1 in the 8th when Harper homered to knock out Mule Watson. This time I kept my mouth shut but a girl about 100 feet away yelled "YAHOO!" real loud and I recognized all at once whose voice it was. I pushed my way through the crowd and there she was in front of me: Rachel. She couldn't believe I was there, too, and gave me a big friendly hug. After yesterday's tough loss she left Boston because she figured she was bringing her Robins bad luck, and they were getting their brains bashed in again on this day, but with the Giants losing too she was in great spirits.

The electric board broke down for a half hour right then, and by the time they got it working again the Giants had scored three times in the 8th and Johnny Couch was now pitching for us instead of Glazner. Huck Betts must have been too tired after yesterday's work, and that was unfortunate. Down 5-4 in the 9th with the Times Square crowd hooting like nuts, O'Connell hit a pinch double for them with one out in the bottom of the 9th. Hack Wilson, who had done nothing all day, then tripled, his mechanical man chugging around on the board the same slow way he is.

Rachel and I got real quiet, and she actually gripped my hand. The game suddenly didn't mean as much, and I started rooting for extra innings so she'd never let go. But no dice. Frisch walked and Irish Meusel hit a fly that scored Wilson's little mechanical man, the crowd threw their hats up and we just snuck out of there quick as possible.

I told Rachel my problems with money and the cop and she offered to let me sleep on her couch for the whole weekend so I could go with her to the Phillies games at Ebbets. We stayed in Manhattan most of the night, first eating at a great Italian place that served the biggest manicottis I'd ever seen, then to a little dancing music club down in an area called Greenwich where she taught me how to do the Charleston till I got dizzy.

Actually she's been making every part of me dizzy, so I badly need to rest up now for tomorrow's adventure. It'll be nice to spend the whole First of May with Rachel and learn more about her. I found out her last name is Stone, not Italian-sounding like I thought it would be. But that's okay. Her name could be Miss Lucifer and I probably wouldn't believe it.

PHL 102 000 020 - 5 11 1
NYG 100 000 032 - 6 10 3

PART TWO
May

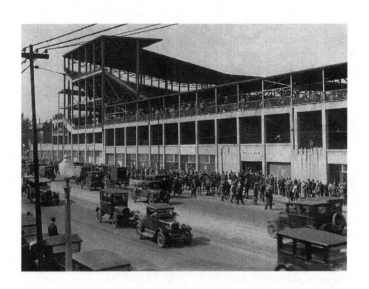

ALL KINDS OF NERVOUSNESS AT EBBETS FIELD
May 1, 1924

I slept real late on Rachel's couch before she got me up with egg and onion smells. She looked a little less cute in the morning but I guess most people do. The Phillies game at Ebbets started at 1 o'clock, and she asked if it was okay if her friend Margie Ginsberg came too. I said fine because here I was staying on a couch for free and eating her food. If I needed to sit with two crazy Robins fans for two hours, at least one of them would be Rachel.

Except I didn't think Margie would be so annoying. She was all skinny and talked forever and had this laugh that sounded like a rooster being pulled through a meat grinder, but I guess her dad was some big merchant in Brooklyn so she had great tickets for us right behind the home dugout. I have to say that Rachel and her did look pretty nice today, dolled up like they were going to a tea party afterwards. Rachel was wearing some kind of perfume or skin cream that smelled like roses, which mixed kind of strangely with the cigar and sausage smells around us.

Just my Phillies luck, Dazzy Vance was pitching again. Jimmy Ring was going for us, and he still hadn't won a game, so I didn't expect much out of this one. We loaded the bases in the 2nd with two walks and a Johnny Mitchell error, but Dazzy beared down and whiffed Ford and Ring to get out of it, Margie braying in my ear. Ring gave up a double to Brown in the 2nd and one to Taylor in the 4th, but escaped both times. In the 5th, Harper and Holke got singles and an error from Johnson loaded the bases with two out. I really wanted to stand and root like I would with Benny, but here I was trying to be a nice guest and it was driving me nuts. Butch Henline was up, and Rachel and Margie were yelling for another Dazzy whiff. The count was 3-and-2 and the next pitch was an inch outside for a run-scoring walk! Margie actually cursed and threatened to whack the umpire, and a security man was called over by some of the men around us to give her a talking-to. I guess it was hard enough for ladies to go to games, and when they did they were expected to act like them.

All was forgotten in the 6th, though, because with one out, Zack Wheat came to the plate. He was readying himself in the on-deck spot right in front of me when Andy High was up, grinding his hands into his brown bat. He was definitely Rachel's favorite player. She said he was 35 years old, from Missouri, and had been on the Brooklyn team for 15 years now. She sent him a love letter once but he never wrote back. Margie said she sent him nine. Anyway, Zack got up there, Ring threw, and he gave the ball a vicious swipe, knocking it high and over the right field fence in seconds. The entire crowd jumped up, even me, and I swear I never even saw Cy Williams hit one that hard. The game was tied, and my lady friends were bubbling over.

Then I started getting nervous. The Phillies kept getting little hits off Vance and I began to worry what might happen if they won. Would Rachel hate me and want me to leave town? Would Margie never stop talking and give me deadly brain sickness? Thankfully it was the Phillies they were up against, and sure enough, Ring gave singles to Neis and High to begin the bottom of the 8th. Wheat flied deep to right but it was caught this time, and after Fournier walked, Huck Betts was called in. He got Brown on a force-play at home, but then Mitchell took four straight balls and the Robins were ahead for good. Vance put the Phils to bed 1-2-3 in the 9th, and that was that. Rachel and Margie both gave me hugs for being such a good sport, which of course was the best part of the game for me other than watching Wheat's homer.

Margie went home after and I had supper with Rachel at a place near hers that made delicious chicken soups. She invited me to stay on her couch again, which was a good thing, and then asked if I wanted to come to her family's house the next night for a Sabbath eve dinner. I looked at her all weird and asked "Are you a witch?" and she laughed, said that's what Jewish people called Friday night dinner. Can you believe that? All this time I thought she was Italian. I said I'd never been friends with anyone Jewish and she said she could tell, and it was a good time to start. She gave me her cute little smile and I wanted to kiss her right there in the restaurant but whoa, I thought: That's how Benny got kicked out of town.

What do you think, reader-people? Should I try kissing her this weekend or not?

PHL 000 010 000 - 1 7 0
BRK 000 001 01x - 2 8 2

SABBATH EVE IN BROOKLYN
May 2, 1924

It was just me and Rachel today at Ebbets, thankfully. Her friend Margie had to work, and my head still hurt from listening to her all of yesterday. The weather was nice and this time we sat down past first base, which gave me a great view of Walter Holke and Jack Fournier as they played the bag. It's incredible to think that not too long ago fielders had to catch the ball with their bare hands. The huge gloves they use now are sure an improvement.

Burleigh Grimes pitched for the Robins, complete with his famous spitter. If the sun was just right I could see a bit of water gleaming off the ball as he threw it. The spray didn't seem to bug the Phillies, because they got their share of hits. The problem is they couldn't score anyone for seven innings. Bernie Neis tripled in the first Brooklyn run in the 3rd which got Rachel hooting and smacking my arm, and then Wheat and Brown got singles to make it 3-0.

Home Run Fournier did it again in the 6th, whacking Bill Hubbell's curve high and deep to right, where the ball almost hit a gull before it dropped over the fence. Rachel yelped with joy, grabbed the side of my face and landed a wet, sticky kiss on my right cheek. So she beat me to it, and made it easier for me to try a real one later.

Then the Phillies woke up. George Harper clubbed a homer to start the 8th, Holke singled, Wrightstone tripled over Brown's head in center, and

Cy doubled him in to cut it to 4-3. Wilbert Robinson waddled out of the dugout and almost sent Grimes home but I guess Burleigh talked him out of it. He got the next two guys, hit Sand, then took care of the next four and that was that. The Phils have only beaten Brooklyn once so far, which might be their undoing if it keeps up.

Rachel tried to cheer me up afterwards by buying me a root beer float, and it worked pretty well. I found out she likes to write short stories and is thinking of trying a novel one day. She worked in the news room of the Brooklyn Eagle once delivering coffee and pop to the writers, and said that inspired her. I promised I'd read something she wrote once, and she got us out of there quick as a flash and onto the first train to her parents' neighborhood.

The Stones lived on a nice shady street in Prospect Heights, in a row house kind of like the ones in Philadelphia except better kept. Her dad's name was Saul and her mom was Lotte, and I also met Rachel's younger sister and brother who were Sarah and Sammy. Anyway, the first thing her mother asked when we sat down in their living room was what my last name was. She made a funny face when I said Spanelli and Rachel said "He's Italian, not Jewish." Her mother shrugged and said, "Well, that's close enough." I think they were happy just to have Rachel bring a boy over who wasn't a troublemaker.

Mrs. Stone lit some candles and Mr. Stone said some things in Jewish language and then we ate a pretty good feast with this brown sliced meat and greasy flat potato things and something that was like sauerkraut except that it wasn't. I also got a chance to drink wine for the first time, and had no idea it was so sweet. I started to feel kind of woogy after my second glass, which was when we went into their parlor room and listened to a play performed on their radio machine. I had a tough time hearing and following it, and because of the wine I mostly just stared at Rachel, who was right next to me on a little couch and smelling as good as the day before.

When her mother asked which hotel I was staying at Rachel butted in and said the Yorkshire, which I think she made up because she couldn't even tell them where it was. Then it was getting late. A friend of mine once told me if you want to get a girl you have to be extra nice to her parents, and boy, I was nice-ing the heck out of them all night and shook everyone's hand on the way out and said thank you maybe twenty times.

And I guess it worked, because the second we got back to Rachel's place she led me up on her roof, where she had two little chairs set up to watch the moon in. We could see its light on the river next to the Brooklyn Bridge from there, with Manhattan's big towers just behind it. Rachel moved her chair closer and put her hand on mine and we had a kiss that tasted like cinnamon and was probably only five seconds long but stayed in my head for the next five hours. We didn't know what to say to each other after except good night, and then it was back to her couch, and the best sleep I'd ever had on one.

Two more Ebbets games left, and right now I don't even care who wins.

SATURDAY FRUSTRATIONS
May 3, 1924

Well, a weekend that started so good for me in the romance area slid into a mud pit today for all kinds of reasons.

The first was when I was eating eggs and toast at Rachel's place in the morning and she asked if I'd read all 200 pages of the novel she was writing, which was only half of the thing. I said okay I would take it home with me and send it back but no, she wanted me to sit there and read it in front of her. So I faked it the best I could, especially since it was on these handwritten pages and her writing was so small I needed glasses to make most of it out. After an hour of this torture she said forget it and pulled it out of my hands and told me to get ready to go to Ebbets.

Then the game happened. The Robins beat up Carlson for three runs in the 1st and like yesterday it stayed that way for a while until Cy Williams belted a homer off Doak in the 5th to make it 3-2. Then it was 4-2 Brooklyn, then 5-2, and I kept making excuses to get up and walk around, because I was starting to not enjoy losing at Ebbets Field, and we were working on the fourth straight time.

Every inning was filled with base runners and nervousness and Rachel and me were afraid to look at each other. We cut it to 5-3 in the 8th, but then Zack Wheat doubled to lead off the Brooklyn 8th and I cursed under my breath and whacked my hand on my seat. Rachel got all huffy and stopped talking to me right there.

On the way out of the park with her a step or two in front of me we heard someone yell our names. We turned and there was Benny! He'd come up in the morning to see the last two games, figuring out from my mama that I'd lied to her and was here myself. Rachel was in no mood to see him, that's for sure, and she said bye and left with a "maybe I'll see you here tomorrow."

Can you believe it? All over her crazy writing! I was pretty happy to see Benny, though, and we took an underground train and then a streetcar all the way to Harlem, where the luggage guy from Philadelphia had another luggage friend named Cecil who had an apartment and put us up.

Benny said to heck with Rachel, there's plenty of tomatoes around, and I guess I agree, except I won't get over this juicy one too quick. Good night from Harlem, reader-people!

PHL 000 020 010 - 3 11 1
BRK 300 011 01x - 6 14 0

GET ME TO THE FIELD ON TIME
May 4, 1924

I woke up kind of late at Cecil's apartment in Harlem, and by the time I washed and dressed, Benny was back with some hot muffins and apples for breakfast. Cecil slept over at his woman's place, which was lucky for him but knowing that didn't cheer me up any.

On the first hand, I felt pretty bad about the way I treated Rachel's book pages. I probably should have just pretended I could read the words and that they were great and writer-like. Then at least we'd probably still be friends. On the second hand, Benny made a good point about not getting too kooky over one girl, not when there was lots more to choose from. Except maybe that was much easier for him than for me.

Anyway, the big news when Benny showed up was that we figured the schedule all wrong. The Braves, just like the Red Sox, aren't allowed to play in Boston on Sundays, so them and the Giants had taken trains back to New York last night. Meaning Brooklyn was hosting the Braves today, and the Phillies were kicked back over to the Polo Grounds for one game before going back to Baker to play four more with those Giants. Benny thought this was a lot better because Harlem is much closer to the Polo Grounds than Ebbets, and also because the Robins have been rubbing our noses in it day in and day out and the Giants are playing like chumps.

But this also meant if I wanted to try and see Rachel again today, I couldn't.

We got to Coogan's Bluff a half hour before game time. I said it might be fun to actually go up on the bluff to watch the game with all the people who couldn't get in, which my dad said was what happened at the end of 1908. But Benny said no dice, the only place to see a baseball game is where you can smell the grass, so he snuck us in under a grandstand fence during the second inning. It was just in time to see the Giants' O'Connell boot one and lead to three Phillies runs in the 2nd and give them a 3-1 lead on Bentley. Doubles by Ford and Parkinson made it 4-1 in the 4th, and with Oeschger going with his 2-0 record, things looked good.

It was another one of those slow agony games with lots of runners, and my mind started thinking about Rachel again. Okay, so maybe she wasn't the easiest girl to get along with, but watching that moonlight on her roof stayed with me like a head cold I couldn't shake. The score board on the far fence read BRK 8 BOS 2 with a 6 beside it, and I knew there was still maybe half of both games left. I fibbed to Benny, told him I promised to buy something for my mama before I left New York and said to wait for me outside the grandstand gate if I wasn't back in time.

I was lucky to remember which train cars to take to Brooklyn, and had no problem slipping or jumping over the ticket booths on every line. I ran like a nut when I got into Brooklyn and ended up on a street behind Ebbets Field. There was a big open area outside the left fence they were just starting to build on, and saw a bunch of wild yellow flowers growing on a hill. I'm not sure what they were and they made me sneeze when I smelled them, but they were sure pretty enough for any girl so I picked the whole bunch.

The Robins were creaming the Braves awful good, 10-2 in the 7th, and fans were starting to leave. This made it a cinch to slip inside the place. I squeezed around the fans in their big coats, the few ladies I saw in their hats, checking every one's face to see if it was Rachel's. It was actually easier to pick out the female fans because of those hats, and when Dutch Ruether pitched Brooklyn out of a little pickle in the top of the 7th, I heard a young woman let out a yelp.

Rachel was in a low third base seat with her father, who I didn't know was a baseball fan himself. I crouched right behind her seat, tapped her shoulder and when she turned I held out the flowers and sneezed. She was amazed and I said all in a rush that I was real sorry about yesterday and really did want to read her writing some time and that I just couldn't stop thinking about her all night and I really do want to be friends, and that she was welcome to visit me in Philadelphia any time during the summer for a tour of Baker Bowl. I put the flowers in her hand, tipped my cap to her father and left the grandstand.

By the time I got back to the Polo Grounds, all out of breath, Cy Williams had dropped a fly in center helping the Giants tie the game 4-4 in the 7th, Frisch had singled in Snyder with two outs in the 8th, and the Phils had lost again.

But I sure hadn't. Good night from our good old luggage car out of New York!

PHL 030 100 000 - 4 9 1
NYG 100 001 21x - 5 11 1

A RECURRING SICKNESS
May 5, 1924

After getting home very late last night during a rainstorm, I woke up in the morning with a scary fever and had to stay in bed. Mama took lots of pity on me and mixed me up some mustard plaster to lay on my chest. I hate that stuff, but when you're sick it's always better to let your mother do what she needs to.

Mama was proud of me for going on my newspaper research trip to New York, and I had to make up a few things about it. Then she was off to the clothes factory so I put up the window and whistled down to little Stinker Delfi who was always throwing dice with his friends on our stoop. I said the Giants were playing at Baker Bowl today and if he'd go back and forth to Mort's for me and keep giving me the score I'd pay him a whole dollar when the game was over. Stinker wasn't too smart but he never could pass up a buck.

I'm not sure he got all the details right, but it seemed like catching a fever was the best thing that could've happened to me. New York got four runs in the first inning off Glazner, and they were ahead 6-1 by the 5th. George Kelly had even knocked in a few of the runs. We were getting bushels of hits off Mule Watson, but couldn't score enough of them, and I'm sure Benny was cursing again in the bleachers and wondering why I never showed up.

Stinker didn't come back until 4:30, when he yelled up to the window to say the Giants had scored eight more times. I was so sick by then and angry at my team that I just slammed the window down. Stinker and his goony friends pelted the glass with dice until a part of it cracked and I heard them run away. He'll be too afraid to come back for that dollar, which is okay, because I'd much rather pay him for hearing about a Phillies win. If we ever get another one.

NYG 400 203 302 - 14 18 2
PHL 010 002 000 - 3 10 2

WE TRIED EVERYTHING TODAY
May 6, 1924

Mama's mustard plaster treatment worked a whole bunch of wonders, and I was up at nine to eat a full breakfast and make plans for another Baker Bowl afternoon. The Phils have been stinking awful lately, and me and Benny promised to see their losing streak end if we had to do it ourselves.

After my morning arithmetic class I smiled at Principal Tuggerheinz and left school to catch the streetcar. I met Benny outside the bleachers entrance at 12, and he was so excited to see me again that he bought me a wiener. Virgil Barnes was pitching for the Giants against our Jimmy Ring. Ring was 0-3 but Barnes had already lost twice to his brother Jesse on the Braves, so we knew he could be had.

We were too far away from the Giants dugout to yell at McGraw but we could see him in there, pacing around with his dinky body and throwing dirt pebbles he got off the top step. Brooklyn's been much better than his team so far, which must be making him cuckoo.

Well, the first inning made us cuckoo instead. Frisch singled to start the game, stole second base on Henline, got singled to third base by Groh, and Youngs walked. George Kelly, who usually bats in their cleanup spot, got knocked down to the 5th position, and Hack Wilson came up instead. He's a tough-looking hitter, but how's he ever going to amount to anything with a stupid first name like that?

"HEY HACK!" yelled Benny right away, "I LIKE YOUR NAME! BET YOU REALLY ARE ONE!" We knew there was no way he could hear us, but it made the fans around us laugh and got some people in the third base stands yelling at him, too, which then spread around home plate, kind of like what an ocean wave does. Hack took two strikes from Ring and we both yelled even louder. "GOTTA BE UP THERE HACKIN', HACK, YOU BUM!" Ring then gave him a pitch that we could tell right away was too good and Wilson clobbered the thing so deep and so far over our heads we lost sight of it in the bright sky. I think I saw the ball bounce up in the air on the street behind us but wasn't sure. Anyway, the grand slam made it 4-0 in the top of the 1st and made Benny nuts.

He got on Irish Meusel right away, who came out to play left field for them straight in front of us. He's the brother of Bob on the Yankees and isn't as good and his name is Irish, so of course he was easy pickings. "HEY O'MEUSEL!" yelled Benny, "HOW MANY WHISKEYS DID YOU HAVE FOR BREAKFAST?" He didn't even turn around, and when the Phillies scraped out a run on a bases-filled walk to Henline, Benny got even louder. "HEY O'MEUSEL! YEAH, YOU! THIS ONE'S BOUNCING OFF YOUR PO-TATO-HEAD, SO WATCH OUT!" It sure sounded good, but Benny forgot that Heinie Sand was up, and he grounded out weakly to end the inning.

Benny calmed down after that because his voice was almost gone, and because the Giants got two more runs in the 3rd and doubles from Youngs and Mr. Hack in the 4th to make it 7-1. Ring has had some bad luck for us, but today he was just a garbage-arm. He did double in a run, after which Harper sacrifice-flied another one to make it 7-3, but that was our last real batting burst.

The only good thing was that Irish got no hits in five times up and ruined a rally in the 7th with a double play ball. Benny came back to life when he took the field after that, yelling stuff about his washerwoman mother and asking how it felt to be the lousier brother but Meusel didn't even flinch. I guess they're trained not to do that, otherwise there would be fights with fans every day.

So that's seven straight losses for us, and we're getting a little too comfy down in the National cellar if you ask me. All I know is I want to be there the next time they win, because it's going to be as sweet as Mama's best cannoli.

NYG 402 100 000 - 7 12 1
PHL 100 200 010 -4 7 1

BENNY THE GOOD MAN
May 7, 1924

So for a change I got to the ballpark before Benny today. He ran up to me out of the crowd maybe a minute before the first pitch and was excited and all out of breath and said he'd meet me in the bleachers later or if not, wait for him over at Bookbinder's Restaurant on Walnut Street. I looked at him like he'd popped a cork, and he just said see you later and ran off.

Gee. As if that wasn't enough to distract me, we had the Giants to deal with again and tough Hugh McQuillan on the mound. Frisch walked to start the game and Youngs doubled him in right away and I said oh boy, here we go again. But Bill Hubbell pitched for us and bore down, Harper tied the game with a sacrifice pop, and in the 4th Russ Wrightstone cracked a first-pitch homer over the wall in right. There wasn't many of us in the bleachers, but we jumped up and made a pretty big ruckus anyway.

And it just got better. Wrightstone singled in a third run in the 5th and in the 6th Youngs dropped his second fly in two days to score Sand and make it 4-1. But these Giants never quit because McGraw would chew out their ears if they did. Travis Jackson homered over my head in the 7th, Youngs made up for his error by doubling in Frisch again in the 8th, and Huck Betts came on to save us.

And did he ever! With Irish Meusel on second, he got the next three guys, then threw a scoreless ninth. Benny showed up in time to watch

Hack Wilson whiff to end the game and join us in throwing our hats, the big losing streak was over and we were out of last place!

Then it was mystery time. Benny was even more excited than he was before the game, but all the way down to Walnut on the streetcar he wouldn't say a word. Bookbinder's is a big famous fish restaurant that's been around since the 1880s, but it was way too fancy to get us in the door in our stinky rags. Benny just smiled at the guy, reached in his pocket and took out a brand new twenty-dollar bill. The doorman's eyes nearly fell out and he got us inside and gave us a small corner table away from the stuffy crowd.

We ordered fresh pasta with giant shrimps and Benny finally spilled the beans. Seems that he had a rich uncle up in Boston who just died and left him over ten thousand dollars, and now he was going to buy himself an automobile, put me in the front seat with him and drive us out west to follow the Phillies on their entire 16-game road trip! I almost fell off my leather chair. It's actually 19 games if you count the three they have to play the Braves at the end, but that would mean us getting from Chicago to Boston in two days, which might be a struggle.

A bigger struggle is what the heck do I tell Mama this time? And how can I miss school? How do we get to these places, and does Benny even know how to drive?

On the other side of my hand, how can I even THINK about passing this chance up? I've never been west of Scranton!

There's one more game with the Giants tomorrow, which I'll try to enjoy while Benny is out shopping for an automobile and hopefully some lessons. The Phils then take Friday off to head for Cincinnati, and if everything goes miracle-good tomorrow, we'll be motoring right behind them.

NYG 100 000 110 - 3 12 1
PHL 001 111 00x - 4 9 0

TIME TO PACK UP
May 8, 1924

Baker Bowl was stuffed solid thanks to this being the Phillies' last home game until almost the end of the month, but somebody else was in Benny's bleacher seat. My friend was off looking for an automobile all day, while I sat there wondering why Mama was so nice to me about this crazy trip I was about to take.

This time I decided to just tell the truth instead of making up a fake story, and it completely worked. Mama was real happy that Benny's uncle left him a bunch of money and said I should stick around with him even more because people with money got more opportunities and I had a better chance of catching one for myself on a rebound. I asked her about my school work and she said she never took much stock in that in comparison to getting a job, and she'd make something up to tell Mr. Tuggerheinz. See, she never got a chance to travel anywhere herself, and said as long as I sent her some letters from out west a few times, she'd know I was safe and could maybe even enjoy the trip through my eyes. I guess I am to her kind of how the Phillies are to me, and she's a bigger fan of me than I thought she was.

Anyway, Benny missed a good game, even though we lost. His best friend Irish Meusel knocked in four of the five Giant runs with two singles and a homer in the 5th that made it 4-0. But Johnny Mokan homered twice for us, making it an all-leftfielder show, and it was 5-3 in the 9th and we had two people on the bases and George Harper pinch-hit for Schultz to try and hit one out off reliever Jonnard.

Nope, he lined out instead, and with the Cubs winning today we're back in last place as we hit the road.

After I got home I was eating dinner with Mama and we heard a loud toot-toot on the street outside. We went to the window and there was Benny, standing next to the most shiny blue auto I've ever seen. He went for the best and gambled with his money on a brand new one called a Model Six, just made by a guy named Walter Chrysler. It was supposed to be lighter than a Buick auto that was similar to it, and Benny's could go from five to fifty miles an hour in an amazing 13 seconds. Benny rode me around the neighborhood all the time with lots of kids jumping on the bumpers for free rides, and I couldn't believe how comfortable it was.

It was real hard getting to sleep later. Mama had my bag all packed up, but all I could think about was the places we'd be going. The Phillies play four games each in Cincinnati, Pittsburgh, Chicago and St. Louis, then three more in Boston. Phew! If we can figure out how to read all the crazy maps Benny's bringing, we might even have time to enjoy this adventure. Good night and see you tomorrow on some highway, reader-people!

NYG 002 020 100 - 5 11 1
PHL 000 020 001 -3 11 0

DAYLIGHT RAMBLERS
May 9, 1924

It was plain scary, that's all I can say. Benny had the Chrysler Six going as fast as 50 miles an hour on that Pennsylvania highway, and I had my teeth gritted for most of the ride. We passed every other car easy, even some big farm trucks, and a couple times we whizzed by families with girls in the back and we could hear them ooh and ahh at the sight of us. Benny sure loved that part, and would take off his cap and salute them like he was one of those Indy 500 drivers. He even bought himself a pair of goggles for the trip, which made him look like some daffy frog.

The seats were made out of velour and were real comfortable, and the car's instruments were all readable on one glass panel instead of small separate ones that I'd seen in most other cars. Mr. Chrysler had also put in a new kind of brakes called hydraulic, which stopped the car quicker and safer than the old drum ones. All in all, the thing was definitely worth the 1,225 dollars that Benny had to shell out for it.

We left the city before sunrise and by the time it was light enough we were way out in the countryside. I had no idea how much of the middle of our state is wild, and I could even smell the spring flowers when the car brushed past them. Benny wanted to get us to Cincinnati before dark, but I didn't expect that to happen. We had to stop for lunch and dinner and buy more petrol and figuring out the big dumb maps was something I needed to be back in school for. We had a specially big one that the Gulf Oil Company put out, and trying to follow my finger along the William Penn or Lincoln Highway or National Road was just plain impossible with Benny swerving around cars like a kook.

Another reason he was driving fast was because he knew the Braves were playing at Forbes Field in Pittsburgh that afternoon and thought maybe we could catch an inning or two. Why bother? I asked him, the Braves stink and the game's probably sold out. Never stopped us in Brooklyn, did it? he said back, and because he was driving there wasn't much I could do.

We stopped at a diner in a town called Breezewood that had petrol pumps, and sure enough, every local man and farm boy in the place had to go outside and drool all over Benny's car. He even let a couple of the kids sit behind the wheel. I guess it was like this when the very first auto rolled into any town, and I had to be careful not to start thinking we were like moving picture stars. Benny, though, was changing before my eyes. When we kept driving he started blabbing about all the pretty girls he was going to meet and I had to yawn and look out the window at a long passing train.

As I thought, we didn't get to the Pittsburgh area until late afternoon, then got lost in some smoky neighborhood and gave up on Forbes Field this time around. But we did pass a general store that had a big sign out front reading PIRATES BALL GAME TODAY!! with a pretty big crowd hanging out the door. We were curious and parked the car. Inside the store was one of those new radio machines, and believe it or not, an announcer named Graham McNamee was telling us about the last few innings of the game, direct from the ballpark! It was hard to hear the words because they were all crackly, but the crowd was excited and we found out the Bucs had a huge lead. After the game finished we bought some snacks and kept on driving, turning west into Ohio.

The Chrysler's lights weren't too bright, and Benny had to slow down to keep us from smacking into trees. He asked if I wanted to try driving and I said forget that so he kept going even though he was getting tired. That was a big mistake because he dozed off around ten o'clock, the car went into a ditch and we had to get a couple farmers to help push us back out. Benny was real mad because there was dirt and a big dent on the side of his new car. Anyway, by the time we got to Cincinnati we were both dog tired and found the crummiest, cheapest hotel we could find, called the Cavalier Arms, and went right to our beds.

WE STORM THE RED BASTILLE
May 10, 1924

What's it like to wake up in Cincinnati? For me it could have been the

Moon. There was ugly flower wallpaper all around the hotel room, different kinds of sausage smells coming in the open window, and looking out I saw at least three or four big hills surrounding the city, and I don't think I ever saw one in Philadelphia.

Benny was snoring until at least nine, and after a pretty tasty breakfast at a place next to the hotel that served something called salt pork and eggs, we got back in the car and started searching for Redland Field. Two different people sent us in the wrong direction, or maybe we just took wrong turns because of our excitement. Anyway, we finally spotted two kids in Reds caps hustling along and Benny slowed down next to them and asked, "How ya get to the BALL-game?" but they couldn't tell us the street names so we let them hop in back and show us instead.

The field actually wasn't that hard to miss, because it was so big it dominated its factory-type neighborhood. Fans were lining up early for tickets, and because it was Saturday there were bunches and bunches of kids, but we only had to stand in line for about an hour before they went on sale. Benny was feeling all high and mighty with the bucks busting out of his pocket, so he asked for the best seats in the house and got us stuck way up in an upper deck behind a post. We ended up spending every inning in a different seat, using Benny's famous method of sitting in empties until asked to move, all the time going in a downward direction. By the sixth we were close enough to Edd Roush outside the Cincy dugout that we could see a blister pop open on one of his hands.

Redland Field is gigantic as far as the fences go, too, over 400 feet to both center field and the right field pole. We also realized that it's about five times more hot and humid in Cincinnati than back home, and we were dying for soda pops before long. Oeschger pitched for us, and he was tough, only giving the Reds five singles for two runs through the 3rd. Then we went to work on Tom Sheehan. Wrightstone and Jimmie Wilson singled to open the 4th, Mokan walked and Ford tied the game with a sharp hit past Boob Fowler at short. "No wonder they call you a boob!" yelled Benny, which I could have bet he would do. But then Oeschger whacked a double to put us ahead and even I was screaming.

Rube Bressler booted one at first to get us going in the 5th, and Wrightstone took the next pitch and shot it out of his bat cannon, deep and high over the right field wall! Burns doubled in a run to make it 5-3 us, but then the starters beared down the rest of the way. When Oeschger gave up a one-out single in the 8th, though, Fletcher brought in Johnny Couch so he could use his snappy bat in the 9th. And guess what he did? Socked a homer deep to left! Critz tripled with one out for them in the 9th, but Couch got the Boob to end it.

A couple of rough-looking older kids with German accents followed us out of the park, but we were able to lose them and find our car in the crowded parking lot. Benny wanted to look for a "beer garden speakeasy" to celebrate our win but I wasn't too sure about that so we drove over to Fountain Square instead and saw a movie and stage show at the Lyric Theatre. The movie was a western story called "The Iron Horse" with actors named George O'Brien and Madge Bellamy in it, and there was too much romance to keep Benny awake, but he sure liked the magician and tumblers that performed after.

There were lots of people in Fountain Square because it was a warm Saturday night, and Benny tried real hard again to find a speakeasy but didn't really want to leave me out so we went back to our hotel room after a while and just rolled some dice. Then as I was getting ready for bed I remembered something, and ran down to the hotel lobby to send a telegram to Philadelphia:

HI MAMA. SORRY I CAN'T BE WITH YOU ON MOTHER'S DAY TOMORROW. HOPE YOU HAVE A NICE ONE. LOVE FROM CINCY. VINNY.

PHL 000 320 001 - 6 9 0
CIN 002 010 000 - 3 11 2

NATIONAL LEAGUE through Saturday, May 10, 1924

Brooklyn	16	7	696	—
Pittsburgh	15	9	.625	1.5
Cincinnati	14	11	.560	3
New York	13	11	.542	3.5
St. Louis	12	13	.480	5
PHILLIES	9	15	.375	7.5
Boston	9	15	.375	7.5
Chicago	9	16	.360	8

BIG TRAIN DERAILED IN THE TWILIGHT
WINGO'S BASE KNOCK WINS 13-FRAME D.C. THRILLER

By Calvin J. Butterworth
Detroit Free-Enterprise
May 10, 1924

WASHINGTON, DC—Ty Cobb stared out at the tall, aging Kansan perched on the Griffith Stadium mound, dug his cleats into the batter's box, and flinched at a passing strike that he barely saw. The first Tiger game in the Nation's Capitol this season began with a pitcher and batter match-up for the ages, and when it was over four hours later, as spring darkness cloaked the ball park, an overflow Senators crowd and handful of fortunate writers would barely recollect all the razor-edged, superlative moments the teams paraded before them.

Walter Johnson battled Cobb hard for that first at bat, and after the infamous twirler's long arm dropped down for a side-wheeling fastball and Tyrus limply popped out, the Train seemed to lose his initial focus. He walked Rigney, gave up a blistering single to Bassler, and Heilman singled hard past Peckinpaugh for a 1-0 Detroit lead out of the gate. Ken Holloway, the lone undefeated Tiger starter at 3-0, pitched in exemplary fashion once again, but after Lance Richbourg doubled with one out in the 3rd, Joe Judge singled him homeward to tie the score.

Johnson then settled into his customary act of pitching sorcery, while the Nats scored another in the 5th on Richbourg's second ringing double of the afternoon and a Peckinpaugh pop safety. Cobb had ripped a single off Johnson in the 2nd but grounded weakly off him to lead the 5th. Now, after Les Burke batted for Holloway in the 7th and made out, the Peach of Georgia dug back in, squeezing the bat handle so tight you could almost see its wood chips fluttering on his shoes. This time he lofted a high fly to right, but Richbourg, perhaps still dwelling on his two-sack hits, jiggled, juggled and finally fumbled the ball and looked up to see Cobb standing at second. Rigney sent the manager home with a sharp single on the next pitch to tie the score at 2-2.

But the keg of exciting gunpowder was just igniting. Bassler roped a double into the opposite corner in left, Goslin raced over like an oafish gazelle, scooped up the sphere and chucked it plateward. The ball flew as a comet would to catcher Tate, who parked his knee on the home dish and tagged Rigney's left collar bone in a cloud of dust for the out! The exultant mob stood and shouted "Goooooooose!" which sounded like "Boooo!" to the untrained ear.

Hooks Dauss relieved and threw two scoreless innings, and then Syl Johnson took the slab for four more. Johnson was weakening, but manager Harris knew that a weary Train was still preferable to any of the relief men waiting in the roundhouse, and left him out for the extra segments. But after an Al Wingo walk and Pratt single in the 11th, Bob Jones hit a deep fly to put Detroit ahead 3-2. Now all base ball fans know the Great Johnson is also a wonderful hitter, yet three separate times—in the 9th, 11th and 13th—he came to bat with a man on second base and could not drive him in. The Nats' Doc Prothro instead was the Brave Knight of the Eleventh, as he singled in front of Manush with two outs to score Ossie Bluege and knot the game 3-3.

Oh, the tension! The score board had long posted a final score from Yankee Stadium, a surprise victory for Chicago, and both the Tigers and Senators were hungry for this win. The 12th went by with no further scoring, but Heilman picked out a dying Johnson curve to begin the 13th and cold-cocked it on a line into the deepest part of centerfield, just below the fine house that graces the top of the zig-zag wall. By the time Wid Mathews tracked down the ball, Harry had huffed into third for a leadoff triple. Manush flied to short center for a harmless out, but then Al Wingo, playing in place of the absent Lu Blue, singled past Harris for the 4-3 lead.

Yet these Nats are one of the toughest outfits in years. Bluege led the Nats' 13th with a double, his fourth hit of the game. Harris took himself out of the lineup for McNeely, but Pillette, now on the hill, whiffed him. The Train batted once more, tipping his cap to the cheering crowd, but grounded out, before Mathews rolled one to Heilman for the exhausting conclusion, as the giant peach of a sun dropped behind the stands.

The Tigers will take their licks against Mogridge tomorrow, while Lil Stoner will attempt to keep the Senators muzzled, but with this uncanny, drama-drenched spectacle still burning in their minds and aching muscles, the players may have a hard time upstaging it.

DET 100 000 100 010 1 - 4 11 1
WAS 001 010 000 010 0 - 3 12 1

BIG TROUBLE IN THE RIVER CITY
May 11, 1924

We got to Redland Field early because it was Mother's Day and we didn't know how many of those mothers would show up in Cincinnati. There actually seemed to be a pretty good amount, and we had to change seats twice because of their big hats in our faces.

We ended up way down in the right field stands about a spit away from the bleacher section. Whitey Glazner was pitching, who's just been plain lousy for us so far, and he didn't change our minds right away by giving up singles to Critz and the Boob and then a loud triple to Rube Bressler for a 2-0 Reds lead. When Roush hit a high fly to score the third run, two whole rows of the bleachers bounced around like a see-saw bench. A gang of young guys all wearing dark shirts and suspenders were making a big ruckus, and Benny went to a seat usher to ask who they were.

The Over-the Rhine Boys were from a tough German neighborhood that went by the same name, and I suddenly recognized them as the guys who followed us out yesterday with their dirty looks. It was 4-0 Cincy behind Carl Mays before long, but when we scored two runs in the 3rd thanks to a big error from Cliff Lee out in right, Benny hooted and waved his cap and made sure the Over-the-Rhine Boys were watching. I told him to keep it down because we weren't back at home but it's hard to calm Benny down when he gets fevered up.

Now Mays is the pitcher who threw the ball that killed Cleveland shortstop Chapman a few years back, and fans of every team except for his usually give it to him good, but today he didn't have to throw at anyone's head because the Phils couldn't have hit him with cave man clubs. And I forget whether I've mentioned it lately, but Cy Williams has been stinking real bad. Today he grounded out twice in the first three innings with people on second base, and with the lineup we got, Cy has to hit for us to have any chance at all.

Anyway, after we lost Benny was moping and cursing Carl Mays and sure enough those German roughnecks followed us out the exit again. We tried to squeeze through the big crowd but they had more friends waiting for us at the edge of the parking places and when one of them mouthed off to Benny in a creepy German accent, he reared back and punched him and then everything went blue. Normally I would have let Benny get himself in hot water but being far from home I just couldn't, and besides I haven't been thrilled with Germans since one of them killed Papa during the Great War so I jumped in and kicked a lot and got thrown to the ground. By the time I stood back up they'd dragged Benny up the street. I couldn't find a cop anywhere so I headed in the direction they took him and found myself in Over-the Rhine.

This part of the city had German restaurants and German hotels and German signs and even sold German newspapers, and I felt kind of sick just looking at them all and smelling the air. After wandering around for a good hour I finally found Benny sitting in an alley with a bloody nose and black eye. He ended up telling the gang his name was Hans Muellerschmidt even though it wasn't, just so they'd let him go, and he was lucky it worked. I helped him up and we found a German laundry where we could both wash up in a sink.

Now that Benny had turned German, he really felt he deserved a good dinner here, so we walked into a fancy restaurant called Mecklenburg Gardens to settle ourselves down, and believe it or not the place had a secret door to an illegal beer garden in the back. We wouldn't have even known it if Benny hadn't put a ten dollar bill in the waiter's pocket.

It was smoky and packed in there and I had to stay calm with all the well-dressed Huns around us, but the big kegs on the wall sure helped that problem. It was the first mug of real beer I'd ever had, all foamy and heavy, and after my second one it didn't take me long to feel poorly. Benny pulled me onto a floor to dance to some oom-pah song with two girls, which only made me run off to a toilet to upvomit.

Bad enough I have to worry about Benny's crazy driving, now I just hope I won't be spoiling his seats. Good night if I can fall asleep!

PHL 002 000 000 - 2 6 0
CIN 310 010 00x - 5 9 3

PHILLIE FANS IN A LOST WORLD
May 12, 1924

Some days you can't get out of bed, or just plain shouldn't. It wasn't until 11 in the morning that I was well enough to eat something, and it was a stale biscuit Benny brought upstairs for me. My first encounter with illegal German beer didn't go all that swell, and I told him I'd be danged if I ever stepped foot in one of those beery gardens again.

The Redland Field sunshine helped my condition, though. This time Benny paid a little extra for good seats between third base and home plate, far away from our bleacher hooligan friends, and when Holke singled in the top of the 1st and Cy walked to the plate to face Rixey, it seemed like the day would turn out fine. But Williams grounded out, and the afternoon went down the drain like dirty bath water.

You see, after Wilson singled with one out in the 2nd, the remaining 23 Phillie batters went down without a fight. I don't know where this Eppa Rixey guy came from or what disease he was named after, but the lefty didn't throw one ball we could hit with a side of beef. Meantime, Cincy put together two of their famous tippy-toe rallies, scoring with walks, sacrifice flies, triples by people who never hit them, and it was 4-0 to stay by the end of the 6th.

The crowd around us was hooting themselves hoarse, and me and Benny just had to sit there and take it. Benny didn't even yell anything after the third inning, and by the end had sunk so low in his seat all I could see was his cap.

What do you do for fun after getting run down by a lorry? I said I'd even go back to Over-the-Rhine and that beer garden just to cheer Benny up, but he didn't want to run into those German goons again. So I said why not Fountain Square and another moving picture? and he said fine.

This time I wanted to find one without kissing and we were in luck because the Lyric was showing "The Lost World", which I think was based on a book by the guy who wrote Sherlock Holmes stories, and it had all these scary prehistoric monsters in it. Benny jumped in his seat and even screamed at one part but mostly laughed and was in a much better mood when it was over and took me to a nice joint for a great spaghetti and meatball dinner. Sometimes when you have an awful day all you need is a good place to escape to, and the Lyric Theatre sure did it for us tonight.

One more Redland game tomorrow and we head to Pittsburgh!

PHL 000 000 000 - 0 2 0
CIN 000 202 00x - 4 7 0

BEER GARDEN OF DOOM
May 13, 1924

Well, the Chrysler was all packed up and ready to head for Pittsburgh after the game, but ain't it funny how things change whenever Benny is part of the story?

We were ready to give those Reds a beating after yesterday's hitless tragedy, and for a while it looked like it could happen. Our biggest winner Bill Hubbell was pitching, and they had Pete Donohue, who's their worst. We were in the upper right field stands for the last game, and the place was pretty crowded for a Tuesday because the Reds were only one game out when the day started, and we were able to move to seats with a good view not blocked by lady-hats. Anyway, two singles, a walk and a big double from Sand in the leadoff hole gave us a 2-0 lead in the 2nd, before doubles from Harper and Wilson and a single by Cy Williams made it 4-0 an inning later!

Cincy has this knack for building rallies out of nothing, though, and sure enough they did it again, Chick Shorten, a spare outfielder batting second because Roush was out along with four other regulars, doubled past Mokan with two outs in the 5th. Then a ball squished past Wilson behind the plate to get Shorten to third. Then Boob and the Rube went to town, a triple from Fowler and a single by Bressler to make it 4-2. I got all worried but Benny said don't worry, this is our lucky day because we deserve one.

How do you explain the 7th inning, then? Shorten singled to start, and Huck Betts came in for Hubbell. Boob and the Rube both singled. So did Pinelli, followed by a sacrifice pop by Bubbles Hargrave, and the game was tied. Then Cliff Lee began the Cincy 8th with a dumb and stupid and lucky homer off the foul stick in left, and we were behind. Dang it to hell! Benny still had faith, though, and cheered himself a little by yelling at the celebrating crowd to shut up.

Then Sand singled off Red reliever Jakie May to begin the 9th. Holke lined out and Harper grounded Sand to second with two outs. Here came

Cy, with three singles already, his best game in weeks. And what does he do? Smoke a two-strike pitch between Lee and George Burns and it rolls all the way to the fence for a game-tying triple! "HUZZAH!" we shouted and jumped so high our heads almost hit the grandstand roof.

We went into extra innings, which naturally had to happen on the day we had to leave early, but they didn't last that long. With two outs in the Red 10th, Betts lost everything he sort of had. May singled, Hugh Critz doubled him to third, and lousy little Chick Shorten ran out an infield hit to give them the stinkin' game.

At least we put up a good battle, Benny said, and I agreed, but now we had a bigger problem because the Over-the-Rhine Boys were on us again. Were we really cheering that loud? They caught us from behind right near our car, dragged us back to their neighborhood. But this time they were laughing and happy and telling us in their weird thick voices that they weren't going to let us leave town without showing us a "gut" time at their "Bock-skellar", whatever that was.

What it was was a private beer cellar of their own, down some narrow winding stairs inside a dark apartment house. They had four large kegs in there and long tables set up and German travel posters up on the wet stone walls, and German music played on a phonograph and an old guy with an apron brought down plates of sausages and then a half dozen big German girls showed up to join the party and Benny was suddenly in nervous heaven.

This beer actually tasted lots better than the Mecklenburg stuff, and it wasn't long before I was patting people on the back more than they did on mine. Three guys actually named Muellerschmidt were surrounding Benny and asking him what village in Bavaria his ancestors were from and Benny had to make up a name that sounded more like a pig snort. I had this 20-year-old fraulein named Ute all over me trying to speak English and butchering every word but I didn't care because she smelled like a morning meadow and kept petting my head like I was her little schnauzer. After my fourth mug of Bock I wrote down my address for her and stupidly said she could write me, which was right before we were forced to stand on a table and sing a few German songs we had to fake so that they'd let us leave. We hugged them and Ute slurpy-kissed me and then we were somehow back on the Over-the-Rhine street and stumbling back to the ball park.

Benny drove like a kook like I figured he would, and I begged him to pull off the road so we could sleep for a while and not kill ourselves, but he said it's easier to drive in the dark because there's less cars on the road and I was too soused to argue with him.

Which is why I woke up at sunrise with the car stuck in the middle of some farmer's muddy field, and Benny snoring on top of the wheel. The farmer came out with his rifle but was laughing too hard to shoot us and finally helped us push the car back onto the highway. Thank God Cincy-to-Pittsburgh will be one of our shortest drives on this trip. Good evening I mean morning. People-readers...

PHL 022 000 001 0 - 5 11 0
CIN 000 020 210 1 - 6 18 1

FORBES, FUNICULARS, AND FANCY DUDS
May 14, 1924

That nice farmer who helped us drag our car back on the highway also sent us off with two chicken eggs apiece, which we broke into big glasses of orange juice at a roadside eatery for our breakfast. Benny had already been on this route on the way to Ohio, so we made real good time and rolled across one of Pittsburgh's dozen or so bridges into the city by half past noon time.

We only had thirty minutes to get a place to stay and find our way to Forbes Field for the game, and it was decided we would just figure out the lodging afterwards. The Chrysler was low on petrol again so we parked it on a back street and jumped on a streetcar that took us to the Oakland section and the corner of Forbes and South Bouquet, where the ballpark was.

It was a fine-looking yard, not that old really, and had a beautiful green park called Schenley right next to it. Benny was real tired and wanted to go in the park and nap under a big tree for an hour but I wouldn't let him, not after we drove all that way, and said he could sleep in his seat.

The Pirates are right at the top in the National League, so of course the park was crowded but we were able to buy some grandstand seats on the right side from a guy whose kids got sick. We sat down just in time to see Harper whack a double off the right fence and Cy Williams single them in, and suddenly Benny wasn't so tired anymore. Hal Carlson was throwing for us which had me worried because he gives up lots of hits and the Bucs don't do anything but collect them. He was tough today, though, and escaped over and over from pickles like a baseball Houdini. First he got Max Carey to pop out with the bases filled in the 2nd, then got Rabbit Maranville and their pitcher Lee Meadows with two aboard in the 4th, then got Kiki Cuyler to rap into a double play with two on in the 5th. Mokan meanwhile singled in Harper after George's second double in the 4th, and when Wilson knocked in our third run in the 6th on a grounder, we had a darn good chance to win!

Glenn Wright hit a sacrifice fly to score their catcher Earl Smith in the 6th, and then it was one heart-stopper after another for Carlson the rest of the way, but the big man came through. Wright doubled to begin their 9th and the Forbes crowd was up screaming and Benny and me were doing the same for different reasons but Maranville grounded out, Jewel Ens pinch-hit and whiffed, and Carey popped out to end it.

We couldn't believe it. Our yucky Phillies team had beaten the league's best, at least for a day, and we skipped out of there like a couple of picaroons. Pittsburgh has all these vertical cable trains called funiculars that go straight to the top of its high hills, and we picked the nearest one out for a fun celebration ride. By the time we reached the top, with amazing views of the city below and all parts of western Pennsylvania, Benny hit on his latest nutty idea. To honor our valiant team, we would find the nicest hotel in town and treat ourselves like kings while we were in town, the heck with this smelly beer garden nonsense.

It sounded like a good plan, except here we were looking like bums and smelling worse than one. Leave that to me, said Benny, I didn't inherit this money to watch it rot. Leaving anything to Benny gets me nervous right away but then I thought, isn't this what an adventure should be?

The first thing we did was buy some suitably nice clothes at a big downtown store called Kaufmann's. Then we drove over to a huge factory called Jones & Laughlin Steel, snuck in a back door and used a shower stall while the factory guys were busy sweating in the next room. We cut out of there with our new clothes on and our hair combed, and then Benny found some street kids to wash his car.

And then we turned a corner and saw the William Penn Hotel, an incredibly giant brick palace which they say that presidents have stayed in. We entered its gigantic fancy lobby and Benny got us a room for three nights, signing his name BENJAMIN C. BOGGS on the register, while I was his young ward VINCENT FOX. What the heck, using fake names in Cincy sure kept us alive so why not here?

The room had two big beds and its own card table and the biggest tub I'd ever seen and I couldn't believe we were there. Benny couldn't either, and stomped around the room singing Great War battle songs for a few minutes until there was a knock on the door. A short, fancy-dressed man in a bowler hat stood there. He had round glasses, a grey handlebar moustache and showed us his card, which said M. CONROY FACE, PRIVATE HOTEL DETECTION on it. He asked a bunch of questions about where we were from and what our business was, and we had to fake it the best we could and make up a raft of stuff and boy, I hope he believed us because the last thing I want to do is lose this room.

And tomorrow? It's Oeschger for us, Cooper for the Bucs, and let's hope another big win.

PHL 100 101 000 - 3 7 0
PIT 000 001 000 - 1 10 1

SWASHBUCKLED

May 15, 1924

Well, our dreams of leaving Pittsburgh with a Jolly Roger flag stuck on the Chrysler turned into dust right away today, but thrills on the high Forbes Field sea were everywhere.

It was a good thing we treated ourselves to a big fancy breakfast in the hotel dining room before that, because otherwise we might not have had enough energy to take it. I had a poached egg for the first time in my life, which was awful strange looking and stranger tasting but they had fresh berry juice that tasted like it had been picked and squashed up in the next room.

Anyway, when Benny got up to go look for a toilet, this lady in a shiny dress and feathered hat started coughing at a table that was nearby us. Her husband was pretty old and in a wheeled chair and didn't know what to do and started yelling for a waiter but no one seemed to hear him. So I jumped up, ran over with my water glass and got her swallowing and breathing normal again. The husband was all grateful and asked my name and asked what room my parents were in so I told him I was Benjamin C. Boggs' young ward and we were in town to watch baseball for the first time.

By the time Benny got back from the bathroom, the old man had scribbled down a name on the back of a small card, someone to ask for when we got to the ball park that day. Benny had an idea what that was going to mean, and quickly introduced himself, shook the guy's hand and gave his wife a weird bow, and I had to almost push him away from their table.

But Benny was right. The scribbled-down man ran the ticket booths at Forbes Field, read the old man's note, smiled, reached in his vest and handed us two tickets to the game. And what tickets they were! Two sniffs away from the field, right behind the Pirate dugout. We could just about reach out and touch a patch of grass that Honus Wagner probably kneeled in once, and we bought lemonade and peanuts from the first vendor we saw. Most everyone was real well-dressed and polite around us, so I told Benny not to get his usual excited this time and he promised he wouldn't.

The first inning took care of that anyway, because we got hit by a volley of Pirate cannonballs that almost made us duck under our seats. Carey led with a single, robbed second base, and Charlie Grimm singled him in. Then Eddie Moore singled, then Cuyler doubled, then Smith singled, then Oeschger committed a balk if you can believe that, then Wright and Maranville singled and it was 6-0 for the Buccaneers out of the dock!

It was one of those warm spring days, though, when the balls fly every which way, and I had a feeling we'd strike back quick. Sand and Williams had singled for us in the 1st, and sure enough in the 2nd, Parkinson, Oeschie and Joe Schultz singled for our first run off Wilbur Cooper. Then in the 4th we got our revenge. Cy led with a monster of a homer ball over the right fence, Wilson and Mokan singled, Parkinson doubled, and with two outs Schultz doubled to make it 6-5! Benny shook off his chains and started clapping and yelping and got about ten dozen dirty looks from the folks around us but thankfully they were too well-heeled to get rude.

There were more hits in the middle innings but nobody scored until Oeschger lost it again in the 6th. Cooper began with a single, Carey doubled, Grimm walked and Moore singled. Fletcher could have yanked Oeschie at that point but he has been one of our biggest winners and the man can also swing a bat, so he stayed in there. When Earl Smith followed an out later with a three-run crack out of the park, it was 11-5 Bucs, the crowd was drowning us out again and Benny was ready to leave. I said forget that, we might never get seats this good again and who knows what else will happen on this nutty day?

I was right. Babe Adams, Pittsburgh's best relief man, pitched two scoreless innings but then Buc skipper Bill McKechnie took a gamble and put in Arnie Stone to finish up. Cy doubled in two runs off him right away in the 8th, and our 9th began with a double by Wrightstone. Ford singled him across to make it 11-8. Oeschie knocked a single like I thought he would. Schultz singled in Ford and it was 11-9! We were shrieking again!

Then the Phillies reminded us they are the Phillies. Sand popped weakly to short, Holke grounded a ball out to Maranville, who started an easy double play and we'd lost another one. But we sure weren't blue about it. The Phils had battled them fiercely with 20 hits of their own, which is all you can ask of your heroes on a losing day. Glazner goes for us tomorrow against something called Emil Yde, and we'll just see how that works out.

After the game we were too tired to do much of anything so we bought pop and jumbo sandwiches, which is what they call baloney around here, and played some cards. Benny started to feel stuffy in the room after a while, got some energy back and wanted to go out to some factory bars down on Carson Street. I wasn't in the mood and didn't want to run into that creepy hotel detective again, so I talked him into going out by himself. Hopefully he'll be back before dawn and in a not-smelly state.

PHL 014 000 022 - 9 20 0
PIT 600 005 00x - 11 16 0

Excerpted from the Detroit Free-Enterprise
May 15, 1924

This scribe must take it upon himself now to say a few words about these Tigers. Halfway through the month of May, they are proving to be a serious disappointment, and I would be shocked to find them part of the pennant flag hunt come July. They simply leave too many runners on the sacks, 279 in 29 games thus far, which computes to 9.62 per game, worst in either league. They have a .303 team batting average, which is reasonably good, but have scored less runs than four other American League teams, and herein lies the sticky issue.

Detroit has struck only seven home runs in a month and a half, one more than the lowly Boston Braves. This is undoubtedly due to the playing and managerial style of Ty Cobb, an aging, surly singles-ripper with a notorious distaste for the long fly. At times Cobb has been a firebrand on the field, but in a league where sluggers like Ruth and Goslin and Ken Williams propel spheres over fences with some regularity, Detroit has been trying to plate runs with rinky-dinkers, walks and donkers. Heilman has been an extra-base terror at times, and Manush has had a few big games, but they are the only large threats. The immortal Tyrus also seems to have little knowledge of pitching, as his moundsmen have conspired to allow 348 hits in 268 innings, and will carry a 5.31 earned run average into tomorrow's contest.

The reading public should not misinterpret my words, though. I am not suggesting Mr. Cobb should be sent a-packing; having him atop our lineup certainly provides a daily spark plug, and his many years of superior service to the Tigers has hardly been for naught. But his famed style of running, slappy play is not a suitable outfit for this current Tiger team to wear, and its continuing fashion may very well produce second division doom for 1924. **—C.J. Butterworth**

CHEAP SEATS AND SOAPY HANDS
May 16, 1924

A knock on our hotel room door woke me up at three in the morning. M. Conroy Face stood there holding a soused Benny up by the collar. "I found him sleeping on a divan in our lobby, which is not allowed," said the in-house detective. Face wasn't wearing his bowler this time, and I noticed he had grey mutton chops to match his giant moustache. I thanked him, helped Benny inside and shut the door.

I let my friend sleep until almost noon. I told him I was worried about the house detective, that he might be on to us, and Benny said it's not illegal to pretend to be someone else, as long as you hadn't stolen their wallet or something. A bigger problem, he said, is that he lost almost half of the rest of our travel money last night playing billiards at Punky Shickelgruber's speakeasy down on East Carson Street, and wasn't sure we'd be able to pay our hotel bill. I got real mad at him but Benny said don't worry because he'd win it all back tonight and I said forget that, just wash up already so we can get over to the game.

It was no surprise we sat in the cheapest seats this time, which were way down in left field in the wide open. It gave us a nice view of Schenley Park, left fielders Mokan and Cuyler and not much else, but our spirits went up when we squeezed out a run off Emil Yde in the top of the 1st. Yde is a rookie lefty with a weird name but lots of potential, so said the old duffer sitting next to us, but Yde sure didn't have it this time. We were getting doubles and triples all over the place for lots of the game.

Unfortunately Whitey Glazner threw for us, and this guy can't pitch his way off a cliff. After Cy Williams dropped his second fly of the game in the 3rd and helped the Bucs to a 2-1 lead, and we took the lead back on a Ford double, Schultz triple and boot by Rabbit Maranville, Whitey got his backside waxed in the 5th. He flubbed a grounder with two outs, then gave up a walk, two singles and triple by the Rabbit and we were losing by four runs. Then it was six runs after Steineder relieved him and Cuyler tripled. Then we got two back when Wright and Carey both made errors and boy oh boy, what crummy fielding today!

Yde ended up going the whole distance even though the Phils got 14 hits off him, and our record on the road is now something like 5-14, but that's okay. It was still a fun game to watch.

Not too sure about Benny, though. We got back to the hotel and he was too blue to eat dinner or even take a bath, but when we went through the lobby the desk man called us over and gave us a personal sealed note from someone named Anthony Quentin Rutherford. Benny and me looked at each other and I ripped it open while the elevator guy took us upstairs. It was an invitation to dinner and cigars at some place called The Duquesne

Club. What the heck? We found out from the desk man that Rutherford was the old guy in the wheeled chair yesterday morning whose wife I saved from choking, and Benny wasn't blue anymore. A free meal? Maybe more Forbes Field tickets? Quick as squirrels we were back up in the room getting washed and putting on our fancy duds.

The Duquesne Club made the William Penn Hotel look like an immigrant slum. The place was built in 1873 and had one giant fancy-furnished room after another, and each one was filled with important-looking men in suits. Mr. Rutherford met us at the dining room door in his chair, and got wheeled inside by his man-servant. We sat next to a stained glass window that went to the ceiling with a big ferny plant in my face, and we ate the same food Greek gods probably did. There was braised quails and plum pudding and caviar from the Persian sea which was pretty darn yucky and Elysian Fields Lamb and me and Benny did our best to hold our forks the right way and put our napkins in our laps and all that, but it wasn't easy.

Anyway, Rutherford was one of the biggest steel magpies in town, and he had a niece he was trying to help get married off and kept calling me a "fine young fellow" because I helped his wife and asked if I could sit with this niece whose name was Lily at Forbes Field tomorrow and explain how baseball works because she'd never been to a game before. It sounded good alright, but with Benny staring at me I then asked if the three of us could go because Benny knew more of the finer points.

Rutherford said sure, and then we were in a drawing room where I tried my first glass of brandy and smoked my first cigar and spent the hour after we left coughing and trying not to fall down. Such is the risk of being a young ward, I guess.

PHL 100 210 200 -6 14 4
PIT 002 152 00x - 10 10 3

EDITOR'S NOTE, DETROIT-FREE ENTERPRISE:

The Enterprise regrets to inform our readers that Mr. Calvin Butterworth suffered an unfortunate personal mishap last evening, and has been transported to North Boston Hospital in Massachusetts, where the Tigers will play the Red Sox on their next road stop, for the finest medical attention.

WE GLADLY WALK THE PLANK
May 17, 1924

So Benny sat there at our little table with his legs crossed, wearing his William Penn Hotel cloth robe, having juice and crumpets for breakfast. I was still half asleep but he kept snapping his newspaper to keep me awake.

Until a story in the sports section did it for him. Seems that this poor Detroit baseball writer named Butterworth got jumped outside Shibe Park the other night by none other than Ty Cobb and got pummeled pretty bad and sent to a hospital with a broken left arm and two black eyes. Now Benny might be nuts but he thinks it's the same writer he wanted to mess up himself when he wrote something nasty about the Phillies before the season began. And here he was in our city getting roughed up by somebody famous! Isn't that ironical?

Anyway, Commissioner Landis is looking into suspending Cobb, something he seems to do a lot, but it might be hard because he is the Tiger manager and they're in the pennant race, though we can't have star players beating up writers because that doesn't look too good. So we'll see.

As it turns out this Butterfield guy was sure right about the Phils, because the Pirates took Jimmy Ring and the rest of us apart like a cheap watch and threw the parts into the gutter. The final score was a 12-0 creaming with the game over after the fourth Pirate batter, but what stunk to high heaven was that we had to sit up close in those good seats with Rutherford's niece and try to be polite to her for all two hours.

Her name was Lily and she was about my age and not too attractive but she had on a white church dress and wore a hat so big that it covered up most of her face. She knew absolutely nothing about baseball and with Benny uninterested and too busy suffering with every Pirate run, it was left to me to explain things. Yes, the defense has the ball, not the offense. Yes, a foul hit is not a penalty hit. No, I have no idea why home plate is shaped like that. No, I have no idea why they call them Pie, Kiki and Rabbit. On and on this went, and what was real bad is that normally we would have left by the 6th inning to start our long drive to Chicago, but we were afraid to strand Lily there and have some rich guy in Pittsburgh who thought we were someone else be mad at us.

The Bucs laid us nicely in our coffins with five final runs in the 8th. Jimmy Ring is now 0-6 for us, while Johnny Morrison, definitely the worst person in their rotation, got his third shutout, is 5-0 and dropped his earned run average to a tiny 0.89. Pittsburgh ended up taking three out of the four games after our opening win, which if you can remember actually made us feel competitive. What thoughts were we having?

Lily invited us over to her parents' house after the game for tea, but we made up some excuse about going to see our stockbrokers, stuck her in a taxi cab, hightailed it back to the hotel for our bags and hit the first road into Ohio. We drove clear across the state until it was almost midnight, and ended up in a town called Van Wert that was just about in Indiana. The 40 Winks Motor Hotel wasn't much, but it was actually a relief for me after the stuffy William Penn. We thought we heard someone snooping around outside our cabin door as we were falling asleep, and Benny was sure it was M. Conroy Face with his evil facial hair, but I said why would that guy ever be following us? Benny got that guilty look he gets and turned over, and then I was suddenly worried again.

PHI 000 000 000 - 0   4 1
PIT 203 001 15X - 12 17 2

OUR KIND OF TOWN
May 18, 1924

We stopped for more petrol outside of Gary, Indiana, and got to Chicago around noon time. What a gigantic city, and there were so many people with cars on the roads, much more than I could remember seeing in New York. We got a city map from another gasoline station and Benny drove us north along Lake Michigan, which looked more like an ocean than a lake.

Cubs Park was in a crowded neighborhood on the north side of town. Benny thought we should get right to the game and worry about a hotel afterwards, which turned out to be good idea as you'll see. The streets around the park were filled with baseball fans that all seemed just thrilled to be going to a game, even though their team hasn't been in a World Series for almost six years now. There were peanut and sausage carts and pennant hawkers everywhere, and the sun was out and the whole area just had a happy baseball feeling I never experienced before.

The best thing was that the Cubs always kept a bunch of good seat tickets available for every game, meaning after standing in a line for just a half hour we had some! They were right behind third base and gave us good views of the city behind the brick outfield walls. Anyway, the second we dropped in out seats, George Harper smacked a homer out to right, scoring Sand from first and we had a 2-0 lead! Bill Hubbell pitched for us, who isn't that great but usually seems to keep us in games. On the mound for the Cubs, though, was Grover Cleveland Alexander, who some people call Pete but Benny and me call a drunk. He pitched for us in the 1915 World Series against Boston and Papa used to tell me how much he loved watering holes after most of the games.

Anyway, he must have been coming off a bender today because he was teetering and tottering out there something awful. With a man on second for us in the 2nd inning, he floated one in to Sand and Heinie smashed it high over the bricks in left and we were winning 4-0. Can you believe it? Heinie Sand homered off Alexander? Well, the man can drink but he can also hit, because after Sparky Adams doubled in the bottom of the 2nd, Old Pete got hold of a fastball, closed his eyes and put it out on Waveland Avenue somewhere.

Then he went back out to give us more presents. He walked Harper and Cy, got Wrightstone on a grounder, but Wilson, Mokan and Ford all doubled to make it 8-2 Phillies. We yelped as loud as we could without upsetting the locals, but they really didn't seem to care anyway. Alexander calmed down after that and pitched darn fine until the 9th when he gave up three more singles and got yanked, but one of the reasons was because he walked and singled and was probably the best Cubs hitter all day. Johnny Couch finished up for us when Hubbell got tired, and we kept up our streak of winning the first game out of four in the third straight city.

We picked out a hotel called the Grasmere afterward, which was close enough to Cubs Park to walk there. The lobby guy said that Charlie Chaplin even stayed there once, which gave us a tiny thrill. As usual, Benny was feeling bouncy after we won the game, and wanted to get out and explore the city. He found out about a big dancing hall on North Broadway which was right in our neighborhood called the Arcadia Ballroom, and I said what the heck I needed to move my legs.

And what a place! It was filled with mostly white people but also some coloreds, because a group of them called Walter Barnes and his Royal Creolians had the stage and boy, could they ever play! Barnes was on a clarinet and a saxaphone and they also had a piano player and a drummer and someone with a trumpet and it was impossible to sit still.

And you'll never guess who screamed my name while Benny and me were trying to buy glasses of flavored seltzer. We turned and there was Rachel! She'd taken the train out to Chicago to visit a girlfriend and see the Robins play at Cubs Park, and it just so happened she was staying an extra day! We hugged each other and she shook Benny's hand and then brought us over to a table where her friend was. Ruby was a pretty young colored girl who used to clean Rachel's house in Brooklyn many years ago and the two of them kept writing letters after Ruby moved away. She was married to Thomas, a colored horse trainer who was also there, and we had a good talk about baseball and horses and jazz music, which had come up from New Orleans and was sweeping through the town. Thomas said he knew some of the colored players from the negro leagues like Smokey Joe Williams and Oscar Charleston, and asked if I'd like to see them play sometime and I said sure, though the prospect for that didn't look good because of our short stay in town.

The Creolians then played a song called the "Jelly Roll Blues" written by a piano player named Ferd Morton, and Rachel dragged me and Benny out on the big wood floor to show us how to do the Foxtrot dance. I was a big failure at that but Benny picked it up pretty good, and he spun away to try it with some other girl he had his eyes on.

Rachel said there was something magical about the way we kept running into each other in different cities, and I agreed alright. I told her all about Pittsburgh and Cincinnati, which got her all excited about the Robins again because I guess they creamed the Reds there today in their first meeting. She said she'd been thinking about visiting me in Philadelphia the next time the Robins were there and I said she'd be real welcome at Mama's house, except she might have to pretend she's Italian for a night.

She left with Ruby and Thomas after a while after giving me a nice long kiss in an alley around the corner, and Benny ribbed me about it all the way back to the hotel like I figured he would. My first day and night in Chicago had been like heaven, a place where you can always count on a good sleep.

PHL 224 000 102 - 11 15 0
CHI 020 010 020 - 5 10 3

ASK QUESTIONS BEFORE YOU GRAB SOMEONE'S COLLAR
May 19, 1924

We let ourselves sleep till almost noon. The Grasmere Hotel was so close to Cubs Park we could walk to the game easy, which was a good thing because the Chrysler Six was making some funny noises on the way into Chicago yesterday and Benny was nervous about driving it for a few days.

It was another beautiful spring day and it was too bad Cubs Park didn't have a bleacher section because we would have enjoyed some of that sun in our faces. An usher in the right field stands told us that Cubs owner Albert Lasker was too cheap to expand the place and was thinking of selling the team to someone else, which I guess could be a good thing. Whoever the new owner is should buy them some good fielding, too, because they sure didn't have any today.

George Grantham booted one at second base in the 1st, and then we got a run off them in the 2nd on a walk and three more errors, two by Ray Grimes their first basemen. Hal Carlson, who has less talent than most pitchers in the league but always seems to come through for us did it again against Elmer Jacobs, and had a 1-0 shutout through the 7th inning. At one point he shot down 16 Cubbies in a row! The fans around us were yelling nasty words at their hitters and calling us bums and meatheads and I had to keep Benny in his seat because he was all ready to go at it with someone.

The fans were also blue because their young, homer-hitting catcher Gabby Hartnett went out with an injured back in the 2nd, and his replacement Bob O'Farrell pretty much stinks. Then the 8th inning started. Holke doubled past Hack Miller in left. Harper singled him to third. Cy doubled deep to right. Guy Bush came on to pitch and he was even worse. He got Wrightstone, but then hit Jimmie Wilson, threw a pitch over O'Farrell's head and the second run scored. Then Mokan knocked in a third one with a long fly. Then Ford doubled, then Carlson singled and Ford was smoked at the plate but it was 5-0 Phillies!

Benny was so excited he offered to buy me a giant pretzel from a wagon he'd seen behind home plate, so between innings we went over there. It was an awful long line but we stood in it anyway because the smell of those hot pretzels was enough to knock you silly. We missed the bottom of the 8th when the Cubs scored a run on a cheap grounder, and Sand doubled for us to start the 9th. Benny was all restless to get back but we were almost at the pretzel cart.

Then this snotty little kid in a fancy suit jacket and tie and his greasy hair parted in the middle cut right in front of us in the line! Benny yelled at him to get lost and the kid turned around and stomped his shoe on Benny's foot. Benny grabbed him by the collar, said where's your parents? and the kid said his dad was in the first row near the Cubs dugout. Benny stuck money for two pretzels in my hand and said he'd meet me at our seats. But the second he hauled the kid away the pretzel man looked at me with this real scared face and asked me if I knew who that boy's father was.

After he told me he gave me a third pretzel for free, and suddenly I was running down to the front row seats. I got there a second before Benny did, and put the free pretzel in the kid's hand. "Hey Pa," said the kid to his dad, "this jerk swore at me." I tried to pull Benny away but it was too late, because Al Capone had already stood up. He wore a shiny blue suit with a white silk handkerchief in it, and he had pearl grey spats on his shoes and diamonds on his watch chain. He was also real short but had cold eyes that sort of froze you to the ground. He also had a pair of large, ugly men sitting in the row behind him, and they stood up with him.

I jabbered quickly that the boy got lost looking for the pretzel wagon and we helped him get back and didn't know you were his dad and so on and so forth and Benny looked like he was about to cry but all Capone said was "What's your name, kid?" So I told him Vinny Spanelli and this was my best friend Benzini Olio and he gave us a big smile and asked if we needed a ride home after the game. Benny said no thanks, Mr. Capone, we already have a car and we need to get back to our seats, right Vinny? Capone then said wait a second and asked if we wanted to make a little money giving one of HIS friends a ride after tomorrow's game. That's okay, said Benny, but my car's a little bit on the fritz so Capone said he'd take care of that for us, and he'd also throw in great ball game tickets for tomorrow. Me and Benny looked at each other and I don't have to tell you what Benny's answer was.

Mr. Capone actually seemed like a decent guy, even though he has what I guess you can call a nasty reputation. Sitting at a ball game for two hours can calm you down pretty good, even if your team loses. He gave us the name of a great steak and hamburger joint in the city, and we ate a huge dinner there after the game which turned out to be free when we told the host who sent us there. I never tasted hamburger meat so fresh and delicious, like the cow had been killed in the next room. The waiter said no, it happens a couple streets away.

Anyway, with all the excitement I forgot to mention that if we beat the Cubs tomorrow we pass them in the standings.

PHL 010 000 041 - 6 9 0
CHI 000 000 010 - 1 6 4

A LETTER TO MY READERS
By Calvin J. Butterworth, Detroit Free-Enterprise

It has been a pleasure to return to the base ball world again, more specifically, to the world of Detroit Tiger reporting I've been a part of for three seasons now.

As most of you are aware, I was the recent victim of a physical attack by manager Ty Cobb for my published comments about his slapping and running style of play, and for my firm doubts about its suitably for our team. I now feel it is imperative to clear the air concerning this incident in these pages, so as to not only prevent other unwarranted attacks, but to express how the incident has altered my general feelings about my profession.

Mr. Cobb has had a long, distinguished career as a Tiger batsman, and if base ball ever constructs a suitable shrine to honor its greatest talents, I imagine he will be permanently housed there. Yet while I found his hair-trigger response to my words utterly uncivilized and reprehensible, I can understand why it occurred. The daily chore of performing well on a ball field while managing 23 other men is not something a member of the press like myself can ever identify with. Add in the constant niggling questions from said press members before and after each contest and the tension of merely staying afloat in a pennant chase, and it is no surprise more players do not walk up behind reporters and beat their heads without warning.

I can sit in my booth seat here and wax eloquently about the statistical sheets that are handed to me by runner boys at game-time, but in doing so it is easy to lose one's sight of how extremely difficult it is to play base ball for a living. The next time we scribes question the thousands of dollars many of these players earn yearly, we should remember that. While I will never forgive Mr. Cobb's flying knuckles, I have a newfound respect for his passion—both for the game and his players—and I trust he and I will approach each other on professional, even footing from now until October's leaves fall.

OUR VERY OWN URBAN SHOCKER
May 20, 1924

Back at Cubs Park for the third game, we sat in incredible seats right behind the Phillie dugout left for us at a ticket window by Mr. Alphonse Capone. Our team was facing a guy named Tony Kauffman who was 0-5 so far, I had a bag of hot salted peanuts in my hand, Benny wasn't yelling at anyone yet and the world seemed wonderful.

Down only 2-1 even though Oeschger had given the Cubs seven hits in the first three innings, we started cracking the ball out of the yard. Wilson homered with one out in the top of the 4th, and an out later Hod Ford did the same thing. With two outs in the 5th, Harper hit one onto the right field street and we were up 4-2. Sixth place was right around the corner!

Then the sky got a little dark and so did the game. With two outs in the Cub 6th they got three singles and a walk off Oeschie and he was gone from the mound along with his 13 hits. Other than the three boingers we hit off Kauffman, though, he was pretty tough, and it was still 4-3 us when Ray Steineder took the hill for the bottom of the 9th. Ray hasn't been used too much but he'd already pitched the 7th and 8th without allowing a hit, which after Oeschger was a huge thing.

Except he lost it somewhere on his way back to the mound. Friberg began with his fourth single of the game. Grantham singled and Grimes loaded the bases with another single. Huck Betts came running in to save the day and our shot at sixth place, but Hack Miller rammed his first pitch deep off the left brick wall for two runs and the shocking Cub win.

Benny and me walked out of there like the stars of our own funeral, and we were so down we almost forgot to drive to this building near a north side pier to pick up Capone's friend. It was some kind of shipping office on a dark street. Thunder and lightning were going now, and we must've sat in the Chrysler for a whole hour waiting for him to come out. Capone had sent a mechanic guy to our hotel that morning and thankfully the car ran like a dream now, but this was getting stupid.

Benny was all ready to leave when we heard two loud gunshots. The door to the shipping office opened and this guy in a black coat and cap came running out with a black valise bag. I opened the back door for him and he jumped in, all crazy, and told us to drive. Benny sure did, but the next thing we knew there were two cars racing after us. The guy sent us down one alley, then the next, and Benny almost hit three brick walls trying to follow his directions.

We ended up in a dark garage and sat there while the two cars went right by. We were both shaking but the guy whose name was Paulie Potatoes and had a face like one gave us three hundred dollars each from the black bag and a bottle of Canadian whiskey. "Mr. Capone says thanks," he said and disappeared around the corner.

I don't have to tell you that we sampled that whiskey when we got back to the Grasmere, and more than once.

PHL 001 210 000 - 4 9 2
CHI 101 001 002 - 5 17 0

SWEATY DEPARTURES
May 21, 1924

By the time I went downstairs to get us a morning newspaper it was 94 degrees and my socks were sticking to my ankles. Summer got to Chicago early and it took me about five seconds to realize there's no way I could ever live in this place, even though it has the best hamburger meat in America.

We took a streetcar to Cubs Park this time to save our energy, and had bought ice cold lemon-limeades before we even got to our seats. Today we waited in line like normal fans and got some way down in left field because Benny was afraid to owe Mr. Capone any more favors. We were still shaking from our getaway driver job last night and wanted to just leave town in peace.

Art Fletcher finally wised up and stuck Johnny Couch in our rotation instead of the lousy Glazner, and it paid off in this one. After Cy gave us a 2-0 lead off the bat with a 2-run single Couch looked like he needed to rest on one because he gave up a Friberg double, Grantham triple and Hack Miller single in a row to tie the game. Then him and Aldridge started pitching zeroes like no one's business.

In the bottom of the 5th, though, with the metal arms of the seats burning us if we touched them and sweat dripping off our hair, we almost fainted when Couch served up a 2-run belt by Grantham that got the Cub fans jumping all around us. A Harper triple and two-out Wilson single made it 4-3, and then in the 8th, Cy took an Aldridge ball and shot it out of his bat cannon to tie the game! Suddenly the heat didn't bother us, and Benny would have ripped off his shirt and twirled it if we didn't have a pair of cops watching us.

Couch got into jams in the 7th and 8th and 9th but got out of them and we went into extra innings. A tall creepy guy with a heavy Italian accent appeared behind our seats around that time and asked why we hadn't taken the free tickets Mr. Capone left for us and we had to explain we were leaving for St. Louis that night and weren't able to give any people any more rides. He said fine, but if we needed any cash while we were in St. Louis we should look up a guy named Big Toe Sam who runs a pool hall there. We said thanks and the guy finally disappeared so we could suffer through the rest of the game.

Turns out we didn't even need to. Cy walked with one out in the 10th, Wrightstone singled him to third, and after Wilson moved the runner to second with a grounder, Mokan ripped a 2-run hit in front of the Hack Man in left. Couch gave up a single to Grimes to start the Cub 10th but then took care of all business and we'd won three out of the four!

To celebrate we decided to cool off by heading over to a Lake Michigan beach, which was packed so tight there wasn't even room to lie down. The water was cool and gave us complete chicken skin, and Benny tried to drown me a few times and followed a couple cute girls wearing bloomers through the water before they told him to get lost, and then we went back to the hotel to start packing.

But when we opened the room door we couldn't believe it: Someone had been in there going through all our stuff.

I can't really call it a robbery because there was nothing stolen or even worth stealing, and Benny kept all his money under a floor mat in his car which didn't make a lot of sense but worked out this time. Was it one of Capone's guys? Maybe someone from that warehouse we drove away from yesterday. Anyway, we were real spooked and packed up in maybe five minutes and got the heck out of Chicago before something worse happened.

No one seemed to be following us, but there were lots of cars on these roads out of town so you never know. The drive to St. Louis isn't that long and with Benny on the gas pedal it'll sure be a lot shorter.

PHL 200 001 010 2 - 6 13 0
CHI 200 020 000 0 - 4 9 2

WAY, WAY OUT WEST
May 22, 1924

We drove to St. Louis most of the night and holed up in the Chrysler in a dirt parking lot behind a roadside eatery so we could be there for our bacon and eggs the second their door opened in the morning. The lady who served us was real chubby and unfriendly and the cook smoked a cigarette that dripped ash on the grille most of the time, but the food was sure delicious.

We read the morning newspaper and saw that our record was 13-22 and just one half of a game behind the Cubs, which made us feel better because at least we had a sixth place pennant race to cheer for. Mama likes to say that even the stormiest sky has a blue patch up there eventually, and I guess that's the way we should look at life.

Anyway, the road down into Missouri was pretty good, and I couldn't believe how far from home we were getting. Benny said he heard a rumor that baseball might even have a team as far west as Kansas City someday, but that would be tough to believe. The weather down here was even hotter than it was in Chicago yesterday, and when we crossed the giant Mississippi River on this bridge we had our first and only breeze of the day and we would've stopped to jump off the bridge into the water if we weren't so high up.

We were in St. Louis awful early so we drove down this downtown street named Lindell Boulevard, where all these new fancy hotels had just been built like the Chase and the Coronado and the Melbourne. Benny said he was sick of the fancy hotel thing and was still worried about our money but he said he had "another idea" he'd tell me about after the game. Oh, I couldn't wait for that.

It was real easy getting a ticket at Sportsman's Park because it was a Thursday and I can't say the Phillies are a team that packs them in. This was great for us because our main purpose was to watch Rogers Hornsby hit, so we paid a dollar-fifty apiece this time to get a seat near the Cardinal dugout. Jimmy Ring and his 0-6 record was going for us, so there was no doubt in our heads that "the Rajah" would knock him around.

Each team went out in the 1st and Bill Sherdel got us 1-2-3 in the 2nd. Then Hornsby came out of the dugout in front of us and we sat up in our seats. He's 28 years old and he's from Texas, meaning he doesn't talk much, but I guess he lets his bat do that part because it's big and heavy and he's got the giant arms to swing it. Benny yelled "Take a good lick, Hornsby!" and he turned for a second with these squinty eyes, spit something brown on the grass and got into the batter box. Ring threw one pitch and Hornsby crushed it with this unbelievable WHOCK sound and it flew past Ring's ear, right between Ford and Sand up the middle for a single. I've heard that he always aims for the middle of the diamond because that's the field area with the least protection and he sure made that work.

Ring was all disflustered from the hit, and threw a wild pitch with Ray Blades at the plate before walking him, Clemons and Cooney got singles and a ball got past Wilson to make it 3-0 Cards. Ring actually got Hornsby out on a called strike three in the 4th, but all that did was make the man mad. After Mokan gave us a dinky run with a homer over the left wall in the 5th, Hornsby walked, singled and singled his next three times up and the score was 8-1 them before we even looked up at the board. We were actually hoping to see a double or homer or triple from him, but what the heck, we still got three days here. His batting average by the way is now up to .453 with 44 runs knocked in.

After the game Benny fished this piece of note paper out of his pocket which had a person's address on it. Remember Thomas, the colored horse trainer we met at that Chicago club? Well it seems that his brother Roy lives in a part of northwest St. Louis called the Ville, and we were to look him up if we needed a free place to stay.

So we did. This was a pretty decent neighborhood filled with mostly coloreds, and they had their own churches and laundry places and everything. There's a lot of great things about St. Louis, such as the World's Fair they had here in 1904, but only seven years ago they had these horrible riots in East St. Louis across the river in Illinois, and a lot of colored people got killed because whites were afraid of them taking their jobs. Roy moved his whole family out of there after it was over and they all seemed much happier in the Ville. He had a nice pretty wife and six kids and they put us up in a bedroom upstairs with three little boys who were real funny and asked us questions about our trip and mostly about the car. We gave them a ride around the neighborhood in it after eating a fabulous dinner of pork and beans and these spicy greens, and then we even played a game of "corkball" in their street. They used broken-off broom handles for bats and corks from wine bottles for balls which they painted white and weren't that tough to hit when you got the hang of it. Me and Benny were on opposite teams and mine ended up winning 28-12 so I was pretty happy.

It had been a fun day even though the Phils lost the first game of a series for the first time on the trip. With Hornsby squinting at us and a game of corkball in the street, how can you go wrong?

PHL 000 010 000 - 1 10 0
STL 030 003 02x - 8 12 2

THE CORKBALL CLASSIC:
Vinny-Ollie-Stinky-Goober & Tim 365 208 4 - 28 22 5
Benny-Roy-Percy-Marvin & Toilet 106 023 0 - 12 31 7

A THRILLER BEHIND CHICKEN WIRE
May 23, 1924

We weren't in the mood for another pasting today, so as we sat having home-made oatmeal with Roy and his family, he said we should try something different—like a big picnic. Before we knew it his wife had put together a big sack of food and the whole family crammed into his old wheezy truck and the back of the Chrysler and we all went to Sportsman's Park together to wait in line for tickets.

The bleacher pavilion in right field was saved for colored fans, and me and Benny got some dirty looks when we went inside because if negroes couldn't get into that section they couldn't see the game at all, and it took me a whole inning or two before I wasn't feeling guilty. Roy sure helped. He was one of the nicest guys and best ball fans I ever met. He was also a huge gambler, even more than Benny was, and there was a friend of his in the section with us named Giggle Face because he had this weird laugh after everything he said, and he gambled even worse. He had a big dirty pair of dice in his pocket and in between innings he'd stand and turn around and whip them against the stone steps without somehow losing either one.

And the game had a lot to bet on, even though we had to squint to see it. The pavilion was about 330 feet from home plate with a fence made out of chicken wire sticking straight up, so when a ball was hit you had to move your head a little to have a better chance of an unblocked view. Harper and Jack Smith were the two right fielders, and it was fun to watch them move after the balls, but it didn't take long before the game started drifting away from us again. Hubbell had ten hits off him in the first five innings, Hornsby with three of them of course, but it was only 3-0 going into the middle innings.

The problem was Leo Dickerman had a no-hittter going for St. Louis, meaning the bets on the first Phillie hit were flying through the pavilion so fast you had to duck. Roy's wife opened the food sack before long and we had delicious chicken and corn and leftover beans but me and Benny were getting too nervous to eat. Even if a no-hitter might be against you it's still nerve-stretching. Dickerman got through the middle game retiring all nine batters and Benny bet on a Cy Williams hit for the 7th but he was wrong because it was Harper, who led with a single! Cy did get one next, Wrightstone was hit, Wilson walked, and two sacrifice flies later we were all tied.

Meanwhile Hubbell had calmed way down, but two Redbird singles and a Wilson error loaded the bases with no outs in the 7th. Roy laid five bucks on two Cardinal runs, I said nobody would score and Benny was too afraid to bet again. Blades grounded one to third and the runner was out at home! Clemons grounded to first and another runner was out at home! When Cooney grounded out I screamed and took Giggle Face's money and couldn't believe he was still laughing.

Extra innings now, the stands all packed and hot with all kinds of home-made food smells, a big crowd of coloreds on the street outside who couldn't get in, with their friends yelling every batter outcome down to them. Dickerman was still in there in the top of the 11th when Wrightstone picked on a two-out pitch and yanked it deep out to our section. We jumped to our feet and the ball bounced off a step below us and went right in the hands of one of Roy's boys! A policeman made him throw it back, and I'm not sure whether it was because a Phillie hit it, or the balls were expensive or because a colored kid had touched it, but it seemed pretty lousy to me.

Huck Betts saved the game for us and we won, even though the Cards had wiped us out in the hit department by 16-5. On the way back to Roy's I made Benny stop at a sporting store where I went in and bought Roy's kid a baseball. He deserved it.

PHL 000 000 300 01 - 4 5 1
STL 021 000 000 00 - 3 16 0

UNCLE ROY REALLY SEES HIS FIRST GAME
May 24, 1924

After another great meal at Roy's place last night, a corkball game in the street that was still going when it got dark and ended in a 31-31 tie, and hot flapjacks and bacon this morning, me and Benny decided we had to do something nice for our host. Roy had been a huge Cardinals fan since he was eight years old but still hadn't seen a game up close for a reason I don't have to tell you.

So Benny got the nifty idea to disguise him up so he could sit in the grandstand with us and nobody would be the wiser. Roy's wife came out with some bandages, gloves, and an old derby hat and we wrapped him from the top of the head right down to his neck. We left giant holes for his eyes and nose and mouth and his wife made sure to soak the bandages in cold water first because it was going to be another scorcher.

I waited with Roy in the Chrysler across the street in a lot while Benny was buying the tickets, and then we walked our friend up to the grandstand entrance. The ticket taker gave us a weird look along with every fan in the line, so I made sure to say real loud that poor Uncle Roy had been in a bad fire at his shoemaking factory and had burns over most of his body and that thinking about going to this game was the one thing he had to look forward to. The ticket guy almost cried.

We bought two extra lemonades but Roy sipped them both down by the end of the 1st inning so we bought him two more. Thankfully the seats were back in the roof shade between third and home or he might've collapsed. It was also good we hadn't done this with Giggle Face or he might've given us away.

Carlson pitched for us, and I'll tell you, he may be the best lousy pitcher around, because he always seems to go deep into a ballgame. Today was his masterpiece of horribleness. The Cards got hit after hit after hit off him but couldn't stick any of them together. Meantime the Phils took a cheap 3-0 lead on a passed ball past Vince Clemons in the 3rd and two walks and a single after Ray Blades botched a Wilson ball to death in the 4th. I guess it was good St. Louis was having no luck because it kept Roy from yelling things through his bandages, but he was sure doing a lot of whispering to me.

"Can't believe the size of Hornsby's arms," was his first thing, "He could knock a buffalo out with those." I had to remember colored folks had no way to see their favorite players up close around here unless they played right field. Roy also kept whispering about the fans around us and how polite and quiet they were and seemed to study the game "like it was grade school arithmetic."

Arithmetic sure wasn't helping the Cards, though. For the second straight game we got outhit by them and ended up winning. A Harper triple and Cy single in the 5th made it 5-0 to stay, and Carlson had a neat little 13-hit shutout. Roy didn't even care because he was having the time of his life. He even ate an entire grilled hot dog which we had to feed him through his bandage hole.

We almost had a little trouble before we left because Roy had to go empty out all his lemonade and was worried about using the park's bathroom with those stupid gloves, meaning me and Benny had to take him in there surrounded by all these angry St. Louis fans and stand on both sides of him while he did what he needed to do. The second we got in Benny's car we helped him rip off the disguise and laughed all the way back to his house. He shared a big bottle of cheap illegal wine with us which made us all groozy and put me to sleep in no time, and we forgot to talk about our long trip back to the East, which believe it or not starts after tomorrow's game. Guess we'll figure it out as we go.

PHL 001 220 000 - 5 8 0
STL 000 000 000 - 0 13 2

NATIONAL LEAGUE through Saturday, May 24, 1924

Pittsburgh	26	10	.722	—
Cincinnati	23	16	.590	4.5
Brooklyn	20	17	.541	6.5
New York	20	17	.541	6.5
St. Louis	20	19	.513	7.5
Chicago	17	22	.436	10.5
PHILLIES	15	23	.395	12
Boston	10	27	.270	16.5

CREEP ME IN ST. LOUIS
May 25, 1924

We packed up the Chrysler outside Roy's house plenty early because they had to get to church, and after we gave him and his wife hugs and handshakes and Benny tossed every one of their kids up in the air we got to Sportsman's Park a whole hour before game time. This meant we were in front of the line and got good box seat tickets because the Cards had lost two straight and people seemed to be taking a break from them.

You'd think a matchup of Oeschger against Jesse Haines would give the Cards the edge this time but both pitchers threw nothing but big eggs for the first five innings. Then Oeschie completely lost it in the 6th. Bottomley, Hornsby, Blades and Clemons all singled to start the inning, one of those weird balk calls was thrown in, and before you knew it we were down 3-0.

Haines then pulled his own plug, and in a similar way. Holke and Harper singled to start the 7th, and after two more singles, a walk and two sacrifice fly pops, it was 3-3. Oeschie then settled down like nothing had even happened in the 5th, but the Phils stayed hot. Heinie Sand began the 8th with a smoky double off the left fence, Holke got him to third with a single, and George Harper, definitely our best hitter after Cy Williams, exploded a Haines pitch high and far and completely over the colored pavilion in right and we were up 6-3! We jumped out of our seats and made loud ruckuses because it was our last day in town and who the heck cared? We got plenty of nasty looks from the St. Louis fans and a few peanut shells flew by our heads but that was it.

At least we thought it was. Five minutes later as reliever Fowler was finishing up the inning for Haines, there was a loud girl's yelp from the aisle next to us. Guess who was standing there? Nope, not Rachel this time but Fraulein Ute from that Cincinnati "Bock-skellar"! She squeezed through the seats and dropped into an empty one beside me and blabbed her whole story. Seems that the Over-the-Rhine Boys went nuts in a bad way after blowing their third straight game to the Giants yesterday and started a riot in their neighborhood and cops were called in to beat heads and anti-German feelings which bobbed up a lot after the War happened again so Ute took a train out to St. Louis to "get from there away" and look for me even though she wouldn't admit it.

She said a lot of other stuff in my ear but half was in German. She smelled more like sweat this time than a mountain meadow, and all I was trying to do was finish watching the game. Ute knew even less about baseball than that rich girl in Pittsburgh, and we bought her a lemonade and pretzel just to keep her from talking for a while.

Betts polished the Cards off easy and we'd won three out of the four from a tough-hitting team, but we were too busy trying to shake Ute to even care. I explained in the simplest English I knew that I had to get back to Philadelphia because my mama and my fiancee missed me, and that's when she got even more crazy and demanded that Benny drive her all the way back to Ohio. He said forget that, he'd pay for her train instead but when she got back to the car with us we all stopped dead in the street.

Someone had broken into the Chrysler. The side window was smashed, and maps and papers and other things in the glove box were thrown all over the car's insides. Me and Benny were suddenly real scared because we remembered this had happened to our room in Chicago, so Benny told Ute to get in and we started driving the heck out of town. "Was ist los? Was ist los?" she kept yelling, while I was looking for the right map and the car was zooming around other cars and ugly dark clouds were straight in front of us and things didn't look too good.

We were a half hour back into Illinois when we saw a black car with its bright headlights behind us, getting faster. We drove through a small town, the thunderstorm hit and this car roared around us, blocked our way and Benny had to throw his brakes on. It was raining so hard we couldn't see who the driver was right away but he got out, threw Benny's door open and stood there holding a small pistol.

It was none other than M. Conroy Face, the Pittsburgh hotel detective. Asking Benny for "all that money." I looked at my friend. Not only had he skipped out of his bill at the fancy hotel back there, but he still owed a bunch of cash to Punky Schickelgruber from the Pittsburgh pool hall, and Conroy also collected for him when asked. Oh boy. Ute started yelling at him in German until he shot the gun in the air, pulled her out of the car and tossed her in a puddle. She got up, all soaked, and ran screaming off down the street of this little town I didn't even know.

Conroy then forced Benny to get out with his hands up and walk down this alley with him. I had no idea what to do. I thought about getting behind the wheel and running him over but I might've hit Benny and the alley was way too small.

So I got out and followed them. I heard kicking and punching and a horrible moaning and the next thing I knew Benny was hobbling back out with a real bad limp and bloody nose and said, "Get us out of here!" I was all confused and looked back down the alley and saw three big guys in overcoats and hats pummeling Conroy Face against a brick wall like they were going to kill him. There was another car parked at the curb, a big shiny blue one, and I saw a guy smoking a cigar in the open back seat with one of his shoes hanging out that must have been a size 20. Benny pulled me away and I jumped behind the Chrysler's wheel and hit the gas.

"Big Toe" Sam, Capone's St. Louis friend, had been watching over us the whole time we were there, which was sure a lucky break for us. Benny said that Pittsburgh Punky probably made payments to Capone, too, so this was probably the end of that business. I sure hoped so, as I did my very first driving lesson and learned the ropes in five minutes flat. Good night from somewhere going east, reader-people!

PHL 000 000 330 - 6 9 1
STL 000 003 000 -3 9 1

SULTAN OF SWAT OR KING OF THE CUE?

By Calvin J. Butterworth
Detroit Free-Enterprise
May 25, 1924

NEW YORK CITY—I was late for my meeting with Babe Ruth this morning, but it mattered little, for the Bambino arrived a full hour after me. No one knew of our secret match planned for 10 a.m. in a private back room at Blatt Billiard on Broadway, and it was a good thing, for Mr. Ruth collects hangers-on as a side of beef collects flies, and it is difficult enough to obtain five minutes of his time for anything, let alone a half hour without further company.

Ruth has been ridiculed almost daily at Yankee Stadium thus far because his team is not five lengths ahead in the American League. Putting this burden on the shoulders of one player is sheer folly; it takes many working together to bring home a championship. Yet when a player produces as much regular awe as Ruth and earns $52,000 a year, nothing less than constant heroism will placate his fans.

"Hey kid, sorry about that," he said, marching into Blatt's and lighting a cigar in one motion. The Babe calls everyone Kid, so I was not insulted despite my older age, and by the time he'd chalked up his cue stick and we agreed on some 8-ball rules, he seemed ready to talk.

"I can take the booing. When you make more loot than the President, people expect results.

What I don't like is newspaper dopes saying I got nothing left. Didn't they see me slug three out of the yard the other day against Cleveland? Can't ring the damn bell every day, y'know." He rammed the cue ball with his pile driver of a left arm and cracked the others around the table. "Everyone forget what happened in '22?"

He was referring to his early-season suspension with Bob Meusel. Ruth was barely batting .100 by Decoration Day, being booed mercilessly and the Yankees still reached the World's Series. "It's a big town here and I'm bigger than the town, but people gotta be patient, that's all. Your shot, kid." I put my pad down, picked out the 6-ball and sliced it just barely into a corner pocket. Ruth grinned, gave me a heavy pat on the back and almost knocked me over. "Heard about your trouble with Cobb last week," he said, "I saw Heilman at the track the other day and he said he didn't mean nothing by it."

I told him thanks, but really just wanted to talk about New York's pennant chances. "Well, we got a bunch of nutwags and maroons but some real bashers in there, too. Long as our pitchers hold up we oughta pick up steam soon enough. You guys are plenty tough but I don't see Chicago lasting and Washington's playing so far over their heads they're gettin' neck strain."

He put the cue stick behind his back and clicked a banker into a corner pocket. I was well on my way to losing our match and Ruth was the proud owner of a new box of cigars, but as the many denizens of Yankee Stadium find, merely watching the Babe perform can be pleasure enough.

GUESS WHERE WE ARE NOW?

May 26, 1924

Dear Mama:

I'm writing this from the lobby of the Lazy Bones Drive-up Hotel somewhere in Ohio to tell you that me and Benny are having a real good time on our trip and expect to be back home as soon as we can!

Benny is a good person to travel with because he is an expert at driving and always seems to make the right decisions about things. His Chrysler has been a great gasoline car and hasn't given us even one problem if you can believe that. On the way home I'm also getting a chance to drive because Benny's foot got real tired, but I'm being very safe and if I had a Kodak I would take you pictures of all the pretty little back country roads we were zipping along on the whole day.

Cincinnati, Pittsburgh, Chicago and St. Louis were beautiful cities to visit and each one had a different way of welcoming us. We mostly stayed in hotels but in St. Louis it was with a very nice family that lived in a less fancy part of town and they made us lots of great healthy food and glasses of milk. I even bumped into an old friend in Chicago, someone I met when I went up to New York for my newspaper delivery research trip last month and we had a bunch of laughs. Benny also made us some extra cash by doing an odd job for an interesting businessman we met at the ball park.

Benny still has lots of money left but we're being careful anyway on the way back east and will probably buy a few days worth of sandwiches be-

cause we're getting kind of sick of big dinners. Boston is the last stop on our trip and I hope we can get there before the Phillies do for tomorrow's game but we might not. We were thinking of skipping that part and just coming home but what the heck, as long as we made it this far why give up?

In case you haven't been following our team, we lost three out of four in both Cincy and Pittsburgh (the Pirates are scary!) but then took three out of four in both Chicago and St. Louis. Boston stinks to heaven so we should do a number on them.

Anyway, I miss you a lot and hope you're okay and if I get a chance to write you from New England in the next day or two I sure will.

—Love, Vinny

HOW WE MADE IT TO BOSTON
May 27, 1924

Benny's Chrysler was leaking black goo on the road the second we got into New York State. And Benny was still passed out next to me from drinking a bottle of something worse than goo which he got from a speakeasy in Erie, Pennsylvania yesterday. He was still a mess because he got beat up by that Pittsburgh detective creep and needed to kill the pain somehow but all that did was put me in charge of the trip at the craziest possible time.

I had two days to drive us all the way to Boston for the 3 o'clock game with the Phillies at Braves Field, and I knew it would be a tough haul but Mama always said the bravest bug gets the tastiest meal so that got me determined enough to try. I was actually in Pennsylvania, not Ohio when I wrote her that letter but we'd been driving for so long that day I had no idea where I really was, only that I was moving away from the sunset as fast as I could.

The road we took back from the west first went under Lake Erie and then Lake Ontario and it was nice to look out at the steamer ships and fishing boats when it was clear enough to see them. Then this car thing happened and I had to stop at a repair shop and have these two guys look at the engine but they knew less about cars than I did and ended up patching what was a bad oil leak with a pound of their chewing gum. It was late morning by the time I got to Albany and I was lucky to not be arrested for speeding so much. We stopped at a diner in a nice little town called Springfield, Mass and I brought food out for Benny to eat in the car, which only made him queasy all over again due to the bouncy road.

It was 3:30 by the time we got to Braves Field and stupidly cold out, and I helped walk Benny into the right field bleacher section they call the Jury Box because it's about the size of one. The guy beside us said all we missed was three horrible errors by the Braves and a run in each of the first two innings for the Phils. Johnny Couch was getting his second start, and he was fabulous again, only giving Boston five hits, and the win was so easy we didn't even notice we were freezing. We thought the Braves would be happy and relaxed to get home but it was the opposite, because they couldn't field a ball if it was delivered to them by Western Union. They made four errors on the day and the Braves fans were even booing the peanut throwers, which is what happens I guess when your record is 10-29.

Anyway, we got back out to the street where I left the Chrysler and guess what? It had been taken away for being in a police horse-parking zone! An Irish-looking cop sitting on a mare was real nasty and I could tell he didn't like Italians but finally told us where we could get the car back the next morning. We ended up sleeping in a flophouse in a part of Boston called Allston, which was probably the closest spot near the ball park we could walk to without passing out.

All I know is that we deserve to sweep the crummy Braves three straight, just for the trouble of us getting here. Hopefully Benny will be better enough to walk around some tomorrow night, because I hear they have great culture and fish in this place.

PHL110 002 010 - 5 9 0
BOS 000 000 001 - 1 5 4

LET JIMMY RING!
May 28, 1924

The first thing we had to do was track down Benny's car, which wasn't easy. There were a few car yards around Allston, but a guy at one of them said because it was the horse police they probably took the car to a big police garage downtown.

So we took the streetcars into Boston and believe me, it wasn't the way we wanted to see the city. Benny still couldn't walk too fast with his bad leg, and the cold weather had left and it was getting muggy by the time we found the police station. The cop at the desk didn't like the looks of us right away and we liked him less, and it took almost a half hour of convincing to make him believe the car belonged to Benny. Then they wanted twenty dollars to get the car back, which left us with about three, barely enough to see the next two ball games. Benny said if we were Irish instead of Italian they would have charged us a dime but neither of us was in a mood to change our names again.

We had to wait another hour for someone to drive the car out of the garage for us, so we killed time by walking over to this giant park called Boston Commons. It was nice out now and pretty ladies and pigeons and swans were all over the place and the trees were all green so we bought a couple ice creams and sat on the grass and talked about how we would pull off the next two days.

We decided we could live with just one game, and Benny was counting on stiffing the old hag who ran the flophouse in Allston, but that still didn't leave us much for gasoline for the drive back to Philadelphia. Then Benny remembered a sign he had seen at Braves Field yesterday, and the second we got the car we headed back over there.

Wednesday Braves games have a special promotion where boys get in free if they are there with their dads. Neither of us have dads, of course, but why would that stop us? "Double-up, mister?" we asked every dad-looking guy we saw that was walking in alone, and after about twenty or so minutes we each had a fake one to enter the park with. The problem was that my fake dad was this real fat guy who said I had to sit with him and describe what was happening because his eyesight was going bad, probably from eating too much.

And he sure ate: sausages and peanuts and pretzels and even a box of gumdrops which stuck to the bottom of my shoes after he dropped a few. Benny had already gotten away from his fake dad and was looking around for me in the left field stands, but I was afraid to move because I was afraid the fat guy would turn me over to an usher.

Oh yeah, the game. Jimmy Ring, 0-7 on the season for us, pitched against Rube Marquard, who is usually very tough or very awful. Rube was both today, taking a 3-1 lead into the 6th before Mokan whacked one of his slow-balls high and deep and out to left to tie the game.

Fat Guy was a huge Braves fan so now he was even nastier to me and made me describe the result of every pitch. This got tiring very fast, but the game went my way in a hurry. Ring doubled to start the Phillie 7th, Schultz singled past Sperber, Ford singled, Holke doubled and when it was over we were up to stay, 7-3. Cunningham, McInnis and Casey Stengel all singled in the bottom half and Fat Guy got all thrilled again. Sperber then crushed their chances with a double play, but I jumped up and yelled "BASE HIT!" Fake Fat Dad screamed with joy and I made sure to knock the peanuts out of his hand so I could run off the second he went to pick them up. He yelled for me to come back but it was too late. I found Benny in no time because he was the only person cheering nearby, and the second Ring wrapped up his first victory of the season we were out the exit gate and off in the Chrysler.

It was a great way to head home. Five wins in a row and we pass the Cubs into sixth place!

PHL 100 002 400 - 7 12 1
BOS 201 000 000 - 3 12 1

BY MUD AND BY THUMB
May 29, 1924

We slept in a classy Hartford, Connecticut hotel last night and celebrated our last evening of the trip with a nice dinner at a steak place. A waiter told us that the writer Mark Twain used to live in a house just up the street, but the person who owned the house now was thinking about tearing it down. Local people are all upset about this, so I hope it turns out okay. Believe me, we would've dropped over to say hello to Mark ourselves if the man hadn't died 14 years ago.

We slept kind of late and hit the road around noon time. It was what they call murky outside, and rain started falling as soon as we got over the New York state line and turned south. Benny wanted to stay away from the crowded roads in the big city by going around it, but the more west we went the narrower and lousier the roads got, and pretty soon it wasn't a road at all but a mud track through farm country. The rain fell harder and the mud got thicker and it got into the Chrysler's engine and the gasoline tank and before you knew it the car just stopped moving in the middle of nowhere. Benny was real mad and made up more blue words than I'd ever heard because he thought the bastard Boston cops did something to the car before they gave it back to us.

Anyway, nobody drove by that could've helped us for the first hour, so we took our bags and just started walking. The good thing is that when we finally came across a small cafe called Hot Eats to dry off and have lunch, the owner had one of those radio machines going with a baseball game on. The problem was that it was the Yankees and Senators, and we didn't give two owl hoots about them. Then we heard the announcing man give scores of other games, and our ears got glued in seconds.

The weather in Boston was still okay, and the Phillies had just scored five runs in the 2nd off Barnes to take a 7-1 lead! We ordered fat sandwiches and colas but had a little trouble digesting things because the next time we heard the score the Braves had come back with four runs and it was 7-5 in only the 4th inning. Cripes, why did we leave town so early? How could they win without us?

Well, they did eventually. The farmers in the place were all rooting for the Yankees, but the game wasn't going their way and a lot of them walked out. The next time we heard a score from Boston it was 9-5 Phils in the 5th, and then the owner decided to close the cafe for the day so we had to leave not knowing what happened. Dang it all, they really need to invent a radio machine that somehow works in your car!

What car? We talked the owner into driving us back to help start the thing because the rain had stopped and hopefully the mud was drying, but guess what? It was gone again, and this time not taken but police but stolen by someone else, probably a crummy New York Giants fan. Benny had had enough of the whole car business and didn't want to get shot looking for it and said it was time to just forget about it and put our thumbs to work.

So the cafe owner drove us south as far as Nyack, then turned us loose. We stood on a busy road for a good half hour before a man in an open truck with his two boys and three dogs picked us up. They were all nice and the dogs almost licked our faces off but the ride only got us down to New Jersey. From there we had a bunch of short ones with different businessmen, because who else could afford cars anyway? There was maybe an hour wait between each ride, though, meaning by the time we saw the bright lights of Philadelphia rising above the dark road it was real late at night.

When I opened the door to my house Mama was asleep already, but she heard me come in and ran down to give me a hug attack. After all, she's a mom.

We'd driven about three thousand miles maybe, been to five cities and seen 14 ball games, and it was hard to believe I was finally back in my own wonderful bed.

P.S. Found out the whole Phillies score from Mort's before I went home. We've won six in a row, and the Evil Giants are here tomorrow for the Decoration Day double-header. Let's get 'em!

PHL 250 204 200 - 14 18 0
BOS 140 000 002 - 7 11 2

SOMETHING TO FIGHT FOR
May 30, 1924

Benny knocked on our door at 8 a.m., excited out of his brain. Oh no, I thought, not another stupid road trip! Mama let him in to have breakfast with us and it turned out he was cuckoo about someone named Ruth Malcolmson.

"Who the heck is that?" I asked. "Miss Philadelphia, 1924," he said, "Don't you ever read the newspaper?" Seems that this real fetching young lady—and I can call her fetching because I saw the souvenir photograph of her Benny had rolled up in his back pocket—was going to make an appearance on the field at Baker Bowl today between games of the holiday double-header, and Benny was determined to get her signature on the back of the photo even if he had to trample people to do it.

"Guess it's always nice to have a goal at the end of your field," said Mama, who was wearing her nicest and biggest hat with the little American flags stuck in it. Decoration Day has been real big for her since Papa got killed over in Europe, and for me too, of course, so we had to calm Benny down so he wouldn't ruin the parade for us.

After breakfast we all took a streetcar over to Broad Street, where bands were already marching, and it was so crowded Benny and me had to stand on mailboxes to see anything. After the bands came the Mayor, and then ranks of soldiers in perfect step wearing those doughboy hats, and I remembered Papa wearing the same outfit when he left on the train and I got pretty sad for a few minutes and Mama grabbed my ankle from below and held on to it.

It took a while to get onto a streetcar to go to the ball field after, because the crowds were all backed up and we had to work our way around drunk guys relieving themselves in the alleys, but we got to Baker Bowl by noon and got in line for our usual left field bleacher tickets.

Boy, it was nice to be back at our second home, especially in sixth place with a six-game winning streak. The players marched onto the field holding their bats like rifles and we all cheered, and then Carlson took the hill with his great 5-2 record to battle the stinking Giants. We could make out McGraw from our seats and he had his typical mad expression, so we knew it would be a rough day. New York has just started playing a little better but they had no luck at all in Pittsburgh so they weren't in the best mood.

Their pitcher Hugh McQuillan sure wasn't. For the first six innings all we could get was four lousy singles off him. Meanwhile the Giants got nine singles off Carlson, good for three runs. Then Cy bonked a deep homer to right to lead off our 7th, we all threw our hats in the air and we were back in the game! Except we weren't. Travis Jackson homered over our heads the next inning, we scratched out another run, but that was that, 4-2 them.

Benny didn't care. He pulled out his Miss Philadelphia photo, ran down to the bottom of the bleacher section to wait for the love of his life. The guy who announces the lineups with a big megaphone came out, announced her to the crowd, and there she was in a red, white and blue gown that must have been awful hot seeing it was close to 90 degrees out. I guess it was good she wasn't wearing the swim suit she had on in the picture or there might've been a riot.

Anyway, Benny had a pen in his hand and was writing something down quick on the back of the photo. What was he doing? She walked out to a little platform at second base to wave to the crowd and Benny just lost it, jumped over the rail and started running across the field right toward her, the photo flapping in his hand. Security cops saw him coming but they were too late and he was too fast. He ran up, pecked her cheek with a kiss and dropped the picture at her feet before the cops dragged him off with the fans laughing and cheering. What a gooner!

I knew I'd have to go look for him either outside or at the police station after the second game, so it was hard to enjoy myself the rest of the afternoon. The Giants sure didn't help, creaming Clarence Mitchell for six runs in his four innings of "pitching" and building a 9-0 lead into the 7th. They had tried blowing some fireworks off after the Miss Philadelphia thing, but half of them didn't work and it was too sunny out to see anything in the sky anyway, so the Phillies then made some of their own. Three singles and a walk gave them one run, and then Harper socked a ball so far over the fence in right that Ross Youngs didn't even move. A grand slam, and it was 9-5!

It was also the end of the scoring, and with the Cubs splitting their games we were back in seventh place again. Oh well. I found Benny outside the park after. His clothes were all torn and messed up but the cops had decided not to throw him in the clinker because it was a National Holiday and they could see he was just in love and not an anarchist or something. I told him it was nice to have something to fight for, even if it was a dream that would never happen. "Ain't no dream if you go and prove it," he said, still glowing like a big bulb, and we went down to Mort's for holiday-sized cherry fizzers.

NYG 000 210 010 - 4 12 1
PHL 000 000 110 - 2 6 1

NYG 101 241 000 - 9 13 0
PHL 000 000 500 – 5 9 1

A FAREWELL TO MAY

May 31, 1924

I promised Mama I would catch up with my lessons in the next two days, because the Phillies go up to Brooklyn for a single Sunday game, and that's the last thing I want to do even if it would mean maybe seeing Rachel. Her team has been in the dumps lately, so it might not be the best time to invade her life again. On Monday the Phillies have a day off before St. Louis comes to town, so I guess I'll spend the whole day in school for a change.

The Phillies might have to go back to winning school, though, because they seem to have forgot everything they learned on their western trip. The Giants knocked Oeschie around today for four runs in the 2nd inning, helped by Parkinson murdering a ball at third base, and we were behind early again. We actually hit the ball well off Art Nehf, getting 14 hits which was two more than they had, but we didn't walk once and couldn't stick any of those hits together.

The Phils did make it close with three runs in the 6th, but all that did was wake up the Giants again, and they put three more across in the 7th with big hits from Youngs and Kelly. Cy hit his 8th homer over the right fence to lead our 7th, but that finished all the scoring on this boiling afternoon.

Benny never showed up at all. I guess he was too blue after the Miss Philadelphia disaster, and didn't want the Phillies to make him any bluer. I'm the opposite. I use baseball games to get me out of bad moods, no matter what happens. What else can beat sitting in the hot sun with a cold pop at a big green ball field?

NYG 040 000 300 - 7 12 0
PHL 000 003 100 - 4 14 2

PART THREE
June

THE LORD FLIPS A COIN
June 1, 1924

Well, I went to church with Mama after breakfast today, and I guess God can't take care of everyone's prayers. I asked Him to do something nice for Rachel because her Robins were stinking bad, but all that probably did was confuse Him, because the Phillies were playing them up at Ebbets later and it's his job to take care of me first.

So I guess He just flipped a coin, because by the time I got over to Mort's to check his baseball ticker, Couch, Sand, red-hot Holke and George Harper had just led off the 3rd with hits and we had a 3-0 lead on Bill Doak, who's been nothing but great so far. A Mitchell triple and Johnston single in the 5th made it close, but Holke singled in another the next inning to put the Phils up 4-2.

Andy High whacked a 2-run homer in the 6th to tie the thing, and that's when Benny showed up with this huge grin on his face. I asked what he was so darn happy about because Brooklyn had just tied the game and he said he was having dinner out with Ruth that night. Ruth who? I asked. He looked at me like I had a faucet on my head. "Miss Philadelphia, you dope!" Seems that she had picked up that photo of her he dropped at her feet before getting hauled off, and it had two verses of an original love poem I saw him scribbling on the back. She was "swooning" the rest of the day as Benny put it, and tracked him down the next morning through the police. Which was why he never showed up at Baker Bowl. They went to Independence Hall, picnicked at the river and came close to smooching in Rittenhouse Square.

Anyway, the Phillies scored a run in the 7th on a Wilson double and another in the 9th on a bases-loaded walk, and Couch beat Brooklyn 6-4 with the help of 15 hits but Benny hardly reacted to it. His eyes lit up like fireflies every ten seconds whenever he most likely thought of the lovely Ruth. He asked if I wanted to meet her and suggested maybe she had a nice friend. So I said sure, but it would have to be after school tomorrow because I couldn't dare skip another day, and that's how I planned my Monday. The good thing is that the Phillies will be off, so that's one less thing to distract me from my school work.

PHL 003 001 101 - 6 15 0
BRK 000 022 000 - 4 9 1

SCHOOL DAZE AND STRAIGHT A'S
June 2, 1924

Like I promised I got up nice and early and took a hot bath, put on my best clothes and went off to school with three apples in my pockets. I had missed so many days because of my baseball journey that I thought Mrs. Crackerbee could use more than one bribe.

Instead she made a big fuss over me the second I got in the room, walked me up in front of the class and asked how my "voyage to the Caribbean

Sea" went. Uh-oh. I guess Mama had made up some cockamamie story about where I went, and now I had to just plain fudge it. All the kids were staring at me, especially the girls, like I was some kind of midget war hero, so I went on and on about my crazy Uncle Percival and his mission to spread religion to the islands down there whether they liked it or not, and how we got attacked by Cuban pirates and had to trade them cigarettes and tonic medicine and chewing gum to save our lives, and how it rained a lot of the time and that's why my skin never got tan. Stuff like that.

For the next hour or so we reviewed a nutty chapter in our physiology book. It described the human body as a house where the stomach was the kitchen, the small intestine was the dining room, and the lungs were the laundry but for some reason it didn't say anything about a bedroom or bathroom. Then right before lunch Mrs. Crackerbee handed out a final history test, which I knew I'd probably flunk. Joey Kopf sat next to me, a smart little kid with blonde hair and thick glasses, and I started working on him for answers. Joey's real name is Josef but the school started giving German kids American school names after the War so they wouldn't get beaten up, and I looked out for him a bunch of times so I knew he might help me.

The test was mostly about the Revolutionary and Civil Wars, and I was getting Lexington mixed up with Manassas pretty quick. If they had questions about the Great War that just ended I might have done better because I'd read every one of Papa's letters from there four times, but I guess they didn't want us to know much about that one and how incredibly stupid and awful the whole thing was. Anyway, Joey traded me six answers for three sticks of peppermint gum, so I guess that pirate story I told made some kind of dent in his head.

I ate my salami and cheese sandwich in the lunch room after. It was broiling hot out and the fans weren't working, so I found a spot right next to one of the windows, and that's when I heard Benny calling my name.

He was standing out in the alley wearing the nicest clothes I'd ever seen on him. His hair was combed and he'd even shaved most of the stubble off his chin. Ruth was right around the corner waiting, he said, and she wanted to take us someplace special for the afternoon. I told him I had to be in school and was already eating lunch, but I knew it was a dumb argument. How could I not meet Miss Philadelphia? Mr. Tuggerheinz had been keeping an eye on me the whole lunch but the second he turned his back I climbed out the window and ran around the corner with Benny.

And there she was—Ruth Malcolmson, wearing a slim blue dress and a cute little hat and good God, she was the most perfect female I'd ever seen. I shook her hand and kissed it because I didn't know what else to do. She had a funny voice that sounded like dripping maple syrup and smelled like a flower vase, and in ten seconds she was getting us into a taxicab.

Benny couldn't even talk, just stared at her and kept his arm around her tiny waist. She said she'd heard about our baseball road trip and wanted to know all about the far-away cities so I serenaded her with that as long as I could before Benny started kicking my shin to shut me up. Benny asked

Ruth if we were going to a park or fancy restaurant and she just smiled and wouldn't give her secret away.

Finally she leaned forward, tapped the driver's arm and said "Twenty-first and Lehigh please," and Benny lost the smile on his face. She was taking us to Shibe Park! He asked her if she was an A's fan and she said "Oh of course! Who didn't grow up rooting for Home Run Baker?" Me and Benny sure as heck didn't, but we kept our fake smiles on as we bounced our way through town.

Shibe is actually just four or five blocks away from Baker Bowl in the area they call North Penn, but it might as well be on the Moon to us. True blue Phillie fans don't want anything to do with those wealthy Mack-heads who follow the upstart American League in their giant cave of a ball field, and it was just our luck that one of the two games being played all day was right in our city. At least it was against first-place Washington, so maybe we could see the Athletics suffer.

Lehigh Boulevard was packed solid. The A's had been playing hot lately, had just beaten up the Yankees three in a row before they lost in Washing-ton yesterday, and their fans were starting to believe again. Heck, they'd won a bunch of pennants in the early 1910s before Mack traded all his stars away, although the Phillies had won a pennant since the last time the A's had. Anyway, Ruth had already gotten us tickets through some society friend and they were supposed to be in a good section, and it's kind of tough to say no to a beautiful lady and a ball game.

This was the first time I'd been to Shibe Park and I have to say it was a palace compared to our dump, especially the outside, which looked like somebody's mansion. The hot sausages were actually hot for one thing, the fans were polite, smelled less like gin and really seemed to understand the game. The team has been hitting like the dickens these days, and they have a rookie slugger named Al Simmons who Ruth couldn't stop talking about. She liked to watch him hit with his "one foot in the water bucket" stance, though Benny whispered to me that she probably just liked looking at his rump.

Anyway, we had a good rump-watching spot, right behind the Athlet-ics' dugout, but the game turned sour right away for the home folks when Eddie Rommel hit Muddy Ruel in the back to start the game. Washington actually had their catcher leading off so I guessed they wouldn't try that again, but getting Muddy plunked only lit their bats on fire. After Judge walked, Goslin singled in the first run and with two outs, Ossie Bluege doubled home two more and it was 3-0 out of the gate. A Dykes triple and Bing Miller single made it 3-1 and got Ruth all excited even though her rump-boy grounded out to end the inning.

Judge then got hit on the side of his head to load the bases, knocking him out for a few days, and Goose Goslin went crazy, tripling in three runs for a 6-1 lead. A walk and four more Senator singles in the 5th kicked Rommel out for good, and their pitcher Ogden sat back on the mound and relaxed while his hitters scored single runs each of the last four innings to take the game 14-4. Wow, those Washingtons can flat out whip your hide, and we were sure glad they're in the other league.

We took Ruth over to this big Jewish neighborhood nearby and had ice cream at a great place called Doc Hoffmans, and her strawberry cone was the only thing that cheered her up. Then Benny made fun of one of the A's players—I think it was Maxie Bishop—and Ruth's face turned from angel to red-hot devil and she said she had to go and told Benny that maybe she'd see him again sometime. Benny ran out the door after her to apologize but she was into another cab before you can say Jack Sprat and that was the end of our date with Miss Philadelphia. Benny felt like a complete dolt of course, so I had to remind him that Hornsby and the Cards were in town starting tomorrow, and I thought I saw him try to smile.

WAS 330 041 111 - 14 16 1
PHA 100 200 001 - 4 8 1

BOMBS AWAY!!
June 3, 1924

This time I left school early, went to lovesick Benny's place and got him going. For the last year he's been living with a poor immigrant family that doesn't speak English about twenty blocks away from me, and after eating their cannolis and drinking some of their muddy coffee I talked Benny out of bed, into his clothes and up to the ball park for some baseball medicine.

Except now *I'm* sick. Jimmy Ring was on the mound after his fabulous first win the last time out, and the Cardinals were in no mood to keep him smiling. Specs Toporcer, one of the only big leaguers brave enough to wear glasses, singled into right to start the game. Wattie Holm tripled off the center fence. Ray Blades doubled. The Amazing Hornsby hit one so far over our heads in the bleachers that we didn't have time to turn around and look at it. Bottomley singled. Clemons singled. Cooney singled. Chick Hafey roped a double and it was 6-0. Art Fletcher finally went out to either talk to Ring or give him a pill, and then guess what? Pitcher Leo Dickerman lined a shot to Wrightstone at third, who tagged Cooney off the base and whipped it to second to nab Hafey for a triple play!

That was the only highlight for us. Hornsby singled and tripled his next two times up, Mitchell relieved and was no better than Ring, and the Cards laid waste to Baker Bowl with a 24-hit bombardment. By the 5th inning it was 14-2 and I had some idea of what Papa must have gone through in that horrible trench that day in France. The Phillies have played pretty darn well on the road, but at home they just can't stop their pitcher-bleeding.

For his part, Benny hasn't given up on Ruth Malcolmson, writing her a 15-page love poem with the words "sorry" and "regret" splattered all over the place. I said don't expect her to reply but he didn't care. I guess it's always good to write something to get your tough feelings out. Like I just did.

STL 611 330 300 - 17 24 1
PHL 011 000 000 - 2 7 2

EVERY BURNT FOREST LEAVES A GREEN SEED
June 4, 1924

Benny was in a much better mood today when he showed up during my mathematics lesson posing as my cousin with whooping cough to help get me out of school. He'd found Ruth's address after much trouble and mailed off his love poem, so he figured in a day or two she'd be reading his love-words and regretting she ever walked away from him for being a lowlife Phillies fan.

It does take a certain brand of life to be one, though, as our team proved again today. It was Sunny Jim Bottomley's turn to whale away on us this time. He doubled in two runs in the 1st to help give the Cards a 3-0 lead off the bat. Cy doubled one back for us, but then St. Louis got two more off Hubbell in the 2nd on doubles from Hornsby and Clemons and another hit from Bottomley.

And then we started coming back. The fans were too worn out from booing during yesterday's massacre so today they were pretty polite, and when Wilson homered in the 4th and Harper blasted a 2-run smack off Haines to start the 5th, the crowd was all up and crazy like we were about to win a pennant. Mokan then singled in the equalizing run with two outs, and when Harper doubled in a run in the 6th to put us up 6-5, me and Benny jumped and almost hugged and peanuts went everywhere.

Hubbell meanwhile had calmed down and seemed to be headed for his seventh win, but you can never expect miracles at Baker Bowl on a warm day—unless you're the visitors. Sure enough, Ford booted a grounder with two outs in the 7th, and Les Bell batted for Haines. Bell just about never plays, but he picked out a Hubbell curve and cranked it way out to left and St. Louis had the lead, 7-6. The air flizzled out of the Phillie balloon the next inning as Blades, Hornsby and Bottomley again singled, Betts came in to walk and hit two guys, and we were down for good 9-6.

It always helps to look for hopeful signs after a calamity, though, and we did have a whole bunch of fight in us after getting trounced yesterday. Who knows? Maybe Carlson will have it tomorrow and Flint Rhem will stink for them like he usually does.

STL 320 000 220 - 9 13 0
PHL 100 131 000 - 6 15 2

AWKWARD MOMENTS ON A BROILING DAY
June 5, 1924

Today was the easiest time I ever had sneaking out of the lunch room, because Principal Tuggerheinz was out sick and Mrs. Crackerbee was too busy making sure the kids were cleaning up their tables. It was about 95 degrees by the time I passed Hecky's Newsstand on the way to the streetcar, and I knew I'd have to talk Benny out of sitting in the bleachers again.

Lucky for us he listened, because this game was almost two hours long and you can only drink so much lemonade, as we found out in St. Louis on our recent road trip. Rhem and Carlson were matched up in a good one so no one was scoring much, but there were runners on base all the time and with the scorchy weather pitchers were being real careful not to throw home run balls.

Cy Williams got us going with a triple that banged off the right field wall and bounced past Jack Smith in right, scoring Harper. It stayed 1-0 until the 4th, when Blades singled, Hornsby walked and who else but Bottomley singled in the tying run.

Rhem dished out three walks in our 7th, and with two outs Holke whistled a single into right to put us up 3-1. I jumped and cheered and ran off to find us two more lemonades. The lemonade guy ran out of them right as I reached him in one of the big aisles, though. He said he'd be right back with more so I stood there in the grandstand shade and fanned myself with a program.

It was then that I turned and saw Principal Tuggerheinz standing in front of me!! I was in shock and wanted to run for cover, but the weird thing was that his face was redder than mine. And then I saw why. A dolled-up young lady who was not much older than Brooklyn Rachel had her hand through his arm. Now I know for a fact that Tuggerheinz has been married for over 20 years and his wife helps out at school functions all the time, and here he was looking pretty darn embarrassed with this floozy.

I said hello and started to walk past but he pulled me aside and whispered, "We will keep our secrets, young Spanelli. Correct?" I nodded and started back to my seat with my heart pounding. Benny was mad that the lemonades were "sold out" and then double mad because the Cards had just tied the game with four straight singles off Carlson and reliever Betts.

I had promised Mr. Tuggerheinz I wouldn't tell a soul about his mistress, but I've known Benny longer than him, so that plan didn't last long. Benny was thrilled about it and said I wouldn't have a problem leaving school early the rest of the year.

So I put my brain back on the game, which happened to be a great one that was going into extra innings with Stuart and Betts on the hill. Hornsby had his usual two hits but completely stunk in the field, booting two balls and not turning double plays a few times. I guess when you're hitting about .460 you can do those things, but when he started the St. Louis 10th with a weak ground out, we all got a shot of hope.

The problem was that Jim Bottomley was stepping up, already with two singles. Right away he creamed a Betts fastball high and deep to center. Cy ran up on the little hill over the underground train tracks but the ball was well over his head and over the center field wall! "Sunny Jim" had clouded up our day again, and after Fowler got us out in the last of the 10th with the help of a big Cy double play grounder to Toporcer, we'd lost the first three to the Cards.

Anyway, it'll be tough to keep my mouth shut about Mr. Tuggerheinz in school tomorrow, but if I can I'm pretty sure I'll have a straight-A report card coming.

STL 000 100 020 1 - 4 11 3
PHL 100 000 200 0 - 3 7 0

IN A WORD: THRILLER
June 6, 1924

Like I thought, school was strange today, but for other reasons. Mrs. Crackerbee handed out our history test scores and when I saw my A minus I couldn't believe it and neither could she. Neither could Billie Jean Smucker, the brainiest girl in class who moved up here from Kentucky back in the fall. She must have seen me getting some of the answers from Joey Kopf and said something to the teacher because that's what snitches do. If I was a hoodlum I would've said the girl is mine and pushed her around after class but I didn't wanna be starting something. Not today.

Mr. Tuggerheinz was in the lunch room this time, and he looked over at me and smiled twice, which was twice more than he ever had before, and I knew why. When I began to make my way over to my usual escape window he nodded and I felt all guilty so I went over and said I had to leave for a dentist appointment and he just leaned over and whispered to me to use the door instead.

There's no better medicine for feeling scared or nervous or sad than taking in an exciting ball game, and we sure had a thriller today. Sothoron was throwing for St. Louis against Oeschger and the toasty wind was blowing out for the fourth straight day so it was clear anything could happen.

Holke doubled, Cy singled and Wrightstone tripled to get us going with two runs, but then the Cards got a Clemons double, Max Flack walk and 2-run triple by the hot Cooney to tie it up. Taylor Douthit sent a long fly to Mokan with one out and we had a great spot in the bleachers to watch his throw, which was a cannon shot that hit Butch Henline on one bounce and got Cooney out in a big dust cloud.

The play seemed to jazz us again, because we whacked four hits for two runs in the 3rd, then Heinie Sand bonked a 2-run poke off the pole to our left and we were up 6-2! But don't forget what I said about the hot wind and Joe Oeschger. The Cards' 5th inning was like sitting in a wobbly canoe and getting run over by an ocean liner. A walk, single and Hornsby double started things, then Bottomley hit his expected double, then a walk to Clemons sent Oeschie packing and brought in Steineder, a reliever Fletcher is using because Glazner stinks and Couch had to become a starter. Max Flack tripled on the first pitch from him and soon it was 8-6 them.

No big deal, because Sothoron had nothing either. Four singles gave us two runs and a tie game right away. Ray Blades tripled to start the St. Louis 6th, but then the strangest thing happened: Steineder turned into a pitcher. He got Hornsby to ground into a force at home plate, then allowed just three singles and no runs the rest of the game. Wrightstone began our

7th with a vicious line homer to right, and adding to his single, double and triple before he had gone through a cycle of all the possible hits!

So we kept the scary Cards from sweeping us and are 4-4 with them as the super pesky Reds come to town after wiping out the Braves in a whole series for the second time. I feel another bout of *eppa rixey* coming on.

STL 020 060 000 - 8 13 0
PHL 202 220 11x - 10 13 0

WHAT A ROUSH!
June 7, 1924

Mama popped a humdinger on me at breakfast: We were going to the New Jersey shoreline tomorrow with Aunt Maria and her two bratty kids. It was okay because the Phillies weren't playing Sunday for church reasons, but I'd be danged if I was going to spend the whole day taking the train back and forth to the ocean with that annoying duo Mikey and Enzo. I begged and pleaded and begged some more to let Benny come along and she finally gave in, though she made it clear she didn't want us running off to the boardwalk and sticking them with the boys.

Anyway, Cincy was in town and they smoked us pretty good out west after we beat them in the first game, so like I figured there was a pretty big crowd at Baker by the time we got there, everyone looking for revenge. I suppose when you lose as much as we do there should be big revenge turnouts all the time, but weekend games always draw more. Also Eppa Rixey was pitching, and the last time we faced him we stayed in a coma for two hours.

This time it was different right off the bat. Mokan singled in a 1st inning run, and after the Reds scored a cheap one in the 3rd on a force play, Mokan did it again with a 2-out single to drive in Sand and put us back in front. Holke knocked one in with a deep fly in the 7th and Sand was gunned down at home plate on a Cy Williams single, but things looked good, and Jimmy Ring was on his way to a glorious 2-8 record.

No sooner had I thought that, though, then Ring gave up three Red singles to make it 3-2 and get us nervous. It was raging hot again, and Benny yanked off his shirt and twirled it in the air as the game went to the 9th inning with Huck Betts now pitching to try and save it. Curt Walker led with a single but Ike Caveney bounced into a Sand-started double play! Someone complained to a cop right then about Benny's bare top, and they made him put the shirt back on but he even didn't care because we were just an out away.

Which is when Rube Bressler, the toughest out in their lineup so far, cracked a ball over Cy's head and it bounced around out by the deepest fence, and by the time the ball got back in Rube was standing on third. Okay, okay, just one more to go, just one more.

Except none other than Edd Roush, probably the most famous Red player ever, was walking up. "Tell me what he does," said Benny, pulling the top half of his shirt over his face. I said I would, but when Roush slammed the second Betts pitch on a deep line to right, the words stuck in my throat. Benny didn't need them, because he heard the cheering turn into quiet all around us. The Mighty Roush had hit it out. Pedro Dibut snuffed us easy in the last of the 9th and we'd lost our 30th game of the year in real nightmare fashion. Benny just sat on our bleacher bench while everyone else left, and it took two trash-pickers poking him with their pickers to get him to finally move.

A day at the shoreline sure seemed like a good idea about then.

CIN 001 000 012 - 4 14 1
PHL 101 000 100 - 3 10 0

NATIONAL LEAGUE through Saturday, June 7, 1924

Pittsburgh	32	16	.667	—
Cincinnati	32	20	.615	2
New York	28	21	.571	4.5
St. Louis	29	24	.479	5.5
Brooklyn	23	25	.479	9
Chicago	24	27	.471	9.5
PHILLIES	21	30	.412	12.5
Boston	12	38	.240	21

I GUESS WE CAN LIVE WITHOUT BASEBALL FOR A DAY
June 8, 1924

We boarded the express to Seaside Park on lower Market Street, meaning me, Benny, Mama, Aunt Maria and her two booger noses named Mikey and Enzo. They're twins with curly brown hair and I can't tell them apart and usually end up calling each one by the wrong name but it doesn't really matter because they're both capable of giving you the same headache.

We bought a morning paper before getting on the train and the baseball page had all the latest batting numbers. I told Benny that Hornsby just got his 100th hit yesterday and was hitting .457 but all he wanted to know about was the Phillie players. So I told him that Cy Williams was at .318 with eight homers and 35 knocked in, and Whitey Glazner's earned run average was down to 9.55, and that's when I felt the pebble hit my knee.

Mikey or maybe it was Enzo sat on the seat across from us with a big stupid grin on his face and his hands behind his back. I told him to give it and he shook his head, so I reached over, grabbed his arm and ripped the slingshot out of his hand. Which is when Enzo or maybe it was Mikey's slingshot marble hit my arm from across the aisle. Benny stepped in, picked the kid up and held him upside down until he bawled and Aunt Maria had to come to his rescue.

That was pretty much what the two-hour train ride to the New Jer-

sey ocean was like. We crossed this long bridge over a bay and found ourselves at Seaside Park, which was mobbed beyond belief but full of cuties
in those new figure-hugging swimsuits that actually stopped midway down
their thighs. Me and Benny had our sleeveless striped tops and dark swim
shorts, and the second we helped Mama, Maria and the brats find a few
square inches on the sand we were running into the sea.

It was nice to have a day off from watching the Phils lose, though Benny
was itching to get scores of the Giants and Robins games if we could. I told
him he could go off and find a place with a ticker machine if he wanted, so
that's what he did while I let waves wash over my head for a while.

There were these five young dames nearby that were splashing around
and at one point two of them waded over and told me that their friend
Madge thought I was a looker. I wasn't sure what that meant but I had
a good idea, so I waded over to meet them. Madge was actually the least
cute of the bunch, but they all had the same bobbed hair style and were going to the same girl college down in Maryland and were full of laughs and
smelled a lot like gin. They said they wanted to play miniature golf and
asked if I was alone, so I said I was just down there with Benny and maybe
I'd go find him and we could all play.

Which was the exact time Mikey and Enzo decided to swim out and
ambush me in the water. I told the girls I'd meet them over at the course,
then dragged both kids out of the water before we all drowned each other,
dumped them back on the blanket and told Mama I had to go look for
Benny.

Naturally I found my friend in the only pool hall on the boardwalk,
where he was all juiced because he'd found out the Pirates were behind by
four runs, and because he was still sobbing for Ruth Malcolmson it took me
longer than usual to talk him into meeting my new friends.

The second he laid eyes on them at Putt-Putt Gardens, though, Miss
Philadelphia went poof in his mind. We bet the gals ten bucks we'd finish
with better scores than them, and because they'd been drinking we knew it
would be no contest. Except we had no idea that Madge, Gibby, Dot, Sarah
and Mitzy had been up to Seaside Park for the third straight weekend and
knew the course like the freckles on their arms. The match was a disaster,
with two of them whomping us by seven strokes, and after they took our
money Benny borrowed one of their secret gin bottles for a loser's swig.

Mama scolded us for being away so long like we thought she would, we
both got sunburns, I had sand in many dark places and the second I sat
back in my train seat late in the day, a fresh pebble hit me in the chest. The
shore can be nice, but Baker Bowl is a lot less dangerous.

SCHOOL BEATS THIS JUNK EVERY TIME
June 9, 1924

The last week of school is always a big joke. We play stickball in the yard,
or hopscotch, or leapfrog, or tiddly-winks, or just bug the girls for five days.
It makes it even easier to slip away to a ball game, not that I've had any

trouble lately with Mr. Tuggerheinz just about pushing me out the door.

But I definitely would've had more fun on a seesaw today, because against Pete Donohue, a rube if there ever was one and by far the worst starting pitcher on the Cincy team, all the Phillies could do was get three measly singles, one of them by pitcher Johnny Couch. Donohue actually had a no-hitter going until Couch's hit with one out in the 8th! In the meantime, the Reds were busy plastering balls every which way, and ended up with 16 hits as they are now right behind the Pirates in the standings again. Roush has been killing us, and he got another single and homer today in front of a much smaller crowd. The way the Phils have been playing at Baker Bowl lately, it's no wonder people are off shooting marbles somewhere.

Benny got disgusted around the 6th inning and disappeared for half an hour to gamble on balls and strikes with his friends in the back row of the bleachers. I've never been a gambling person but I can see how it can help pass your time when something horrible or boring is occupying the rest of it, like this icky game. Hubbell throws against the Cuban guy Dolf Luque tomorrow, so let's hope for no Benny-gambling.

CIN 020 020 200 - 6 16 2
PHI 100 000 000 - 1 3 0

BOOB AND THE RUBE ALMOST DO US IN
June 10, 1924

A couple of the punkier kids in school cornered me today before I escaped from the lunch room and asked me where the heck it was I go every day. I made up something about a sick cousin, but then Mucky Hoag told me he had a friend whose father owned a German Luger, and that got me to spill the truth in no time.

I suppose it's always better to not fib, but maybe not in this case because suddenly there were half a dozen kids in the lunch room who wanted to go to the ball park with me. Heck, I said, it's the last few days of school and Tuggerheinz is looking the other way on purpose so come on.

Benny was sure shocked to see me hop off the Lehigh streetcar with a gang of boys, and it all worked out because the Tuesday tickets were always half price, the weather was beautiful and the game was exciting from start to finish. Bill Hubbell was lousy for a change and the Reds got four hits in the first three innings off him, with Rube Bressler whacking two doubles. We jumped right back in the 4th with four singles and an error by Boob Fowler, who me and the bunch serenaded with "boob-calls" for the rest of the inning.

Then the Phils built themselves a good picket fence, scoring single runs in the next three innings, including the go-ahead score on a homer just to the left of us by Mokan. Lefty Clarence Mitchell came in with the first two Reds on base in the 7th to get Roush on a liner, and then Steineder wiped up the rally when Hugh Critz hit his first pitch for a ground ball double play!

Mucky and his friends hadn't been to a game all season and made more noise than me and Benny as we went to the 9th inning. They just didn't understand that a lead at Baker Bowl at the end of the game is practically useless. Sure enough, Boob singled to begin things, and then Bressler crashed one over the center field wall to tie the game with his fifth hit. Steineder gave up a Roush single, but then got the next three guys to keep us all from weeping.

Jakie May, one of Cincy's three great relievers, gave up singles to Harper and Cy to start our 9th, and wild-pitched them around to second and third. Parkinson grounded into a home plate force, but the second Pedro Dibut came in, Jimmie Wilson skied a fly out to Roush, and the throw was too wide and too late as Cy slid in with the winning run! Mucky jumped so high he snapped a suspender, and I almost wished the Over-the-Rhine-Boys were there to get rough because this time we had a fighting force to take care of them.

It felt great to beat the Reds again, and we have one more with them tomorrow before the big bad Bucs come to town. I made it pretty clear to Mucky that him and his pals would have to sneak out on their own next time, because I had a reputation to protect, whatever the heck that was.

CIN 020 001 002 - 5 11 1
PHI 000 211 101 - 6 12 2

HEADHUNTING THE HEADHUNTER
June 11, 1924

Well, what I was afraid would happen went and happened today. Word got around school pretty quick that sneaking out of the lunch room to go to Baker Bowl was not only a possible thing to do on the last week of classes but a sensible one. I thought I was doing it on my own this time but by the time I got off the streetcar there were already a dozen kids I knew who had gotten there ahead of me, and by the time Hal Carlson threw the first pitch we'd taken over the left field bleachers.

All the punks from yesterday came back with a lot of their friends, and except for Billie Jean Smucker, most of the girls from Mrs. Crackerbee's room had even showed up. I figured Mrs. Crackerbee was probably having a good fainting spell over this, and I hoped Mr. Tuggerheinz was there to whisper in her ear that sneaking out to a ball game was a healthy and natural kid thing to do. After all, he had a motivation.

Lucky for us, the bleachers had a good villain to get riled up about. Carl Mays was throwing for Cincy, the Indian shortstop-killer. To be honest, even though there were lots of people who wanted him kicked out of baseball for that, I didn't. It was just an accident after all, and at the time umpires didn't even care how dirty the dumb ball got during a game. Mays was only doing his job throwing the thing sidearm and Chapman didn't see it in time.

But being part of a mob can be fun sometimes, so my Mays opinion didn't keep me from getting in on our razzing action, with good old Benny tossing out the first insult: "Hey Carl! Gimme a shave but watch the head!" Our kid-crowd was a little nastier. "Hey Mays! Your firing squad is outside Gate B!" was one of the nastier ones, along with "Murdering Mays! Murdering Mays!" and my favorite from one of the girls: "Oh Carl, PLEASE write me from the scaffold!" The fact that the pitcher's mound was so far away that Mays probably didn't hear a word didn't seem to bother us, and when Mokan hit a sacrifice fly off him in the 2nd for the first run of the game, the ribbing got even louder.

If Mays didn't hear anything, his teammates sure did, because they started going nuts with the bats in the top of the 3rd. Lee walked with one out, Mays himself doubled, and then Walker, Boob and Rube all singled, Critz doubled and we were behind 4-1 just like that. Three singles, a Ford error and Rube triple the next inning made it 8-1 and shut us up for good. Carlson was so bad he made Whitey Glazner look like Ed Walsh in relief. In almost four innings the Reds couldn't get one hit off him, which makes me think Fletcher has found himself a new middle-of-game rescue man.

We got two runs back in the 7th on two singles and two walks with nobody out, but then Ford kept his horrible game going with his second double play grounder which finished off our rally. Mays walked off with the complete win, a 7-2 record and a fantastic earned run average of 1.77 for the year. On top of that, Cincy is back in first place thanks to us!

The whole mob of us tried to squeeze into a nearby soda shop after and buy root beer floats, but the owner kicked us out for excessive hooliganizing. Tomorrow when the battling Bucs come to town I think I might just call in sick and sit on the other side of the park.

CIN 004 400 000 - 8 10 1
PHI 010 000 200 - 3 6 1

HOW TO ENJOY A SLAUGHTER
June 12, 1924

Getting beat by a shortstop-killer yesterday was bad enough. Today it was Wilbur Cooper's turn, coming back from a long injury, to make the Phillies look stupid. But that's why Benny is my best friend, because when either of us are down in the dumps, it's the other's job to make the sun come back.

We sat way down deep in the right field grandstand to avoid another flood of kids from my school, though it turned out that Mr. Tuggerheinz put his iron shoe down and kept everyone there because there were so many complaints from parents. Of course I was able to get out my favorite window again because Tuggerheinz wasn't looking on purpose and there was no way I was going to spend six hours playing hopscotch or something.

Instead I watched Jimmy Ring de-prove his record on the year to 1-9. What a worthless wallahonie he's turned out to be. And because our bullpen was used so much lately, Art Fletcher made him stand out there and get machine-gunned for nine whole innings.

I don't care how bad a time the Pirates just had up at the Polo Grounds, they still look like the team to beat to me. They have eight tough hitters, some great pitchers, tight fielding and plus they never seem to ground into double plays, which we do like breathing air. They're also relentless against us, and here's an example. One out in the 1st, Moore and Cuyler single and Earl Smith walks. Ring whiffs Traynor and you think great, we got their number today. Uh-uh, because Glenn Wright whacks a homer off a bleacher plank to start the very next inning. They load the bases again with two outs, Ring whiffs Cuyler and you think great, we're gonna come back and win this thing but uh-uh again. Smith, their brutal catcher who looks and hits you like an oil truck, crushes a double to start the next inning. Wright singles him in and it's 2-0. Then 3-0 on a Cuyler sacrifice fly the next inning. You see what I mean? Relentless.

Ring singled in a run for himself in the 5th, but all that did was get the Buccaneers bloodthirsty. Moore walked and Smith homered to begin their 7th, Traynor, Wright and Rabbit Maranville all singled, and the slaughter was on. A walk, hit batter and two more singles later it was 10-1 and fans were running to the exits.

Most of them, anyway. Benny seems to get more fun to be around at times like this, and sure enough, here he was stuffing dollar bills in my hand and dragging me up to the back row, where his incredibly fat friend Rollo Briggs was busy betting on balls and strikes. Rollo is up there for every game with his back leaning against the same wood post like he was glued to it. Benny told him we wanted to bet on batter results instead of balls and strikes so I took the Bucs and bet on hit after hit because that's the way the win was blowing, and right about then Pittsburgh decided to go to sleep and I began losing money. Ring and Ford got doubles in the 8th and of course neither of us bet on that, either.

Rollo was giggling in the fat way he does when his whole body shakes, and he just kept taking our bills, but then the 9th happened. Carey and Jewel Ens singled for the Bucs with one out. I bet Moore would get a hit, too, Rollo didn't, and Eddie tripled in both runs! I doubled down for four straight hits, Rollo said nuts to that and Cuyler singled!

Benny got in on it now, and we gambled on Earl Smith. The oil truck singled! I was nervous suddenly but Benny was drooling like a mad dog, grabbed all my bills and threw everything down on a sixth straight hit by Pie Traynor. Ring had nothing left but he wasn't going anywhere, reared back and threw and Traynor blasted a single into center! We had ourselves a steak and ice cream dinner! Rollo almost exploded all over the grandstand, wanted to keep betting but we were already running down the aisle as Wright grounded out.

Tomorrow is the last day of school, praise God. No more sneaking for three whole months, and no more glares from Mrs. Crackerbee. What the heck will I do with my mornings?

PIT 011 100 705 - 15 19 1
PHL 000 010 011 - 3 6 0

ENOUGH OF THIS SCHOOL STUFF ALREADY
June 13, 1924

It was a perfect Friday the 13th if there ever was one. The luckiest thing that happened was that I graduated public school even though I skipped class almost every afternoon since April. Guess that's what happens when your principal is afraid to do you wrong.

Mr. Tuggerheinz had his picture taken with us while Mrs. Crackerbee was off in the school kitchen making a hundred apple tarts for everyone to eat at the reception. We all got flimsy paper diplomas that said we were "bound to continue on to an institution of higher learning" which I suppose makes sense if you can afford that. More likely I'll be getting a job to help out Mama before long.

Anyway, it was hellish-hot, and we had to line up out in the yard next to the flagpole and wait for Tuggerheinz to call every graduating kid up to get his flimsy paper. Naturally I was the only graduator not to wear a tie and with the heat and all it paid off. Mama was there with a big hat on, fanning herself and grinning the whole time and when I shook Tuggerheinz' hand I grinned back at her which got all the girls in the class giggling. They can think what they want, but I'm never ashamed to be Mama's boy.

The part afterwards lasted for hours and about sixteen other moms and dads took turns patting my head and mussing my hair. I wished Benny was there to help me escape but as it turned out, it was the best day I could've decided to skip going to Baker Bowl. We lost to the Bucs 15-3 yesterday, so even though I figured we wouldn't get creamed again that badly, I wasn't exactly in the mood to watch another loss.

Boy, was I ever wrong. This was even worse.

PIT 300 205 311 - 15 20 2
PHL 101 000 000 - 2 8 1

GETTING OUR HEADS SMASHED IN WAS BETTER THAN THIS
June 14, 1924

I knew something strange was up when I hopped off the streetcar. The bleachers were sold out already and the grandstand ticket line was around the block. Then Benny found me and clued me in. It was Saturday, it was Flag Day, and because the Pirates had murdered us 15-3 and 15-2 the last two games, every fan who had never seen a team score 15 runs before had shown up.

But I wasn't gonna accept that. Heck, summer was officially here, I was a school graduate, and I'd had enough of these dumb Bucs making us look bad. We can certainly do that on our own.

We got pretty good grandstand seats just past first base, and when speedy Max Carey beat out a single to start the game off Johnny Couch, the crowd said oh geez here we go again. But then he took off for second, Butch Henline rifled a throw and Sand tagged Carey on the hat for the first out of the game! Of course Moore tripled and Cuyler was hit by a pitch with two outs, but Earl Smith flied out and it looked like we had a chance.

It looked more that way with two outs in our 1st. Holke singled off Lee Meadows and Cy Williams clubbed one onto the train tracks past the right field fence. Yowsa, we are up 2-0! A Hod Ford error helped the Bucs get one back in the 3rd, but then the Great Kiki really messed up a fly for them in the 4th. Cuyler dropped and then kicked Henline's ball like it was a football, and Butch got all the way to third, where he scored on a Mokan double.

Everyone was nervous the whole game because we knew how dangerous the Buccos are. Benny went through four lemonades and even ate some peanuts without taking off their shells. Wright tripled and scored on a Rabbit sacrifice fly in the 6th, and because we couldn't get anything else going off Meadows, the game stayed 3-2 us going into the 9th.

Couch has been a great plug for our starting rotation leaks, and he was real tough again here, getting Rabbit and pinch-hitter Bigbee out to begin the Pirates 9th. But if there was any cheering going on at Baker Bowl, it was the quiet, teeth clenching type. Sure enough, down to their last strike, that crumb-head Carey banged a double off the fence in right that just missed being a homer. Pie Traynor ripped a single and the game was tied, and it got so quiet in the stands it was like fifteen thousand people just died. Sure it was tied and we had last ups, but who the hell thought we had a chance?

We did get Ford to second with a two-out double, but with our relief team a tired mess and no good hitters on the bench, Couch batted for himself and grounded out. In the 10th Glenn Wright made a 2-base error with two outs, but the chicken face walked Cy on purpose and Parkinson lined out.

Top of the 11th, reliever Babe Adams singled and Carey walked him to second. Moore singled and Huck Betts came on to face Cuyler. Who walked. And Smith walked. And that, sad reader-people, was that.

PIT 001 001 001 02 - 5 12 2
PHI 200 100 000 00 - 3 9 1

NO GAME TODAY, JUST A LETTER
June 15, 1924

Dear Rachel:

It's been almost a month since we bumped into each other at that music club in Chicago, so I was wondering how you were doing and when I can come visit you again.

I finally graduated public school, which is a big load off my mind. I was able to finish with pretty decent grades somehow, even though I did more studying at ball fields than in the classroom. I'll explain why this happened at some later point.

Anyway, it sure seems like your Robins are back on the winning track after their tough trip out west, so that must be exciting for you. Has your father gone to more Ebbets games with you or do you just go with Margie? My Phillies as you probably read in the newspaper are a lousy team in their home park, maybe because the dinky fences can't keep the other teams from bombing homers. The Pirates put 30 runs on the board in two games against us and I'm sure glad they finally left town. I think they're up in Boston starting tomorrow, and the Braves are the worst team in years so that should keep their winning vacation going for a while.

Now that I'm out of school I have to start thinking about getting some kind of job, but I really don't have an idea about that yet. Maybe you can help me if I come visit you again.

Benny is doing okay, even though he's still a little blue after his two-day romance with Miss Philadelphia Ruth Malcolmson fizzled like bad seltzer. His head was pretty much in the clouds about her, but I have to say I had a chance to meet her myself for an Athletics game with Benny and even though she was cuter than a peach I thought she was a little snobby.

How are your parents and brother and sister doing? I sort of forgot their names because I didn't see them for too long. I'll be sure to remember them next time, if I ever I come visit you again.

So write me back soon if you can. I miss dancing and looking at the moon with you. There was no Phillies game today because of church reasons and I've been mostly sitting around my house. But I just looked at the schedule and saw that they have a three-game series up at Ebbets Field starting on June 20th. Isn't that interesting?

Good night, Rachel!

—Vinny

WAY TOO MUCH GABBING FOR MY TASTE
June 16, 1924

Well, we had to like our chances against the Cubs today. We took three out of four from them out at Cubs Park, our biggest winner Bill Hubbell with his six wins was pitching, and their guy Vic Keen's record was a crummy 2-8 going in.

So Heathcote doubled to start the game. Grantham tripled with one out, Gabby Hartnett singled, Butch Weis doubled, Friberg walked, Hollocher singled and they were up 3-0 before I tasted even one onion on top of my hot dog. Then with two outs in the 2nd, Grantham singled and Gabby smoked one deep into the bleachers to make it 5-0.

This Hartnett guy is one of the best young backstops to ever come along. Last year he only hit .268 with eight homers but already has 13 knocks this season and might get 100 runs batted in at this rate. They call him Gabby because he's always talking to the hitters and bothering them, and if he wasn't such a jolly dope he probably would have had a bat planted in his head by now. Anyway after Mokan homered for one run and doubled in another to make it 5-2 going to the 7th, Hartnett started another Cub rally with a double of his own. A Wrightstone single made it 6-3 them into the

8th, but that's when Hubbell lost his marbles.

A walk and three straight singles—the last by Gabby, of course, for his fifth run batted in—brought on Huck Betts, and he should have stayed home in bed. Friberg singled and Hooks Cotter walked with two out, and then Hollocher, one of the weakest shortstops around, blasted one over the right fence for a grand slam homer! Glazner mopped up the mess but we were deep in our caskets by then. Our home record now is a sickening 7-19, and we all know the only other team with a worse one.

CHC 320 000 170 - 13 17 0
PHL 010 001 10x - 3 11 0

ROLLER COASTER THRILLS FOR THE BAKER BOYS
June 17, 1924

What a game today! All the schools were out by now in Philadelphia, so Baker Bowl was flooded with kids, and me and Benny decided to stand in the grandstand area behind home plate so we wouldn't go deaf from all the screaming weemies.

It was a good idea, because the Cubs and Phils staged maybe the most exciting game of the year for us, like being on a carnival ride for almost two hours. Jimmy Ring was determined to get his second win but fell behind like he usually does on a Gabby (him again) Hartnett triple, Weis single and Friberg double in the 2nd. Chicago first baseman Ray Grimes butchered a Cy ball with one out in the 4th, and two singles and a walk followed for three Phillie runs. Cub starter Kauffman singled home the tie run in the 6th, but Ring hit a sacrifice pop to match that and we were up 4-3 going to the 7th.

Then things went nuts. Three walks and a double by Weis put the Cubs back in front 5-4 in the 7th. Holke slammed a deep homer to right after a Harper walk in the bottom of the 7th, and so many people stood up in front of us we couldn't even see where the ball landed. But who cared? We were back ahead 6-5!

Uh-oh. Here came a Ring slow-ball to Friberg to start the 8th and Bernie roped it for a double. Grantham hit with one out, everyone in the park afraid to look, and then we knew why. George lined it onto the rail tracks in three seconds flat and the Cubs were back ahead 7-6! Steineder came in to put Ring out of his misery and finish the inning.

With both our catchers hurt, third-stringer Lew Wendell had to play the game and singled to begin the Phillie 8th off Cub reliever Wheeler. Then Ford rapped into an easy double play and we all groaned again. Steineder got out of the 9th without worry, and came up for our last three outs. Normally we would have sneaked down to great seats by now but no one in the park was leaving. Harper reached on a walk to begin, Holke fanned, and Cy rolled one to Grimes' right but he threw it away for his second horrible play of the game, putting men on second and third. Chicago brought all their infielders close, and when Wrightstone dribbled one between short and third, Harper had to hold at third base even though it was a single.

Mokan then grounded one but the Cubs couldn't make a double play and the game was tied again. Two outs now, Wendell cracked a ball into center, Williams ran home from third and we had the 8-7 win! Yahoo! Benny jumped around a few seconds, slapping my back and knocking my wind out.

Excuse me, reader-people, but us Phillie-stines have been wandering in the loser desert for a while. A happy good night!

CHI 020 001 220 – 7 14 3
PHL 000 301 202 – 8 11 0

THE SHOOTOUT AND THE TELEGRAM
June 18, 1924

The weather finally cooled down today. Benny planned to buy just two lemonades at the game instead of the typical six, and right after the game started there was more good luck spilling all over us.

Pete Alexander, that old souse, went on another bender last night apparently, because after Carlson pitched like junk for us in the top of the 1st and gave the Cubs five runs on six hits, old Alex grounded out to end the inning, tripped over his own feet on his way down the base path and knocked himself out. That's right: Guy Bush and Sheriff Blake were forced to pitch the whole game for them, and it was only a matter of time before we got back into the thing.

Well actually, it took about four innings. See, Carlson was still a big joke out there, and after Friberg, Heathcote and Grantham began the 2nd with hits it was 7-0 Chicago. Then we grabbed our lunch pails and went to work. Holke homered to start our 4th, Williams walked, Wrightstone singled and the Sheriff walked into Pitching Town to save the day. Except he didn't. Wilson said howdy with a double, Mokan singled, and after the next two guys went out, a wild pitch and three more singles tied the score 7-7!

Now Blake is a horrible pitcher, but because Rip Wheeler was used too much in yesterday's clubbing party, manager Bill Killefer had no choice except to use him the rest of the way. The problem was that our bullpen was just as stretched, so Fletcher was refusing to change his pitcher, too, like a pair of smelly drawers he just couldn't take off. Three walks, a single and plunked Butch Weis began the 5th and we were behind again 9-7. This drove Benny crazy and he started cursing at Fletcher from the grandstand until a cop came over to shut him up.

The Sheriff gave us three runs right back, though, and after a Holke single we had the lead for the first time 10-9! Then Ford booted one in top of the 6th, Grantham whacked a ball onto the train tracks and we were losing again. Cripes. Ray Grimes then popped a ball right toward us in the stands, and Benny jumped over two old men to snatch it. "I'm keeping this baby," he said, even though all foul balls are supposed to be thrown back on the field to save the team money. Sure enough, the cop who shut him up before appeared again and asked for the ball back. Benny decided it wasn't worth getting arrested and missing the rest of the exciting game for, so he handed it over.

Unfortunately, that's where the thrills stopped. The Cubs scored a run in the 7th, two in the 8th on a Grimes homer off Huck Betts who finally replaced the sickening Carlson, and another in the 9th on a Grimes triple while Sheriff Blake turned into Davey Crockett out there and roped us to a tree for the last four innings.

I was able to calm down Benny a little after with a root beer float at our favorite parlor, but I could tell his head was still cooking. What I wasn't expecting was the telegram from Western Union that was waiting for me when I got home. Mama gave it to me with a worried look on her face, saying she just "had to open it." I sat down at the kitchen table for a read:

DEAR VINNY:
READ YOUR LETTER TO RACHEL. SHE COULD NOT RESPOND AS SHE HAS GOT SERIOUS ILLNESS. CANNOT DISCUSS FACTS NOW.
BEST, SAUL STONE

Mama and me looked at each other. My words could barely come out, but it was clear I was missing tomorrow's game for an emergency trip to Brooklyn. And not the way I wanted to be going there. Good night if I can even sleep!

CHC 520 022 121 - 15 18 1
PHL 000 730 000 - 10 15 1

VINNY THE "MENSCH"
June 19, 1924

Thankfully my baggage friend at the train station remembered who I was and got me a nice spot between a stack of steamer trunks and carton of pickle jars. I was on my way back to New York first thing to visit Rachel, who was sick with some disease her father couldn't even tell me about in his telegram. So because I was anxious to get up there the train trip seemed to take three times longer than the last few times.

When I got to Pennsylvania Station I took an elevated train over the river to Brooklyn, then got on the Franklin Shuttle line that went to her neighborhood. It was crowded with Robins fans heading to Ebbets Field for their last game with the Reds, and if I wasn't worried to death about Rachel I probably would have been joining them.

It took me a while getting lost on foot before I could locate her street in Prospect Heights. Her little brother and sister answered the door and said she was in the Brooklyn Jewish Hospital not too far away, with a bad case of something called red fever. Her parents were there watching over her and didn't want any other visitors but that sure wasn't going to stop me. I bought some flowers from a girl on a corner and went straight to the hospital.

A nurse at a desk told me what room she was in, then changed her mind and said it was off limits and I couldn't go up. I said okay, then found some back stairs and went up anyway. I peeked into the room, saw both her mother and father sitting there holding hands with these creepy white masks on their mouths, so I looked around until I found a supply closet and grabbed one for myself.

Lotte was shocked when I walked in, but when she saw the big bunch of flowers it calmed her down. Saul shook my hand three times and kept calling me a "mensch", which I guess is a Jewish word for a good thing. The "red fever" was actually scarlet fever and Rachel looked awful, her face all pale and sticky and these little red sores around her mouth. She smiled when she saw me but it was one of those weak ones and her throat was so swollen up she couldn't even talk. I got a chair next to her and rubbed her arm for a few minutes through her hospital dress.

She slept for a while, then seemed kind of thirsty when she woke up so I went out with her glass to try and find more water for it. I went past a room with some colored clean-up guys sitting there, and they were listening to a scratchy radio machine that had the Reds-Robins game on it, right from Ebbets Field. I asked the score and one guy said Carl Mays had a 6-2 lead on Brooklyn just an inning ago and now it was 6-5. I brought the news back to Rachel with the water and she gave me a weak nod.

Her father fell asleep after a while, her mother sat there and knitted, and I went back for more water and a few more scores but things were getting worse down the street. Cincy had scored four runs in the 8th to put the game to bed. I couldn't bear to tell Rachel this, so I just said the score was tied and that the Robins were getting lots of men on base. She held the sleeve of my shirt and fell asleep with a smile.

Saul and Lotte shooed the nurse away when she started asking who I was, then invited me home for dinner with them when the visiting time was over. I really liked them, even though her mother served those weird flat potato cakes again, and after the meal before they put me up in their spare room I had a chance to teach little Sammy and Sarah a card game or two. The doctor said that Rachel might be able to come home tomorrow or Saturday if her fever drops below 100 degrees, but there's a good chance it won't.

An announcer on Mr. Stone's radio machine mentioned that the Phillies got mauled by the Cubs today, but you know what? Even though they're now on their way up here for a weekend at Ebbets Field, they are the farthest thing from my mind. Good night reader-people, and especially you Rachel.

CHI 505 001 210 - 14 19 0
PHL 100 000 000 - 1 6 3

TORN UP AT EBBETS FIELD
June 20, 1924

Mrs. Stone cooked a giant pot of homemade oatmeal for breakfast, and I read the sports page with Saul while we ate. He's worried a lot about the

Robins, mainly because the Pirates and Reds have been so tough, but also because after Wheat and Fournier the Brooklyn lineup doesn't have much to be afraid of.

He told me some stories about the 1920 World Series when they lost to the Indians, how impossible it was to get tickets and how nobody went to work or school during the games. He saw Game 1 when Coveleski beat Brooklyn 3-1 and was glad he missed the unassisted triple play Bill Wambsganss made, which was in Game 5 out in Cleveland, "or I probably would've killed myself."

We went back to the hospital after breakfast and the first thing they said is that we didn't have to wear those creepy masks anymore. Rachel was feeling a lot better, and was ready to go home. We rode with her in an ambulance wagon and fixed her up in her bedroom, and that's when she said I could go over to Ebbets if I wanted and watch the Phillies play. "Bring me back a victory," she said, and kissed my hand. I said okay, but wasn't sure which team she was talking about.

It was easier getting a ticket to the game than last time, when Brooklyn had started out so hot, and I got a good seat in the lower grandstand for a dollar-fifty. A tasty sausage roll with onions did me right, and I made a brain note to find something to sweeten up my breath later, just in case.

Johnny Couch was throwing for us against Dutch Ruether, an old lefty who has a problem with hit-giving. He was at it again early, as a Wilson triple and Ford single gave the Phils a 1-0 lead in the 2nd. Mitchell booted a grounder to start the 5th, and singles by Schultz, Holke, Cy and Wilson put three more on the board. The crowd got quiet, and I was hoping Rachel wasn't listening on her father's radio machine because I didn't want her to have a relapse. Then Mokan doubled in a run, it was 5-0, and I was torn in half about whether to cheer or not.

Milt Stock tripled for Brooklyn after that, Loftus batted for the crummy Ruether and doubled, and after an Andy High triple it was 5-2 and the Ebbets folks were alive again. Art Decatur relieved for the Robins but he floated a pitch in too slow to Heinie Sand and the doinky shortstop lined it over the left field fence to put us up 6-2!

But Couch finally fell apart in the last of the 9th. High led with his second triple, Fournier singled him in with one out, Taylor singled Fournier to third and Huck Betts came on to get Tommy Griffith. Griffith was only in there because Bernie Neis was hurt, but he walloped Betts' first pitch way out to center field. Cy ran to the fence and it bounced off the very top for a double, and missed tying up the game by a mere inch. Fletcher yanked out Betts in no time and put in Steineder, who got Stock to roll out to third and end the thing.

I felt bad that Brooklyn lost for Rachel's sake, but when I got back to her house she was sitting up in bed eating homemade soup with chicken in it, and had a lot more color in her face. She was thrilled the Phillies won because I deserved it for coming up to Brooklyn to see her, which got me all embarrassed of course.

After I rinsed the onion breath out of my mouth for about ten minutes with something called Klenzo Dental Creme, Saul set up their Victrola in her room and we listened to phonographs of Paul Whiteman and Al Jolson with a nice breeze blowing in through her curtains, and she held my hand for at least an hour of this until I heard her snoring. I pulled my chair closer and stretched out with my feet on the bed touching hers, and I'll tell you something, there's no better way to fall asleep.

PHL 010 031 010 - 6 11 0
BRK 000 002 002 - 4 8 2

MIRACLE BROOKLYN RECOVERIES
June 21, 1924

The Stones went off to the synagogue in the morning for their Sabbath stuff, and I was left at the house to cook breakfast for Rachel. I would have been probably better off trying to learn Yiddish. First I cracked a couple of eggs into a pan and spent two minutes picking out the shells while the things were burning. Then I poured her orange juice without shaking up the bottle first so it came out thicker than the bottom of a swamp. I was real happy they weren't bacon-eaters.

Rachel had started working on some short stories because she figured they might be easier to sell than a long novel nobody would want to take the time to read (with a hint-wink toward me), so I was nice and read one of them after breakfast. It was called "The Tragedy of Harriet" and was about this orphan girl who gets left on the doorstep of a rich guy in a big bread basket and he ends up taking her off to Europe and leaving her with the family of his French mistress, where she becomes a drunkard and whore-lady and gets sent to prison the rest of her life for knifing someone. I told Rachel there might be too much plot in it for a short story, so she said she'd try to cut it down and didn't even bite off my head this time.

It earned me another trip to Ebbets, where I sat in the left field bleachers and was afraid to cheer again because the Phillies took a 3-1 lead on Dazzy Vance with the 1-9 Jimmy Ring on the mound, if you can believe that. Dazzy's curve sure wasn't dazzling, as Harper doubled and Holke homered in the 1st inning. Ring got out of jams in the first six innings but during that Vance calmed way down and suddenly the Phils were whiffing a lot.

As a matter of fact, Dazzy was suffocating them to death slowly, giving them just three puny singles the rest of the game as the Robins waited around for Ring to lose his nerve. Which he did starting in the 7th. A walk and two singles gave them a run. Stock's double tied the game at 3-3 in the 8th and Steineder relieved to whiff Vance and Johnny Mitchell. But the great Fournier, quiet the whole game, smashed a triple off the fence right near me with two outs in the 9th. Brown was walked on purpose to bring up the much-weaker Taylor, who ripped a single anyway to give Brooklyn the game!

As you'd figure, I was sad for myself but thrilled for Rachel, who was following the action in bed on the radio machine. Her mother cooked a nice hunk of meat called brisket for dinner, and Rachel even joined us at the table. We paid another visit to her roof later on to stare at the city lights, and she asked me if I was going to college. I said we probably couldn't afford it and I wasn't much for learning things out of books anyway, which got her quiet and made me think she was looking for some kind of smarty husband. There's lots of ways to get smart, though, so I guess we'll see how this issue turns out.

PHL 210 000 000 - 3 6 0
BRK 100 000 111 - 4 13 2

NATIONAL LEAGUE through Saturday, June 21, 1924

Pittsburgh	40	21	.658	—
Cincinnati	39	26	.600	3
New York	36	27	.571	5
St. Louis	35	29	.547	6.5
Brooklyn	33	29	.532	7.5
Chicago	30	33	.476	11
PHILLIES	24	39	.381	17
Boston	15	48	.238	26

DOUBLE FATHER'S DAY
June 22, 1924

Rachel had planned to take her father to the game, it being Father's Day and all, but she still had a few drops of scarlet in her and figured she'd just sit the thing out. Sarah and Sammy were too young for that crowd and her mother wasn't a fan, so guess who got elected to sit with good old Saul Stone?

Well, even though the Phils lost again it turned out to be one of the best times I had at a ball park, because from the first Burleigh Grimes spitball to the last, I felt like my own papa was sitting with us.

Mike Spanelli, or "Micky" as his drinking pals called him, got killed over in France six years ago, maybe a week before the Big War ended, and it just about killed me because I had my baseball mitt all oiled up and ready with a ball in it, just waiting for the day he would walk back in the house. See, he got me into baseball when he gave me a Rube Waddell player card from his pack of cigarettes when I was around seven, and before long we were out in the alley every weekend day and summer night after his job, whipping a ball back and forth or showing me how to choke up on the bat to hit bottle caps better.

He took me to a good amount of Phillies games but they were real bad back then and I could barely remember the players' names. He hated the Giants worse than Benny does now, and he wasn't crazy about the Athletics either though I still haven't figured that one out, but I used to love going to Baker Bowl with him on hot days because he would always sit on my left and keep me in shade with his big body.

Anyway, Saul had a small body so it didn't matter where he sat, and our seats at Ebbets were mostly under a roof so nobody got baked—except the Phillies of course. Grimes had his loogy-ball going pretty good. We only got four hits off him the whole game, a single, two triples and a double, but they were spaced far apart to not cause trouble. Bill Hubbell meanwhile pitched another bad game, giving a cheap homer to puny Mitchell to start the Brooklyn 1st and a 2-run smash to Fournier an out later.

Saul really enjoyed himself and bought me five pretzels, and kept dropping nice hints about Rachel all through the game, like he was waiting for me to ask him if I could marry her or something. Not that I won't one of these days, but gadzooks—I haven't done anything but kiss her yet!

Zack Wheat's his favorite player and when he doubled in the fourth and fifth Robin runs in the 2nd inning he pounded me on the back a few times and threw his boater up in the air. He was acting like a little kid, but I guess that's what baseball does to you sometimes. It's like drinking a big tall glass of youth juice, and in the summer, you can have one almost every day.

Rachel couldn't stop hugging me after dinner when I got up to leave. Tomorrow's Benny's birthday and I promised I'd go to the Braves-Phillies game with him at Baker, so I needed to catch the next luggage car back home. She was real happy I took her dad to the game, and she actually had a different look in her eye than I'd ever seen. It was a long delayed twinkle, like the North Star, and it got me feeling all warm in new places. If anything, it'll be something new and nice to think about all week while we're hopefully destroying the Braves.

PHL 000 000 102 - 3 4 2
BRK 320 000 01x - 6 13 0

AS IF WE WERE LAYING IN HAMMOCKS
FIVE TIGER TALLIES AT THE OUTSET MAKE FOR A RELAXED FATHER'S AFTERNOON

By Burgess Bannister Butterworth, PhD
June 22, 1924

DETROIT—My son Calvin has been working quite hard of late, and while I am slow to commend his choice of a profession when there are far more important arenas he could be toiling in than a ball yard's writing roost, I must say I was honored to receive his Father's Day invitation to report today's Cleveland vs. Detroit game at Navin Field. I am anything but informed when it comes to our alleged national pastime, being a Professor of the Physical Sciences at the University of Michigan, yet it is my firm hope that you will enjoy my attempt at sports documentation.

With thousands, or perhaps hundreds of fathers in attendance, Mr. Frank Brower struck a triple against Mr. Rip Collins almost immediately but never left the comfort of the square cloth sack he stood upon. Sherry Smith, the Cleveland thrower of balls with the ladylike name, then had the misfortune of surrendering consecutive hits to the following: Mr. Rigney (a single), Mr Cobb (a single), Mr. Heilman (a single), Mr, Manush (a double), Mr, Woodall (a double), Mr. Pratt (a single), and Mr. O'Rourke (a single). This resulted in five Detroit runs, the total confirmed by the giant wooden number slotted into the board five feet beyond the right-centerfield fence.

From this juncture the offensive force of the assembled home team lessened considerably, as a Mr. Cobb single and Mr. Manush double in the 7th frame of reference provided the only other scoring digit of the event.*

*It was at this point that I was forced to attend to private bodily matters, having earlier consumed a warm sample of possible pork meat that my son delivered to me in a bread cylinder soaked in questionable mustard.

The affixed outcome of the contest kept the denizens from raising any audible excitement, and Mr. Collins carried his run-less performance into the final frame, only to have his acumen suddenly evaporate. A ball batted by Mr. McNulty became a single and error off the hurler's leather sphere-catcher. Mr. Burns pinch-hit a double, before an aborted athletic play by Mr. Rigney and two four-ball base tickets compressed the score to 6-2 and created the need for Mr. Cole to complete the effort.

He did by projecting one solitary pitch, which Mr. Myatt bounced harmlessly across the soiled inner field to Mr. O'Rourke for a play that produced two outs rather than the accustomed one, and the Tigers had finished the sample series with three marks of victory alongside their one defeat.

The team journeyed thereafter to their St. Louis train, while my son drove me back to my home in Woodbridge to enjoy my wife's robust Father's Day dinner of wild quail. Thank you, Calvin, for this fine, if laborious gift, and may you derive some comfort from penning words while visiting Missouri.

A SHUTOUT FOR BENNY'S BIRTHDAY
June 23, 1924

I was sleepy-eyed after my late trip back from New York, but couldn't lollygag around at home because the game at Baker Bowl with the Braves was an hour earlier than normal and I still had to figure out a present for Benny.

He was turning 19, which I figure is a big deal with that bigger 20 just around the corner, but as usual with Benny he wasn't thrilled. "Come on Vinny," he said when I practically had to drag him out of bed, "I don't have a steady girlfriend, my team stinks and I can't even rub two nickels together." I told him it was his birthday, the sun was out and there was a brand new ball game to see, but all he did was complain about the flapjacks that Dotty his rooming house lady made special for him and tasted like "burnt Goodyear tires." But when I reminded him we were playing the awful Braves he cheered up a little, and when I said everything at the ball park was going to be my treat, he shook my hand and actually smiled. I had him back.

Hal Carlson with his lucky 5-5 record was throwing for the Phils. I say lucky because he gives away hits like candy canes on Christmas and still manages to pull games out. Jesse Barnes, the unlucky brother of the Giants' Virgil, won his first three games of the year but then lost his next eight and I knew we could get in some tasty licks off him.

The left corner bleachers were packed, probably because everyone else had the same hunch that we could beat these rubes, and sure enough, with two outs in the 1st, Butch Henline singled, Cy Williams walked and Russ Wrightstone clanked a ball off the Lifebuoy sign in right field. Henline scored easy but Cy couldn't outrace Ray Powell's throw from right. We saw the giant cloud of dust erupt, lost our view of Cy and catcher Gibson, but then the umpire's thumb shot up and we groaned.

The 1-0 lead went on forever, it got real hot in the bleachers, and with every runner we left on base Benny got glummer. He had no clue what to do with his life and I reminded him I didn't either and we could knock our brains together all summer to come up with something, but that didn't help.

Then Jimmie Wilson stepped to the plate to lead off our 7th. Barnes spun and threw and Jimmie cold-cocked one high and deep to left. The ball was coming right at us! Benny climbed on the bleacher row, knocking me aside, leaped over the hats and heads of six fans but the thing nicked off his fingers and landed in the lap of some little girl who wasn't even watching the game! The crowd cheered the homer but Benny just sulked from missing the ball, so I had to re-direct his attention back to Carlson, who was throwing a 2-0 shutout into the 8th. Heck, even Casey Stengel was hitless.

A Harper double and Holke triple in our half of the inning made it 3-0 and seemed to perk him a bit, and then Oscar the Peanut Man edged himself into our row. He handed Benny two bags of hot nuts tied together with a blue ribbon and said "Happy birthday, Benny!" Right after that Benny's grandstand gambling friend Rollo Briggs showed up, gave Benny a couple of cigars and wished him the same thing. He was followed by Sidney, our favorite Baker Bowl security cop, who reached up from his stool on the field and handed him a rolled-up paper: a giant signed photograph of Ruth Malcolmson, the Miss Philadelphia of 1924 who Benny embarrassed himself over back on Decoration Day. Benny was blushing silly and asked me how all these people knew about his birthday and I told him I visited a few folks right before game time.

I even said I talked to the Phillies' equipment man, who knew Hal Carlson real well and that the pitcher had promised to throw Benny a shutout. Of course this was just a big fib, but with the score the way it was and the Braves being the other team I figured I had a good chance of getting away with it. Hal got the first two guys in the top of the 9th but then Cotton Tierney scratched a single. Some bum named Herb Thomas pinch-hit for Barnes and Carlson hit him in the back. Art Fletcher went to the mound and I thought oh no, what if he lifted "Benny's friend" before he could finish the shutout? This could wreck Benny's mind for a solid month! Instead, Fletcher went back to his dugout hole, Carlson got Bill Cunningham on an easy grounder and that was that! The place erupted, and lots of the bleacher fans around us who overheard my fib pounded Benny on the back with birthday wishes.

Benny was all smiles after and treated me back with some Bassett's ice cream dishes at the Reading Terminal. He vowed I would be his best friend forever, and that I could be his best man if he was ever lucky enough to meet a real girl. Before he could start dwelling on this again, I reminded him Cooney was facing Oeschger tomorrow.

BOS 000 000 000 - 0 8 0
PHL 100 000 11x - 3 9 1

PHILS NOT TOO LOONY OVER COONEY
June 24, 1924

I should've known yesterday was an extra special day, like finding a gold dubloon in a gutter, because today was just plain dismal. You have to expect this to happen when your record is 25-40, but it still isn't much fun when it does.

Joe Oeschger threw for us, showing off his usual nothing, and after four innings the lousy Braves had seven hits, a walk and four runs on the board. The Boston pitcher was Johnny Cooney, a tough lefty who sometimes plays the outfield and had a 2-9 record when the game started because his team never hits for him. Well, he couldn't use that excuse in this one.

The truth was that he looked like Mathewson out there, giving up nothing but a Hod Ford double in the first six and two-third innings, and the Baker Bowl crowd was so quiet you could hear the clouds roll by. Oeschger calmed down pretty well for him, and when Mitchell relieved him to face lefty Stengel with the sacks stuffed and two outs in the 9th, pinch-hitter Les Mann popped up to the catcher to get us out of it.

Benny had gone off to gamble in the grandstand with Rollo after the 6th inning, and I hope he was watching the last of the 9th, because that's when our only fun of the day began. Cooney walked Parkinson and Holke on eight pitches, and Cy Williams roped a single to load the bases. After Wilson singled in our first run, Skinny Graham ran in to take Cooney's place, and whiffed Mokan right off the bat. But Hod Ford rammed his second double down the line in left, two runs scored, and it was 4-3!

I thought about making my way from the bleachers over to Benny in the stands, but was afraid I wouldn't make it in time. I'm also superstitious like you wouldn't believe, and because I was opening a peanut with one foot on my seat when Ford doubled, I had to keep that foot right where it was and get another peanut ready. So why did Heinie Sand then ground out and keep Ford at second? And why did Wrightstone then pinch-hit a weak fly to right to end the stupid game?

I guess when your record is 25-41 and you can't even beat the Braves, you don't really have to ask questions like that.

It's a real battle of the champions tomorrow, with the 2-8 Benton facing our 1-10 Jimmy Ring. At least it'll be Ladies' Day.

BOS 100 300 000 - 4 11 0
PHL 000 000 003 - 3 7 0

NOT FOR THE FAIREST OF HEARTS
June 25, 1924

Benny was not only at our front door early, he was up in my room and dressed like a dancing hall sap in a blueberry shirt, suspenders, and striped silk tie stuck with a big pin. I asked what the heck he was doing and he just threw up his arms and said, "It's Ladies' Day!"

And so it was, one of two the Phillies held on Wednesdays where females over 16 could get in Baker Bowl for free. But I'd never seen my friend so excited about one. He said he was sick of being alone and was going to find a girlfriend this time come hell or an avalanche. He was also bent on finding me one, so before long he had me in my closet, throwing every piece of clothes that might be fancy on my bed so he could choose an outfit for me. I told him it was almost 90 degrees out there, but all that did was make him choose something white.

We went with a starchy shirt and eight-plus knickers under my pants, which is what I only wore to church on holidays, and then Mama got involved, which is always a mistake. She put some kind of paste in my hair and combed it for so long I couldn't tell where my head ended and my hair began, stuck some fresh plums in my pockets to give to any "nice girls" I met, and sent us on our way.

It's always nice to stare at attractive girls because after all we're naturally built to do that, but at a ball park I much prefer staring at the game. They'd reserved the entire grandstand section with the most shade for the free ladies, and the lady-hunting men who showed up had to fight for the rest of the tickets, most of them young and nearly as slicked up as we were. Benny, of course, was thinking way ahead of all of them and was at the park at seven in the morning to be first in line for bleacher tickets. "How do you expect to meet ladies sitting out there?" I asked and all he did was wink at me and pull some rolled up paper out of his tail jacket pocket. Tear some off and hand it to me with a small fountain pen. "Just get their orders, and any addresses and telephone numbers you can." I said he was nuts, that the vendors would get us thrown out. "Which is why we need to be smooth about it," he said.

A lot of the vendors went down to re-fill their trays after the third inning, and by that time Cy Williams had given us a 1-0 lead with a monstrous poke onto the train tracks, so I felt good about trying this out. We split up and took different parts of the grandstand, but I was too nervous and shy and honestly more interested in watching the game action to have much success. I was sweating mightily in my stupid outfit, and a cute red-haired girl with round glasses who was probably 16 but looked no more than 13 handed me her handkerchief so I could wipe my forehead. Her name was Mopsy and she was there by herself because her sister went home with heat stroke, meaning there was an empty seat next to her. So I took it to keep from fainting and she gabbed in my ear forever about her classes and her jigsaw puzzles and dolls and her recent time at a lake with her cousins and here were the Braves on the field, suddenly tattooing Jimmy Ring for five hits and three runs and taking a 3-1 lead.

I quickly asked Mopsy if she wanted something to eat or drink just to get out of there and she asked for a lemonade and peanuts. I reached around the rotting plums in my pocket, pulled out the paper and scribbled it down. Mopsy got all excited seeing my pen and blurted out her telephone number right there, so I wrote that down too just to keep her happy. The vendors were coming back right after I got the peanuts and lemonade, so I hurried back to Mopsy, gave her the goods and kept walking.

Meantime Boston had knocked out the horrible Jimmy Ring with two more runs, and were about to make the score 6-1 with a run off Huck Betts and I was in a very sour mood. I opened three buttons on my stiff shirt and went looking for Benny but he found me instead, all thrilled because he had numbers and addresses of ten women already. But the heat was doing a real number on him and he looked like he was about to pass out, so I grabbed his arm and hurried him back to the bleachers.

The Phillies had collected just five measly hits off a bum with a 2-8 record named Larry Benton, so the day had become just a big fat loss for me. Then when we walked out after the game ended, Benny pulled out his rolled up list and dropped to his knees in pain. The sweat dampness had turned every name, number and address into impossible-to-read ink blots!

We ended up down at Mort's for cherry fizzers, and so I could get the scores of the other games, but even the Giants losing again couldn't cheer him up. I reached in my pocket, gave him Mopsy's readable number, and said, "Good luck. She's real nice." I think he appreciated that.

BOS 000 003 210 - 6 14 0
PHL 010 000 000 - 1 5 2

CREATED TO DRIVE US NUTS
June 26, 1924

This time it was Mama who shook me awake this morning. "There's a girl downstairs named Maria asking for you." I rolled over and said I didn't know any Maria and she said "The girl sure knows you. Maria Stonetino from Brooklyn?"

Oh lord. I tiptoed out, took one peek at the front room from the top of the stairs and saw Rachel standing there, all dolled up in a sun dress and yellow hat and carrying a little yellow sun umbrella. What the heck? I ran in the bathroom, washed up so fast I almost brushed my teeth with hair grease, threw on some clothes and hurried down to meet her.

Her face was full of color and she looked as sweet as a grape in her outfit and gave me this giant hug. Mama didn't know what to make of all this so I introduced "Maria" to her as "a friend I met up there I was meaning to tell you about." The second Mama went off to finish breakfast I asked Rachel what she was doing in Philadelphia and she looked at me like I was a big kook. "We got four games in three days here with you! Isn't it time I visited you for a change?" Honestly, the Phillies have been so busy losing lately I haven't been up on their schedule as much, but it was true. The Robins were at Baker Bowl today, tomorrow, and Saturday for a double-header, before the teams went back up to Ebbets for a Sunday game.

Mama called us into the kitchen for breakfast, which was when I noticed Rachel was talking with a fake Italian accent to go along with her fake Italian name. She even said her father worked down at the docks in New York hauling around vegetables. I was certainly thrilled to see her, but this masquerade stuff was ridiculous, and I told her so when we started off to the ball game. "Well, I wasn't sure your mother would like who I was," she said, "and me being Italian is a lot easier than you pretending to be Jewish." I asked where she was planning on staying and she said Mama had already promised her the downstairs couch, and that her little travel suitcase was in the hall closet. I couldn't believe any of this, but as the streetcar got close to Baker Bowl I started to think about the game, with Burleigh Grimes facing Johnny Couch, of all the strange things, and how fun it was going to be to give someone a tour of my daily field.

Benny met me outside as usual, tried to kiss Rachel's hand and missed, then asked if she had brought one of her girlfriends along. Realizing this was a solo journey for her, he gave me a little wink and said he'd see "you lovebirds" afterwards. I sprung for dollar grandstand seats, of course, and pointed out my favorite Baker items to her, like the dinky right field fence and the little hump in center field that went over the train tunnel. I bought her a sausage roll and lemonade, and promised her a dessert at Bassett's after the game.

The Phillies jogged on the field in their creamy white uniforms and red caps, the Brooklyn players in their drabbier grey colors, which delighted Rachel to no end because she had gotten tired of seeing her Robins in the same outfits every day, and she leaned over between sausage bites and gave me a wet cheek-kiss right before the first pitch with a "good luck" smile. Life was wonderful, even in seventh place.

And then Johnny Couch threw the ball, Bernie Neis singled, and we were off. One out later, Wheat singled, Fournier got hit by a pitch, shooting Rachel out of her seat with a "You can't do that!" with everyone laughing around us. Brown singled in two runs and it was 3-0 Brooklyn. A Holke triple and Harper single cut it to 3-1, easing my stomach a bit, but Couch was even worse in the 2nd inning, giving up two sharp singles, a loud double, and sacrifice fly for two more runs. Rachel could tell I was annoyed and held my hand with both of hers. It was warm out again but she didn't sweat like a normal person and her palm was actually dry and soft.

And then the Phillies went cuckoo on the old spitballer Grimes. Mokan singled, Hod Ford tripled. After two whiffs Holke singled, Harper tripled and Cy singled and we had tied the game 5-5! I hooted and jumped up and Rachel let go of my hand. "We got a war now!" I shouted to her trying to be funny but she hardly laughed. A Ford error helped give the Robins a 6-5 lead in the 3rd, but Holke got ahold of one in the 4th and belted a 2-run homer and we were up 7-6! But not long because Grimes singled and Neis homered with two gone in the 5th! When Holke drove in his fourth run with a scoring fly in the 6th it was 8-8 and the place was insane.

Rachel and me had pretty much stopped talking, as we took turns jumping out of our seats like yo-yos. Sometimes men play baseball and other times baseball plays the men, and this was one of those times. The game stayed tied until the 8th, when Rachel's heartthrob Fournier walloped his major league-leading 18th homer and she cheered so hard I almost went deaf. Then Brown doubled, scored when Wrightstone butchered a Zack Taylor single, and Steineder came in to put Couch to bed. And that stopped nothing. A single, three walks and two wild pitches with the same hitter up later, Brooklyn had a 12-8 lead and pretty much the game, right?

Nope. Ford tripled and Steineder singled in our 8th to make it 12-9 and bring in their best relief man Rube Ehrhardt. Brooklyn got another run in the 9th, but then we went even more cuckoo. Cy singled to begin our final ups, and so did Wrightstone. Neis flubbed an easy fly in right for a two-base error and it was 13-10. Rachel hid behind her sun umbrella. Two ground outs followed, but one scored our 11th run. Joe Schultz hit for Steineder, our only home run threat on the bench. Ehrhardt reared and threw, Rachel peeking out, and Schultz creamed the ball on a line toward Benny in the left field bleachers. Mokan ran back but the ball bounced off the wall in front of him for a double and it was 13-12! Rachel couldn't take any more, said she had to find a lavatory and left the grandstand, missing Heinie Sand's weak fly to right for the final out.

I sat waiting for her in my seat after half the place had left, and when she finally came back she was dabbing her face and neck with a wet handkerchief and was all smiles again, as if nothing had happened. But I was in a sour mood now after being thrilled and tortured for nine innings and still coming up short again. I told her the Phillies home record was a horrible 9-24 so she really had no business being worried, and if she was lucky maybe Brooklyn would just win 12-0 tomorrow and we wouldn't have to go through with this again.

She got as cool with me as I was with her, and we never went for ice cream, and during Mama's spaghetti feast that night I just sat and let Rachel Maria tie herself in knots with her fake Italian answers to Mama's questions. I knew I was being a dope, a jerk, and a bad host but come on, that game was just a brutal one and I need a full day to get over the brutal ones. Believe me, if the Robins had lost she would've left town on the first train.

We played some cards with Mama after dinner and Rachel let me win

but I was still pretty much a wet blanket. I did give her my room and take
the lumpy couch, though, hoping I could get all of my suffering out in one
night, so I suppose I'll be ready to have fun again by morning.

BRK 321 020 041 - 13 19 2
PHL 140 201 013 - 12 17 3

A REAL ENDURANCE TEST
June 27, 1924

Rachel was just a chipper little june bug in the morning, sitting with
Mama and talking about shoes. I never quite got what girls find so interesting about feetwear, but get them started and you might as well go out
for a walk yourself. Today I still needed one after losing yesterday's slugging party, but I had told myself lying on the downstairs couch that it was
just over a dumb game, and that getting on good with Rachel was much
more important.

So after breakfast I took her for a stroll along the Schuylkill River,
where the trees were nice and shady. We sat for a while and watched some
tugboat captains and Schuylkill Navy rowers sweat their way by us, and it
was a nice way to mend things up before heading back to the ball park. I
apologized for being such a bad sport yesterday and she said it was no big
deal, and agreed with me that we should just enjoy the game together and
not let the fact we're going for different teams bother us. What we actually did was hold hands and make a pact to make it through nine innings
without once letting one thing on the field get us upset. We both knew that
would be tough, but if we were going to stay close friends and especially
any kind of romantic ones we had to learn how to do that every day.

Dutch Ruether was facing Bill Hubbell, two pitchers who can either be
hot or cold, and Hubbell was the first cold one. Three singles, a walk and
hit batter put Brooklyn up 2-0 in the 2nd, and I patted Rachel on the shoulder and said "Good for you!" when she managed to not jump out of her seat
with a cheer.

Joe Schultz knocked in a Philly run with a single in the 5th, and in the
last of the 7th, with two of our guys aboard, Sand grounded one out to
Mitchell at short, but Johnny first kicked the ball, then whipped it over
Fournier's head and into the seats for a tie game! Rachel's face turned red
and crinkled up like a rotting tomato but she kept a frozen smile and pretended everything was just fine.

But then the game entered some kind of zone that was almost like twi-
light. Ruether kept putting us on the bases but we kept hitting into double
plays, while Hubbell turned into Houdini himself. Fournier and Wheat
were getting aboard almost every time but the last five spots in the Robins' lineup couldn't buy a hit for a thousand dollars. The game went into
the 10th, then the 11th, then the 12th, Rachel buying one lemonade after
another from the vendor to keep from fainting, while I just kept nervous-
munching on pretzels.

"Amazing game, isn't it?" I asked her when we went into the 13th. "Yeah, sure is," she said, afraid to look at me too. Wilson doubled in the 13th for us after Williams singled, but Cy got gunned out at home plate and we didn't score. Two Robins got on with singles in the top of the 14th but Fletcher walked Wheat on purpose and Griffith grounded out. Woehr pinch-ran for Parkinson at second in our 14th, but got thrown out at home two outs later. It was clear that me and Rachel were either going to not see each other again after this game or be together forever.

Steineder finally took over for Hubbell in the 15th inning and got Brooklyn 1-2-3. Then Holke walked to lead off our half. Wilson singled him to third with one out and up stepped Mokan. I peeked at Rachel and saw she had her eyes shut, the sick smile still stuck on her face. Mokan lined a single over a jumping Mitchell, Baker Bowl went loony, I yelped out a small huzza and threw my arms around Rachel. "I'm so sorry, beautiful", I said, words I didn't even know could come out of me. She turned with her eyes all wet, gave me a real three-second kiss and whispered, "Thanks Vinny..."

We held hands all the way to Reading Terminal for that ice cream we ditched yesterday, and we glanced at each other all through another Mama spaghetti dinner, and afterward I ripped some boards off an upstairs door so we could get up to my roof and sit on a wall to look at the city lights and a bunch of bright stars off to the west. We'd made it through another punishing game, and tomorrow there would be two, but for now there was just us, and sweet dreams all ready to go.

BRK 020 000 000 000 000 - 2 13 3
PHL 000 010 100 000 001 - 3 16 0

WHAT THE HECK JUST HAPPENED??
June 28, 1924

What a wonderful world, I thought, as I squeezed my fresh orange into a glass this morning. Rachel blew me kisses at the table every time Mama turned her back, and made sure to knock her knee against mine the rest of the time.

Our mission today was a Saturday double-header in 85-degree heat, but Rachel could only go for the first game because she had a 4:30 train to catch back to New York. I asked why she couldn't just board a later one, and then realized it was because she already had a coach ticket, instead of riding in the luggage car like I always did.

The ball park was packed to the gills, and luckily Benny met us out front with grandstand tickets he'd bought early in the morning. He said he had a mystery lady friend meeting him there, and wanted to make sure she had shade. Benny noticed me and Rachel were holding hands, completely unembarrassed, and poked me for fun in the ribs four times in the next hour.

Anyway, the love pact I made with Rachel yesterday lasted less than one inning. That's because Hal Carlson gave up two quick singles, a Fournier double, Brown single, and 3-run Zack Taylor homer for five Brooklyn runs. How could I be happy about this, no matter how stuck I was on Rachel? She was very nice about it and was afraid to cheer at all, but then I got her right back. Tiny Osborne walked Sand, Harper and Holke to begin the Phillies 1st, Cy and Wrightstone creamed back-to-back triples, and we had four runs before one out was made. All we could do was laugh.

But the chuckles stopped in the top of the 2nd, when after a single and walk, Carlson gave up two doubles and four straight singles and the score was 11-4 Robins. Rachel threw up her hands over and over the deeper I sunk in my seat, but guess what? It was one of those loony days.

Three singles, two walks and another Wrightstone triple made it 11-8—after two innings. "Can you believe this daffiness?" I yelled, and Rachel just shook her head. After a Neis triple and Brown double in the 3rd it was 12-8, and then things calmed down for a while. Benny was all hoarse from screaming, but found his voice again when a young red-haired girl in glasses arrived and gave him a big squeeze. It was Mopsy, the jabbering little tomato I met on Ladies Day whose number I gave him later out of pity. "I didn't miss anything, I hope!" she said, and the laughing began again.

So did the scoring, but this time all for the home side. Holke began the last of the 6th with a single. Williams singled. Wrightstone singled. Wilson walked. Mokan doubled in two and the score was suddenly 12-11. Dutch Henry came on, not to be confused with the crummy Dutch Ruether who pitched for them yesterday. And we made a Dutch pie out of this guy. Ford, Carlson and Sand all singled, making that eight in a row reaching base to start the inning. After Harper hit a long sacrifice fly we had seven runs on the board, a 15-12 lead, and Rachel was standing up to leave. "I'd rather read a book at the train station then watch any more of this nonsense!" she said. Don't go, I told her, "Carlson is rotten today and you're gonna come right back. Your team needs you."

After Benny and Mopsy made her feel even more guilty, she gave in, just in time to see three Brooklyn singles and a double tie the score 15-15 in the top of the 8th! Harper doubled in our 16th run after that, and Benny did a little jig in the aisle to keep Rachel entertained and not crazy.

Huck Betts was in for the top of the 9th, and Zack Wheat opened with a single. Fournier bounced a ball in front of the plate but Wilson kicked it for an error. Brown then hit into a fast double play, Rachel groaned in agony and I had to throw my arm around her waist to keep her in the seat. "Look, Rachel, you got a man on third." She said she couldn't look, so I did it for her. Zack Taylor whacked the ball hard to right. She looked up, saw the ball sail out to George Harper, who parked himself underneath it, lost the thing for a second and had it bounce off the top of his mitt for a 2-base error and tie game! Rachel screamed with delight and hugged me, but I was too shocked to feel anything. Benny turned, walked away from us and down toward a restroom, probably to upvomit.

Johnston singled to begin the Brooklyn 10th, but Betts got the next three men. Mokan started our inning with a walk, and with one out, Betts bunt-ed him along to second. Up came Heinie Sand, without one game-winning hit the entire season, but Art Decatur threw him a curve that didn't curve enough and Sand shot it right into the left-field corner for the Phillie win!! I jumped out of my seat, whooping and yelling because it's my instinct but forgot all about Rachel. She was slumped in her chair, hat yanked off and sobbing into her hands.

"You don't care about me at all," she cried, "Your team stinks and your heart's even worse!" She stuffed her hat back on, got up and excused her-self past us. I looked at Benny in surprise, then ran after her. Turned her around when she was halfway down the grandstand tunnel, grabbed her hand and dropped on one knee. My feelings from the last two months had gotten to the edge of the cliff and the words just fell right off.

"Rachel? Would you...wanna marry me?"

Her mouth opened wide and stayed that way for what seemed forever, even after her tears froze on her face and fans walked by us on both sides to stock up on food and drink for the second game. Finally she pulled me out of the way of everyone, took my hands and put them around her thin waist and whispered "If you can really stand being with a Brooklyn fan... sure!" I couldn't even talk for a second, then blurted out "How soon?" and she shrugged her cute shoulders and said "I don't know. First you have to ask my father, don't you?" I said I had forgot about that and she took my hand and said "Don't worry, my love," so I held my cap up for a little bit of privacy and kissed her for a good thirty seconds. It was heaven in a ball park, which is kind of a redundancy thing, but it sure made the sight of her disappearing down the tunnel easier to take.

I was in a romantic fog for most of the second game, and after the Phils took a 2-1 in the 4th with the awful Glazner on our hill I hardly noticed. I didn't tell Benny I had proposed yet because I just wanted to swim in the idea by myself for a while. Heck, the Phils even had a chance of beating the Robins twice in one day! How much more good luck could I have?

As it turned out, not much at all. Glazner gave up the lead in the 6th with a single, walk and double, and after a 2-run single off Steineder by Taylor put Brooklyn up 4-2, I was annoyed all over again. Ivy Olson lined a foul ball back off the grandstand roof, and it bounced straight down into our aisle. I snatched the thing, stuck it in my pocket and said to Benny, "I'm saving this one for Rachel."

But as I think I've mentioned, foul balls are supposed to be thrown back on the field to save the home clubs money. I was feeling like a pretty big cheese today, though, and when a cop came up the aisle and asked for the ball I just stood there and shook my head. "Vinny? You better fork it over," said Benny, but I said nope, not today. The cop tried to reach in my pocket and I pushed him away and said "Get lost!" He whistled for two of his cop buddies, and before you knew it I was getting dragged right down the aisle and down the exit tunnel with the crowd cheering me the whole time.

"My girlfriend said she'd marry me!" I kept yelling, "and she's getting this ball!" They just laughed and said the hell she is and next thing I know

I'm carted out to a paddy wagon, thrown inside and driven right to the local police station for making a public disturbance.

So I had to scribble out this report on a piece of paper the jail guy gave me through the bars. They're just a couple old drunks in here with me, thank God, but who knows who else will show up before morning? Mama was here an hour ago but didn't have enough bail money and went off to find more from her cousins. At least she managed to bring me the other ball scores from Mort's.

And I didn't tell her about Rachel either. But the good thing was that there was a dirty foul ball still in my pocket.

BRK 561 000 031 0 - 16 24 0
PHL 440 007 010 1 - 17 17 2

BRK 100 003 001 - 5 10 0
PHL 001 100 000 - 2 8 1

THE WORST OF TIMES AND BEST OF TIMES
June 29, 1924

Well, Mama wasn't at the jail cell this morning with my bail dough, but there were a few more drunks to keep me company. One of them had relieved himself in his pants and the place stunk something awful, and when a guard opened the door and waved me out I just about ran.

I figured Mama had paid the bail, but I was wrong because she wasn't even there. They walked me down a bunch of halls and into a small court room, where I got sat with about six other kids between 10 and 18 who looked more dirty, sleepless and sad than I did. I felt like Oliver Copperfield or one of those other Charles Dickens characters, getting ready to be sent to some big depressing workhouse.

One kid was sent to a juvenile home for robbing people on a streetcar, the next went back to jail because he stole a car and was actually 20 years old. Then I was called up and had to stand in front of this creepy-faced judge. The charges were resisting arrest and public disorderliness, and when they asked the room who paid the bail money and agreed to take custody of me, a tall man with glasses who I hadn't noticed stood up in the back row.

It was Mr. Tuggerheinz, principal of my school and my secret guardian after I caught him and his mistress at a ball game back in May. Well, wasn't that a humdinger? He was actually at the game yesterday, saw me get arrested, and had already spoken to Mama about some kind of "proposition."

He walked me out of the police station and onto a streetcar but wouldn't tell me where we were going. "I trust you'll be satisfied," he kept saying with this goofy smile, and before long I could see we were heading back to Baker Bowl. The Phillies had gone up to Brooklyn to play the Sunday game, and it was strange seeing the streets around the park so empty. We got to the door of the Phillies' offices and I stopped in my tracks. "What the heck is this about?" I asked.

And then Tuggerheinz told me. One of his oldest friends was Thomas Crane, a very successful Philadelphia businessman who was also an old friend of Phillies owner William Baker. Anyway, it seems that the club had gotten some bad notices in the newspaper today for arresting a minor over a lousy ball, and when Tuggerheinz had talked to Crane about it, some kind of meeting was set up. The one I was walking into right then.

Crane was in the room, and so was Baker, a tough-looking former New York policeman. "Our security fellas might have been a little rough with you yesterday," he said, then walked over and held out his hand. "Still got that ball, Vinny?" I was in love with Rachel but figured it wasn't worth going through that jail business again, so I fished the thing out of my pants pocket and put it in his hand. Baker grinned and mussed my hair. "We've had this old clubhouse man named Grover who's about to retire, and thought with our next big road trip starting today it might be a good time to take on some younger blood." He looked at Crane, then at Tuggerheinz, whose little smile was suddenly big. And then he crouched in front of me.

"How'd you like to be the Phillies' bat boy?"

I almost fainted right in my chair. "Bat boy?" He said the Phillies had never had one because Grover was doing a good enough job and there was no need "spending the extra cash," but this was going to be a real long trip with the team not coming back until July 24th, and in the hot western towns he just thought having a kid instead of an old man was a safer idea. "If you do a good job, maybe you can stick," he said, and I was out of my chair and shaking his hand, followed by Crane's hand and Tuggerheinz's hand and if a secretary walked in right then I probably would've kissed her.

ME! The Phillie bat boy!!

I went straight home and hugged Mama, who already knew about it and was thrilled for me. Then I figured why the heck not? and told her I was getting married to Maria Stonetino whose real name was Rachel Stone and she was Jewish, not Italian. Mama was shocked for a second, then said "So? Isn't that the same thing?" and we hugged all over again. I had to be up at Braves Field in Boston for a double-header tomorrow, so there wasn't much time to pack suitcases for my clothes and typewriter and eat something.

On the way to the train station I stopped at Mort's to catch the Phillies' ticker score up in Brooklyn and give Benny the big news. Mopsy was sitting on his lap and Benny was real excited because Jimmy Ring, of all people, had a 5-1 lead on Dazzy Vance in the 5th inning. He was blown over by both the Rachel and bat boy news, and didn't know whether to cry or be envious. More than anything, he said, he was going to miss me and I promised I'd write him once a week.

The Robins scored four runs to tie the game right as I was sitting there, but then Cy Williams clubbed his second homer of the game two innings later, Ring with his 1-10 record beat Vance with his 10-3 record, we celebrated the Phillies and toasted the events with double cherry fizzers, and I was off to the 30th Street Station to begin both of my new lives.

PHL 400 010 010 - 6 9 0
BRK 001 040 000 - 5 9 2

THE BOYS OF LUMBER
June 30, 1924

The first part of heaven turned out to be the train ride up to Boston. It was the first time I got to ride in a fancy coach car with business men and normal people, and it felt great to actually stretch my legs instead of having to fold them up inside a luggage crate or something.

I sat next to a mother and her little boy, who wore a sailor suit and nibbled a giant lollipop for at least two hours. When the mom asked me why I was traveling alone I told her about the Phillie batboy job and her kid's eyes just about popped out. It was still hard for me to believe I was actually going to do this for money, even though it wasn't too much, but seeing the way the kid reacted made me feel even more special about it.

I dozed off for a while, and when I woke up it was almost dark and the mother and kid had already gotten off in New York. I could see pieces of Long Island Sound go by off to the right as we went up through Connecticut, and then darkness rolled over and the coach car's lamps came on. I figured I should probably get as much sleep as possible, but it was tough because the train kept stopping with its loud screeches, first in New Haven, then in Hartford and Springfield before turning east. I was also too excited to even think about sleep.

A geezer with baggy eyes and suspenders met me in Boston when I got off the train after midnight. It was Grover, the Phillies' clubhouse man who was retiring, and this guy didn't stop blabbing at me on our entire walk over to the team's hotel. He ran through about ten different things I was supposed to do every day in the clubhouse, but after the floor-sweeping and shoe-shining I started not listening. He said no big deal because I could learn on the job the way he did twenty years ago.

The hotel was on a street called Tremont, and even though my room was about as big as a stowaway's closet on an ocean liner, I didn't care. The Phillies were sleeping or playing cards in rooms nearby, and I faded off hearing a few of them curse.

Braves Field had a pretty good crowd in the streets by the time I got there around eleven this morning. It was a double-header, which always draws more, and the Boston fans knew their team had a fighting chance against the likes of us. Grover let me into the visitor clubhouse when I knocked, and I met manager Art Fletcher right away. He was a former player but didn't seem braggy like a lot of them, and I couldn't bring myself to tell him how many times I'd yelled at him from the stands. He walked me past the lockers, where a few of the players were getting dressed, and

I recognized Mokan and Wrightstone, who were busy sharing a joke and didn't even turn to say hello. My hero Cy Williams was over in a corner, rubbing ointment on a leg bruise, and I nervously went up and introduced myself. "Well hi there," he said, and felt both of my hands with his beefy ones. "Okay, kid. They're warm. Don't want no cold hands touching my lumber all day."

Grover showed me how to polish each player's glove with neat's-foot oil and hang each uniform in the right locker, and then it was bat duty in the dugout. Most of the players had their initials painted or carved into the wood, and I had to stick them in the bat rack in order of where they were hitting in the lineup for the first game. It was taking me forever, and I kept looking over into the Braves dugout, where THEIR batboy was doing the same thing a mile a minute.

By the time I finally got all the bats in the right slots, the players came out and started grabbing them anyway to practice their hitting. George Harper asked if I was there to bring the team some luck, and then Heinie Sand asked pretty much the same thing, and all I could do was nod because the last thing I wanted was to get tossed out of the dugout.

Then the game started, and tossing sure seemed possible. Oeschger was terrible for us and the Braves had a 4-0 lead after four innings. We finally scored a first run off Benton in the 5th, but I missed how we did it because I was too busy moving the bats around. One of the things I never realized about batboys is that it's always more fun when the other team is up.

Harper broke his bat in the 7th with Ford out at second, and he waved at me to fetch him another. For some dumb reason I couldn't find the right lumber, brought him one of Wilson's bats instead and he just about tore my head off. Fletcher finally fished out the right one for me and I got it out to Harper. He stepped in, Benton threw, and George whacked the next pitch high and far into the right field "jury box". George gave me a big wink when he ran by me, Fletcher said he owed me a cigar, and I never felt so good.

Unfortunately, Skinny Graham put us away the last two innings and we lost by one run. Between the games I dug dirt out of everyone's cleats, swept the whole locker room floor, and got back out to set up the bats in the nick of time. Hucks Betts threw for us against Al Yeargin, and we were behind again by the 5th, 2-1. "Lose one of MY bats this time," yelled Walter Holke at me, while Harper just stared.

Fletcher talked me into faking that I couldn't find Harper's bat when he came up in the 7th with Sand on first, but I was a bad actor, and Harper came over to rip his bat away from me. And then he did it again, ripped a Yeargin ball way over the right fence, and we had a 3-2 lead! We scored another in the 8th, Betts and Glazner held down the Braves, and I had two cigars coming to me.

The players went to the fancy hotel restaurant for dinner, while me and Grover ended up at a hamburger joint down the block, but I didn't care. I needed to relax after that opening ordeal, and the taste of cheese-covered

greasy meat took me back to Philadelphia for a half hour or so, and that did
the trick.

PHL 000 010 200 - 3 8 2
BOS 001 300 00x - 4 9 1

PHL 000 010 210 - 4 11 1
BOS 000 020 000 - 2 7 1

PART FOUR
July

THE HAVANA GRIT FACTION AND OTHER PHILLIE SECRETS
July 1, 1924

The Phillie players were making a ruckus most of last night at the hotel, but it was easy for me to nod off after all the bat and club house work I was doing. Any kid who tells you being a batboy is the most fun job in the world doesn't know what he's talking about.

There's only one game today and tomorrow so I should get through those no sweat, and then we have a day off to take the train down to New York and play the Giants starting with a big July 4th double-header. Before heading over to the field today I sent Rachel a telegram and told her to meet me behind the Phillies' dugout at the Polo Grounds and didn't say a word about my new job. She'll probably be over the moon about it.

Johnny Couch was facing Jesse Barnes today, and because I was able to finish my bat setups earlier this time, I had a chance to learn a few things about what players do before a game. Namely, they play cards, cuss at each other a lot and look at girlie magazines. Heinie Sand, who it turns out is a nice guy from San Francisco and is just a little taller than me, told me that most every club in baseball keeps a stack of swimsuit magazines and cheap detective tales around, thinking the players will get satisfied with them and not want to go out carousing for girls after the games. As I watched Hod Ford poke through a copy of *Detective Classics* with an almost-naked girl on the front, it seemed to me it just made the players want to hit the town even more.

The other thing that happens is nobody talks to the starting pitcher. Unless you're the manager or coach, you have to treat him like he isn't even there. I made the mistake of looking at Couch's face today when I handed him his polished shoes and I thought he was going to murder me.

The good thing is that my look didn't wreck his performance today one bit. For the first five innings all he did was give the Braves two singles. The problem was that Barnes was throwing just as good, even though he'd lost ten straight times after winning his first three of the year.

Sand, Harper and Holke then singled in a row in the top of the 6th to put us ahead 1-0. I was running bats around with Cy up at the plate and I missed the pitch he whiffed on. Wrightstone popped out to end the inning, but in the last of the 7th Couch got tired real fast. Bill Cunningham tripled to their canyon of a center field, Frank Gibson doubled and after a Wilson single, Cotton Tierney hit a sacrifice pop fly that put them ahead.

The dugout mood got dark and crabby then. Cusses were aimed at the ground or sky instead of at other players. Harper came up to me in the 8th and said "Rub my bat, kid." I said "Aren't I supposed to lose it again?" and he said "Rub it and if I get another hit you're in the HGF." I asked him what that was, but he didn't answer. Sand singled again to start the inning and Harper went to the plate. Where he singled! Holke followed with a loud double and we were tied up 2-2! Sand came in the dugout after scoring so I asked him what the HGF was but he went right past me like I suddenly had a disease.

Couch pitched a scoreless 8th, but Cunningham started the Boston 9th with his second straight triple off him. The small crowd was going crazy. Fletcher waved the infield in close but it didn't matter. Gibson skied a ball out to Cy, but his throw was late and weak and the winning Braves run scored.

I was afraid to look at anyone in the club house after. Harper talked a bluer streak than I ever thought was possible and threw his roast beef sandwich across the room. "We should NEVER lose to these rubes!" he screamed. I went back to that hamburger joint by myself because Grover had gone back to Philadelphia to retire, but when I opened my hotel room door later there was a note on the floor:

HGF. 10 p.m. RM 609.

Naturally I was up there five minutes early and knocked. There was some low whispering inside, and then Russ Wrightstone opened the door. The room had so much cigar smoke I could barely see who else was there, but it was Harper, Holke and a weasel-looking bench guy who almost never plays named Andy Woehr. They all had big Cuban cigars, glasses of light brown stuff that looked like whiskey, and two young girls dressed in underthings were sitting on the bed painting each other's nails.

"Welcome to the Havana Grit Faction," said Wrightstone, and yanked me inside. It was him and Harper's secret society that Fletcher didn't even know about, and to get into it you needed a special invitation. Harper said I belonged because I'd brought him nothing but good lumber luck on my first two days on the job. So in the next hour I smoked my first cigar (which I'm still coughing over as I write this), drank my first Canadian whiskey from Wrightstone's private jug, and learned that Holke liked to be called "incredible" whenever he got a big hit. I thought that was kind of dumb, calling a guy The Incredible Holke when he was only hitting around .300, but if I was going to stay in this faction I had to play along.

I also learned how to paint a girl's toenail, but I'll keep that one under my hat and use it on Rachel.

PHL 000 010 200 - 3 8 2
BOS 001 300 00x - 4 9 1

DOUBLE-DUTY SPANELLI HAS A NICE RING TO IT
July 2, 1924

I woke up today with that Canadian giggle-water still doing the Charleston in my head, and there was a copy of *Weird Tales: The Unique Magazine* next to my pillow, folded open to a story written by Harry Houdini himself. It was nice of Heinie Sand to slip me the magazine, but all it did was give me strange dreams about spirit mediums.

I also dreamed these big, shadowy guys were in my room performing some secret ceremony on me, which I guess explains the letters HGF that I saw inked on my ankle when I was washing up. Those crumbs! I threw on my oversized Phillie top which wasn't getting washed until after today's last game here in Boston and was really beginning to stink, nabbed some biscuits from downstairs and high-tailed it out to Braves Field.

Harper and Wrightstone and Holke and Woehr were all snickering at me when I came in the locker room but I didn't say a word because I was still pretty honored to be included with these lunatics and needed to get through the summer with them. But then Art Fletcher called me over and said the Braves batboy was sick, and I had to work for both teams in the same game! Were they kidding me?

Nope, they weren't. The breeze that comes off the Charles River a lot took the day off, and it was over 90 degrees even in the shade. Dave Bancroft, the player-manager of the Braves, seemed like a good egg but he was out of his lineup with a bad shoulder so wasn't in the best mood and stood right next to me when I was setting up all the Boston bats, like it was going to be my fault if they lost the game or something.

From what I could see of the game, it was another close battle. Incredible Holke doubled in a run for us in the 1st, and Bill Hubbell tripled in Sand in the 2nd, but four Brave singles in their 2nd tied it up in no time. I was running back and forth between the dugouts like a nut, at the same time fetching balls to the umpire at home plate, and my wool top was so drenched with sweat it felt like it was pushing me into the ground.

Rube Marquard was throwing for Boston, a guy who used to be pretty tough for the Giants, and he still pitched good games once in a while but we had his number today. Mokan doubled, Ford tripled and Hubbell got another hit to put us ahead 4-2 in the 4th, and then Hubbell began getting out of pickles like he usually does. I tried to spend less and less time in the Braves dugout because it was getting deadlier in there and not one player or coach had a friendly look for me. Finally, after Mokan whacked a homer in the 8th and Harper pinch-hit a single after he had me rub my hands on his bat handle, we had three more runs and the easy win—our 30th one!

Leaving a town after a victory has to be the only way to travel in baseball, as I'm sure I'll experience after the opposite happens, but tonight everyone was in a great mood at the hotel. The Havana Grit Faction was out carousing somewhere, but Sand and Ford and Frank Parkinson invited me into a room to throw some dice, and they told me some great stories about playing ball, and how'd they'd do it for free if they could. I said the game looked kind of easy from up in the stands and Heinie said oh no it ain't, and promised to get me in the batting cage one of these days to prove it.

That's sure something else to look forward to, along with my first train trip with a big league team tomorrow morning—straight down to big old New York.

PHL 110 200 030 - 7 13 1
BOS 020 000 000 - 2 13 0

SPEAK EASY AND CARRY A USEFUL BAT
July 3, 1924

The ride down to New York lasted most of the day but didn't include anything overnight, meaning I'll have to wait for the trip out to Cincinnati to see where I'll be sleeping. The players were mostly in their own special car, playing cards or reading magazines or smoking, though Heinie Sand and Hod Ford strayed out to the dining car for lunch and invited me along.

What a fancy spread and what service! Colored waiters were all over the place and they served the best grub I've had in a long time, even from Mama. Heinie recommended a roast beef and melted cheese sandwich so I took him up on it and the meat was so delicious and fresh I thought I heard it moo when I chewed it. Ford was big on seafood and ordered fresh clams and oysters that were still in shells, and we all had vegetables even though I just picked at mine, and something called birch beer that tasted more like strong root beer and went down like frosty butter. I'll tell ya, hanging around with wealthy ballplayers is sure a nice way to live!

We stopped in the players' lounge to watch a huge game of Mississippi 7-Card Stud that seemed to involve every other player and even Art Fletcher. There was lots of shouting and cussing and five-dollar bills being smacked around, and I asked Heinie if the players went easy on their manager in these games. "Only if we lost that day," he said, which I figured was most of the time. Harper came out of the bathroom to rejoin the game, nudged me aside and invited me to join the HGFs for a little tour of New York night spots after we checked in at the hotel. I said thanks but I probably wasn't old enough and he said "If you walk in with us you can be in diapers."

Our hotel was on a nice street in midtown Manhattan called Fifth Avenue, but by the time I got pulled into a taxicab with Harper and Holke and Wrightstone and Woehr it was dark, and we were heading west, then east, then north so fast I had no idea where we were most of the night.

And there was another reason for that, because every place we stopped was a speakeasy, and I got introduced to many kinds of whiskey, a few kinds of vodka and quite a bit of beer. Much of the stuff was shipped to the city from boats off the coast of Long Island, rumrunning as it was called, and as Holke explained, every ballplayer worth his salt knew where to find the stuff after games. As I sat and stumbled around with them, it struck me that if they ever invent a way to play ball games at night, it would probably help keep the players from becoming drunks.

On one place we walked over to a big guy sitting alone at a table with a girl passed out on his arm and it turned out to be George Kelly of the Giants! Their talented first baseman was having a real bad year for himself with the bat, and he was all out of sorts with Brooklyn having just crunched their behinds three straight at the Polo Grounds, and when he saw the Phillie players he got all chummy and started ribbing us, saying we were going to pay tomorrow for what the Robins just did, and Harper bet him fifty bucks right there on the spot that they'd be lucky to win one of the double-header games. Kelly then saw me, grabbed my arm and yanked me close to his drunky mouth. "Whaddya think, junior? Giants got a chance tomorrow?" I said sure, why not? and he winked at me. Wrightstone pulled me away, said "Don't be fraternizing with enemies," and that was that.

Anyway, I think I remember us eating steaks and bread somewhere, which is probably why I didn't upvomit until I got back to my room later, and I also think I was dancing with a girl to a jazz band at one point but it wasn't Rachel because too much of her legs were showing and she smelled like an open gin bottle. We were in a club called Connie's Inn up in Harlem, and I knew that because I'd stayed up in that area with Benny one time early in the season and I remember all the coloreds in the streets. They didn't allow coloreds in the Cotton Club or this place unless they were playing the music, which I think is stupid and unfair but who the heck am I to change things? I'll tell you who I am, damnit, I'm Vinny Spanelli, star batboy for the Philadelphia Phils, and I'm gonna dance with flazzies and drink speakeasy juice and fraterize with whoever the hell I want and no one's telling me different, so g'night...

GODAWFUL IN GOTHAM ON AMERICA'S DAY
July 4, 1924

Heinie Sand knocked on my door at ten this morning while I was still drooling on my pillow. When I told him I was skipping breakfast because my stomach felt like there was a thunderstorm inside it, he understood who I was out with last night and reminded me to be at the Polo Grounds in an hour because the double-header was starting at noon and McGraw would be watching me. "John McGraw? What does he care about me?" Heinie said the famed Giants manager was as hard on visiting batboys as he was on players, so don't mess up.

That didn't sound good, but then I remembered I'd asked Rachel to go to the park so I could surprise her, and that got me going. I took a quick cold bath to wake myself up, grabbed some muffins downstairs in the cafe and wolfed them as I ran down the street to the elevated train station. The train ride up to 155th Street only took about fifteen minutes, and I could see the bright green field of the Polo Grounds get closer, including the high bluff behind it, already covered with fans ready for free ball-watching and their holiday picnics. I was here earlier in the season but the crowds were nothing like this. The el train was so crowded I had to stand the whole way, and my Phillie jersey got a few funny looks from Giants fans.

The players were all excited to take on a New York team that was seven games above .500 but after three pennants in a row was expected to be much better, certainly as good as the Pirates. Jimmy Ring was pitching for us in the first game, after finally getting his second win the last time out. Virgil Barnes was up against him, and Cy Williams especially was talking while he got dressed about how many homers he'd hit off "that mucker" down the short right field line.

I hurried up the tunnel and popped my head carefully out of the Phillies dugout, looked around for Rachel and spotted her, cute as a button in a light blue blouse and long white skirt. She wasn't facing the field at all, just checking the grandstand for a sign of me. "Hello there, beautiful!" I yelled. She turned, saw me and just about fainted. I told her the whole story about getting arrested, and how I got the batboy job, and even though she was happy for me she was also pretty sad I'd be traveling around the country again for almost a month. I promised I'd come talk to her father about us getting married as soon as I could, and that seemed to calm her some. She said she was there with a girlfriend, and gave me a little smooch before going up to sit with her. Hod Ford saw the kiss and made a weird honking sound at me from the field for the next ten minutes.

Anyway, Heinie was sure right about John McGraw. As soon as I finished setting up our bats in the dugout, I turned and there he was on the field behind me, hands on his hips, snarling at me with that little fighter's face of his. "Grab those damn bats right after they're dropped," he said, "I don't want my fielders tripping over them and snapping ankles." I said "Yes, Mr. McGraw!" He walked off without a word, and I almost wished I'd told him something nastier but what the heck. I'm liking my job.

After a scoreless 1st inning, Frisch booted one at second, Mokan doubled him home and our dugout was jumping like a tub of crickets. Then Ring went to work...and got himself fired. George Kelly, looking pretty awake seeing how drunk he was last night, singled to start their 2nd. Jackson, Groh, and Snyder did too, and we were down 3-1. A Hack Wilson homer in the 3rd and it was 4-1. Then a Ring wild pitch with Youngs at the plate and it was 5-1. Then triples from Frisch and Wilson and a Kelly double and it was 8-1.

Then the Phillie hitters started snatching their bats out of my hand, and whipping them further away after every bad swing they took. I tried to lug some new baseballs to the umpire behind home but I guess I was too slow because the snotty Giants batboy grabbed them from me and did it himself, McGraw smirking in my direction from his dugout. Then the Giants scored three more times in the 6th. Then the Giants scored three more times in the 7th and the rout was finished.

There was no sound in the club house between games. I thought at one point I heard Jimmie Wilson cough but it might've been a rat sneezing in the corner. Heinie gave me a nice pat on the back, like I actually had something to do with us being creamed and felt sorry or something.

In Game Two we had to face Wayland Dean, who hardly ever starts, and we got eight hits like we did in the first game, but this time scored one less run, meaning nothing. And how did Clarence Mitchell do for us? Well, he was losing 6-0 by the 4th, before Steineder came on and gave the Giants five more runs in the 6th. The dumb Giants fans were cheering and hooting and cussing us like they'd won the stupid pennant or something, and I guess they deserved a little fun after getting swept by Brooklyn, but we weren't in any mood to hear it.

Nope, when you get outrunned 24-1 for the day, you're in no mood to hear a bird chirp. Harper and Wrightstone threw their equipment all over the place afterwards, while Art Fletcher escaped from reporters by going into his office and locking the door. I took my time cleaning up so I could avoid most of the players, but Walter Holke was standing there in his street clothes when I finally finished sweeping. "I don't care what good luck you gave us in Boston, buddy. If we play this bad out west we might just have to throw your little scooter pie off the train." With that he walked out, and I was left in there all alone, without anyone to go get an illegal drink with.

So I went back to my hotel room, stripped down to my boxers and just laid on the bed. I ordered a hamburger from the room service, which cost a ridiculous dollar-fifty, read until I couldn't concentrate, and then just fell asleep early.

A knock on the door got me up close to midnight, and I threw some pants on and opened it. Rachel stood there. She'd snuck into the hotel past the doorman and asked a player what room I was in. She had a darker outfit on that looked just as good as the other one, and said she thought I might need some kind of hug. Boy, did I ever.

PHL 010 000 000 - 1 8 2
NYG 031 133 30x - 14 15 2

PHL 000 000 000 - 0 8 0
NYG 104 105 00x - 11 12 0

ESCAPE TO LUNA PARK
July 5, 1924

So Rachel and me snuck out of the hotel first thing in the morning. I left a note on Heinie Sand's door telling him I was sick and was checking myself into a hospital for the day but the truth was that this batboy job was getting to me already, and I needed to think about how much I wanted to be a human bowling pin every day that the Phillies lost.

Rachel kept saying as I tossed and turned all night that I should do what I liked to do for a job, and I sure don't like batboying at the moment. So we took a morning train across to Brooklyn, where I caught a few extra winks on her parlor couch. I figured it would be a good chance to talk to Mr. Stone and ask him about marrying Rachel, except I forgot it was Saturday and that he was going to Jewish church again and expected the whole family to go. Meaning it was then Rachel's turn to pretend being sick. I said I'd stay there and put wet cloths on her head and Mr. Stone and his wife seemed to buy it, so off they all went after breakfast with their little books.

And off we went on the train to Coney Island.

Rachel actually wanted to take me to Luna Park, which was a newer amusement place there that was built in 1902 and now had about 90,000 visitors a day during the summer. Sure enough, it was packed solid, and the perfect place for both of us to hide out for the day. We went on all sorts of rides, like Shoot-the-Chutes, Helter Skelter, and the Dragon's Gorge, which was a roller coaster that ended up going under a waterfall. We ate sausage rolls and popcorn and even threw each other in the ocean waves with our clothes on a few times to cool off. We took a dark boat ride through a tunnel and set our own record for kissing, and there wasn't one moment when I wondered what my Phillies were doing.

Unfortunately, Rachel started thinking about the Robins some time after lunch, and made me look for a newspaper stand where they might have an electric scoreboard. We finally did, after walking for what seemed like two miles, and the guy's board was awful dinky and kept lighting up the wrong bases, but we got all the scores there were. Up in Boston, Brooklyn's Osborne was beating Barnes of the Braves 2-1, while Snyder had two homers already at the Polo Grounds and McQuillan was taking care of the Phils easy enough 4-2.

When I saw we were behind again I began to feel bad. Who knows? Maybe I would have handed Harper his lucky bat today and he would have walloped one. We hurried back to Rachel's place, and explained to her father that she suddenly felt a lot better after they went to the Jewish church and if we sat around the hot apartment she night have gotten sick all over again. Anyway, they invited me for Sabbath dinner but it was still a bad time to start asking him marrying stuff when he was so busy doing his prayers, so I said I'd "stop by" on Sunday sometime, kissed Rachel good night and went back to my hotel.

There was a note under the door again:

Dear Vinny:
Hope you're all finished puking because we need you to set up our bats again for tomorrow's last game and send us out west with a big win. That Giants kid helped us today and he's a complete fish. —HGF

You know what? As much as I enjoyed Rachel and Luna Park, I missed those big dopes, too. Good night!

PHL 020 000 002 - 4 7 0
NYG 010 201 02x - 6 14 0

NATIONAL LEAGUE through Saturday, July 5, 1924

Pittsburgh	51	24	.680	—
Cincinnati	48	32	.600	5.5
Brooklyn	46	32	.590	6.5
New York	43	33	.566	8.5
St. Louis	38	38	.500	13.5
Chicago	34	42	.447	17.5
PHILLIES	30	49	.380	24
Boston	19	59	.244	34.5

THE IRISHMAN VS. THE ITALIAN, NINE ROUNDS
July 6, 1924

By the time I woke up this morning there was no time to go to Brooklyn, do my proposal bit again for Mr. Stone and high-tail it back to the ball park, so I packed my bag for the long road trip and picked the batboy job instead.

It was a good thing, because the Giants batboy was out sick, no doubt sneezing into his already snotty nose, and McGraw needed me to work for his team, too. If he had his way I suppose he would rather have the players take care of their own bats, because it was pretty clear before the game even started that he didn't like anyone he didn't really know touching Giants equipment.

"Did you wash those things?" was the first thing he asked me. "You mean the bats?" I asked and he grabbed both of my wrists with his little meat hooks and shook them. "No you dunce, your hands!" I said not yet and he sent me back to the visitor club house to scrub them. The Phillie players saw me at the sink, knew what I was doing and started to needle me. "Tell that buzzard there ain't enough time to wash off smallpox!" yelled Harper, who seemed to be in a real good mood, which was surprising seeing we'd just lost three straight. Sand told me that the team was always kind of lively before a big trip because lots of the players had their dames lined up for the different cities.

I sure had the Phillie bats lined up right. Holke singled off Art Nehf with two outs in the 1st and Cy Williams cranked a ball into the high deck in deep right, and we were up 2-0! Oeschger was throwing for us, and believe me, he probably never pitched this good. The first eleven Giants went down without a fight before Youngs singled with two outs in the 3rd, and with every out I was less in the mood to go near the New York dugout. McGraw just stood there with his arms folded, staring at my hands every time they touched a Giants bat. Heck, it wasn't my fault his team is eight or so games out of first and his second best hitter George Kelly is playing like gutter swill with his average down to .262.

Jimmie Wilson hit a solo homer to start the 6th, it was 3-0, and I could feel McGraw's eye-heat on my neck without even looking at him. When I ran back to the Giants dugout to fish out Travis Jackson's bat, McGraw ripped it out of my hand, inspected the handle, then my hand again, then gave it to Jackson himself. "You're doing something here, kid, and I better not find out what it is." I said how do you know and he kicked over a ball bag, wheezed in my face and pointed out to Oeschger. "That bum's given up 149 hits in 101 innings, and we can't knock a gnat off his sleeve, that's why!" I shrugged and just said, "Well, baseball can be kind of funny" and I thought he was about to knock my head off. At that moment Jackson swung and lined a homer way out to left, the crowd went crazy and McGraw got out of my face. He didn't smile, because I'm not sure he ever has, but at least I'd live for another inning.

A Mokan sacrifice fly made it 4-1 us in the 8th, and Oeschger went back to spinning his best-ever game. After Jackson's homer he didn't allow another hit, gave them only two, and we had a big win to leave town with. The Phillies club house was just a big party and I was the girl on the cake. The Incredible Holke had four straight singles and proclaimed me the best good luck charm we'd had in a while. That was exaggerating too much, but it was true that this might've been McGraw's worst day of the year, which always meant for something.

Benny sure enjoyed it. He sent me a telegram right from Mort's where he must've been following the game:

GOOD WORK BEATING UP IRISH THUG, SPANELLI. HAVE FUN TRIP. I'LL FIND YOU SOMEWHERE.

One thing was definite: There was no way I could get over to Rachel's house like I thought I might. Our moving celebration carried me right to Pennsylvania Station, where we boarded our liner for the whole night and day trip to Ohio. I got a sleeping berth right above Heinie Sand, which was great because I wanted to hear all about San Francisco from him, and if I'm lucky the singing and card games and cigar-smoking might end by midnight.

PHL 200 001 010 - 4 11 0
NYG 000 001 000 - 1 2 1

THE ONLY WAY TO TRAVEL
July 7, 1924

We boarded the express to Cincinnati last night close to eleven, and I was so excited I almost broke out in hives. Heinie Sand had been filling both of my ears about how much he loved the team's train trips, which I found surprising when you figure how many times the Phillies travel after a loss.

But when we boarded it all got clear. The team had three Pullman cars, lettered A, B, and C, with C being the one in the back that gets whipped around the curves. Of course, that's where me and Heinie's upper sleeping bunks were. Fletcher, the coaches and Cy Williams were in lower berths in the A car, but I didn't care at all because it sure beat a cabbage carton or whatever the heck I got stuck in during those early trips to New York this year. Each berth even had a little hammock thing to put your clothes or toothbrush or whatever else you want in while you sleep.

Some of the players had trouble nodding off, so they tried different ways to do this. The easiest of course was having some bootleg liquor in the club car, the one just in front of the sleeping ones. Even with booze still illegal, every baseball team train somehow got bottles of the stuff aboard, and the porters weren't shy about serving it if you tipped them enough. The other way Phillie players used was to recite the name Sherry Magee over and over. Magee was a player on the Phils and Reds about ten years ago, and if you matched the clackety-clack train wheel sound with "Sherry Magee...

Sherry Magee...Sherry Magee..." you'd fall right asleep.

I was all ready to try that, but Heinie Sand was too busy keeping me awake with his gabbing. Heinie's only in his second season, but because he's 27 he has a bunch of minor league stories to tell. The best tales, though, were about growing up in San Francisco, a city that to me just sounds wild and magical. I can't even imagine living somewhere that doesn't have snow.

After a while, Heinie even got tired of his own stories and fell asleep, and when I woke we were just about in Ohio. It was amazing to think that the last time I was headed to Cincinnati I was driving with Benny and sleeping in some farmer's field, and now here I was eating eggs and ham steak and little roasted potatoes at a back table in a ballplayers' dining car! Russ Wrightstone was at the next table with his fellow HGFers, reading anti-McGraw articles out loud from a New York newspaper. "The Giants are a disgrace to New York ballhood," wrote one wag, and Harper piped up, "If I ever find out what ballhood is, you better not mess with mine!" and everyone cackled.

There was time for some gin rummy games in the club car after that, though the Harper gang didn't let me anywhere near the table. Rookies and clubhouse help weren't really welcome with the high-rollers on the trains, so I ended up back in Car C with Heinie and a pair of dice and another hour or so of amateur baseball stories. Heinie was worried about keeping his job in the big leagues because he was told he strikes out too much, but I told him from what I've seen he also walks a lot, and getting on base sure accounts for something. I think he appreciated that.

Talk to you tomorrow from Cincy!

THE AGONY AND THE EPPA RIXEY
July 8, 1924

We rolled into Cincinnati late yesterday and split into a bunch of taxi-cabs for the drive over to the Palace Hotel on Vine Street, which was built in 1882 by someone who must've thought he was a French king. It was eight stories high and had elevators and marble grand stairs in the lobby.

It also had three hundred or so rooms, but because there was a big party of sausage-makers in town, there wasn't any space for me. Art Fletcher argued with the desk man for about ten seconds, and they ended up clearing out an extra mop closet and throwing a mattress on the floor. Harper felt bad and gave me a cigar, which I wasn't about to light up in there, while Wrightstone went down to a store and bought me a calendar with pictures of German countryside on it to hang on the closet wall. Real nice guys. The water pipes also happened to run up one of the walls, so when someone used a toilet, took a bath or washed their teeth, which was most of the night, I would hear it.

I was so tired in the morning that I had my first cup of coffee with Heinie Sand in the hotel's breakfast room. It was awful bitter and I have no idea how so many people drink the stuff every day, but it did wake me up some. By the time we got to Redland Field I was all hopped up and took care of our bats five times quicker than usual. Johnny Couch was pitching for us, which probably meant a close game, except then I looked toward the Cincinnati dugout and saw scary Eppa Rixey tossing warm-ups. The Reds have been in the pennant chase all season, and this guy has been the main reason with his 11-4 record. He's also wiped us clean at least three times, and I could see most of our players drop their heads and shoulders just by taking a look at him.

Holke tried to make us forget about him by hitting a sacrifice fly in the 1st inning, but the Reds took care of that business right away with two-out singles from Bressler and Roush and the favorite Cincy weapon, the clutch triple, by Pinelli for a 2-1 lead. Heinie got himself a run-scoring fly in the 2nd to tie us again, but then Cincy went ahead 3-2 on a double play grounder by Walker...

And we were never heard from again.

Mokan singled in the 4th, Holke led the 6th with a double and Cy bashed a long out in the 8th that would have been a homer anywhere but here, and Rixey got everyone else out. The Reds scored single runs in the 4th and 7th but didn't need them, and then something even worse happened.

One of the Over-the-Rhine boys me and Benny had run into back in May recognized me while I was lugging some bats to the Phillie dugout and ran up to the rail. "Hey!" he shouted, "Aren't you Hans Muellerschidt's friend?" Muellerschmidt was the fake name Benny had given them to keep us from getting beat up, so I said "Ja" in a fake German accent and before you knew it, six more of those little thugs were squeezing into the good seats to pick on me before a cop finally made them move.

I stuck to Sand as close as I could after the game and we went for hamburgers. He didn't like losing but felt pretty good about his sacrifice fly off Rixey. "That guy is 12-4 now. It's a good thing when your bat hits any of his balls." I said from the stands it doesn't look all that hard and he just laughed, toasted me with his root beer glass and said, "Meet me on the ball park diamond tomorrow morning."

You bet I will, reader-people!

PHI 110 000 000 - 2 6 2
CIN 210 100 10x - 5 10 1

EASY DOES IT, SORT OF
July 9, 1924

Heinie got me up early and out to Redland Field a whole hour before any other players showed up. I knew what this was about.

After yesterday's game I had to shoot my mouth off about how easy it looked to hit a baseball, and now Heinie wanted me to swallow those dumb words. He knew the Cincy equipment man from his days in San Francisco, and talked him into throwing some practice balls my way on the big diamond, something he did once in a while for the Reds.

Heinie handed me his "lightest bat", which still felt heavier than anything I'd ever swung, and I walked up to home plate in the morning shadow. Solly the equipment guy was almost 60 but had an arm like a tree-cutter's. He reached into a wicker basket with it, took out a ball, wound up and chucked it over the plate. By the time I got around to swinging, Heinie was crouched in back of me holding the ball.

"Now I'll try a fast one!" yelled Solly, and I almost fainted. I dug my shoes into the dirt but it didn't do any good because the blur-ball was past me before I even took a step. I told them I got the point and had had enough, but Heinie wouldn't hear it, and said I was standing there until I made some contact. Twelve or thirteen more pitches went past until I finally shut my eyes, swung as early as I could and felt my bat nick one.

That was amazing, I thought, as I was finally allowed to trudge back to the Phillie club house. How does any big leaguer ever hit a baseball?

It sure got me watching the hitters closer during today's game and had me respecting the heck out of them. Seeing Wrightstone, Wilson, Mokan, and Ford begin our 2nd with two doubles, a triple, and a single off Pete Donohue was mighty special, and gave Jimmy Ring a 3-0 lead for a change. Jimmy was 2-11 to start the game, so everyone in the dugout was waiting for him to start throwing it all away.

Except it was the Reds that did the bad throwing. George Burns muffed a ball in left and Bressler booted one down at first to help give us two more runs in the 3rd, and it seemed to give Jimmy a boost because Cincy could do next to nothing with him the rest of the afternoon. Harper tripled and Holke singled him in the 9th just to rub it in, and the Reds played so awful even the Over-the-Rhine Boys stayed in their bleacher seats. It was an even tougher day for local fans because the Bucs actually lost a game to the Boston Braves at home, which is about as likely as Benny marrying Miss Philadelphia.

The Havana Grit boys invited me to a speakeasy downtown afterwards to celebrate me giving the Reds the whammy, and I went along with it all for a German beer or two before I started getting a lead stomach and had to crawl back to my hotel closet. I was too gone to even let the rushing water-pipe sound bug me, and reciting "Sherry Magee" a few times sure helped.

PHI 032 000 001 - 6 12 1
CIN 000 000 200 - 2 4 4

GREETINGS FROM ONE OF THE QUEEN CITIES
July 10, 1924

Dear Rachel:

Sorry it's taken so long to write, but we've had a busy time of it out here in Ohio beating up the Reds. Actually they got us in the first game because of that dang Eppa Rixey, but we skunked them yesterday and today was even more fun.

Bill Hubbell threw for us, and he must be the worst pitcher in the league with the best record. He has this Carlson-like way of getting out of predicaments, and the 2nd inning was a good example. Roush led with a double, and Jake Daubert tripled him in with one out. Wingo then hit a ball to Holke at first, who whipped it home to snuff Daubert. Critz then singled, but Dolf Luque, their pretty good hitting pitcher, whiffed. The Reds have been in a hitting slump lately, because normally they would have scored two or three runs there, but that's also Bill Hubbell for you.

George Harper, who seems to like me a lot and invited me to be in this little club of players who get together after games and do things like go out to eat, whacked a deep homer in our 5th inning, and believe me, whacking is what you have to do to the thing to get one out of this place. Harper then led off our 8th with a single, Cy Williams doubled, and Wrightstone got one in with a deep fly and the 2-1 lead was all Hubbell needed to put Cincy to bed. They got five singles off him in the last four innings but couldn't do a thing with them.

What really had to hurt for the Reds fans was the Bucs amazingly losing to Boston again and missing a chance to get closer to them.

After the game tonight, Harper's little player-club took me down to a downtown area called Fountain Square, where all the best restaurants and dancing clubs and theaters and cigar stores are. Wrightstone mentioned a secret speakeasy he knew about where they serve German beer in these big icy glasses and there are even half-dressed women walking around trying to make friends with the men, but we made sure to stay far away from that place.

From being here before with Benny and now this time, I'm really starting to like Cincinnati. They call it the Queen City, but from what my best friend on the team Heinie Sand says, that's kind of dumb because there's about twenty other "queen cities" in America, even Burlington, Vermont and Dickinson, North Dakota. I think these towns need to announce which queen gave them permission to do this.

Anyway, I wish I didn't have to leave New York so fast. I promise when I get back to the East I'll meet with your father about our marriage idea and it won't be on a Saturday. Maybe I should just save time and send him a telegram. What do you think?

Good night, Rachel-love!

—Vinny

PHI 000 010 010 - 2 9 0
CIN 010 000 000 - 1 8 1

BACK TO THE LOSING BUSINESS
July 11, 1924

I woke up with a scattered cloudy head, which is usually what happens if you spend most of a night in a secret speakeasy drinking German beer out of icy glasses and keeping half-dressed women away from you. Heinie got me going with a bigger cup of coffee than usual, and we grabbed a streetcar out to Redland Field.

Carl Mays was throwing for the Reds, meaning everyone on our team could have used their own pot of coffee. George Harper especially has it in for Killer Karl, and joked in the club house about walking up there with a bullet-proof vest under his uniform shirt. The truth is that even though Mays killed that Chapman guy, the way they were letting dirty balls get used in games back then it's a surprise no one else got their lights knocked out.

Anyway, even if it disturbed Mays to no end, it sure seems to have bothered the teams he pitches against, because he was 10-5 going into this one. Harper snatched his bat out of my hands, walked up to the plate to start the game, and drove the second pitch clean out of the ball park! Roush doubled in Boob Fowler in the last of the 1st to tie things, but then Mays settled into his typical groove slot, wiping out the next eight Phillie hitters with ease. Harper singled with two outs in the 3rd and stood on first base clapping his hands at our dugout like some nut, but it didn't exactly get us going. Heinie weakly popped out to end the inning.

Carlson threw his usual tough game, but Cincy wasn't about to lose three in a row to us. After a Roush single leading off their 6th and a wild pitch, Al Wingo doubled in the go-ahead run. Four straight singles got them two more in the 7th, Roush driving in his second and third runs on the day, and then Mays got even better. Except for a Wilson double and Cy Williams walk in the 9th, he retired everybody else and finished us off in less than seventy minutes.

The players were nice to me after because Harper had a homer and single and couldn't exactly blame my bat-handling , but the worse news is that now we're on the train to Pittsburgh for a Saturday double-header with the first place Bucs, who are 6-1 against us. No one plays baseball on Sunday there, which is why we had to double up, and by the time they're through with us, we might all need to recover in church.

PHI 100 000 000 - 1 3 0
CIN 100 001 20x - 4 13 0

SEASICK ALL DAY ON A PIRATE SCHOONER
July 12, 1924

The good news is that our Pittsburgh hotel was the Schenley, not the William Penn where Benny and me ran into that creep house detective and almost got nailed for impostering. The bad news was that we had two games to play with the first-place Bucs at Forbes Field, and after getting shut down yesterday by Carl Mays in Cincy, no one was really in the mood to take two beatings.

The Schenley was sure a posh locale, though. Marble and chandeliers were all over the place, and Heinie told me that Presidents Taft, Roosevelt and Wilson all stayed there. We could also walk to Forbes Field, which we did on the early side, all split into groups so Pirate fans on the streets wouldn't bother us. Pittsburgh fans are basically good loyal ones anyway, and they're too excited about their team being good again to even notice opposing bums like us.

Forbes was stuffed to the rafters for the twin games, and when the first one started at high noon, the last thing we played like was bums. Meadows pitched for them, and Glenn Wright began by making what must have been his thousandth error in the last month, Holke singled with one out, Cy singled, and Wrightstone clubbed one into the right field stands for a quick 4-0 Phillie lead! Meadows was all rattled because then Wilson singled, Mokan got plunked and Ford doubled in another.

And we weren't done. Cy and Wrightstone hit back-to-back doubles in the 2nd, and Wrightstone knocked in our seventh run in the 4th with a single. Our pitcher Oeschger couldn't believe he had a 7-0 lead against these guys. In fact, he couldn't believe it so much that he started giving it away. The Bucs got one run in the 4th on a double play ball, then went to town on us in the 6th. With one out, Grimm singled, Moore and Cuyler walked, Smith singled, Traynor doubled, Maranville singled and avast ye dang mateys, it was suddenly 7-6.

The Phils then gave up the sea battle and went back in their hammocks, because we couldn't score a run for beans the rest of the game. Traynor tied the thing at 7-7 by singling in Cuyler in the 8th. Arnie Stone took over for Meadows and we couldn't score on him either. I'd never seen our dugout so tensed up. Huck Betts pitched three tough innings of relief for us after Oeschger was sent packing, but then he got tired in the 10th, walking three Pirates in a row. Steineder took over to face Traynor, and we all knew this game was far lost. Pie sliced one into right field to Harper, but Moore tagged and scored easy and we had probably our worst defeat this year.

Art Fletcher showed what a good manager is like between the games, though. He told the players they should only think about the 7-0 lead they took early, because that didn't come from nowhere. Harper said yeah, but Whitey's pitching the second game for us and he hasn't won all year. Glazner was in the next room getting a rubdown, so it's good he didn't hear that, but then I remembered Mama saying that even a blind bear finds a fish once in a while and it didn't pay to have that attitude.

So out went Whitey Glazner with his 0-5 record and 7.28 earned run average to face the scariest lineup in the league, and guess the heck what? NO ONE could touch him. I mean, there was one walk, two hit batters, three singles and a double, but not once was he in real trouble. Meanwhile we knocked around Jeff Pfeffer enough to build us a 3-0 lead by the 7th and held on from there.

As we ran back to our hotel to start card games and plan dinners and whatever else tonight, all I could think about was how unpredictable baseball can be. It's almost like a box of candy, because you never know what flavor you're going to end up with.

PHI 510 100 000 0 - 7 17 0
PIT 000 105 010 1 - 8 10 2

PHI 000 110 100 - 3 9 0
PIT 000 000 000 - 0 4 2

AND ON THE SEVENTH DAY...

July 13, 1924

"Hey Vinny!" It was Hod Ford, our second baseman, calling me over to his breakfast table at the Schenley this morning. It seems Heinie Sand had met up with a young "Baseball Mollie", which is what the Phillie players call girls who follow them around, and still hadn't come out of his room. That got me a little disappointed in Heinie, because I swore he told me he was married once, but maybe I was wrong. Either way, said Hod while he munched his toast, you can't expect guys like us to be away from home for a month three times each summer and not "sample the local fare."

There was a kitchen help lady who kept coming over to re-pour our water glasses, and when Hod got up, left his quarter tip and headed upstairs, she came back and stood next to the table. When I looked up at her I noticed she was staring at me sort of funny. I also noticed that under her white cloth hat she had rolls of bright red hair and an amazingly beautiful face.

"What position do YOU play?" she asked, and it took me a second before I realized she thought I was on the team. "Oh, I'm kind of a backup everything," I said, because I enjoyed playing along. "You're awful young-looking," she said, "even for a rookie." Harper and Wrightstone were calling her from the next table, and she stared at me with a big smile for a little longer until finally turning away.

I finished my eggs and juice and started to get up and suddenly the lady was back. She re-poured my water glass again, but this time very, very slow, like she had to watch every drop go in. "I'm Gretchen Slattery," she said in her calmest, sweetest voice, "Want to go canoeing with me today?" I didn't know what to say, so I just sat there. "I know you fellahs aren't playing," she continued, "Nobody in Pennsylvania does on the Lord's Day." When asked if she had her own canoe she said "Yes, and I even have an auto."

I was tempted to say I was engaged to somebody right then and there, but being around these wild players was rubbing off on me, and I figured what was wrong with a little canoeing, anyway? So when she got off from her job around noon time, I met her around the back of the hotel, and we climbed into this rickety half-truck jalopy, which she had to start with a crank and blammed its exhaust out every couple of blocks.

It was hard to tell how old Gretchen was. She was able to drive herself so she obviously wasn't too young, but she had this sweet little girl face that made it hard to take your eyes off her. She drove pretty fast out of Pittsburgh and headed in an east direction, up and down these hilly, curvy roads along a river. There were less and less houses and more and more trees, and after at least an hour of this we bounced down this narrow, muddy trail and stopped at a dead end.

I didn't see any canoe anywhere, just a sorry-looking cabin perched on these flimsy wood poles stuck into the riverbank. There were smoke wisps coming out of its little metal chimney and a collection of fuzzy animal skins hanging between two trees. When I asked where the heck the canoe was she just smiled and led me inside.

There was no electricity, and she lit about twenty candles around the room before she answered one of my questions. She said she did have a canoe once but it tipped over and she almost drowned and she just let it float downstream. She also had a rowboat once that did the same thing, so no, she never went out on the water for fun anymore. I asked why she lied to me and she just pulled me close and took off her cloth hat and her red hair spilled out of it like flowing lava and the next thing I knew she was kissing me and tugging at my shirt. Don't leave me, too, she kept saying and I pushed her off and said "I don't even know you!" and then she got real calm and sweet again.

"Do you know of the Johnstown Flood?," she asked. Of course I did, what Pennsylvania kid doesn't know about that? Well, it turned out that Gretchen was four years old when it happened and her entire family drowned, "and now I'm waiting for the next flood to take me, too, but I need someone to go with me..." Can you believe this? Fetching Gretchen was not only close to 40 years old, but living like a hermit by herself, trying to snag a man she could drown with. Or in this case almost a boy.

I told her I was just the Phillie batboy and not a player and really had to get back but that only got her to start grabbing me again. I began to feel bad for her and let her hold me in her arms for a while, and I even had some of her stewed raccoon for an early dinner. But there was no way I was going to wait around for another flood and miss the rest of the Phillies' road trip. She drank a small glass of moonshine whiskey after we ate, and I faked drinking mine, and the second she fell asleep I snuck out to her jalopy, cranked it up and drove away from the cabin with her running out after me screaming. I left the auto for her at the edge of the main road a few miles away, and hitchhiked a ride back into Pittsburgh from there.

I told Heinie the story later, but he was all giddy from the time he spent with his normal girl and could only laugh about it. I guess it was a little bit funny, but if you think I'm going anywhere near the Schenley Hotel breakfast room again you got another thing coming.

ANOTHER DAY OF INDEPENDENCE
CHURCH FOR SOME, REFLECTION FOR OTHERS, BASEBALL-FREE FOR ALL

PHILADELPHIA, July 13

Dearest Bonnie,

I am writing this to you on a shady park bench in Rittenhouse Square. On a long base ball road trip such as this it's always a decided pleasure to have a full day's respite, so a healthy huzzah goes out to Pennsylvania for enacting their Sunday "blue laws" that prohibit ball-playing.

I have the same room at the Warwick I was given on my last visit, and it seems vast and empty without you here to share it with. Many of the fellows on the team make special plans on days like this to see old friends or new ones that I am not at liberty to speak of, but for me it is always a simple, though bittersweet trick to give myself a fine walking tour of the city and pretend my darling wife is on my arm.

I visited Independence Hall and the Liberty Bell this morning, and enjoyed a walk along the Schuylkill until the hot sun felt like it was crisping the top of my boater. A polite young man named Benjamin who delivered your telegram to me in the press row after yesterday's game met me at the hotel this morning to give me a rather inexpensive shoeshine, and told me exactly how to get to Strawbridge and Clothier's. I hear they are a fine department store that has been around for quite a while, and look forward to buying you the hat you asked for.

It has been a wild and exhausting pennant chase for our Tigers, even without our four-game debacle in Washington. A 154-game season is just too long, and base ball would be wise to insert some kind of mid-campaign vacation for the players and writers and followers, if only for a few days. It would be a joy to spend those days with you and the wee ones without a moment's thought of batting averages and ornery personalities.

As we did on our last eastern sojourn, from here we will travel to Boston and New York before I rail back into your arms on July 25th. If only I could persuade you to join me with the children in Manhattan next week I would be a happy man, or even happier if you could leave them with Aunt Sue and come on your own. But I realize travel and the bigger cities don't agree with you, so please don't think of me as the pushy sort.

For now, I will just enjoy your sweet, wispy presence on this historic bench.

My deepest love,
Calvin

GET ME OUT OF THIS BURGH
July 14, 1924

I peeked into the Schenley breakfast room on my way out to the street to find a pastry wagon and didn't see that cuckoohead Gretchen girl, but it didn't make me any more relieved. Between yesterday's nightmare and the thought of us facing the Bucs again, I was eager to get out of this town and on to Chicago.

So were the Phillies, I bet, after today's game at Forbes. Jimmy Ring has been pitching better lately but he was still 3-11 going into this one, and Pirate pitcher Wilbur Cooper, even though he never looks any better out there than Ring, was 10-4 somehow.

An hour and a half later, I knew why. Ford and Parkinson started our 3rd inning with singles and were left there by Ring, Schultz and Sand. Rabbit Maranville began the Buc 3rd with yet another triple and came home on Carey's double play ball. Even when Pittsburgh makes an out it gets something done.

Best player in the league Kiki Cuyler then whacked a homer to left with one out in the 4th, and the Forbes Field crowd went nuttier than Gretchen. Just for fun, Kiki doubled in the 6th and singled off Steineder in the 7th for the third and last Pirate run of the day.

Meanwhile the Phils were really busy doing nothing, and I didn't mind keeping my back turned to the field when I was setting up the bats because I knew every inning had another tragedy in it. Schultz walked with one gone in the 6th and got erased on a double play. Holke singled to start the 7th and was left there scratching himself. Ford and Parkinson again singled to begin the 8th and Henline hit a pinch double play. Even my buddy Heinie Sand singled to lead the 9th and was wiped off the bases with a double broom.

It was a sickening afternoon all around, and even a fun game of gin rummy in Ford and Parkinson's room later where a few of us won a couple of bucks didn't cheer anybody up. Maybe we'll get lucky and leave Pittsburgh with a win tomorrow, but if I were you I wouldn't bet my lunch on it.

```
PHI 000 000 000 - 0 6 0
PIT 001 100 10x - 3 11 0
```

YDE GADS!
July 15, 1924

Heinie Sand was all out of sorts this morning because the floozie he spent Saturday night with wanted nothing to do with him after yesterday's loss, and according to him that's when ballplayers need loving stuff the most. Of course from what I've seen so far players seem to need it when they win or lose, but it sure isn't my place to give them a hard time. Heinie and me have gotten pretty close and the last thing I wanna do is mess that up.

But the first thing I wanted to do after today's disaster was bury my head in a ball bag. Johnny Couch started for us against this very tough young rube named Emil Yde, and it was downright bloody by the end. After the Pirates scored twice in the 2nd without getting a hit (three walks, error from Heinie and a scoring fly) we got three right back in the 3rd with almost exactly the same garbage (three walks, error by Wright and a single).

Couch probably thought this was his lucky day at that point, but before long he needed to lay on a couch, because these Buccaneers take no prisoners. Moore singled right off the bat, Cuyler tripled, Smith singled and they had the lead back. Two walks, a single and double after that and they were up 7-3. Cuyler started the next inning with a triple just to show off, Smith got him home with a deep fly and it was 8-3.

Things calmed down from there, but mostly for us. After Couch singled in the 4th we got no hits off this Yde joker the whole rest of the game. Three walks and three singles in the 8th polished us off for good, and we were off to Penn Station like hay through a horse.

Nobody on the train seemed to care all that much, because I guess it's always easier to get clobbered then lose by one run and be thinking about one or two plays you flubbed for the whole ride. Wrightstone gave me my first taste of Caribbean rum and I kind of liked it, even though it didn't mix too well with a rocking sleeping berth. Anyway, I sure look forward to getting back to Cubs Park tomorrow.

PHI 003 000 000 - 3 2 1
PIT 025 100 04x - 12 11 1

HEINIE'S BAD FALL
July 16, 1924

We got to Chicago on the very late side last night, and the engineer pulled us off onto a side rail so we could get some extra sleep. Kind of a nice privilege if you ask me.

Heinie Sand was all business while we ate breakfast later in the stopped dining car. He knew he'd be leading off in the first game against the righty Vic Aldridge, and was determined to have a good day. The Phillies actually had a winning record of 4-3 against the Cubs, and Harper had a juicy bet going with their first baseman Ray Grimes that we'd finish the season in front of them. This morning they were in 6th place, six full games in front of us in the losses column, so we had a bunch of work to do.

It was nice to get back to Cubs Park, which had a fabulous baseball-flavor neighborhood and fans perched in trees and on walls all around the place. Hubbell was throwing for us, and he's been tough all year but Aldridge can be even tougher. Heinie didn't care, ripped his favorite bat out of my hand, marched up to the plate and lined the first pitch from old Vic clean into left field for a single! I gave a little shout, then saw everyone in the dugout looking at me and realized it probably wasn't okay to do that. Harper rapped into a double play ten seconds later and I thought oh great, now they'll blame that on my stupid little cheer.

Grantham hit into a twin killing in the bottom of the inning for the Cubs, but that one scored Heathcote from third base and they had a quick 1-0 lead. We got singles in the 2nd and 3rd but nothing else, then put men on second and third in the 4th but Mokan left them there with a ground out. A Friberg single, Grimes grounder and single by Hack Miller then made it 2-0 Cubs, and we could see the way this one was going. Heinie lined out, struck out and grounded out in his next three times off Aldridge, and paced around in the dugout like a crazy chipmunk when he wasn't hitting.

The big shame was that Hubbell pitched one of his best games of the year, giving up only one single after Miller's and getting everyone else out. Cy Williams got us thrilled for a second with a deep homer in the 6th, but we wasted a single in the 7th and one in the 8th after that. Sometimes things don't go your way in spite of ten tons of evidence that they should, and this was one of those times. Down 2-1 in the 9th, Wilson led with another single, our ninth hit to their four. Mokan whiffed, Ford got Wilson to second with a grounder, and Butch Henline pinch-hit a hard single that only got him to third.

Up walked Heinie, grinding his skinny bat handle into sand. He fouled off a couple, got the count to 3-and-2...and popped weakly out to Hack Miller in left to end the game.

Heinie kept his back and heinie turned to everyone in the club house while he got dressed, and didn't even react when a half dozen players patted him on the shoulders or slapped his back to try and cheer him up. The players were going off to their favorite speakeasy on Rush Street but he didn't want to go, so I leaned in and asked if he wanted to get dinner with me. He said no thanks, let's just play us a little cards in my room at the Knickerbocker and order food up.

So that's what we did, helped by a flask of illegal brandy he took with him on the trip for just a night like this. The stuff tasted pretty awful, but after a swig or two it didn't really matter. I asked if he'd heard from his floozie and he said no, and then I asked if he was worried about his wife finding out with newsmen all over the place and he said are you kidding? Press folks make it their rule to never write about a player's personal life. He then told me about his little baby boy and I told him all about my papa getting killed in the War, and before long we were singing European trench songs and flipping the cards up in the air.

"Heck with it," I said, "We're 34-55 now, but seventh place is sure better than last." Right, he said back, "just think about how many bottles of this swill the Braves have to go through every night!" And that got us laughing all over again.

PHI 000 001 000 -1 5 0
CHI 100 100 00x -2 9 1

PHILLY HOUDINI AMAZES AGAIN
July 17, 1924

There was scattered drizzles all day in Chicago, which is pretty rare in summer here but darn refreshing after all the heat we've been playing in. The crowd was a little less but because they were afraid of the game getting called off everyone was yelling at the players and umps more to try and keep it moving.

And what better pitcher to throw for us on a dark and stormy day but The Amazing Carlson, scoring rally escape artist extraordinaire! Hal had given up 168 hits in just 120 innings, but his record somehow was still 6-7 with a not-too-awful earned run average of 4.71. How did he do it, you ask? Well, let's go to Cubs Park's center stage and watch!

Heathcote began the Cubs 1st with a wicked single, but Carlson got a double play grounder from Friberg. Grantham then walked and Grimes singled, but Hack Miller flied out for Escape No. 1. With one out in the 2nd, Weis walked and Adams singled. Pitcher Keen bunted them over, but

Carlson got a grounder out of Heathcote for Escape No. 2.

In the top of the 4th, we went to work on Vic Keen, who's been pitching great lately but looked like his 5-12 record in this one. Cy Williams led with a booming triple, Wrightstone followed with a banging double, and Wilson pinged a single for a 2-0 lead. After Mokan grounded out, Ford doubled and The Amazing Carlson chipped in with his second single for a 4-0 lead.

Hartnett and Weis doubled to begin the bottom half, but after Adams walked and Keen bunted, Carlson got Heathcote and Friberg on infield balls for Escape No. 3. Want some more? Okay. Weis and Adams singled to start their 6th, but Carlson got Keen on a whiff and Heathcote and Friberg on grounders again. If they made a new statistic called PPF (pitching in a pickle factor), Carlson would lead the league every year.

And Keen would be at the bottom of the list. He has three times the talent Carlson does but always throws the wrong pitch at the wrong time, and it happened here in the 7th to put the game to bed. Holke and Cy got on base with two outs, and Jimmie Wilson picked a fat fastball and rammed it over the left field wall for a 3-run smash and 7-1 lead! Carlson gave up a scoring fly to Miller, got out of another jam, then got his fourth hit of the game, a long homer which got the Cubs Park crowd booing like I've never heard. A bunch of hits and walks later Keen was gone and we had ten runs on the board, the most we've scored in ages.

Hal was the toast of the club house of course, and everyone wanted to take him out for food and illegal drink. The party started in Harper's room at the Knickerbocker but we ran out of whiskey bottles before long and headed out. I got stuffed into the back of a taxi with Heinie and Holke and Henline and we ended up at a chop house that had a speakeasy in the back over on North Broadway, where Benny and me incredibly bumped into Rachel at a dancing club back in May.

As usual, I had too much to eat and even more too much to drink, and the cigar smoke was making me gag and I had to step out the back door of the place, where I saw Heinie kissing some waitress to death under a lamp post. At least he was happy again, though we'd all be paying for it tomorrow. Heck, though, when you're seventh place material you gotta get your good times whenever you can. Good night—hic!—reader-folks!

PHI 000 400 330 -10 14 0
CHI 000 100 110 - 3 13 1

CURSE OF THE FRONT ROW SEATS
July 18, 1924

"Vinny! Spit on my damn bat, will ya?"

It was Heinie, red-eyed and wobbly, so hungover he couldn't even spit on his own bat handle for the gooey grip he liked to have. I told him I wasn't a good spitter and he said that's baloney because all kids know how to spit. It took me four tries to call up a good one because I was just as hungover as he was, but I got it done.

The sun was back out today and it was a perfect low 70s, and the good Cubs Park seats close to the field were all filled. I even saw my old pal Al Capone back in his front row spot next to the Chicago dugout. Me and Benny ran into a peck of trouble when we did a driving job for him last time here, and I didn't even want him seeing me so I pulled my hat way down over my eyes before the game started and kept it there.

Elmer Jacobs was on the hill for the Cubs, and he's no good. Fletcher switched Harper and Heinie in the lineup, with the idea I guess that Harper had a better chance to get on base and then Heinie could bunt him over. Well, guess what? Ten seconds after I spattled on his bat handle, he swung at an Elmer curve and popped it high and deep to left. Hack Miller went back to the wall but the ball floated right over for a home run! Heinie ran so fast around the bases he almost reached third by the time the ball had bounced twice in the street, and when he ran by me he grinned and yelled "patooey!" at me.

Jimmy Ring and his stupid 3-12 record was going for us, so we knew a 1-0 lead had little to no chance of lasting, But Sand's homer just gave everyone in the dugout hope. Mokan did a little jig before he ran out to left field, and I swear I saw Wrightstone smile. Ring meanwhile was the best anyone had seen him in a while, scattering three singles, three walks and nothing else for his first seven innings.

In the top of the 6th, everything got sunny for us. Cy led with a double, Wilson singled him to third, and a Mokan fly got another run in. Then Ford and Ring both singled, and a ball hit out to Sparky Adams at short by Harper went right through the Spark's legs for a two-base error and we were up 4-0!

It was then that the first peanut shells hit my back. I didn't turn around, because I knew it was some wiseacre Cubs fan taking out his losing worries on me. "Go back to Philly-dilly, you punk!" a voice shouted, and I stopped, because there was something familiar in the accent. I whipped my head around, and there was Benny! He'd snuck right into an empty front row seat and had his shoes up on the rail while he whipped shells at me. "You bum!" I yelled, ran up and shook his hand. He'd been riding boxcars all the way from Pennsylvania, just to spend a few days in Chicago with me. I asked him why and he said, "I'm your best friend and isn't it your birthday tomorrow?"

Geez, he was right! I'd been so busy batboying I'd forgot all about it. He said he got me something special, and it was tied up in his sack which he'd hidden a few blocks from the park, so we made plans to hook up after the game outside the visitor club house.

Heathcote doubled and Grimes homered in the 8th to put the Cubs back in the game and put Ring back in his usual trouble, but Wrightstone socked one out in the 9th, Huck Betts finished up for Jimmy and we had the 5-3 win. We were now just four games behind Chicago in the standings, so Harper's bet was still alive, and everyone wanted to celebrate again with me as the honor guest because I had spit on Heinie's bat. I told them about Benny and they invited him along, but when I went outside to find him he wasn't there.

I waited a good ten minutes, and was about to give up when two scary-looking mugs in hats and suits came up on both sides of me and stood there.

"You the bat kid?" asked the shorter, uglier one. I nodded and they took my arms, walked me to the corner and shoved me into the back of a long, fancy car.

Where Alphonse Capone was sitting. Not looking all too happy and smelling like garlic. He said one of his boys had recognized "your buddy Benzini Olio," when he leaned over to talk to me, and then he recognized me too. Just what I was afraid of. Benzini was what Benny called himself when we met Capone out here last time, and he wasn't nuts about the way we left town so fast without thanking him for our last job. They had Benny a few streets away in another car, and according to Capone he'd already agreed to "help us out" again and wanted to make sure I would too. He also didn't seem too happy about the Cubs losing to us again, and didn't give an owl's hoot that I was their batboy.

There was "an associate" who was being fitted for some new "very heavy footwear" and needed to be dropped into Lake Michigan late that night to "test them out". I said I was too scared to do something like that, then got an idea and asked Capone if we could "warm up" by doing something else, like helping them get some bootleg whiskey. Al looked at his creepy guys a second, who chuckled at each other, and Capone seemed to buy the idea.

They let me duck back in the club house to "get my things," and I told some players I would meet them at the hotel later with a "bottle of something wicked". Heinie saw a scared look in my face but I was afraid to mention anything about Capone and said everything was fine. Capone's creeps then walked me to their own car, where Benny was stuck in the back with his hands and feet tied. They let me untie him and explain what we were doing, and it took a good five minutes for me to calm him down.

Benny had his bulging sack with him, and as we got drove up the north end of the lake, he took out my birthday present, a brand new Royal typewriter and three new pens. He said he got them from that rube of a Detroit reporter named Butterworth who he was still angry at for writing bad things about the Phillies in his before-the-season report. You mean you stole them, I asked? Yeah, but I don't think he knew it was me, was his weak answer.

I then made the mistake of asking Shorty Creep how and when we were getting the whiskey, and he said, "2 a.m. Which one of youz can drive a boat?" Oh criminy...Help us, reader-people!

PHI 100 003 001 - 5 12 0
CHI 000 000 021 - 3 8 1

I WASH MY HANDS OF THIS EXCREMENT
TIGERS SLIDE INTO FOURTH PLACE HOG PEN WITH RANK DEFEAT

By Calvin J. Butterworth
Detroit Free-Enterprise

BOSTON—With a grand chance to redeem yesterday's tragedy dropped in their laps, our foolish gang of athletic jesters proceeded to flub away a certain win in a manner that was fouler than a farmer's back yard.

The often unreliable Ed Wells was staked to a 5-0 cushion after two innings, with Cobb and Heilman each knocking in two off Fullerton. It was 5-1 Detroit in the last of the 4th when Joe Heving, who replaced Picinich at catcher earlier, tripled with one out. Ezzell grounded right back to Wells, who gunned down Heving trying to score from third. Wambsganss then singled, and pitcher Fullerton popped a lazy fly out to Cobb. The great and wonderful Tyrus dropped it, and two were aboard. Geygan and Harris followed with singles, Pratt booted another ball at third, Flagstead doubled, and the Red Sox had five unearned runs and a 6-5 lead.

As is so too often the case with this unit, the Tiger offense then dropped dead, while Boston pecked away with single runs in the 6th, 7th, and 8th. Cobb's next three at bats came with men aboard, and he grounded out each time, once into a killing double play.

Watching this ungodly spectacle unfold, it became apparent to me that I can no longer write daily reports on this dreadful, dreadful team. Cobb is futilely piloting a sinking barge without heads or hearts, one that recently proved in Washington it is not ready to compete for a league crown. In short, this is a wildly inconsistent amalgamation of ninnies, and they would be better served if they performed in a newsless realm where one would not be subjected to their daily pitiful ways.

Cobb can crack open my skull if he wishes, and the newspaper can excuse me without pay. I do not care. When the sun rises tomorrow I will be sailing on the Charles in a rented canoe, or hiking in the mountains of New Hampshire, or sipping a glass of absinthe en route to a long-sought reunion with my lovely wife. But I will not be watching the Detroit Tigers attempt to play baseball.

NOTHING LIKE A GOOD WATER SPORT
July 19, 1924

Well, neither of us had driven a motor boat before, so one of Capone's creeps filled it with gasoline and showed us how to yank it started. We were at the edge of a far north part of Lake Michigan, behind some trees in the pitch dark, and I stepped into the drink twice trying to climb aboard.

I elected Benny to be pilot because he was the jerk who showed up in the front row seats and got us into this mess. Our job was to ride three or four miles straight out until we saw flashing blue lights, and those would be from the Canadian whiskey smugglers. I asked Capone's creep how Canadians get here if the whole lake is in America and he said shut up and get going and handed me a fat zippered pouch which I knew was filled with cash. The creep was going with us to make sure it all went smooth and we didn't take off with the loot, and we had two hours to make the swap and get back or we'd be "a gull's breakfast" by morning.

Luckily the waves weren't bad, but it was dead cold and we weren't dressed warm enough. We motored out for a while, afraid to talk with the goon sitting there watching us, and then we suddenly went straight into a huge fog bank! Benny panicked at his outboard helm, yelled "Where do I go?" and Creep said "Shut up and listen!"

We did, but the fog made everything even more quiet than it already was. We cut the motor off and listened again. Tiny waves lapped at the sides, and there was a far off horn, but nothing else. I said maybe we should head back just to get our bearings and Creep pulled out a snub nose gun and pointed it at me.

Benny saw the gun and went crazy, leaped out of his seat and knocked the guy down. The gun went off and the two of them fell into the lake! I yelled for Benny and could hear them splashing around but couldn't see a damn thing. Then Benny's hands appeared on the side of the boat and I tugged him back in. He was wet and freezing and had no idea what happened to the creep. "I guess...he couldn't swim..."

Oh great. I yanked the motor back on and just started driving the boat in the direction of anywhere. "They're going to kill us!" Benny yelled. No they're not, I said, because we're escaping through Michigan. To heck with the Phillies and everything else, I just wanted to survive.

And then two flashing blue lights hit us through the fog, and we almost motored smack into the side of a long trawler. A man on top was shouting something at us we couldn't make out, and a rope ladder dropped over the side. Me and Benny looked at each other and we realized we'd better do this part of the job just in case and make up answers later.

The boat captain was a dark-bearded guy in a knit cap, and him and his small crew spoke in French accents. Benny nudged me and asked how people from France even got here and I had to explain that they were probably French Canadians. Benny seemed confused about that.

"My name is Payette. Show me ze money!" is all the captain said, so I gave him the pouch. He zipped it open, smiled, and handed it to a crewman to count it. "Where is Louie Lips?" he asked, and we guessed that was probably the name of Capone's guy who was drowning at the moment. "He didn't make it," is all I said, and he squinted at us. Nodded at another crewman and they started pulling out whiskey crates and lowering them into our boat.

I was shivering cold, so pulled out my Phillies cap and put it on. The captain saw it and suddenly flashed a big smile. "You like ze baseball?" I explained that not only did we love it, but that I was the Phillies batboy and got kidnapped to do this job. He was amazed, and invited us down into his cabin for glasses of French wine.

It seemed that his father played for the 1898 Montreal Royals, the team that won the old Eastern League that year with a 68-47 record, and he'd followed "ze baseball" ever since. We felt pretty safe at that point so told him about Louie Lips falling into the drink and how much trouble we were probably in. "I will take care of this mess," he said.

And boy did he ever. Two of his crew took the motor boat back to Illinois for us to unload the whiskey and tell Capone's guys we were all killed and thrown overboard when Louie pulled a gun on the crew, and then the trawler turned south and took us close to northern Indiana. Payette gave us a rowboat and enough cash to get us to St Louis, where we could rejoin the team tomorrow. I gave the captain my Phillies cap as a souvenir and took off his knit hat right away, pulled the cap on over his salty locks with a big grin. "Baseball has been tres tres bon to me."

And us, too! Bonne nuit, reader-people!

The Phillies game today we found about on Captain Payette's wireless:

at CUBS 5-13-1, PHILLIES 2-6-0

See what happens to our lineup when I'm not arranging the bats? Nothing. Tony Kauffman, the worst starter in the Cub rotation, throws his best game of the year and Oeschger stinks for us. I wonder if Fletcher contacted the FBI to look for me yet. All in all, it's been one hell of a birthday.

NATIONAL LEAGUE through Saturday, July 19, 1924

Pittsburgh	58	30	.659	—
Cincinnati	55	37	.598	5
Brooklyn	53	39	.576	7
New York	51	38	.573	7.5
St. Louis	45	45	.500	14
Chicago	40	50	444	19
PHILLIES	36	56	.391	24
Boston	24	67	.263	35.5

From the July 19, 1924 edition of the Detroit Free-Enterprise:

TIGER SCRIBE FEARED MISSING IN BOSTON
"MENTAL FATIGUE" MAY BE FACTOR; AUTHORITIES SEARCHING

By Percival Q. Mellon, Publisher

Calvin Butterworth, a Free-Enterprise employee and one of the more respected men of sports letters in the nation, has inexplicably left his position as daily Tigers reporter and vanished in the city of Boston.

Apparently distraught over the sinking stature and uninspiring recent play of the Detroit club, Mr. Butterworth was not to be found in his luxury suite at the Copley Plaza this morning, or anywhere else in the fashionable hotel. "He rang the valet at 8 p.m. last evening to have his shoes picked up and polished," related Copley desk manager R. P. Simmons, "but when they were returned this morning, he had already vacated his suite with all belongings."

Boston police immediately commenced a search of neighborhood streets and alleys in the hotel's vicinity, as well as at all local train stations, known speakeasies, reefer dens and gambling halls, but at press time the writer had yet to be found.

According to other members of the sporting press Butterworth worked alongside, he was especially homesick for his wife and family on this current road trip, which resumes in two days at Yankee Stadium. He was also disturbed by the recent theft of his typewriter and personal fountain pens from the Shibe Park press row in Philadelphia. In some quarters it has been rumored that a blow to the head he received earlier this season from player/manager Cobb may have caused him headaches and occasional delirium, but this has not been substantiated.

BOUNCY NERVES TO MISSOURI
July 20, 1924

"What?? Give me that!"

Benny snatched the newspaper out of my hand at the roadside cafe in the middle of Indiana we were eating breakfast at. It was true. That Tigers writer Butterworth who Benny was complaining about months ago disappeared in Boston yesterday because he was upset about his missing typewriter and pens! My friend Benny was not only a thief, but he might have made someone nuts!

"I had nothing to do with that," he said, throwing the paper back at me, "the guy is obviously a mental case and can't take his team losing. Look at our crappy Phillies and how normal WE are!" I didn't want to get in an argument about what being normal was, so we threw some change down for our eggs and went back outside into the broiling morning.

We had gotten the rowboat ashore around dawn and hiked through some woods to a main road, where a farmer took us south a few hours to a more mainer road. The plan was to try and get to St. Louis for the 2 p.m. Phils and Cardinals game, even though we knew we probably wouldn't make it. We stood on the highway until the heat started melting our clothes and sat down and kept shirts over our heads with our thumbs sticking out. Benny was still lugging his clothes sack and the dumb typewriter he swiped for me, and I thought about trashing the thing but it was a real nice one and wasn't mine anyway, so I just couldn't.

A really fat guy wearing nothing but overalls drove up in a stinking, shaking fuel truck and invited us up in the cab. It was hard to tell what smelled worse, the gas or the driver. His name was Dobbs and he burped or farted with every bump in the road, and there were quite a lot of bumps. He was from Kansas and headed back in that direction, so I knew we had a chance of making the game. The problem was that Dobbs wouldn't shut up so it was impossible to take naps, and all he talked about was how much black people and Catholic people and Jew people were ruining America. He said he was in some kind of national group that wore white outfits at night and burned crosses like they were some kind of special spooks or something, and he was a pretty disgusting human.

He also smoked one cigarette after another which didn't make us too comfortable with the giant tank of fuel right behind our seat, and it wasn't long before I wanted to stop and hitch with someone else. Benny thought I was crazy, that we'd never make St. Louis in time, but I didn't care.

Suddenly we came up on two coloreds walking along the road with their thumbs out. Dobbs' eyes bugged out and he swerved the truck right at them! I yelled, jerked the wheel the other way and the next thing we knew he was pulling off the road and shoving us out. Good riddance.

So we ended up getting to Sportsman's Park in the 7th inning, which at least got us in one of the gates for free. We were losing 3-2 to Jesse Haines and I hurried down to the Phillie dugout to get Hod Ford's attention as he came out to the on-deck circle. "Vinny S!" he yelled, and then Harper popped out to help me over the rail and throw me my jersey. It was nice to know my new family was actually worried about me, and the team got inspired on the field right away. Johnny Couch hit for himself and singled. So did Harper. Heinie gave my hand a big shake, went up to the plate...

...and popped out to the catcher. Holke grounded out, the inning was over, and they didn't get a hit the rest of the way. According to Fletcher's scoring pad we hit into two double plays, left runners everywhere, and Cy Williams made a terrible error right before Ray Blades tripled to give the Cards three unearned runs and the game, but who cared? I was safe and sound and back in home sweet losing home.

PHI 000 200 000 - 2 9 1
STL 000 030 00x - 3 8 1

JIM CROWS OF A FEATHER FLOCK TOGETHER
July 21, 1924

Me and the team were put up at the famous Chase Hotel here in St. Louis, while Benny went over to Roy's house on the colored side of town. With me being missing for almost two days, I didn't want to push my luck by getting Benny into my room, and besides, Roy is a great guy and Benny had been looking forward to seeing him.

We met his brother first in Chicago the last time the Phils were out west, then stayed with him and his family, sat in the Negro pavilion for one game, then bandaged Roy up and snuck him into the regular white seats for the next game. This time, with me having to batboy all day, I didn't have a chance to see Roy until I spotted him back behind the pavilion chicken wire in right field, sitting with Benny again.

Cy got us a 1-0 lead for Bill Hubbell with a long sacrifice fly in the 3rd off Sherdel. The Cards are back over .500 again but they never seem to go much higher than that. Like us they play in an easy hitters' park, so road teams come in and knock their heads around regularly.

Except us, naturally. After we take the lead we can't do a lousy thing for three straight innings, and then Hubbell loses it in the last of the 6th. The Great Hornsby whacks a single with one out, and the ball hitting his bat is so loud it makes my ear ring being so close to him. Sunny Jim Bottomley then clubs a pitch high and deep over the pavilion, and I can make out Roy jumping up and down while Benny sits like a monk right next to him. The smash makes Hubbell batty because Clemons singles, Flack walks, and Cooney and Sherdel single for a 4-1 Cards lead!

From there it's all frustration. We had nine singles off Sherdel in the first six innings but only could score one run. Now we start hitting doubles and triples off him, but still can score just once in the 7th and 8th. Poor Heinie rolls into double plays to end two of the innings, which doesn't help and makes me think there will be more drinking later.

Butch Henline bats for Huck Betts to start our 9th and singles. Schultz whiffs but a ball gets past their catcher to move Butch to second. A two-out cheap single from Holke gets him to third, and ace St. Louis relief man Jesse Fowler enters to take care of Cy. Williams makes it easy for him, fly-ing out to center on the first pitch, and we all trudge back in the club house. There's a lot of cussng and equipment throwing and food being knocked over and Fletcher slams himself in an office and nobody talks to reporters. Outhitting the other team 15-9 and losing by one run is one of the worst baseball things that can happen.

And then Benny picks the wrong time to walk into the room with our friend Roy. "Who let that nigger in here?" asks Harper, and "Shoo, Darkie!" yells Wrightstone, and before I can even think about introducing him, two other players are shoving him and Benny out. I'm embarrassed and real angry and I don't even know what to do. Will I still be the Phillies batboy if I defend him in front of the Havana Grit Faction? Should I even care?

All I know is that I need to see my friends, so I make a dumb excuse to go down the hall and catch them just outside the park, where Benny is getting ready to punch a security cop. We had saved a couple bottles of Canadian whiskey we got from the smugglers to give to the team tonight, but after that bit I'm in no mood to give them a thing. Instead I apologize to Roy, give him the bottles and we go over to Roy's house for a huge chicken dinner, more corkball in the street, much whiskey drinking and long talks about the way America just has to get rid of these Jim Crow laws some-day.

Benny actually asked me who this "Jimmie Crow" was at one point and I had to give him an education right there. My best friend isn't too bright about important things but has a good sense of what's right and wrong, and to him, walking Roy right into the Phillie club house seemed as natu-ral as mailing a letter. If everyone else only felt that way.

PHI 001 000 110 - 3 15 1
STL 000 004 00x - 4 9 0

CAN'T BLAME THIS ONE ON ME
July 22, 1924

I had put a note under Heinie's door at the Chase last night to let him know I'd be staying over at Roy's so they wouldn't think I got kidnapped again, but to tell you the truth I was so mad at the team for shoving my friends out of the clubhouse yesterday I didn't care if they thought I was dead.

Roy and his family took good care of us again, and because it was incredibly hot and muggy this morning we sat out on their shady front porch for breakfast, something every other person in "the Ville" was doing. It was great. If someone on one porch ran out of butter or syrup for their flapjacks they'd yell across and send one of their kids over to borrow some.

Anyway, Roy and us got talking about the dumb Jim Crow laws all over again, and then about how good some of those colored players are that play around the country. Roy's brother Thomas asked us in Chicago on our last trip out here whether we wanted to watch some of them play sometime, but there wasn't enough time. Thomas actually knows Oscar Charleston and Rube Foster, and Roy told us that a friend of an old girlfriend's brother-in-law knows Judy Johnson, the star third baseman of the Hilldale Daisies, the champs of the Eastern Colored League who play in Darby which is right next to Philadelphia!

This got us thinking all over again, and before you knew it we had this nutty idea about collecting enough money to set up a game between some colored players and the Phillies in one of their off-days, just so they could eat their own jim crow. Benny thought it was the best idea anyone had ever had, and promised to start "working on it" right away.

With that hot little secret on my mind, I took a trolley back over to Sportsman's Park to get our bats ready for game time. Jimmy Ring and his luckless 4-12 record was going against Leo Dickerman, and we were about due for a win against these guys. But there's something about brutal hot weather that turns everyone into ghouls, and by the time I had the bats set up in the dugout my wool jersey felt like it weighed two tons and nobody looked like they wanted to play. There were so many people in the stands waving fans it seemed like the whole ballpark was going to fly off.

Then things started off great for the Cards. Ray Blades tripled with two outs in the first, and Fletcher decided to walk Hornsby on purpose. Not a bad idea, except when Sunny Jim Bottomley is up next, and I started grumbling to myself by the bat rack that this wasn't going to work. One of the coaches overheard and told me to shut up and sure enough, Bottomley cracked the next pitch out of the park and we were down 3-0.

We couldn't do a thing with Dickerman for four innings, then squeezed out single runs in the 5th and 6th with the help of a Cooney error and Ford sacrifice fly. The energy came back in our dugout, maybe because by then everyone was pouring cold water on their heads between innings, and we finally started hitting. Holke and Cy singled and Wilson walked to load our bases with two outs in the 7th. Mokan then shot one down the left field line to score the farm and put us ahead 5-3!

In the 8th, Harper, Holke and Cy all singled to make it 6-3, and Wrightstone yelled at me to get his bat. Russ was having a lousy day with no hits in four tries and I think he was still mad because I was friends with a colored because he'd never been this nasty to me before. When he lined out on the first pitch he came back in the dugout, shoved me out of the way and said "See what you did to me by bringing that coon in the club house?" I stood right up in his face, said "Don't you ever call my friend that!" and Heinie and Ford had to get between us to keep a fight from starting. Fletcher told me to go back to the hotel and cool off, as if that was possible. Instead I got dressed and went up in the stands and found some shade.

And it was just in time to see the Cards wake up. A Hornsby double and three singles off Ring and Steineder made it 6-5. Hi Bell shut us down in the 9th, and then the bottom of the 9th happened. Quickly. Specs Toporcer singled, Douthit doubled, Ray Blades tripled them both in, and we'd exploded to death with a 7-6 loss. To quote Wrightstone a little differently, that's what they get for kicking me out of the dugout.

Back at the hotel later where it was too hot to eat, Heinie showed me how to cool off the sheets by dumping ice buckets on them. He felt bad about the way Wrightstone was treating me, but said not to worry because him and his Havana Grit bunch were probably out drinking and cavorting all night and they wouldn't remember a thing by morning. Doesn't mean I won't.

PHI 000 011 310 - 6 13 1
STL 300 000 022 - 7 13 2

HOW TO HIT ROCK BOTTOMLEY
July 23, 1924

There was a knock on my hotel room door at eight this morning, and I knew it was too early for Heinie. When I asked who it was I heard "room service!" so I opened the door and two big carts filled with breakfast food came rolling in, pushed by Harper, Wrightstone, and the rest of the Havana Grit Faction, with Heinie and Hod Ford bringing up the rear! Even Cy Williams was there, and at first I thought it was some kind of late birthday present, but it wasn't.

"Russ has something to say," said Williams, who I realized for the first time was probably the quiet spokesleader of the club house. Wrightstone walked up, shook my hand with me still in my night shirt, and said, "Sorry for everything I said to you, Vinny." After the Cards scored five late runs to beat us yesterday the second I was booted up in the stands, Cy and some of the other players believed it had given the team bad luck, and that I had to be apologized to if we were ever going to turn that stuff around. So here they all were.

We had a huge breakfast in my small room for the next half hour, even had time to play some cards before we had to pack up and get to the ball park. It was the last game of the long road trip and in two days we'd be back at Baker Bowl to play the Cubs. All anybody wanted was a nice, normal game and hopefully a win to board the train with.

Benny showed up in the box seats before game time to tell me he was sticking around in St. Louis and Chicago for a while to try and get Roy and his brother and some people with money to set up a Phillies vs. colored players exhibition game. I wished him luck with that, but there was no way I was going to bring this up with anybody on the team after what's happened the last few days with our colored business.

Bottomley booted Harper's grounder to start things, and Holke blasted a 2-run homer to put us all in a good mood already. A Harper triple and Holke single in the 3rd made it 3-0, and it was 3-1 when we started throwing the ball in weird directions. Errors by Holke and Wrightstone helped the Cards tie it in the 4th, and after Bottomley homered off Carlson to put us behind 4-3, Ford flubbed one, Max Flack doubled, and Carlson was called for a balk by the home umpire for sneezing as he was throwing a pitch.

So we were suddenly down 5-3, and Cy Williams walked by every player sitting in the dugout to punch his arm. I had no idea he had anger like this in him. Wherever it came from, it sure worked. He picked out a Flint Rhem fastball to start he 6th and creamed it over the pavilion in right. Wrightstone then got plunked, and Wilson hit one out to Douthit in center, who dropped the ball. Mokan singled in two. Carlson doubled with one out, Harper tripled in two more, and Johnny Stuart took over on the mound for them.

It didn't help. Heinie singled, the Incredible Holke bombed another homer, and we had eight runs and an 11-5 lead! There was lots of huzzahs in the dugout, and everyone was looking forward to the train party tonight, but Fletcher reminded us we still had a game to win.

Boy, was he ever right. The Cards got two runs back right away and one in the 7th, and the score was then 11-8. Ray Blades tripled to start the St. Louis 8th, and Steineder took over for Huck Betts, who had relieved Carlson. But Ray was worse then awful. Hornsby walked right away, and Bottomley sent his second smash of the game over the fence for three runs and an 11-11 tie!

Jesse Fowler came in for the Cards, and people haven't been hitting him all year. Sure enough, a Ford double was the only thing we got off him for the last four innings. Steineder did his best for us, but it was a lost battle. With one out in the 11th, he walked Fowler, and Toporcer and Douthit singled to give them the exciting and sickening win.

Lucky for us, Mokan had bought some gin bottles from someone in town, so we were deep into those before the train pulled out of Missouri. It'll be nice to have a full train day tomorrow, because after going a crummy 6-14 on this trip we all could use one.

PHI 201 008 000 00 - 11 13 3
STL 001 222 130 01 - 12 19 2

RIDING HOME WITH A DEEP CY
July 24, 1924
My head was foggier than the stuff we saw from our train windows this

morning. After yesterday's ridiculous 12-11 loss in St. Louis, we had a full day of travel to flush it out of our brains, and it all started when Cy Williams roused me out of my upper berth and invited me to have breakfast with him.

Cy hasn't had as good a power season as he did in 1923, when he hit 41 clouts, but I didn't realize until he made Wrightstone apologize to me that he's really the quiet leader of our club house. He's over six feet tall with a hard but friendly face, and he looks right in your eyes when he talks so you tend to listen.

We had one of those fancy dining cars again with white tablecloths and fresh flower vases, and we ordered steak and swiss cheese omelettes and potatoes with herbs on them and grapefruit juice which I never get to have, and the other players sitting around us stayed clear the whole time. Cy asked me about my family and what I planned to do after the season ended so I told him about Papa dying in the War and my plans to marry Rachel if I ever got around to asking her father, and so on. He laughed, said that "baseball and wives aren't always the best marriage," and I said don't I know that already from seeing how some of the married players carry on.

Cy perked up all of a sudden as we entered Indiana because he's from a town there called Wadena. He went to Notre Dame and studied architecture, of all things, and even played football with Knute Rockne before the Cubs drafted him for baseball. I had no idea he was so smart, and I guess you learn stuff like that about athlete people when you have a meal with them. He told me how important it was to learn a trade you can make money at it in case your "fun job" never pays off, and asked how much I liked batboying. I said except for the last few days, an awful lot, and he went on to tell me about how you had to be careful not to make enemies of anyone and just do what I was supposed to do day in and day out.

By the time the meal ended I was a little sick of all the lecturing, and joined him and some of the players in the smoking car for some poker. I did my usual losing, and it was horrible-hot so Henline and Ford set up a big cake of ice at one end of the car and blew it in our direction with a fan.

"Did you tell Vinny about the shoe thief yet?" Harper suddenly asked Cy, and Williams leaned over and told me that some joker on the train had been stealing some of the players' shoes at night, so tonight it would be my turn to stand guard and watch for anything suspicious.

That sounded exciting, so when midnight rolled around there I was hiding inside the rest room in the front sleeping car, waiting for the snatcher with a knife in my pocket I'd grabbed from the dining car. Benny would sure enjoy this, I thought, except I kept nodding off and had to splash cold water in my face a bunch of times.

Finally around 1 a.m. I heard a noise in the hall, looked out and could see this shadowy figure reaching into one berth after another to take the players' shoes! "HA!" I yelled, jumped out of the bathroom, and knocked the guy against the wall.

It was one of the colored porters, as surprised as I was, and every sleeping player in the car had woken up to stick out their heads and laugh at us. Players leave their shoes out every night for the porters to collect and polish, and here I was holding a butter knife to the poor guy's throat.

Thanks a lot, Cy. Mr. club house leader. I'll get you back somehow.

BACK IN THE CITY OF MOTHERLY LOVE
July 25, 1924

We pulled into Broad Street Station late last night and Mama was there to hug the stuffing out of me, the first time she'd actually been there to greet me from a trip. I guess she missed me more than usual, probably because I stupidly didn't write her any letters. I guess what Cy told me yesterday about baseball not being good for marriages can also be said about mothers and sons.

Anyway it was good to be back in a bed that didn't roll, and eat Mama's oatmeal and spiced eggs again. She asked me about Rachel a half dozen times before I got out the door and I said I'd write her again soon. I think Mama's nervous about me marrying myself off and would rather have me around for a while, but until I actually talk to Rachel's father there's no sense even worrying about that.

Baker Bowl never looked so good, the horrible heat was gone and a decent crowd of five thousand or so fans were there to welcome us back from our long, tough trip.

And then we thanked them by playing like circus clowns again.

Joe Oeschger was the ringmaster, and he threw a walk out to Friberg with one out in the first. Grantham then tripled down in the right corner for one run, Oesch kicked a grounder halfway to the street for another, and the mauling was on. Hack Miller bombed one over the bleachers to make it 4-0 in the 3rd, and three runs with the help of Oeschie's second error made it 7-0 in the 5th.

Meantime we were busy getting no hits off Vic Aldridge for the first four innings. Mokan started the 5th with a line single, but then Ford erased him right away with a popout double play. What a bad comedy all around. Glazner took over for Oesch and spat up three more Cub runs in the 7th before Clarence Mitchell gave them a few more in the 9th.

So here we were down 12-0, half the fans already hurrying home, we were about to go ten games behind Chicago in the losses column, making our bet to finish in front of them another stupid dream, and I looked at our blue dugout and suddenly yelled, "C'mon guys!!"

They looked at me like I was in a strait jacket. "C'mon what?" asked Harper. "We can't let these dopes shut us out, right? We gotta take something into tomorrow!" Hod Ford shouted out "I'm game!" grabbed his bat out of my hands and ran up to the plate. Aldridge threw and Hod whacked it into left for a single. So did pinch-hitter Schultz. The dugout was alive again. Harper drove one high and deep to Heathcote in center but after he caught it both runners advanced. Heinie swung as hard as he could three times but whiffed, and with two outs, here came the Incredible Holke.

"No shutout!" yelled Cy from the on-deck spot, and whaddya know! Holke ripped the ball over Grantham's head for a two-run single. Ford and Schultz got pounded on the back when they came in while the Cubs just stood out there tryng not to laugh at us. But we sure as hell didn't care. Cy singled just then and Wrightstone rolled out to end the thing, but we'd showed 'em how tough we can be when we put our minds to it, even if just for ten minutes.

Afterwards I got a new cigar for my inspiring from Harper, and even Art Fletcher shook my hand. Maybe I should try and be a coach or manager when my batboy career is over.

CHI 202 030 302 - 12 20 0
PHI 000 000 002 - 2 7 3

A JOURNAL OF DESPAIR AND ELATION
July 25, 1924

by C.J. Butterworth
A Reporter Bound to No One

The call of an annoying blue jay woke me at dawn. The musty folded blanket I had been sleeping on these two days now had spiders darting across it, and I jumped to my feet in the chill, lake-dampened air.

For a moment or two I had forgotten where I was, and why I had come to this isolated spot, and then it all returned to my head: the train ride from Boston, the hike up to the lake from Dorset village, the wonderful quiet and lampless nights in my found cabin.

But loneliness and hunger then settled in, and yesterday morning I trudged back to Nutter's Sundries for a bit more food and human conversation.

Two men in suits, looking quite lawful, stood on Nutter's porch talking to him. I knew they were searching for me, that I'd be snatched and returned to the torments of daily baseball reportage in no time. I had to flee, and quietly slipped back up the mountain path.

Imagine my dread, then, to reach the cabin again and find its rightful owner, a stocky Vermonter and his teenage son, hauling supplies through its front door from their small truck. They both had hunting rifles. It was only a matter of seconds before they found my belongings...

Deeper into the woods I went. The trail switched back and forth over a series of ridges, and before long I was in an even more remote valley. Deer pranced by, beavers worked away at a stream, and for a time I marveled at the sights and sounds nature was providing.

But my hunger was genuine. I tried a few berries along the path but they tasted foul and I spit them out. If I had a hunting instinct I imagine I could have throttled a furry forest inhabitant and dined on its meat and innards, but outdoorsmanship has never been my forte.

So I walked on...and on. The sun climbed in the humid sky, and I wished I had filled something with stream water earlier. The bugs here were insufferable, and I soon found myself scratching small lumps on every inch of my body.

To say I was lost would be understated. Thick black clouds rolled in, making it impossible to tell which direction I was even moving. Then a summer thunderstorm hit, deafening and deadly, and I sheltered myself in a grove of birch trees. A lightning bolt cleaved one in two just yards away, and I covered my head, burrowed under an embankment and wept for myself.

It was Bonnie's darling face that kept me alive, that gave me the strength I needed to endure the ferocious storm. She was states away, pouring her heart out to me, wishing and praying for my safe return. How could I ever do myself in like this? Groveling in mud like a young peccary?

The thunderstorm rolled on ten minutes later, and spots of sun made the woods around me glisten. I rose, sopping wet, and walked on.

The mosquitoes were back in force after the rain, attacking me from all sides. I staggered in what seemed by the returning shadows, a northerly direction. My throat was parched, my stomach screaming for substance. I reached the edge of a vast open clearing that seemed larger than an ocean, staggered and fell. In my delirium I thought of Thoreau, and words he wrote at Walden Pond:

> I have heard of a man lost in the woods and dying of famine and exhaustion at the foot of a tree, whose loneliness was relieved by the grotesque visions with which, owing to bodily weakness, his diseased imagination surrounded him, and which he believed to be real.

And here I was eighty years later...his inspiration. Soon to be dinner for squirrels and a colony of ants. I lay on my back and stared up at the mocking clouds, waiting for my merciful end.

Then the buzzing of bugs and caws of pestering birds suddenly receded, and a new sound filled the heavy air.

The crack of a wooden bat.

I painfully sat up, looked around the high grass. Boisterous male shouting followed. Someone yelled "Don't stop, Rudy!" I rose to my feet, moved in the direction of the sounds. There was a second, even louder wooden crack, the shouts returned, and something fell with a thud nearby. I walked a few more steps to the edge of the high grass, and nearly tripped over something.

A scuffed baseball. Instantly a gaunt young man in bare feet and farmer's overalls bounded into the grass, out of breath, a worn brown mitt on one hand. He looked at me oddly for a moment, then yelled "Toss it!" and I scooped up the ball, threw it to him. He turned, hurled it back in the direction of a sandy home plate area with incredible force, but the opposing hitter had already rounded the bases.

It was a collection of local men, mostly farmers, having an uproarious game of ball in a flattened, tree-lined pasture. Emptied flour sacks served as bases, and home plate was an overturned metal pie cooker.

In a flash I had forgotten my hunger and thirst, my idiotic flight from daily responsibilities and the Tigers' futile pennant struggle. These men were not playing for flags or cash or a city's hopes, but for the sheer enjoyment of the game. It was a revelation, and I made my way around to the home plate area, where a farmer's wife gave me a cool washcloth, poured me a giant glass of lemonade and fed me a chicken leg.

It was the most enjoyable ball game I'd ever witnessed, and I had no stake in the outcome. One of the men crouched down and asked who I was and where I came from. I stared at him a very long time and then said, "I am a writer of baseball games."

A FINE BUNCH OF CLOUTS
July 26, 1924

Okay, enough of this already. The Phillies had lost six games in a row, and hadn't won since we beat the Cubs 5-3 nine days ago in Chicago. Heck, me and Benny had even been kidnapped by Al Capone's men and ridden to Indiana on a smuggler's boat.

Well, luck finally showed up today for us in the personing of Vic Keen. With his crummy 6-13 record, the Cubs hurler has loads of talent but never seems to catch a break. Ring is the same kind of black cat pitcher for us, but Johnny Couch was going instead so I knew we had a chance.

The players all have their own ways to fend off the spooks, though. Mokan always stops to grind his shoe into the foul line chalk when he runs out to left field. Holke starts wearing his underwear inside out whenever we lose three straight, and even Art Fletcher puts a dollar bill under his cap if we have a lead in the 9th. I personally don't believe in that stuff, and got no problem walking under a ladder on 13th Street on Halloween night, but I can see why baseball people do it, because sometimes there's almost fifteen seconds between pitches and they get a lot of time to think about things.

That blabbermouth catcher Hartnett got things going for the Cubs today with his 21st homer in the 2nd inning, but doubles from Wrightstone and Ford got the run right back. Then it was high time for Cy Time. After Heinie singled with one out in the 3rd, Williams crushed a Keen lob over the Lifebuoy sign in right and we had a 3-1 lead! We were all kind of expecting for Chicago to jump on us then, because like most teams, Baker Bowl is sort of an easy firing range, but a 1-run shot by Hack Miller was all Couch gave them for the next five innings.

It was another beautiful afternoon without too much humidness, so the players had more energy than usual. Especially Cy. In the 5th with one out, he knocked another ball out of the park, his 17th smash of the year. Couch nearly did the same thing but doubled instead to begin the 6th, and then Harper blasted a ball toward Delaware and it was 6-2! It was a good-sized Saturday crowd watching all this, and when they realized they might have an actual win to watch they got even louder.

Harper promised Cy he would hit a second homer, too, and off Guy Bush in the 7th he did exactly that, knocking the thing the other way into the left bleachers and making the place cuckoo! It was like we'd won the pennant. Of our sixteen hits, over half of them were for extra bases, and it was nice to get some decent pitching for a change. Sticking Couch in our pitching rotation and kicking out Glazner was the smartest thing Fletcher's done all year.

After the game I passed up going out for trouble with some of the players because Mama was baking manicotti, but I missed not having Benny around to stop off at Mort's with. I wonder, is he still out in the midwest fishing around for money for that colored game idea? Soon as I get a chance I'll have to write Roy a letter, because he's too poor to have a telephone.

CHI 010 100 001 - 3 8 0
PHI 012 012 21x - 8 16 0

NATIONAL LEAGUE through Saturday, July 26, 1924

Pittsburgh	61	33	.649	—
Cincinnati	58	40	.592	5
New York	55	40	.579	6.5
Brooklyn	55	43	.561	8
St. Louis	50	46	.521	12
Chicago	44	52	.458	18
PHILLIES	37	61	.378	26
Boston	26	71	.268	36.5

From July 26, 1924 edition of the Detroit Free-Enterprise:

HATS OFF TO OUR BRAVE BUTTERWORTH!
MISSING BALL SCRIBE RETURNS TO NAVIN PRESS DUTIES AFTER NARROW ESCAPE FROM NEW ENGLAND WILDERNESS

By Percival Q. Mellon, Publisher

It is with unbridled joy this publisher announces the miraculous return of our esteemed Tigers reporter Calvin Jedediah Butterworth. Following a three-day nightmare of thirst, famine, deadly insects and torturous solitude in a wild, largely uninhabited region of Vermont, Mr. Butterworth has returned to the bosom of his family and the eager eyes of his breathlessly waiting readers.

Before today's home-stand opener with Philadelphia at Navin Field, he was introduced to the overflowing crowd and received a thunderous standing ovation, usually reserved for heads of state or a command Stravinsky performance. So many straw boaters were tossed on the field that the start of the contest was delayed at least fifteen minutes while they were collected.

TAKING CARE OF DREAM BUSINESS
July 27, 1924

Dear Roy:
Hello again. Is it still swelteringly hot out in St. Louis? It's real nice to be

back here and only having to change shirts once each day instead of three times.

Is my friend Benny still there? He said you and him and maybe your brother in Chicago were going to try and get some money from business people or whoever to help stage some exhibition ball between some white major league players and a bunch of colored ones, but I haven't heard from him since I left on the Phillies train so I was just wondering.

I still think it's a great idea, though as you could tell when you stepped into our club house out there, it's going to take some convincing of most of these players to look at you people as their equals, even as athletic types. I have gotten to know some of the Phillies well, but none of the ones who seem to hate black people, so I hope you guys can raise enough money to pay them well and shut their traps.

Anyway, if Benny is with you or you can reach him, tell him to write or telegram me. Thanks!

—Vinny S.

Dear Rachel:

I had this weird dream the other night that the Phillies were playing in a future World Series against the Yankees and I was around 100 years old and you were sitting with me at a ball field where they were actually playing at night. It all seemed so real and amazing that I think I'll go to sleep early for a few days and try to get back there...

So I just returned from my first batboy road trip, and I guess I survived or I wouldn't be writing this. The Phillies are off today for church reasons again, which is too bad because we finally won a game yesterday with a whole bunch of home runs and it's not a good thing to take a break when you're just starting to play well.

Not that it matters. We're stuck like glue in seventh place now, probably for the rest of the year unless the Cubs break their legs or the Braves grow some arms. At least your Robins are still fighting for something, which makes going to Ebbets more than just a day in the sunshine for you. Hopefully I'll be able to join you for another game there soon.

Which brings me to more romantic things. Even though you haven't seen me in a while, I do hope our secret engagement is still a real thing, and that you still think of me as warmly as I do to you. There were many times on our road trip when I could have enjoyed an illegal drink with a local miss, but purposely did not. You would have liked riding the train around with us, though it probably would have been too cramped in my sleeping berth for two of us.

I know I still haven't talked to your father about our marriage plans, but I promise I'll do that in person as soon as possible so we can start talking about planning what we will do.

Write back to me please, so I can cherish the words.

With love and all that,

—Vinny

WESTERN UNION TELEGRAM
To: SAUL STONE
From: VINNY SPANELLI

DEAR MR. STONE:
AM BACK FROM FIRST BATBOY TRIP. WOULD LIKE TO HAVE PERSON-
AL TALK WITH YOU BUT CAN'T GET AWAY UNTIL HOME STAND WITH
WEST TEAMS IS OVER. SUGGEST WEDNESDAY AUGUST 13. I WILL BUY
YOU LUNCH.

SINCERELY, VINNY S.

DUEL OF THE DUNCES
July 28, 1924

Who on earth can find entertainment in watching two crummy teams
out-stink each other on a muggy afternoon in late July? Me, that's who.

Tony Kaufmann for the Cubs and Jimmy Ring for us have been two of
the sorriest pitching specimens all year in the National League, because
they both have talent enough to win but never seem to. With Tony's 3-9
mark going against Jimmy's 4-12 today and almost every ball popping out
of Baker Bowl at batting practice, it was going to be a long day for me.

It was going to be longer for the players, though, and Harper got a side
bet going with Cliff Heathcote on Chicago for a steak dinner. We already
had a losing bet that we'd finish ahead of these guys, but Harper never
knows when to stop.

And Heathcote must've not eaten breakfast or lunch, because he ripped
a single off Ring to start the game, got singled over to third by Grimes and
homered in by Hack Miller and we were down 3-0 just like that. And Ring
was more worthless than he usually is. With a guy on first and two outs in
the 2nd, he walked Heathcote, Friberg, and Grantham. Grimes and Miller
then singled in a row and he hit Hartnett before finally getting out of the
mess down 7-0.

Every Phillie hitter was mad. They were snatching their bats out of my
hands so fast I was getting blisters. At least they started to put them to
some use. Holke bombed one over the right fence in the 4th, before two singles, two walks and a plunked batter got us three runs back. A bases-filled
walk to Friberg made it 8-3 them, but then we started smoking. Harper
began our 5th with a double, Sand singled him to third, Cy tripled deep to
center for two runs and a Wrightstone grounder scored another and it was
suddenly 8-6!

Ring finally threw a 1-2-3 inning in the 6th, and our dugout was hopping. Ford got his third single with one out and went to second when Grantham chucked it away. Ring zipped a double down the line, Harper got him
to third with a hit and none else but Heinie Sand poked a single into left to
tie the game! Harper could taste that sirloin as he raced home to try and
give us the lead on a Holke fly to center, but guess who shot him down at
home plate with a cannon throw? Cliff Heathcote. Grrrr.

When you lose your last out at home something bad seems to happen right away, and it sure did. Weis doubled to begin the 7th, Hollocher singled him in and we were behind again. Steineder finally relieved to put Ring out of his misery in the 8th but he wasn't much better, giving up a triple to Hartnett and three straight walks to make it 10-8. Mokan cracked one into the bleachers to bring us close again, but Kaufmann took care of us in the 9th and as usual at Baker, we'd gotten 15 hits and nine runs and still lost.

I wasn't even the one having to foot a steak bill after the game, but I have no interest in eating cow for a while.

CHI 340 010 110 - 10 16 2
PHI 000 332 010 - 9 15 0

From July 28, 1924 edition of the Detroit Free-Enterprise:

PUBLISHER'S NOTE: It is with new regret that the Free-Enterprise announces the immediate suspension of base ball reporter Calvin Jedediah Butterworth. As evidenced by his flighty approach in yesterday's "game story," by his adamant refusal to write in the past tense favored by all trustworthy press men, and by his rebellious behavior when questioned by his superior editors on the above matters, it is apparent that his recent wanderings in the wild state of Vermont have irreparably impaired his reporting faculties, and he can no longer

AND THE FANS SHALL DECIDE!!
July 28, 1924

By C.J. Butterworth
Base Ball Writer of the People

Publishers! Editors! Who needs these blind, bloated buffoons? Followers of this glorious game hunger for freshness and daring in their daily accounts, not stodgy, predictable grammar lessons! Some dark day the newspaper form could perish altogether, and it is the craftsmen with vision, the ones who speak for the ordinary base ball fan, who will survive.

OKAY, SO THE PHILLIES STINK
July 29, 1924

Not that I thought we'd be able to beat old Pete Alexander today, but the guy is a famous drunkard and all. The older Phillie fans who remember what he did to get us to the '15 World Series gave him rousing cheers as usual, though after Cy singled in a run off him in the 1st, then bashed a 3-run homer off him in the 3rd we were up 4-2 for Bill Hubbell. Heinie even chipped in with a scoring fly in the next inning to make it 5-2, and it seemed like we'd be sending the dumb Cubbies out of town with a loss.

But things haven't been going our way since around April. Hollocher hit a sacrifice fly in the 6th, and three Chicago singles and a ground ball in the 7th tied the game 5-5. Huck Betts relieved because Steineder is exhausted and Fletcher doesn't trust Clarence Mitchell to hold a baseball, let alone throw one.

Betts is anything but a sure bet, though. Weak little Hollocher popped a homer over the Lifebuoy sign to begin the 8th, Grantham tripled home another, Grimes fired his second cannon shot of the game into the left bleachers and that was all I wrote. Meanwhile, after Heinie's scoring fly way back when, old Drunk Pete put his sauce away and plowed through our lineup like a hell preacher for the last five innings, giving us nothing but a Harper single and Mokan walk.

There were the typical angry players and knocked-over food after the game, and now we get Hornsby and the Cardinals for a nice long visit, a team much hotter than the Cubs. Looks like I'll need a new reason to smile pretty soon.

CHI 011 001 240 - 9 15 0
PHI 103 100 000 - 5 7 0

LADIES DAY, AND THEN SOME
July 30, 1924

It was the first Ladies Day I ever batboyed for, and let me tell you, it's pretty different from sitting in the stands. So many of the players peek out to eye-sample the girl pickings it's a wonder they don't get conked on the head by foul balls.

"Section 12, fourth row!" yelled Henline down the bench to Ford, who picked up a small pair of field glasses probably meant for operas and squinted at whoever Butch was talking about. "Eyes on the ballgame, fellas!" shouted Fletcher, but only because he was being paid to do it. I caught him peering out of the dugout at least five times during the game.

But the real shocker came when I finished getting our bats back in order after the scoreless 1st inning. I took a peek behind the dugout right after our starters ran back on the field, and there's Mama, sitting there knitting a sweater! "Hi there, Vinny!" she said with a big nutty smile. I told her I thought she didn't even like baseball and she said she didn't but she was missing me since I got this job and wanted to see what I actually do here all day and the tickets were half price so...

So I spent the entire day answering her dopey baseball questions and being ribbed by the Phillie players.

Thankfully there was a game going on I could try and distract myself with. Carlson gave the Cards a 2nd inning run on a Bottomley double (him again!) and single by Max Flack, but Mokan bombed one off Rhem in the 3rd to tie it up. After a Bottomley walk and Clemons double in the 4th, Flack scored Sunny Jim with a deep fly, which got Mama asking "How can he run home if the fielder caught it?" about four times until I had a headache. Usually I stand just outside our dugout so I can run up to home plate and grab the tossed bats, but today I just tried to stay clear of Mama.

We strung a great rally together in the 4th, though. Cy singled to begin, Wrightstone got him to third with another single and Wilson walked. "Who's that tall one on the third base?" asked Mama, and I said it was Cy Williams, our best player. "Ohh!" she said, and stopped knitting to stare at him. Seconds later Mokan got him and Wrightstone home with a single and we had a 3-2 lead. "Yay Cy!!' Mama yelled, like he had done something important, and I swear I saw Cy wink at her as he jogged into the dugout.

A crappy Wrightstone error in the 6th helped the Cards go back on top, and then a ball squirted past Wilson behind the plate to make it 5-3 St. Louis in the 7th, and the crowd got quiet again.

Not Mama though. "Swing those things, Phillie boys!" I swear she yelled, making our bench whistle and laugh and turning my face the color of tomato sauce. "How much did you pay your mother to do this?" Holke asked me, which got everyone cracking up even more.

But we suddenly started hitting again. Schultz pinch-hit a single. Harper singled. Heinie ran up there, still chuckling, beat out an infield hit and when Cooney threw the ball into the stands both runners scored to tie the game! The play got him to third, ladies were screaming all around us, and with Cy coming back up against relief man Stuart, Mama was standing on her chair and waving her knitting needles. Cy turned, gave her a nod, and whacked a ball deep the opposite way. Left fielder Blades caught the ball but Heinie ran in to give us the lead!

This time Huck Betts was relaxed and perfect, retired all five Cards he faced, even hitless Hornsby to end the game, and we'd opened the series in winning style.

The players all patted my back after and thanked me for bringing "Good Luck Mama" to the game and I went along with it. By the time I got home after stopping at Mort's for the other scores, the house was empty, and there on the kitchen table was a note next to some leftover sandwich meat:

YOUR FRIEND CY TOOK ME OUT FOR DINNER AND A SHOW. HELP YOUR-SELF!   —Mama

Oh boy...

STL 010 102 100 - 5 9 3
PHI 001 200 30x - 6 8 2

ANYBODY FOR SOME TRENCH BALL?

July 31, 1924

Thank God Mama got home before ten o'clock last night and with her clothes still unwrinkled, otherwise I don't know how I could've walked into the Baker Bowl club house today. Cy Williams staying out all night with my mother? I wouldn't know whether to grin about it or find a gun.

Speaking of guns, today we had one of those games where you're being barraged with one hit after another for nine straight innings. I can only imagine what those trenches were like in Europe for poor Papa during the War but they must have been like this, except with deadly shells and mustard gas instead of doubles and the stuff you put on pretzels.

We know Oeschger's always in trouble, but Sothoron usually pitches okay for St. Louis so he was the surprise stinker. Good old Cy, in a happier mood than I've ever seen him, smacked a long homer shot in the 1st to put us up 3-0, and after five Card hits and two runs in the 2nd, we got two more on four singles and the second passed ball of the game by their catcher Clemons.

Oeschie's arm must've been made out of gunpowder, because the Cards seemed like they were getting three or four hits every inning. The problem was that Steineder and Betts had been overused by Fletcher the last few days and really had to rest. All we had were terrible Glazner and ridiculous Mitchell to bail us out. Sure enough, a Flack triple and Cooney single got them two runs in the 5th, before singles from Smith, Hornsby and Bottomley tied the game 5-5 in the 6th.

I kept looking around for Mama back in her front row seat, but she never made it. She was still sleeping this morning when I got up and made my own breakfast, but Cy did just fine without her watching him all afternoon. His single was one of five straight hits we began our 7th with, and four runs later we were up 9-5 and looking good.

Except Oeschie was still out there. He walked the first guy in the 8th, booted a grounder, and then Fletcher put Glazner in anyway. Two singles and a deep fly came right away, and it was 9-8!

Miracles can even happen on a sleepy Thursday in July, though. Whitey whiffed the scary Ray Blades to begin the 9th. The not-so-mighty-lately Hornsby and Bottomley both rolled out and we'd pulled off a second straight squeaky win!

St. Louis had fired off 20 hits, and if baseball players ever wore helmets we'd have a bunch of dents in ours. The Cards also left 16 runners on the bases, which is a good reason why they can't seem to get higher than fifth place.

STL 020 021 030 - 8 20 0
PHI 320 000 40x - 9 15 2

PART FIVE
August

A MORNING SURPRISE AND AFTERNOON DELIGHT
August 1, 1924

Me and Mama both got woken up this morning by an auto horn honking its head off. I stuck my head out my bedroom window and who do I
see down in the street? Good old Benny! Sitting with Roy in the front seat
of a fancy topless car, both dressed like traveling wiseacres and smoking
cigars.

"Breakfast's on us, kid!" he shouted, and in seconds I was throwing on a
shirt and overalls.

It was about a week since Benny had stayed behind to try and cough up
money for a colored vs. white players exhibition game, and by the looks of
his rented car and new duds I figured he had a bit of luck. Except Benny
was in a mischief mood and wouldn't tell me dirt until we got to some little
restaurant uptown where our "guest" was meeting us.

Lizzie Mae's was a homey little breakfast spot in a mostly colored neighborhood, and when we got there, a huge, friendly-faced colored man in a suit
and tweed cap was waiting for us in a large back booth. I thought I recognized him from a photo once but wasn't really sure, but when he introduced
himself as Rube Foster everything clicked into place for me. Rube was the
same Foster who ran the Negro National League and the Chicago American
Giants, and he used to pitch, and here he was buying us flapjacks and eggs
and fat bacon strips and whatever the heck else we wanted.

Like most people involved with colored baseball, he'd been wanting to
see how some of the black-skinned players would fare against some of the
whites. Benny and Roy and Roy's brother in Chicago had spent the last
week tracking Rube down and talking him into bankrolling a game, and
now it was all set. All he needed was an "inside person" like me to get the
word out to the Phillie players. I said none of them would probably do it
and he said for the right amount of cash a ballplayer will do anything.

They even had a place and time all set up. A week from this Sunday, on
August 10, only four National League teams play, and the Phillies aren't
one of them. It seems that Foster made a deal with people in Pittsburgh
and with Ed Bolden of the Eastern Colored League to book either Forbes
Field or Hilldale Park in Darby for the entire day and into the night.

That's right, the night. They know a way to rig up electrical generators
and searchlights like they have outside motion picture theaters, and with
most ball games being less than two hours, there's a good chance the players can have at each other three times. The only thing I needed to do was
keep everything secret, because of the baseball commissioner ever found
out he might try and shut the whole thing down.

So my brain was doing somersaults all day at Baker Bowl as I tied to
figure out who to talk to. Heinie seemed like the right person but he wasn't
close to a great player, and even though I didn't even know who the colored team was going to be yet, I knew he wouldn't stand a chance against
them.

Either way, it had to wait till after our game with the Cards, Ray Blades
got it going for them with a 2-run poke off Jimmy Ring in the 1st. Ring gave

them two singles and a walk to start the 3rd, but then whiffed the slumpy Hornsby and got killer Bottomley to rap into a double play! From there Jimmy became a classical music conductor and put them to sleep.

Meantime, we were pecking away at Bill Sherdel, with single runs in the 2nd, 3rd, and 4th and a monster of a 3-run bash by Jimmie Wilson in the 5th to put us up 6-2! I was glad because I could crouch there by the bat rack and go over my upcoming words to Heinie for the rest of the day. Ring gave up only one more hit, a pinch single to Les Bell, and might've had his best start of the year. The other good news is that the Cubs lost again, and we picked up more ground on them.

So there I was leaving the club house with Heinie afterwards. As I figured, he thought I was completely nuts for bringing up an idea as crackers as an exhibition game with coloreds, but when I mentioned that Rube Foster was in town and had the cash to do this, he got a lot more excited and said he'd bring it up with a few of the less-dumb Phillie players later on.

I found Benny down at Mort's, buying cigars and drinks for his cronies, and told him what Heinie was doing, and that it might be a good idea to save whatever cash Rube had given him because we might need it. Knowing how fast he lost his dead uncle's money earlier this year, it seemed an important thing to do. Good night if I can sleep!

STL 200 000 000 - 2 5 1
PHI 011 131 01x - 8 12 1

TRIPLE SPECS AND A BUNCH OF SUSPENSE
August 2, 1924

At breakfast Mama was more interested in asking me Cy Williams questions than eating. Is he married? Does he drink bootleg liquor? Is he nice to the other players? That sort of thing. I had nothing to tell her and wasn't interested anyway because my head was spinning with dark thoughts about this upcoming exhibition game Benny and me and Roy got involved in. Heinie Sand was supposed to talk to some of the Phillie players about it last night, and after the horrible day in St.Louis when Roy got kicked out of the club house for stupid racism reasons I didn't know what to expect when I got to the park today.

For that reason I took my time getting there, and dressed and set up the bats when everyone but Frank Parkinson was already on the field, and I made sure he was in the toilet first. The weather had gotten all humid again, and some of the players were shagging balls with wet cloths around their necks.

And none of them were talking to me. I finally cornered Heinie when he ran in from infield practice and when I asked how it went his voice got real quiet and he just said, "Somebody's gonna talk to you later." Oh great, big bigots Harper and Wrightstone were going to play the piano on my face and stuff me in a locker or something.

Good thing I had a ball game to watch and try not to think about this. It was a typical swatting party between these two teams, and skinny, glasses-wearing Specs Toporcer got it going for the Cards with a deep and loud triple on Johnny Couch's first pitch. Specs was already 8-for-13 in the series before this and Jack Smith knocked him in right away with a single. A Smith single, Hornsby double and scoring Bottomley fly made it 2-0 in the 3rd, and when Specs came up with a guy on second and two outs in the 4th, I could hear Benny yelling "You stink Four-Eyes!!" at him all the way from the left field bleachers.

Four-Eyes whistled a second triple over Cy's head right then to shut Benny up, scored on a third Smith single and it was 4-0 for St. Loo. We started hitting Jesse Haines in the last of the 4th, a guy who never looks sharp but somehow has a 12-5 record. This game showed why, because every time we put runs on the scoreboard they piled on more of their own. It was a Cardinal triples festival, as Hornsby and Bottomley both whacked 3-bag hits to begin the 5th, before Max Flack doubled in two more in the 7th.

Wilson knocked in two for us with a triple of his own in the 8th, and when the base path smoke cleared we were down 10-8. All this did, though, was bring on tough reliever Jesse Fowler, who after giving up a single and three straight walks got our last four guys to ice the day.

It was a rough one to lose on such a broiling day, and nobody felt like talking about anything afterwards, let alone colored ballplayers. Hod Ford walked right into the shower with his whole uniform on. I kept my head down while I cleaned up the place, waiting for a big hand to yank me aside, but it was just a bunch of thick suspense in there.

When I finally washed up, put my regular clothes back on and stepped outside, who was standing outside the door but Cy Williams. He smiled and jabbed me in the arm. "Heard about this big colored game you got going. If he's good on that cash, count us in."

I could barely talk. "Count WHO in?" I asked.

"Who do you think?" he said. "Me and Rajah. Let's get together on the day off tomorrow and talk about it." And he walked away.

Rajah? Did he mean Rogers Hornsby? The best dang hitter in the league?? I don't remember how I made it home.

STL 101 210 320 - 10 17 1
PHL 000 220 040 - 8 12 1

NATIONAL LEAGUE through Saturday, August 2, 1924

Pittsburgh	65	35	.650	—
Cincinnati	62	43	.590	5.5
Brooklyn	61	44	.581	6.5
New York	58	44	.569	8
St. Louis	53	50	.515	13.5
Chicago	46	56	.451	20
PHILLIES	40	64	.385	27
Boston	27	76	.262	39.5

TABLE FOR SIX, PLANS FOR TWO DOZEN
August 3, 1924

It was Mama's nutty idea. "There's no ball game today, right? So why not invite your friend Cy over for late breakfast or early lunch? Benny can come, too, and also those negro men you've been talking about."

She of course meant our friend Roy from St. Louis and Rube Foster. Cy Williams did tell me he wanted to get together, so why not give it a try? All Mama had to do was control herself around Cy and it would probably go fine, and our kitchen was probably the best place in town to meet and not be bugged in.

So I got a hold of Cy through Heinie and set the whole meal up for ten-thirty in the morning. What we didn't figure on, though, was Rube being almost an hour and a half late because he was in a negro church somewhere across town. That was sure fine with Mama, who got extra time to sit in the parlor with Cy and make eyes at him. I had to keep reminding her that things on the stove were burning and boiling in order to keep my head on straight.

Mama had baked hot muffins and fried eggs and bacon and even cooked a big pot of oatmeal. Rube was starved by the time he showed up, but the second he joined us at the table he took one look at the Cream of Wheat box with the old-time negro cook on the front and almost walked back out the door! "That's just the junk I've been tryin' to change!" he said, and Roy and Benny had to jump up and calm him down and lure him back to the table with a piece of Mama's yummy bacon. Mama apologized about six times and tossed the oatmeal box in the trash basket even though it still had a serving or two left.

And then we got down to this exhibition baseball business. I was dying to bring up what Cy said yesterday about Hornsby wanting to play, but kept the lid on the pot by asking Rube which colored players were on board so far. The big name I'd heard of was Oscar Charleston of the Indianapolis ABCs, who'd been around for almost ten years and could do anything on a ball field that was possible. Turkey Stearns of the Detroit Stars and Cool Papa Bell of the St. Louis ones were other fabulous outfielders who'd said yes, and some of the "hurricane-fast" pitchers I'd never heard of were Bullet Joe Rogan, Nip Winters and Smokey Joe Williams. Cy gave me a funny look about then, thinking the same thing I was, and said, "Well, all we got so far is Hornsby, so I'd better get on the telephone. Cuyler's coming into town this week to play us, so I can probably scratch his ear a bit." Benny couldn't believe what he was hearing, and didn't stop grinning and poking me for the rest of the meal.

It seemed more and more that we'd be using Hilldale Field in nearby Darby for the game, because one of the colored catchers Biz Mackey played on the Daisies team there, and he knew the Hilldale owner well. I asked how we'd be allowed to play on a Sunday with all the church laws in the state and Rube said they let that thing go in Darby sometimes and besides, ain't this thing gonna be secret?

Yeah, I thought, but this little secret idea was starting to blow up right in front of us, and I nervously poured myself another bowl of oatmeal. Mama kept coming over to refill Cy's coffee cup, asking how much money "my Vinny" can make on this. Rube only gave fuzzy answers about that, but I didn't care. We had a week to bring in as many good players as we could, and then if everything went okay we'd get to watch one of the best exhibitions ever played.

I asked Rube if I could batboy for both teams and he just laughed, swallowed down the last of his eggs and said, "Son, why you wanna batboy when can you be a damn coach?"

I don't even remember finishing my oatmeal.

BABES IN BAMBINOLAND
JOINING THE KNOTHOLE QUEST FOR HOMER BALL 30
August 3, 1924

By C. Jedediah Butterworth
Base Ball Freescriber

DETROIT—With Ruth and the Yankees back at Navin Field, and with my feelings for Tigers management still at a low ebb, why not take in today's game through the squinty eyes of our local "knothole gang"?

The St. Louis Cardinals began the first organized free admission for children in their bleacher section back in 1917, though it's been said that Abner Powell, owner of the New Orleans Pelicans in the 1880s, allowed city youth in for free once a week if they showed good behavior.

The Tiger knotholers are neither organized nor well-behaved. With the Bambino afoot, they are more like swarms of army ants, rabidly climbing over each other to gape through and under Navin Field's right field fence. A patrolman vainly attempts to keep the peace but gives up five minutes before game time to no doubt stroll a more peaceful neighborhood.

The gaggle of boys eye me with trepidation, imagining I must be one of their fathers, until I produce my writing pad and introduce myself. My guides for the afternoon will be Mickey from Warren Corner, scruffy of dress and hoarse of voice; "Brainy Eyes" Bradley from Highland Park, a slight boy in a white dress shirt with glasses thicker than hockey pucks that fog up in the heat every ten minutes, and the energized, hyena-laughing Beesum brothers, who hitch-hiked all the way to Detroit from Pontiac to see the Babe. Mickey seems to be the knothole veteran, the aficionado, so being new at this sport I tend to follow his lead.

"We're supposed to take turns looking through the holes, but with the Babe here, crap on that." he says. I ask him what he'll do if he somehow ends up with Ruth's 30th homer ball, and he says probably sell it to some other kid, or trade it to a man for cigarettes. "He's hit over fifty before, but he might not do that again, so this one has to be worth something. Hey! I was here first—" He shoves a blonde kid about three feet with one meaty hand, turns his cap around and peers through the prize hole. "Rip just took the mound!" he yells, and his junior disciples cheer.

The Yanks are back to playing the dull, ineffective ball they've been showing most of the season, but thankfully have their ace Pennock going against ours, Rip Collins. The Ripper is tied with Walter Johnson for the circuit lead with 16 wins, yet even the little rascals around me know that New York fares better against right-handers.

"Bambino's up!" Mickey shouts, and I'm suddenly drowning in boys. All available viewing portals are gone in seconds, a few new ones are created with pocket knives and fingers, and a handful of wee ones climb on each other's shoulders or risk leg abrasions by scaling telephone poles. Collins walks Ruth on four pitches, though, the throng deflates, and sanity returns to the sidewalk. "Rip's just afraid of the big dope," says one of the Beesums, which brings on a "Rip's not afraid of anybody! YOU'RE the dope!" from a nearby wag, and little fists are flying in seconds.

When the Babe jogs out to play right field, the kids go even more crazy, shouting encouragement at him until he apparently turns, says Mickey, and doffs his cap. The game must be a sterling hurler's duel in the early innings, for little crowd noise emits from the grandstand. So do frankfurter smells, though, and when a sausage roll street vendor rolls his wagon by between innings he is nearly attacked. Most of the boys have coins to spare for the much-needed nourishment, though I'm honored to help a few poorer-ones out of my own pocket.

Another mad rush to the knotholes occurs for Ruth's second at bat, and this time he reaches on a Collins boot but in true Yankee fashion gets stranded on base. On his third time up, though, a rally has been brewing. Ernie Johnson walks to fill the bases in the 5th with one out and bring on Dugan. "Jumpin' Joe at the plate!" yells Mickey, the signal for an imminent Ruth appearance. Dugan grounds into a force at home, bringing up the Bambino with a possible grand slam in the making. Shoving, kicking and squeals erupt, and Brainy Eyes Bradley somehow worms his way to a viewing hole.

"Strike one! A soft curve, I believe." he chirps, then "Ball one, high and outside and nearly off Woodall's mitt!" Two more balls follow, then a strike. Brainy Eyes has to pull off his glasses and wipe them off on his sweaty shirt again. "He hits it! A sharp grounder! And it's past O'Rourke for a single!" Groans fill the sidewalk air, and they have nothing to do with the 1-0 Yankee lead.

A Rigney double and Cobb's second single of the day tie the score 1-1 in the 6th, but when Ty is erased by Schang trying to nab second, curses never before heard by this writer out of budding mouths make me wince. Apparently Mr. Cobb also has his profane talons embedded in the younger set.

Ruth's fourth trip to the plate is a short fly to center, which has our gang briefly buzzing, but with the game moving to the last of the 8th, a new recipe for suspense is cooked. Pennock and Collins are locked in a classic low-score engagement, one not often seen between these thrashers, and it's the kind of affair not often appreciated by young fans. So after bribing Mickey with a hot, salty pretzel, I am allowed access to his prize spot for the Tigers' eighth scoring attempt.

I need to crouch to Mickey's level, and before long remove my jacket to set my knees on. The view takes in home plate and all of the infield, and I witness a Rigney walk and Cobb's third single to start things. Haney whiffs, but Heilman walks to fill the bases, and Manush moves to the plate. "Heinie with the bases loaded!" I announce, and my nose is pushed against the fence. The Tigers have hit very few home runs this year, so even the threat of one, particularly by a lefty, drives the knotholers into fevered anticipation.

I lodge my eye back into the hole just in time to see Manush swing viciously. The crack of bat is delayed a moment by my distance away, and I can make out the ball vanishing into the sky. Ruth turns, speeds to his right, disappears, and seconds later the grandstand explodes in cheers. "One run scores! Two! All three!" as Heinie slides into third with a triple! Little hands yank me away from the hole, and some child I can't see announces Woodall's single to make it 5-1 Detroit. Beall finally replaces the battered Pennock...

...and then the unthinkable happens. "Pratt hits one deep to left!!" yells a Beemus, "Oh geez, it's outta here!!!" The swarm leaps away from the fence as if hit with an electric charge, scampers en masse down Trumbull and around to National Drive. I give chase, weaving around tiny legs to keep up, and am nearly out of breath when I spot a pig pile of boys wrestling for something against a stoop. Out pops Mickey from Warren Corner, hair askew, scratches on his face and Del Pratt's home run ball in his hand. "I got five of these this year now," he boasts, though Ruth's 30th is still in the offing.

The six-run Tiger outburst puts the game's fate to rest, but with Dugan aboard with two outs in the 9th, the Babe tries his last licks against Collins, and the knotholers have swarmed back to the right field corner. Brainy Eyes has the announcing honors. "The Babe hits it deep! Heilman's running back...back...and catches it right in front of me with a nonchalant gesture!"

The game is done, and the boys evaporate from the sidewalk. By the time I've flipped shut my notebook, Mickey and Brainy Eyes and the Beesums have vanished into the bigger and older crowds exiting Navin Field.

And I find myself a year or two younger.

WE'LL CATCH THOSE CUBBIES YET!
August 4, 1924

With all my thoughts from yesterday on my brain, it wasn't easy concentrating when it came to lining up baseball bats in the dumb rack.

The pesky, pitching-heavy Reds were in town trying to stay alive under the Pirates, and even if players always are more energized against the good teams it don't mean us batboys are. We had Bill Lucky Hubbell throwing against one of their Cubans Dolf Luque, and with the warm wind blowing out at Baker Bowl again I figured I was in for a long day. Dolf had light skin and blue eyes, which is pretty strange for a Cuban, and I guess it's helped him stick around in the big leagues because no one ever thinks he's a black.

Hubbell gave him a 2-0 lead today when the Reds walked, doubled, singled and doubled in the 1st, even though Roush was shot down at the plate on Daubert's two-bagger with two out. It gave us hope, and good old Cy ripped one into the corner to lead off our 2nd. After Wilson brought him in with the fourth double of the game, Luque got all nervous and stupid and kicked Mokan's easy grounder to put guys at first and third. After a force at home, Hubbell singled, Harper singled, and presto—we had three runs and the lead!

Luque is pretty famous for his bad temper, and after he didn't get a strike three call on Wilson with two on in our 3rd, he started chewing at the umpire. Wilson tagged the next pitch for a scoring fly and it looked like Dolf was going to pop a bolt. Sure enough, with two outs in the 4th, and the Reds able to put people on but not knock any home, Luque got the first two men and then Harper and my buddy Heinie whacked doubles for a 5-2 Phillie lead. The Incredible Holke then pounced on a boring curve, creamed it over the Lifebuoy sign, and we were up by five!

Cincy skipper Jack Hendricks wouldn't have left Luque out in the sun for another inning even if he was a blonde bathing beauty blowing him kisses. And the move paid off for him. Hubbell fell asleep with his suddenly big lead, gave the Reds three singles and a walk to start the 5th, and Chick Shorten came up to bat for the pitcher. He wasted no time, scorched a triple between Cy and Mokan that rattled around some dropped trash from the bleachers, and after a Walker scoring fly and Bressler single it was 7-7!

The scoreboard showed the Cubs losing up at the Polo Grounds, and that got the Phillie players all hopped up again because we still had that bet with Chicago we'd finish in front of them. If we won this we'd only be seven behind in the losses column. Well, Cy took care of that in the 7th. With lefty Jakie May in to face him, he belted a no-doubt-about-it ball high and far over the train tracks in right, his 20th smack of the year. Harper added a run-scoring single in the 8th, and even though Hubbell gave up 16 hits we won it with 14 because more of ours went higher and further.

Cy was all grins and chuckles in the club house, and players and writers were taking up his time so I didn't get a chance to ask him if he'd heard about any more white players signing on for our secret game. Then Benny took me aside down at Mort's later and asked me pretty much the same question, so I guess I'll have to get to Baker Bowl earlier tomorrow to see what's been happening. I asked Benny if Rube Foster was serious about me being a coach and he said I could ask him myself except he went back to Chicago for a few days to take care of some business. Ain't that great.

I'll tell you, it's nervous-making to be a baseball organizer.

CIN 200 050 000 - 7 16 1
PHL 030 400 11x - 9 14 0

CARLSON THE MAGNIFICENT
August 5, 1924

Mama ran out of the house this morning before I was even done with my bath, and left a note about meeting Cy at the Reading Market for a "light pastry." So much for me getting to talk to him when I got to the ballpark. I guess I'm happy for Mama having met someone she liked, but why did it have to be the star of the team I'm batboying for and someone I'm trying to do business with?

I rode the streetcar to Baker Bowl with Benny this time. Roy was down at the Western union office waiting for a telegram back from his wife in St. Louis, who he'd wired to try and get her and his kids to join him for Sunday's secret game. I told Benny maybe Roy should wait until the whole thing is officially official, but Benny didn't want to hear any negative stuff right now and said he had all sorts of good feelings about it and I should too.

Speaking of good feelings, Heinie Sand was hopping around our dug-out like Felix the Cat. The Pirates-Brooklyn game had an earlier start for Ladies Day (Hello, Rachel! I haven't forgotten you!) and Dazzy Vance had already beaten them 2-1. "That means we're going to win today!" screamed Heinie. I asked how come and he said that the Reds lose whenever the Pirates do, or at least 95 percent of the time lately, "meaning all we gotta do is take the field and the game's in the bag!"

That seemed a little too braggy for my money, but we did have the best pitching escape artist in the league going, Hal Carlson. Still think I'm crazy? He's given up 200 hits in 140 innings and somehow has a 7-7 record. Ain't no other way to explain it. Tom Sheehan was pitching for the Reds, and he hasn't exactly had any Irish luck lately. Sure enough, Jimmie Wilson popped one of his sleepier curves over the bleacher wall to lead off the 2nd, and we were ahead 1-0. Boob and the Rube (Fowler and Bressler) got the game tied in the 4th with a double and single, but we went back up 2-1 on a Harper scoring grounder. Ford ran in from third on that and I nearly bumped into him picking up Harper's bat, which got most of the Phillies laughing. Edd Roush even went out of his way to jog past home plate on his way in from the field and give me a wink.

Then Houdini Hal went to work. Critz and Sheehan opened the Reds' 5th with singles, and up stepped Curt Walker. He destroyed a fastball but it was right at Ford, who nabbed it, stepped on second base to put out Critz and whipped the ball to Holke to get Sheehan. It was a triple play! The first one I'd ever seen! Maybe Heinie was right about this Cincy Curse after all.

Bressler and Pinelli singled in the 6th but Carlson got out of it. Wingo led off the 7th with a hit but Carlson got out of it. Boob began the 8th with a single and Rube hit a double play. Hal came in the dugout screaming that he had to do all the work, and the Phillie players must have heard him. Holke singled and Cy tripled. Sheehan got the next two guys, but then Mokan and Ford doubled. Carlson walked. Harper crushed a 3-run homer that was never seen again and Bill Harris took the mound. Heinie tripled! Holke, Williams and Wrightstone all walked in a row, and we had seven runs just like that.

Cy slipped me a folded-up note when he came into the dugout, but I had to stuff it in my pocket because the Reds were already back up in the 9th and knocking the feathers out of the ball. Single-triple-single-triple-single-single and they had four runs but Fletcher wouldn't take Hal out. Either because he'd been shooting his mouth off or because he also believed in the

Cincy Curse.

Well, we all do now. Boob flied out, Rube hit into the fourth Reds double play of the day, and the thing was over. Houdini Carlson: 216 hits in 149 innings, 8-7 record.

And then I was in a corner of the club house, reading the note Cy had slipped me:

ALL IN SO FAR:
Me
R. Hornsby
D. Vance
J. Fournier
Z. Wheat
P. Alexander
G. Hartnett
E. Rixey
C. Mays
E. Roush

I almost fell over. No wonder Roush winked at me!

CIN 000 100 004 - 5 16 0
PHL 010 100 07x - 9 13 1

THE MICHIGAN LORD AND HIS SUBJECTS
A MID-WEEK RESPITE AT HENRY FORD'S ESTATE

By C. Jedediah Butterworth
Base Ball Freescriber
August 5, 1924

Few were as shocked as I to receive a phone call from Henry Ford's staff manager this morning, inviting me to a spontaneous dinner banquet for "American Legends" at Fair Lane, his grand Dearborn mansion. I imagined he had been reading my daily reports in the Free-Enterprise for some time, and thought I was worthy of covering the event. Or maybe he had another motive. Regardless, after today's dreadful game at Navin Field (Yankees 8, Tigers 3, Ed Wells wretched, Babe Ruth typically impotent) Bonnie helped outfit me in my finest supper attire, and off I rode down Michigan Avenue.

I doubt there are even a handful of dwellings in this country as opulent as the one Henry Ford assembled. Not only are there 56 rooms, but as you drive through the high gates onto his 1300 acres, you pass a man-made lake, summer house, pony barn, a skating arena, entire working farm and the five hundred birdhouses that satisfy the owner's ornithological interest.

The carved oak entrance hall, library and living room are stuffed with guests and tobacco smoke. I only recognize a few other local wordsmiths, but do catch a glimpse of Thomas Edison conversing with Clara Ford, motion picture star Will Rogers telling a story next to a stained glass window, as well as Michigan State football coaching greats Chester Brewer and John Macklin.

Then I hear a familiar bellow of laughter coming from a cavernous fireplace across the living room, and I walk over to see Babe Ruth, looking unusually stiff in his bulging suit, puffing on the largest cigar in North America and telling a no-doubt randy joke to a crowd of reporters. He recognizes me instantly from our one-sided billiards match in New York back in May, yells "Hey, kid!" at me, and takes me aside for a private word.

"Can you believe the size of this joint?" he begins, flicking a dollop of cigar ash on the carpet and making sure to snuff it with his heel. "All from making that joke of a Model T. I'd shoot another rack with ya but I hear old Clara took over the pool room 'cause she needed a place to write her girlie letters." Will Rogers strolls by to shake his hand, and he pulls me further away, against a window.

"Hey listen. There's a rumor floatin' around that a bunch of star players are gonna play against some pretty good coloreds outside of Philly this weekend. Hear anything, kid?" I am flabbergasted, and profess my ignorance of such an event. "Well, keep those big ears open and let me know tomorrow if you do. My club rots this season and I can't seem to hit my weight when it counts, so a nice little fake game with them colored boys might relax me a tad."

A dinner bell gongs, we're whisked into a lavish main dining hall, and take seats around the long grand table. Ford enters, takes the end seat at the far end, raises his glass of Maine spring water (which we have all been served), thanks us for coming, and toasts each and every "American legend" at the table. Then he fires his steely gaze straight at me.

"And from the esteemed fourth estate, we have none other than Calvin J. Butterworth. While I cannot condone his recent anarchistic behavior, I have admired his writing skills for some time, and see now that his inherently rebellious spirit harkens back to the brave patriots of Lexington and Concord. I salute you, sir!" Glasses clink, tears flow from my eyes, and I settle before my braised duck stuffed with soybean pate.

To my immediate right sits one Dean C. Smith, a young, handsome and notorious air mail pilot, famous for delivering a letter after crashing his plane last year. His senses appear to be juiced with illegal liquid from a hidden flask in his vest pocket, but I enjoy his humor and company and being a loyal follower of air achievements, it isn't long before I discover it was he who buzzed his de Havilland biplane over Navin Field yesterday. He offers to take me on a ride any time I wish and write about it, but my height-challenged nerves and lack of incentive force me to decline.

Ruth stands before dessert is served to rekindle laughter and offers "a big thank-you to Hank Ford over here for not inviting Ty Cobb." Most of us know Ruth and Tyrus get along just fine, but despite his reputation as a Jew-hater, Henry Ford is a most devout man and has no interest in entertaining a notorious scaliwag like Cobb in his home. Ruth himself may be as safe to have around as a grizzly bear on a motor cycle, but he is still universally loved.

As the crowd departs, after I thank Ford for his blessed honor, and with the taste of soybean and duck still gracing my palate, all I can think about is the Babe's inquiry about this rumored Negro game. What if it were true? The publisher of the New York Sun, who has already contacted me concerning writing occasional dispatches for his paper, would certainly enjoy reading about it...

WISH YOU CAN BE HERE
August 6, 1924

Dear Rachel:

Good work on your Robins smacking around those dang Bucs the last few days! Keep up the winning and maybe your boys will make a race of this thing yet, because all we can do at this point is probably spoil things for whoever.

Anyway, the reason I'm writing this today in the dugout between innings of our boring stinker of a game against Carl Mays is because I wanted to tell you about a different kind of thing I've been working on with Benny and our friend Roy from St. Louis who we met out there.

I'm sure you know that coloreds play baseball, too, and from what I hear a lot of them are awful good, maybe as much as the players we know in the big leagues. We've all had a pretty big desire to prove this, so this Sunday the 10th we're putting on an exhibition game (or maybe a few of them depending on time) out in Darby at Hilldale Park, which is where the colored Hilldale Daisies of the new Eastern Colored League play. The Phils are off that day so I shouldn't have any problems, except some of the white stars who have said they're playing will have to call in sick as a big group or something. The important thing is that Commissioner Landis somehow doesn't find out because I don't think it would make us his favorite people.

I would just love it if you could come down from Brooklyn that day to take the game in. I haven't seen you in a while and it would mean lots to have your support and see your face in the grandstand if they actually have one there. Maybe you could even bring your father along and I could ask him that big question I've been meaning to right there on the spot or afterwards. I don't think Sunday is the big Jewish day so he'd probably be free to go with you.

Anyway, Rube Foster, who runs the Negro National league and I think is paying most of the dough for this idea, will be back tomorrow with some of his players and hopefully he'll have his whole team picked. We have a bunch of great players so far, meaning the white team which I'm going to help Cy Williams coach, so it should be a heck of an extravaganza, or at least an interesting one. Today I even learned that Tris Speaker from the Indians wants to play!

Let me know as soon as you can and I'll have Mama fix up a guest room for you. She's been dating Cy, by the way, even though I'm not supposed to tell anyone.

Loving and missing you,

—Vinny

CIN 201 400 000 - 7 14 0
PHI 000 000 000 - 0 5 2

RAGING STARS: EPPA KNOCKS OUT CY IN EIGHTH ROUND
August 7, 1924

So today we all went to a baseball game and a boxing match broke out. Everyone inside Baker Bowl and probably for the surrounding twenty miles figured on a big Reds picnic, with the 15-5 Eppa Rixey going against the 6-9 and usually bullet-riddled Joe Oeschger, but that's why these dang things are played, right?

Four Cincy singles in a row started it off, and their 2-0 lead held up until Cy Williams said enough of this malarkey and bammed a homer to deepest center leading off the Phillie 4th. Cy's been all pepped up lately like I've never see him, and I'm sure the thrill of him player-managing these white all-stars on Sunday has a lot to do with it.

Roush got his third single in the 5th to put the Reds up 3-1, but then got too full of himself and dropped Oeschie's easy fly with one out in our 5th to put Phils at second and third. Part-timer Joe Schultz then whipped a hit into left and the game was tied! Take that, Eppa! Seriously, this Rixey disease has had us sick all year, so it was nice to see us getting some good licks in.

Of course, so were they. Oeschie gave up two quick singles and a scoring fly to put Cincy up 4-3, but then Cy creamed another Rixey pill high over the right train tracks, and it was 4-4. We were in a great one here, and for a while I actually forgot about Rube Foster and this Sunday and all the headaches going with it.

But then Cy came up to start the Phillie 8th. Cincy had knocked Oeschie out with three hits and a run in the top half, but Steineder got out of the mess that was left. Rixey was 15-5 for a reason, though, and wasn't about to let Cy take him out of the park a third time.

So the first pitch knocked him in the head! It wasn't a fastball thank God, but it sure didn't feel good. The crowd moaned as he dropped in the dust. I think I even heard Mama scream thirty blocks away.

Cy got up all wobbly, dusted off his uniform and headed straight to the mound! Eppa ducked the first punch but Cy is a big fellow and had him in a headlock in no time. By the time every player on both teams had reached the fight Eppa and Cy were tearing at each other like mad dogs.

It took almost five minutes to get them apart, and park policemen had to help. Cy was booted out of the game, but was too dizzy to play anymore anyway. Unbelievably though, the umpires allowed Rixey to stay in! Fans hurled trash and a few bottles from the stands, and he had to duck a few other things to make his first pitch to Jimmie Wilson.

Well, he should have come out for his own good, because we weren't about to let him get away with throwing at anyone's head, let alone our best hitter's. Wilson singled. Mokan singled. Parkinson singled. Steineder popped a deep fly for a third run and we were suddenly ahead with justice 7-5! Skinny bastard.

The Reds aren't exactly in second place because someone gave it to them for Christmas, though. In the 9th with one out, they got more patient at the plate than they were all game, and waited for Steineder to crack. Walker,

Bressler and Roush all walked. Pinelli made it 7-6 with a single. Bubbles Hargave ripped a 2-run single to put them up 8-7. Daubert singled and it was 9-7 and the crowd was moaning all over again.

Dibut relieved to keep Rixey from being shot, and after a Ford single, Holke dribbled into a double play, Harper who replaced Cy in the cleanup hole, grounded to third and the bout was over.

The doctor checked Cy's noggin after the game and said he had a little concussion and won't be able to play for a few days. Naturally, Mama had heard the news from someone on her block and showed up outside the clubhouse to escort him down the street to who knows where.

He might be okay by Sunday, but this makes two other problems now. Rixey thinks he's pitching with the white stars, so he and Cy better drink some moonshine together, and quick. The other thing is that our best slugger just went out with the first-place Bucs coming in tomorrow. And nobody following this National League race is surprised by that.

CIN 200 011 014 - 9 15 1
PHL 000 121 030 - 7 12 1

THE HOME INVASION
August 8, 1924

Oh boy. So Cy was holed up in our guest room all night with dizziness and headaches. Rube called this morning to say he was on his way over with some of his colored team, Rachel telegrammed to say she's probably going to be coming tomorrow for the weekend, and then I open the newspaper with my toast and read this headline:

BASEBALL'S LANDIS WARNS OF NEGRO THREAT TO BASEBALL

Well, we didn't need that. I'm telling you, if school was open today I'd escape to Mrs. Crackerbee's class and bury my head in a Greek history book. What was I supposed to do? Cy was still too deloozy to talk about anything, Mama was busy laying ice-cold strips of cooking foil on his head, and Benny and Roy were nowhere to be found.

So I did the only thing I could, which was distract myself from the whole mess by reporting to Baker Bowl for two hours to watch the Pirates blast us into pieces. With Cy out of our lineup we didn't stand a chance, right?

Well, that's what I thought. But Earl Smith, the most fearsome hitting catcher in the league after Hartnett, was out of their lineup for a while, and Johnny Couch was making a good habit out of putting Bucs on the bases and squirming out of trouble. Heinie started two double plays in the first four innings, and Harper gave us a 1-0 lead with a homer off their ace Kremer in the 1st.

But these rubes don't have 67 wins for no reason. After Kremer bunted Johnny Gooch over to second with two outs in the 5th, Max Carey got himself plunked, Grimm walked and so did Moore and we were tied. Meantime we loused up two great scoring chances in the third and fifth, so it was just a matter of time before the noose broke our necks.

The snap came in the 7th. Kremer, already with two good bunts, whacked a ball to deep right-center for a triple to begin the inning. Carey walked, Grimm singled and we were behind. All that was left was for Wrightstone to thrill the crowd for three minutes with a leadoff double in the last of the 9th, only to have Henline pop out, Wilson line out and Mokan screw himself into the ground whiffing on a bad pitch to end the game.

I didn't even sweep the locker room floor this time, just bolted back to the streetcar to see if our home was still standing.

And that was the problem. All you could do was stand. See, Foster didn't show up with some of his players, he showed up with ninety percent of the team, and there they were sitting around on every piece of furniture or on every untaken inch of floor, eating their hamburgers and chicken and beans and Italian sandwiches that they'd bought from vendors in the neighborhood. Mama was trying to help out by pouring drinks for any of them that didn't bring pop bottles, but I could tell she was rattled and would rather have been on cold cooking foil duty upstairs with Cy.

Rube was excited to see me, shook the heck out of my hand and introduced me to his players. I had only heard of a couple of them and didn't even know where they played on the field, but they were all pretty friendly and joked with each other non-stop. Sam Streeter and Webster McDonald and Nip Winters were pitchers, Dobie Moore and Rev Cannady were smaller so were probably infielders, while Tubby Scales looked like he ate baseballs for lunch instead of just hitting them. Willie Wells, Pop Lloyd and Mule Suttles were all hilarious, and Oscar Charleston had more of a dignity look about him, like he knew he was the best of the bunch and didn't have to act it.

I showed Rube the Commissioner Landis story in the paper, but he'd already heard about it and said it was nothing new. He was sure that if he forked a little more cash over to every white player there wouldn't be a problem getting them to play. Plus there seemed to be a scheme that "acquaintances" of ours were working on.

It was right about then that our door got knocked, and there was a Western Union man. I grabbed the envelope and tore it open, all excited because it might have been from Rachel again. But no, it was from Benny in New York City. What the damn was he doing up there?

WITH ROY IN BIG CITY. MEETING TONIC MAKER ON FERRY BOAT
TONIGHT. LANDIS WILL SLEEP LIKE BABY. WE PROMISE.
—BENNY

Rube was all smiles, but I just stared at the telegram in shock because there was nothing I could say.

PGH 000 010 100 - 2 9 0
PHL 100 000 000 - 1 6 1

THE BITTERS AND THE SWEET
August 9, 1924

I had to tiptoe over two dozen pairs of hands and feet this morning on my way out the door. Rachel missed the late train last night, so I headed over to Broad Street as soon as the bugs were out of my eyes to pick her up.

She had asked her father Saul to come, him being such a huge ball fan, but she said he wasn't feeling well again and wasn't really interested in seeing any kind of "schvartza" game, whatever that was. So there went me asking him the Big Rachel Question again.

Rachel looked as cute as ever, even that early in the morning. She was also real hungry and asked if Mama had made anything for breakfast. "Aw, the house is kind of a mess" was all I said, and hustled her straight to Reading Terminal to get us fresh pastries instead...

By Benny Zepp
Whites vs. Coloreds Organizer

Good old Rube. Me and Roy still had usage of the fancy convertible he leased for us, meaning we had gotten up to New York lickety-split and a half. Our mission was to make sure Judge Landis didn't know our big exhibition was going on tomorrow, and lucky for us, Roy had an old Caribbean friend to help out.

Skitch Thomas had about twenty kinds of British, Dutch, Jamaican, Bermudian and whatever blood in him, and now lived in New York where he delivered bottles of health tonic made by some old German family living in Venezuela named Siegert. If you can keep THAT straight. The stuff was shipped up from the Siegert factory in Trinidad, where Skitch was from, and was made with something called Angostura bitters that were supposed to clean out your stomach problems if you put it in liquor.

Anyhows, it seems that Landis is a longtime fan of Siegert bitters, and Skitch sometimes delivers bottles of it to his hotel room when he's in from Chicago. And he was in New York again this weekend for some baseball writers banquet at the same hotel.

So we met Skitch out on a Staten Island ferry boat today. He had a little derby hat and blue-tinted glasses on and spoke the worst English I ever heard, and had a little pouch inside his coat packed with bottles he had re-filled and capped himself. You see, Skitch had gotten hold of some of Siegert's bottles and what he thought was their secret formula and had made his own special illegal tonics in his apartment basement as sort of a hobby. According to Roy, he had one that could put a nervous rhino to sleep. So for a decent price we had two bottles of "Sleep-aider XX," one each for me and Roy just in case, and the address of the hotel. Now it was all up to us...

Rachel and me went straight to Baker Bowl after our pastries, where the Big Bad Bucs were there for a Saturday double-header. Cy wasn't around because of his dizziness, so I had no idea what was going on back at my house, but I knew the plan was to get out to Darby later and make sure the field was all set for tomorrow.

As far as I was concerned, I was ready to ditch being batboy after three innings. Lee Meadows gave us a single and error on Harper's first at bat to get us going, but Sand, Holke and Wrightstone left him out there at second scratching his bum hole. Then, as usual, the Pirates scored out of nowhere. Johnny Gooch, the second-string catcher filling in for Earl Smith, tripled, singled and doubled his first three times up to start one 3-run rally and knock in their fourth run. Meadows cruised along from there, winning for the eighth time in his last nine starts. Hubbell was lucky because they more than doubled our hit total and still only scored five runs.

Rachel was bored beyond tears and asked if she could sit in the Phillies dugout with me for the second game. I told her she was cracked, that Art Fletcher was a nice guy and gentleman and would probably let colored Roy sit there before a woman. So Rachel sulked in her great behind-the-dugout the whole time while we tore up Jeff Pfeffer for 13 hits to their eight and still managed to lose. The Bucs went through a miniature slump in the last week but are back to winning ridiculous again, and for the 70th time no less.

I was thrilled when Cy showed up in street clothes near the end to tell me that the colored players needed help hauling the lighting equipment out of their trucks in Darby. Fletcher believed my fake coughing and in a flash I was dressed and back down the street with Rachel. I had no idea what Benny was up to at the moment, but I figured he was busy messing up whatever that crazy plan was he came up with...

Me and Roy snuck into the hotel through a back door and nabbed waiter uniforms from a storage closet. Skitch had given us the number of the room Judge Landis stayed in every time, so I elected myself to deliver a tonic bottle.

There were lots of fancy-dress people walking around, but I have to say I looked awful snappy myself in my long white waiter coat. I knocked on room 381 and waited. And waited. And waited. Then I heard someone coming and ducked around the corner.

It was a chambermaid, who unlocked the Judge's door and brought in some fresh towels. I snuck in when she wasn't looking and left the tonic bottle on a napkin next to his bed.

But then Roy was missing. Or at least from the place in the back alley where we were supposed to meet. I looked and paced around for an hour almost, until he finally came out, all huffing and sweaty. He said he served the tonic bottle to Landis right at his table but it just took a while. "What?? You told me to bring one to his room!" He said he saw him cross the lobby and go into the banquet room so decided he could get him the stuff before I could.

Yikes and a half. We never got away from a place so fast in our lives...

It was nice to discover a trolley line that went all the way to Darby, a township just southwest of Philadelphia. The trolley wasn't even that crowded and the weather was nice, so me and Rachel had time to get off for an ice cream on the way.

Hilldale Park was a funny-looking place with a dinky grandstand that even had a big tree in deep right field. The lights were big and heavy and everyone hoped they'd work. We were only supposed to play three games at the most, but the way the two teams could probably hit, who knows when the games would finish. Rachel got a chance to meet all the colored players and they were all pretty polite to her, but as soon as she took off her hat and jacket and rolled up her shirt sleeves to help haul out the lighting stuff, there was hooting and chuckling for a good five minutes. I guess there'd never seen a white girl doing muscle work before, especially one as nice and smart as Rachel.

We all went to a colored chop house after, and I tried to start a conversation with Oscar Charleston, but he never took the serious look off his face. Rube said he wanted to beat the whites tomorrow something bad, and wouldn't smile about anything again until that happened.

Cy went back to his own place tonight for a change, so Rachel got our guest room to herself after Mama cleaned it up. Benny showed up at midnight to tell us that him and Roy had gotten Judge Landis two bottles of this home-made sleep tonic instead of one. Great. Hopefully they didn't kill him for their troubles.

What would happen tomorrow? I realized Judge Landis might be dead to the world for a day or two, but I was starting to worry that no one else in the country might realize these games were actually played.

I hate to say it, but I think we need a reporter person.

PGH 003 001 001 - 5 15 1
PHL 000 100 000 - 1 6 1

PGH 002 001 001 - 4 8 1
PHL 000 010 101 - 3 13 1

PERMISSION FROM THE CLOUDS
August 9, 1924

By C. Jedediah Butterworth
Airborne Base Ball Freescriber

SOMEWHERE OVER OHIO—Flying at 18,000 feet is not the choicest place to learn what cold rain feels like. In two words: icy daggers.

Aviator Smith had lifted us off from our foggy airfield outside Detroit without incident this morning, despite my wobbly nerves, and once we had broken above the cloud layer and caught the eastern sun in our faces, I was finally able to marvel at the wonders of flight.

The marveling has been going on for hours now. Smith's Airco D.H. 9A is a mere 45 feet from wing to wing, and as I sit in the nose seat of the biplane I enjoy an eagle's view of the sky. Buildings below are mere match sticks, and autos slow moving ants. The wind stings my cheeks, futilely tries to slip under clamped goggles, and I have to drop my head on occasion to warm my vision back up.

"Cal! Take this!" It is Dean, holding out his silver flask behind me with a gloved hand. I shake my head as a fierce wind gust drops us fifty feet and right back up in less than five seconds. I suddenly understand his imbibing and grab the flask from his hand.

We have been following the south edge of Lake Erie for some time, and I can make out farms and small crafts through the cloud wisps. I assume Dean has telegraphed the Philadelphia air field ahead of time, but at our speed of 120 miles an hour I have no idea how long this route will take.

We cross over Buffalo and the beginnings of Lake Ontario, and Dean veers us southeast. Within minutes, the sun vanishes behind a bank of black clouds, and the ice-rain commences. Dean tries to lift the plane higher, thinking we can stay above the foul weather, but the engine strains horribly as he attempts this.

We have no choice but to endure the barrage and pray for the best. Nature's fury reaches its pinnacle, and the rising and falling and bumping seem to last forever. I lean over the edge at one point to empty my stomach. Dean ducks the flying contents at the last moment but seems obscenely calm. I long for a photograph of Bonnie and the children mounted on the panel before me, and am reduced to imagining one there. The wind in my ears howls angrily. I am cold and drenched beyond belief, and sick to my bones.

Then, without warning, as if a stage curtain has risen on a third act, the rain lessens, dissipates, and glorious patches of blue sky appear above. Dean lets out a whoop and lifts us heavenward. We are over the rolling green of New York State, heading south into Philadelphia. I may in fact live to see this white-colored classic!

Yet there is still the small matter of landing. Dean apparently never wired ahead to announce our arrival, so as the spires of Philadelphia gleam at us in the afternoon sunshine, Dean is forced to drop the plane severely and eyeball the landscape. The clouds are now stacked cotton balls, guardians of the sky, and I almost feel we need to ask their permission to land between them.

The little airstrip on Hog Island is just past the center of the city, and I shut my eyes when we seem to be on a collision course with William Penn's statue atop City Hall. Wind gusts pick up again, though, and we are forced to circle and circle the field at a hellishly low altitude.

"Tell me when we are on terra firma!" I yell to Dean, but all he does is laugh. When our wheels finally bounce on the grass and settle down for good, I say blessed thanks to every deity I can think of. A small gang of air field attendants are there to shepherd us in, as well as a handful of local reporters. For reasons I can't begin to fathom, Dean and I are suddenly minor celebrities for doing this flight. When asked why I've come to Philadelphia, I cannot lie, and mention a certain whites-coloreds game out in Darby tomorrow. The reporters stare at me for all of five seconds, then rush off en masse to find telephones. Hmm.

THE FIRST-EVER HILLDALE/DARBY WHITE-COLORED CLASSIC
August 10, 1924

By Vinny Spanelli
Phillie Batboy and White Stars Coach

Well, the nice, quiet trolley car I took out here yesterday was nothing but a big, rolling crazy house today. It seemed like every real ball fan, every nearby sports reporter worth his salt and a few more hundred curious types were making their way southwest to little Darby to see how Rube Foster's Colored Stars would fare against our Whites.

Chester and Cedar Avenues were so packed it took me and Rachel fifteen extra minutes just to find where the entrance gate was, Benny and Roy ran out of tickets to sell by ten o'clock this morning but the mobs wanting to get in wouldn't let up and they finally decided to let folks in for free. The Hilldale Park grandstand was puny, so they put ropes up in the outfield, there were people up in a big tree planted inside the park in deep right field, and at least a hundred more people sitting and balancing on gravestones in the Holy Cross Cemetery past right field.

The great thing was that the crowd was a complete jumble of both races, and everyone seemed to be getting along, making bets and laughing and just happy to be part of such an amazing thing. Rube and Cy had decided to try a two-out-of-three series, and when they flipped a coin, it came up tails to make the Whites the home team for the first and third game, if it went that long. I was wearing my Phillies jersey and cap, and joined Cy in front of our bench to pep talk the players.

They sure didn't need one. There was the Babe, right in front of me and slapping Hornsby's behind. Tris Speaker spat into his hands and worked a bat handle. Goslin and Fournier and Eddie Collins and Heilman and Zack Wheat were sitting a few feet away and I was so dizzy just watching them I didn't hear one thing Cy was saying. The great Walter Johnson hadn't shown up, which didn't surprise anyone, and Mays and Vance were coming late because they had to start in their teams' early afternoon games today.

Looking over at the other bench, where Big Rube was holding court, I could see the colored players were wearing K.C. Monarchs uniforms because Rube won the Negro National championship with them last year. None of them seemed to mind.

Then two umps, a white one and a colored one, called the players out from home plate, the crowd went nuts, and old Pete Alexander grabbed the cleanest ball he could find and headed to the mound.

GAME ONE

The great Oscar Charleston led off for the coloreds, and Pete got him on a short fly to left. Half the crowd cheered, the other half booed. A black Cuban guy named Cristobal Torriente lined a single to reverse all the cheering, and after Bullet Joe Rogan flied out, Mule Suttles, as scary a hitter as

I've ever seen, singled Torriente to second. Turkey Stearnes grounded to Hornsby, the Whites were coming up, and there I was running out to coach third base.

It was kind of scary being that close to the action. Joe Beckwith was taking ground balls at third base, singing under his breath in between throws. I turned and caught Rachel's face behind our dugout, smack in the middle of three or four fancy-dressed colored ladies. She looked as excited as me.

Cy noticed how bouncy the Babe had been all morning, and to get him up to bat as much as possible and put the jeebies into the opposition, he stuck him in the leadoff spot. Smokey Joe Williams, a blazing fast right-hander, looked about as scared of Ruth as he would be of an ant, took a big windup and whipped one over the plate.

The Bambino swung. The ball went soaring, up and up and completely over the big tree, bounced off a dozen or so gravestones and finally stopped when two fans fell on top of the thing. Ruth took the slowest home run trot of all time, waving at the stands and winking at Smokey Joe. If he didn't get his chin buzzed the next time it'd be a miracle.

The homer rattled Dobie Moore, who muffed a grounder out to short by Speaker. Hornsby then singled Speaker to third, and after Fournier forced Tris out at home on a grounder, Goose Goslin did what he's been doing all year and lined a 3-run homer right down the line for a 4-0 Whites lead! I'm telling you, you never heard such a happy and angry ruckus.

Beckwith tripled to lead off the Colored 2nd and scored on a Moore fly, but our big rally had taken all the steam out of the park. It got worse in the 4th when with two outs and nobody on, Alexander singled, Ruth crushed a double and Speaker singled them both in. Torriente golfed out a solo homer in the 6th, but then Traynor singled, Ruth kept his mashing fever going with a triple and Speaker doubled to put this massacre to bed.

Rixey and Adams gave Alexander some late relief, but there was no softening up the truth. Us Whites had whipped those Coloreds bad.

COLOREDS 010 001 000 - 2 8 1
WHITES   400 202 00x - 8 13 0
W-Alexander L-Williams HRS: Ruth, Goslin, Torriente

GAME TWO
By C. Jedediah Butterworth
Base Ball Freescriber

It is close to 5 o'clock in pleasant little Darby, and after the unexpected bludgeoning of the first game, few know what to expect in the second. A pair of southpaws, Herb Pennock for the Whites and Nip Winters for the Coloreds, will have at each other from the mound, with the darker team enjoying the home advantage. If anything, the number of onlookers has increased, the outfield ropes bulging at the seams, the back-and-forth cheering reaching an operatic crescendo.

The noise shakes the old wood grandstand I am perched atop when with one retired in the

Colored 1st, Tubby Scales lofts a fly out to Ruth in right. Whether it is the late afternoon sky or his proximity to the big leafy tree, the Babe drops the ball for a two-base error! Bullet Rogan then pummels a Pennock pitch high and deep and gone out to left, nearly two-thirds of the mob erupts like it's New Year's Eve, and the Whites fall behind for the first time. The Coloreds then load the sacks with two out, but Pennock gets catcher Biz Mackey to line out to Dykes and end further bleeding.

Not so in the 2nd inning, a frame as horrific as anything experienced by this year's National League Boston club. Winters begins it with a sharp single and Jimmie Lyons matches him with another. Scales clubs a double. Rogan skewers a triple. After a Beckwith fan, Mule Suttles singles. After a force out Baby Doll Jacobson drops an easy fly in center. Wright kicks a ball at short and five runs are across with lightning speed.

There is little left to discuss about this one. The Coloreds rack up five more doubles after that, Winters pitches the game's entirety, and the Whites trudge back to their bench inning after inning like scolded children. Meanwhile the stands throb with euphoria, and delicious smells permeate the late summer air as picnic dinners break out everywhere, even on grave-stone taple-tops in the adjoining cemetery. The event takes on the air of a country carnival, with everyone eagerly awaiting tastes of the third and deciding match.

Between the contests I am visited at my viewing spot by two fine lads who helped Mr. Foster organize the spectacle, Vinny Spanelli and Benjamin Zepp. I instantly recognize young Ben as the one who absconded with my typewriter and writing pen on my last working trip through Philadelphia. Well, it is a pleasure to report that after issuing a heartfelt apology, he has made amends by presenting me with a new writing machine and two replacement fountain pens. Obviously, the boy has been blessed with a fine upringing.

```
WHITES      001 000 001 - 2  5  3
COLOREDS    250 120 00x - 11 17 0
W-Winters L-Pennock HR: Rogan
```

GAME THREE
By Vinny Spanelli
Phillie Batboy and White Stars Coach

I made Benny give this Butterworth writer a new typewriter to replace the one he stole before, and even though it was used and bought at a pawn-shop the guy didn't seem to care. The important thing is that he came all the way here on an airplane to report the games, so he must be something special, and it's important that the Colored players have a special person to write about them, and not just one of these dozen or so clowns who showed up from eastern newspapers.

Well, guess who joined us on the bench between games? Yup, Big Train Walter Johnson, straight from Chicago. Eager to show these Negro fellows his buggywhip fastball. I made a dope out of myself before he took the mound by asking him to sign a baseball, but he was actually quiet and friendly and hard to believe he's so competitive, too. Charleston got him for a walk with one out in the 1st, but when Oscar leaned too far off the bag, Walter turned and shot him down in one motion! No one on our bench could believe it even happened.

Dick Redding took the hill for the Coloreds. The big Georgia man played for the Brooklyn Royal Giants, had the nickname of "Cannonball" and sure threw like one. Watching his balls explode in catcher Beckwith's mitt it seemed like he was a perfect match for the Big Train, and he was. Both of them gave up a few singles, but the game was scoreless into the last of the 4th, when Hornsby worked a leadoff walk. Fournier golfed one the opposite way out to left but Turkey Stearns got all confused and dropped the thing for an awful 2-base error. Might as well have thrown some blood in shark water while he was at it. Cuyler hit a scoring fly, Myatt got plunked, Sewell singled, the Train drove in two with another single and the Whites were up 3-0.

Johnson then retired ten of the next eleven Coloreds, whiffing four of them, until Torriente ripped a homer down the right field line with one out in the 8th. Charleston came up, still miffed about being picked off, and started barking things under his breath to try and upset Walter. The Train's face didn't even twitch, but the first ball he threw knocked Oscar right square in the back! Both benches jumped up, along with the fans, but the umps ran in before anything violent could happen. Suttles fouled out to end the inning, and lefty Sam Streeter took the Colored hill.

He shouldn't have bothered. Speaker pinch-hit a walk. Hornsby singled. Fournier rattled the gravestones with a booming homer, before Cuyler hit a fly out to poor roasted Turkey, who dropped it for another error!

You get the idea. Dazzy Vance relieved Johnson for the 9th to keep the colored players from hitting liners at him, and got out of a small pickle to end the sad game and the little series. The sun was just about down, but strange enough, the folks didn't seem to want to go anywhere.

"Not so fast!" said Rube, hurrying over to Cy from the Coloreds' bench. "We spent a lot of dough to haul these searchlights down here, and we got a big old crowd none too happy about those last two innings."

"Well," said Cy, "Train didn't hit Oscar on purpose and you know it."

"Hey, my friend, never said he did. But a plunk's a plunk, and it's a sure sorry way to end a great day. How 'bout we make it three out of five?" Cy just gave him a funny look.

"C'mon," Rube said with a giant smile, "Ain't this supposed to be fun?"

Cy or me or Benny or Roy sure couldn't argue with the man.

COLOREDS   000 000 010 - 1 5 2
WHITES   000 300 04x - 7 8 0
W-Johnson L-Redding HRS: Torriente, Fournier

WE CAN'T BELIEVE WHAT WE JUST WROTE
August 10, 1924

By C. Jedediah Butterworth
Base Ball Freescriber
DARBY, PENNSYLVANIA—Thrilled by the anticipation of two additional games in this fascinating match, due to be played beneath a set of modern search lights acquired just for the occasion, I leave my grand stand perch prior to the fourth game for some sidewalk vendor nourishment.

It is while standing beside Minky's Frizzled Beef, Onions and Cheese Sandwich wagon that I overhear two colored gentlemen discussing rumors of Commissioner Landis' "drug coma." I rush to the nearest newspaper box containing a local evening edition, and indeed, the rumors are true in the sporting headlines:

LANDIS HOSPITALIZED!!
--Base Ball Czar Felled by "Mystery Tonic"--
Shenanigans Investigated

Newspaper under my arm, dripping and scrumptious Minky's sandwich in hand, I return to my Hilldale Field seat, secure in the knowledge that our spectacle will continue uninterrupted. I certainly had been wondering how Mr. Landis would be kept in the dark...

GAME FOUR
The prodigious field illuminators, leased from the Kliegl Brothers at New York's Universal Electric Stage Lighting Company, have not fully taken effect when Eddie Collins steps into the batting box against Big Bill Foster. Large William is actually Rube Foster's younger half-brother, and has a left-handed fast pitch that I can barely see, even against the green infield grass. Collins does not, either, nor does Joe Sewell, who both walk away after three straight bullets. Speaker flails at an offering and lines it into right for a single, but the Babe looks more helpless than anyone and mopes out to his position in a humiliated fog.

Foster's sizzler is still on his mind in the last of the 1st, it seems, because after Torriente singles, Stearnes drives one deep to right but the Bambino turns the wrong way, drops and kicks the ball and Turkey gobbles around the sacks on the 3-base error and 1-0 Coloreds lead. Fournier evens matters right away with a loud solo blast to begin the 2nd, but all this does is anger Big Bill.

We are now all the better for his lividness, for with two aboard and two outs, Foster fans Collins to end the threat. He then whiffs Sewell to begin the White 3rd. He then renders Speaker superfluous with another third strike. Ruth has at him again and screws himself into the ground with three airy swings. The crowd erupts, but Big Bill isn't finished. In the 4th, Fournier is called out on strikes. Brooklyn teammate Wheat swings at a pitch as invisible as a telegraph signal, and SIX mighty white hitters, all at the top of their sport's heap, have been eviscerated.

For his part, Detroit's Rip Collins proves why his mark of 18-3 is no fluke. Aside from a second Torriente single and his own flubbed grounder, the Ripper gives the Coloreds nothing but frustrating outs for some time. Night is upon us now, river moths ballet-dancing in front of every search light. The tension on the Colored bench and among the majority of dark-skinned fans intensifies. Can Big Bill keep this up? Speaker and Ruth finally reach him for singles in the 6th, but Bill bears down and whips a third strike past Fournier, clearly paying the price for his early clout.

It falls on short-stop Willie Wells to crack the scoring ice in the last of the 7th with a seemingly innocent free pass. Collins then walks Tubby Scales. Biz Mackey drops a bunt in front of the mound but Rip and Hartnett mix up on the coverage, and Mackey hustles out the hit. All sacks are stuffed, with no one retired! Foster is due at the dish, but Rube cannot let family relations interfere. He needs this victory or the series is finished. Up strides Bullet Joe Rogan, and Pittsburgh's sterling relief man Babe Adams is hailed.

Rogan digs in. Adams hurls. The ball is cracked out to Speaker in his usual shallow center field spot, but his throw to the plate is slightly off-kilter, Wells scores and the Coloreds lead! One out later, Adams bounces a pitch past Hartnett and Scales bounds home to make it 3-1!

Lefty John Donaldson takes over the Colored mound duty, and the Whites fare no better. Lefty-mashing pinch-swingers Hornsby, Wright and Jacobson go down on two whiffs and a weak grounder to the box. Adams simply cannot focus after that, as Stearns singles, Mule Suttles clubs a ball off Minky's aforementioned food wagon, and the lead surges to 5-1.

Ruth reaches on a Judy Johnson error to start the 9th, but Fournier fans for the third time, Heilman bounces to Wells for an easy double play, and the series will go five games! Big Bill Foster is nowhere near the pitching slab when the game concludes, but is mobbed by his mates in front of the bench regardless.

Pete Alexander and Smokey Joe Williams will be called upon again to decide this lovely war, and with the probable weary state of their arms, I would be shocked if we witnessed a tight hurling exhibition.

WHITES   010 000 000 - 1 5 3
COLOREDS   100 000 22x - 5 5 1
W-Foster L-Collins HRS: Fournier, Suttles

GAME FIVE
By Vinny Spanelli
Phillie Batboy and White Stars Coach

With the Coloreds pulling out a scary and rugged fourth game to tie the series again, no one in the place knew what to expect for the finale. One thing we did know is that the home team had won every dang game, so it was up to the Coloreds to change that business around.

Charleston said not a bad idea and singled off Alexander to start things. Torriente singled him to third. Tubby Scales pounced on the first fastball he saw and bammed it high and deep over the left fence and it was 3-0 Coloreds just like that. Suttles and Stearns followed with doubles to make it 4-0 before Alexander even got an out.

Not thinking he had to pitch again tonight, old Pete had obviously gone down the street to find a speakeasy and succeeded with that mission, because he had nothing. After he gave up a Charleston walk and Torriente smashed homer in the 2nd, it was 6-0, the whites in the stands were booing, and Cy walked out to the mound. Pete barked something at him and I could see Cy turn away from his boozy breath. He stayed in to get Scales and Suttles out, but after Hornsby muffed a grounder to start the 3rd, Pete plunked Beckwith and finally got yanked. A Mackey double off Rixey made it 7-0, and three singles, a walk and Suttles triple in the 4th off Mays put us down 10-0. The Colored players were running past third so fast and so often we were all getting cool breezes.

Most of the white crowd had started to head home, and as they gave up their seats, more and more coloreds took their place and made the park even louder. Babe Ruth by this point was managing for Cy, walking up and down the bench and hollering everyone to death. He had a walk and single off Smokey Joe his first two times up, and doubled Traynor over to third with one out in the 5th. Speaker got a run in with a deep fly, Hornsby doubled before a Fournier single, and we had three on the board.

But the Coloreds wouldn't let up. Biz Mackey singled home two more in the 6th off Sherry Smith and it was 12-3. Now Bullet Joe Rogan's a guy who can hit and pitch, and sure enough Rube sent him out to the mound after he hit for Williams to end that inning. But we weren't all that impressed. A Myatt double, Traynor walk and Wheat pinch single loaded them up, and Ruth got two in with his third hit of the game. After Speaker hit another sacrifice fly it was 12-6 and nothing was safe!

Make that 12-7 in the 8th, because the Bambino mashed one out off Sam Streeter, and a few whites came back in the stands to try and re-get their seats. Dazzy Vance had taken over for us in the 8th, our sixth pitcher of the game, but he was more out of gas than Old Drunk Pete was. Luis Santop pinch-hit a double off him with one gone in the 9th, and Oscar Charleston hit a ball that left the park faster than I've ever seen a ball leave a park. 14-7 was now the football score, and Webster McDonald came in for the Coloreds to try and finish us off. Hartnett singled with one out, but Joe Sewell grounded one out to Scales, who flipped the ball to Willie Wells without looking to start the double play and end the series!

We heard that the Coloreds went back to their chop house to celebrate, and Cy and Eddie Collins proved good sports by going along and buying them the food, but none of the other Whites seemed too happy. I mean, did this really happen? An incredible team of 28 big leaguers beaten in a five-game series by 28 colored players? Benny and Rachel had the same reaction as me: happy for the Coloreds but a little scared about what this could mean. We're dying to see what these reporters say in the newspapers tomorrow. It seems like this Butterworth guy from Detroit will tell what happened pretty fairly, but who knows? None of us really know him.

The search lights got unplugged around midnight, the grand stand and graveyard emptied out, and crickets chirped again in the outfield grass. We walked back to our trolleys and houses under a curious moon, peeling food wrappers off our shoes. The first and maybe only Hilldale/Darby White-Colored Classic was over, but its moments would burn into our eyes forever.

COLOREDS 421 302 002 - 14 18 0
WHITES   000 033 010 – 7 13 2
W-Williams L-Alexander HRS: Scales, Torriente, Charleston, Ruth

MUTINY ON THE BAKER
August 11, 1924

I never thought it would feel so empty to be home again. Yesterday and last night out in Darby was so exciting and magic-making, and now Mama was shouting me out of bed again, and Rachel had gone back to Brooklyn, and I was back in Baker Bowl to lug bats for my lousy 7th place Phillies against the sickeningly good and lucky Pirates.

One thing Cy and me hadn't figured on was the reaction from the other Phillie players, especially the biggest Negro-haters Wrightstone and Harper. Art Fletcher was okay with us going to Darby but it didn't seem like a lot of his team was because they flat out quit on him today.

The worst Pirate starter Wilbur Cooper was throwing, and we made him look like Eppa Rixey out there. The Bucs scratched out a 1st inning run on a Carey walk, stolen base (Pittsburgh has stole 71 bases and been caught just 11 times, by the way), an on-purpose walk to Cuyler and a single by Pie Traynor. After that Jimmy Ring pitched the hell out of the ball and got out of every little mess he began.

Us? Forget it. Cy singled to start the 2nd and Wilson hit into a double play. With second and third and two outs in the 3rd, Parkinson grounded out. Holke walked and Cy singled to start the 4th but Wilson hit into another double play to kill that one. Ford singled to lead the 5th and went nowhere. Ring singled with one out in the 8th and was left there. Still 1-0 in the last of the 9th, the worst one happened. After Carey dropped a fly in center for a two-base error with nobody out, Cy popped out, Wilson dribbled to the pitcher and Mokan grounded to Traynor and our mark against the Bucs went to 2-13.

Fletcher was so mad he wouldn't talk to one player or reporter. Cy had words with Wilson and the catcher shoved him, which brought Wrightstone and Harper over to stand up to Cy, saying "Anyone who'd rather be playing darkies got no right to criticize us." Cy went straight to Fletcher, who finally came out of his office to yell at Wrightstone, who knocked the manager right over a chair and said "I quit this slag heap of a team. Who else is with me?" Harper and Henline walked out with him, and then everyone else in the clubhouse. Heinie gave me a torn-up look, said "Gotta stay with the old pack, Vin," and left, too.

Fletcher was really upset, and I actually thought he was going to cry. Cy sat him down and got him a bottle of pop and it was just the three of us sitting there in the mess of a club house for the longest time. "We still got one to go with the Pirates. Who the Christ is gonna play for us tomorrow?" was all Art asked over and over.

Then I got a big thought—maybe my biggest ever.

"Hey Cy. Ain't Rube and those colored players still over in Darby?"

Cy looked at me and snuck out a grin.

Hee hee...

PGH 100 000 000 - 1 8 2
PHL 000 000 000 - 0 5 1

MEET THE BLACK PHILLIES
August 12, 1924

Cy was exhausted after his Phillie teammates abandoned ship yesterday, and went back to his hotel to sleep everything off. This meant our spare bedroom was open again so I invited none other than Calvin Butterworth over to fill it. And Mama sure didn't care, being used to a new person almost every night these days.

It seems that Cal isn't welcome in the Detroit press row anymore, and his paper doesn't like him much either, so with the Tigers in town and starting with a double-header at Shibe Park tomorrow, he needed a place to stay that wasn't the usual luxury team hotel.

Rube and Cy were also due for breakfast with hopefully most of the colored stars, and lots of discussing had to be done. Cy was real close with Fletcher and Phillies owner William Baker, who also must like me or he wouldn't have given me this batboy job a few months ago. Anyway, the plan was a simple one: put the Negro players in our uniforms, call them the Black Phillies and let them play as long as the real players sit home being babies. Baker hates the Pirates' guts, anyway, so even if the Black Phils only get one game in at least they'll have a good chance of trouncing the Bucs.

"You are traversing on most dangerous ground," is all Butterworth told me last night when I spilled it out to him. I wasn't used to such fancy language, and knowing that he took an aeroplane to get here, it seemed like he was the one that was traversing. I reminded him that Commissioner Landis was in a coma and even if he woke out of it tomorrow, the ball game would be over before he ever found out about it. Butterworth was more worried about the "larger scope," as he said, meaning how big league baseball and the public would take something like this. I told him I had no idea what would happen, but that's kind of the way life's been going for us all year, one weird happening at a time, and all you could do was roll with them.

So Butterworth had a glass of warm milk before he went to sleep, and by the time we got up this morning, Rube, Cy, Fletcher and Oscar Charleston were over for pancakes and coffee and everything got figured out. Baker had assigned extra police in case the Phillie fans started a riot, but with our 42-70 record they didn't have much more they could complain about.

Bill McKechnie and his Pirates had already been told they were playing coloreds, and with Cuyler and Adams and Traynor filling their teammates in they didn't seem all that worried about it.

The Baker Bowl crowd was a-buzzing because the rumor had spread like a disease, and the stands were more stuffed than I'd seen in a while. When Bullet Joe Rogan took the mound looking darker than ever in his white Phillies jersey, the fans either cheered or booed or just plain gasped. Carey bounced the first pitch to Charleston at first, who booted it and made the boos take over. Moore and Traynor singled to load the bases, but Wright grounded out and it was our turn.

A speedy guy named Cool Papa Bell, who didn't even get to play out in Darby, led with a walk and danced around on the bag but Buc lefty Emil Yde kept him close. Lloyd, Wilson and Stearnes all went out and we went to the 2nd scoreless. Yde singled with two outs, Rogan wild-pitched him to second, and when Carey rapped a sharp single the Bucs had the lead.

Mackey hit into a double play to kill our 2nd inning rally, and then the Pirates fired their cannons. After Moore walked, Cuyler added to his 1924 legend with a smash homer deep into the bleachers. Bullet Joe was rattled and gave up a double to Traynor and single to Wright and it was 4-0 just like that. Bell and Pop Lloyd got mad and doubled with one out in our 3rd, and when Jud Wilson creamed a Yde pitch over the right fence, the place went nutty-cake.

But if anyone's been doubting how good this Pittsburgh team is, look at the rest of this game. They scored two in the 6th and two more in he 8th, Cuyler adding two more singles and driving in five on the day, while Yde blew through the great Negro lineup, tossing them only five scattered single-crumbs after Jud's homer. Charleston was even picked off first at one point and Cool Papa whiffed with two outs to end the thing.

There was a bunch of angry racist yelling from the stands after, and I thought I even saw Wrightstone and Harper in their street clothes helping out the crowd. The colored players went back in the club house with their heads down. Butterworth, who watched the game from our dugout, was scribbling notes like a lunatic and we'll have to wait and see what he writes about or who will even publish it. All I know is that I just saw the Pirates shellack the best Negro players around without anybody starting a riot, so I guess that has to account for something.

```
PIRATES       013 002 020 - 8 13 0
BLACK PHILS  003 000 000 - 3 10 2
```

THE BUTTERWORTH ADDRESS
August 13, 1924

Quayle P. Rutledge
Acting Base Ball Commissioner
381 Fifth Avenue, Sixth Floor
New York, New York

Dear. Mr. Rutledge:

We truly never know what brand of curve ball life will hurl at us, and it is apparent from here in my modest Southern Philadelphia accommodations that base ball suddenly has a chance to whack a fluttering willy-nilly of a pitch straight out of its park.

For as you may have heard rumored, a best-out-of-five exhibition series was played a short way from here on Sunday afternoon and into the night, pitting a team of eager big league stars against a squad of equally talented colored ones.

There; I said it. Equally talented. Whatever blind prejudice you and others in our fine sport's upper berths may possess—and I know that Commissioner Landis has more of this foul hatred and fear of a colored base ball integration than anyone—it would stand a fair chance of being dissolved instantly had you witnessed those games at Hilldale Park in Darby, or the one I witnessed yesterday at Baker Bowl, when a trimmed-down version of the Star Negroes wore the Phillie uniforms in place of their mutineering owners, and bravely battled the first-place Pirates in a losing cause.

There; I said that, too. Battled the Pirates. And all without incident in the grandstand and streets, and all without a shred of outrage being uttered, and all without the sun failing to rise today. I have discussed the situation at hand with team owner William Baker, with team manager Art Fletcher, with Negro National League President Rube Foster, and with White/Colored entrepreneurs Vincent Spanelli and Benjamin Zepp, and it seems perfectly possible to have these talented colored athletes fill the Phillies' shoes in our National League campaign for as many games as the base ball world will allow them. Judge Landis is unfortunately restricted to a bed-ridden, comatose state for the forseeable future, and while this may be a sad burden for he and his family, it is a glorious opportunity for the rest of us to step in and shatter the archaic barrier between white and black ball foolishly erected by Cap Anson and others of his ilk many years ago.

Let us call it "The Grandiose Experiment" if we must. I shall call it "scintillating base ball" and enjoy every moment. Messers. Charleston, Scales, Suttles and Beckwith, et al. are ready and willing to display the skill and entertainment a city as rich and storied as Philadelphia deserves, and a country that treasures its freedoms should be ready to embrace it. If we let this historic, God-blessed opportunity pass today, we may regret our blunder for decades to come.

Please consider this heartfelt proposal, and we await your response.

Sincerely,
Calvin Jedediah Butterworth
Base Ball Freescriber

HOW WE SPENT OUR SHIBE PARK VACATION
August 13, 1924

Butterworth's letter to the acting baseball commissioner was pretty great, and gave me and Benny hope that we wouldn't get arrested for mixing races right away. Cal also telegraphed the letter to some big newspaper editors, even some guy named Robert Lee Vann who runs the *Courier*, which is the black paper in Pittsburgh.

The Phillies were off again today, and were supposed to leave for Chicago tomorrow for their last western trip. This meant that the real Phillie players were all wondering what was going on with their jobs, but William Baker has been doing a great job of telling them nothing while trying to keep Rube's colored boys hanging around just in case. I'm telling you, it's a heck of a job being an operator.

Anyway, Butterworth invited me and Benny out to Shibe Park today where his Tigers were playing two with the A's. Cal still isn't welcome in the Detroit press porch, so we all got tickets to the grandstand. Connie Mack's guys have a better record than us but are sure no closer to being in the pennant race, so we pretty much had our choice of seats.

It was nice being back at Shibe. The last time was when Benny had this date with Miss Philadelphia, who turned out to be such a big A's fan it wrecked Benny's relationship before it even got started. Now we were sitting with a real baseball expert, a guy who could tell us things about the game we never even bothered to see. Like the way the fielders all tense up together right before every pitch. And the way the shortstop signals the second baseman sometimes by kicking pebbles at him. Cal also bought us pretzels and lemonade, which was nice of him. That time he got lost up in Vermont really seemed to have some good effects.

Rip Collins was going for his 19th win with only three losses, so it was fun to see him throw. The Tigers made it easy for him by scoring five times in the 2nd, helped by A's catcher Sammy Hale letting two balls get past him. Harry Heilman, one of the scariest-looking hitters after Ruth, doubled in two to give him 107 runs knocked in on the year, second to Goslin's 114.

Mack's guys tried to get back in the game but Collins wiped out every big scoring chance, and Cobb started another rally in the 9th with his second single off Roy Meeker, and Detroit took Game One easy. The fans seemed happy to have their A's back home, but weren't expecting much out of them. A few people around us were talking about the "Black Phillies," some even asking how good they really were because they had lost to the Pirates. Benny spun around and said "Pittsburgh can beat anybody, pal!" and I had to calm him down to keep another fight from starting. Benny's never been a big Athletics fan.

Between games, Heilman saw us sitting near the field and ran over. "Hey, Cal. They want you up in the press row." Butterworth asked who wanted him, and Harry just said, "The whole gang, I guess. There's a telegram from New York." Well, this got the fans buzzing around us and got Cal out of his seat in no time. We had a good feeling about this...

SUCCESS!

By C. Jedediah Butterworth
Base Ball Freescriber

My letter has produced the desired result, and the base ball world can only benefit. With acting commissioner Rutledge's blessing, the "Grandiose Experiment" will take place. Base ball and Phillies owner Baker is apparently suspending the entire Phillie team indefinitely for insubordination, and Foster's "Black Phillies" will take their place on the field of play! Cy Williams and young Spanelli will be the coaches and Oscar Charleston will player-manage, and in Rutledge's words: "Any clubs or players refusing to participate in this experiment will be fined severely. All of base ball stands to reap the rewards of this temporary race-blending, and we would be foolish to not let it occur."

Oh joy! The reporters of Detroit and Philadelphia glad-hand me before running to their phones, happy I supplied them with wonderful news stories for the duration of this pennant race-starved season. They even allow me to sit with them again.

Meanwhile, the Tigers thank me by pouring it on the hapless Athletics in the second contest. 'Lil Stoner, of all people, hurls a complete victory while defensive fill-in Bob Jones drives in three off Slim Harriss. The Philadelphia denizens are none too happy, and begin chanting "We want the coloreds!!" over and over by the 6th inning. I look down on the field and see Ty Cobb's shoulders sag as he listens to this out in center field, knowing we have no room left in our minds or hearts for his hateful thoughts.

Yet in some ways, I understand him. Who ever thought America would support such a courageous attempt at human harmony, coming only sixty-one years after the abolition of slavery?

I did, readers. I did.

THE SMOKEY AND BOOJUM AND CANNONBALL EXPRESS
August 14, 1924

Why did I ever think I could sleep?

"Out of bed, darling!" said Rube Foster, standing at my berth with his suit still on at a little after midnight, "Cannonball's taking every cat's money and we need some white man's luck to cool him off."

The special train Rube and Pop Lloyd had helped get for the Black Phillies' first and maybe only road trip was somewhere in Ohio, and the parlor car's dice game showed no signs of ending. The colored stars had been joking and eating and liquoring and playing since the time we pulled out of Philadelphia, thrilled beyond belief to have a chance to prove themselves against big league pitching in a regular season way.

Acting commissioner Rutledge might've done a great thing by letting them replace the lousy white Phillies, but he was no dope. With the Bucs beating them at Baker Bowl the other day and still as hot as firecrackers, he knew darn well it would be almost impossible for these black players to catch them at the finish line and embarrass the heck out of the sport.

Our player/manager Oscar Charleston sure didn't care, and neither did

Cannonball Dick Redding, Smokey Joe Williams or Boojum Wilson. These guys were deadlier than poison darts on a baseball field, and even if they didn't catch the Pirates they could make an awful big dent in people's race views by getting our record up close to .500.

"This is one big historical stew we're all cookin' up here," Cannonball told me and Benny as we ate our yummy chicken dinners hours earlier. Roy had gone ahead to Chicago a day ahead to meet his brother and get things set up for our first game at Cubs Park, so Benny was all mine for a change and loving every second of his first "luxury" train trip. From what I could tell he was more excited about maybe making a living at this game promotion thing than any sort of history, but he went along with what Cannonball said just to be nice. Redding was over six feet tall, a blazing fast thrower from what I saw out in Darby, and had this habit of never taking off his sweatshirt on long trips. After a while the armpit smell kind of mixed in with the chicken one so I passed up dessert and left the table.

By the time I saw Cannonball again he was in the parlor car after midnight whipping dice against the wall with Biz Mackey, Pop Lloyd and Jud Wilson. Jud was called Boojum because that was the sound his line drives used to make off the fence, and he had the biggest shoulders and smallest waist I'd seen outside of Babe Ruth. He also looked like he could squish me like a plum if I got him mad for some reason so I stayed clear of him.

Pop Lloyd used to push a train wagon when he wasn't waiting tables down in Florida, and him and a friend named Phillip Randolph who knew a lot of porters and train folks worked with Rube to help get us our own spiffy express. Pops was also a nice guy, and wouldn't even use bad language. "Gosh bob it!" he yelled when his dice came up wrong, then turned to me and asked, "Ain't your pal the one who put Judge Landis to sleep?" I told him it was actually two of my pals, and he should keep that business under his hat. "How long before that old coot wakes up, you think?" I said I had no clue, and Biz Mackey said, "If he does we'll just invite him to a game and let Smokey Joe put him in another coma by throwing those lazy curves."

Mackey seemed like a great person. He'd been catching on the Eastern Colored League's Hilldale team all year, and one of the reasons they were in first place was because of him. His fingers were all bent and twisted from taking foul tips but he's supposedly got a shotgun arm and can throw a man out at second even after a slow curve from his pitcher. He was also drinking like a fish on a fish's birthday, and his questions to me about the Cub hitters were so slurry I just made up some answers and he seemed to buy them.

Cy Williams was on the train too, even though he was asleep in his berth with blankets over his head. Rube named me and him honorary base coaches, I think to show the crowd that whites and coloreds could be "on the same team", but Cy had other problems, namely how the real Phillies would treat him as soon as this big experiment ended. I didn't care much about those jerks Wrightstone and Harper, but I did feel bad for my buddy Heinie Sand, who would have a tough time finding a place on any other team.

Me and Benny also talked with Smokey Joe Williams a little about what the Chicago crowds might be like. Smokey wasn't worried, because colored baseball is big in that town and Rube Foster is pretty well thought of. I figured it could get rough because the Cubs were playing real good lately and had a chance to jump in front of the Cards, and the last thing they needed was to get whupped by a bunch of colored fellas.

"Well then," said the tall, half-black and half-Indian Smokey while he puffed on his cigar, we'll just have to whup those Redbirds, too."

I threw my dice, which came up freight cars. Cannonball screamed in pain and handed me one of his twenties. Who the heck needed sleep, anyway?

BLACK PHILS ROAST CUBBY BEARS FOR LUNCH
August 15, 1924

Uh-oh.

I never thought it was possible to destroy an enemy team and feel scared and guilty about it at the same time. Until today...

The first matchup at Cubs Park was a good one, Smokey Joe Williams against Vic Aldridge, and after the easy way the Bucs took care of us a few days ago, I was expecting another tough battle. The whole city of Chicago was too, because every seat was gone by ten this morning and all eight local papers had shouting headlines like CUBS BRING SHARPEST CLAWS OUT and INVASION OF THE COLOREDS. The regular bad Phillies would have been lucky to fill half this place, and there was Benny and Roy and Roy's brother Thomas, forced to stand at the back of the left grandstand and choke on everybody's tobacco smoke.

Aldridge got Torriente, Wells and Charleston 1-2-3 on easy grounders in the 1st, and the crowd went cuckoo. Williams had one-fourth of a cigar in his mouth until he walked out to pitch, and it was my job to keep it safe somewhere. Smokey walked Friberg with one out but then whiffed Grantham on a high fastball and got Grimes on a fly. Mule Suttles singled and Jud Wilson got hit due to his usual plate-crowding in the 2nd, but Aldridge got out of the minor mess pretty easy.

Then the 3rd inning happened. After Smokey whiffed for starters, Torriente ripped a single to right. Wells got him to third with a single, and Charleston completely hammered a ball over Heathcote and off the center field wall for a double. Mule then singled and I never saw a human run so fast as Oscar did getting across home. The fans, who were happy and buzzing when the game began, were suddenly crabby and quiet.

Grimes singled in a run for them in the bottom half to get them going again, but the resurrection didn't last long. It seemed like the Black Phillies must've liked scoring those first three runs, because they did it three more innings in a row and in the 8th inning did it a fifth time. And the balls couldn't explode off their bats fast enough. Wells hit a 3-run cannon shot after Aldridge got the first two guys out. Jud Wilson remembered Aldridge plunking him in the 2nd and got him back with a 3-run rocket onto Sheffield Avenue with nobody out the next inning. Turkey Stearnes gobbled up a fastball and put it in the bleacher oven and one out later Tubby Scales did the same.

Standing in the third base coach box I was expecting bottles to be thrown at us, or certainly more racist yelling than I heard, but it just got weird and quiet, like parents who had just watched their kids get run over by a truck. After Tubby's homer some fan in the bleachers yelled something I couldn't make out and whipped the ball back on the field—kind of a new, funny idea if you ask me—but that was the only peep out of the crowd.

Smokey Joe finished off the poor Cubs by getting the last five, two on strikes, shook some of his teammates' hands, grabbed the cigar butt from me that I was carrying in my pants pocket, lit it back up and smoked the rest of it in the shower.

There were extra police there to make sure no one jumped us on our way out, but that wasn't going to happen here. Chicago people know their baseball, and sure know how to take a clubbing. If this happens again tomorrow, though, we'd better keep our bags packed.

BLACK PHILS 003 333 030 -15 21 0
CUBS   001 000 000 - 1 10 3

OSCAR DOES THE CHARLESTON
August 16, 1924

The Black Phils took over the Arcadia Ballroom last night, getting all kinds of free drinks, free food, and not-as-free girls. At least that's what I heard. Cy and me and Benny were a little too scared to show our faces in white public after the beating we gave the home team, even though a lot of coloreds went to this dancing club, as I remember from back in May.

"This was just a one-game thing, right?" Benny asked Cy, who just shrugged his tall shoulders and chewed on a toothpick. "Probably. Pittsburgh didn't to seem have any problems with us. Guess we'll know after tomorrow."

Well, tomorrow just happened, and I'd say we knew after the top of the 1st inning. Willie Wells doubled with one out off Vic Keen, Charleston got him to third with a grounder, and Super Mule Suttles went to town with a booming triple over Jigger Statz' head in center. Stearnes and Scales doubled around a Jud Wilson walk, and four of our runs were on the board.

I guess scoring three runs most every inning yesterday wasn't good enough for these guys, because this time they racked up four more in the second. Torriente singled and stole and with two outs Oscar bashed one way out of there, snickering at me as he rounded third. Suttles then doubled and Turkey homered and I thought Keen was going to drop dead before his manager Bill Killefer had a chance to pull him.

We got a little less greedy after that, scoring only one run in the 3rd, two in the 4th and three in the 5th. Keen was actually left on the hill for

201 AND YOU ARE THERE!

all of this, and I can't blame Killefer. Why stick in worse pitchers and wear everyone out for the next one?

The crowd that was just shocked yesterday was five times more angry today. A bunch of times Turkey had to run around trash that was being thrown from the bleachers, and the umps even stopped the game once to get it cleaned up. The Cubs got mad enough themselves against Nip Winters to get homers out of Grimes and Hartnett later (Gabby's 25th!), but a lot of the fans left by the 5th inning and missed them.

Rube Foster gathered everyone in the club house after, and even he wasn't happy. "We gotta give 'em more of a chance, darlins," he said "Oscar? Better put on some bunt plays tomorrow or there won't be any fans left and they won't let us do this any more." Oscar said OK, but we all could see he wasn't doing cartwheels about it.

They dragged me and Benny back to the Arcadia tonight though, and we got a good look at Oscar being plenty happy. We'd heard he was popular with the ladies, and they were all over him like ants on a muffin crumb. He just kept smiling and grinning at each one and whispering things and soon enough he'd pulled one out on the floor and was doing a full-blown Charleston Chalreston with her. They say Oscar's the most talented colored player because he can hit for average and power and run and field like the wind, but I bet they didn't know he can also skate on polished hardwood.

```
BLACK PHILS   441 230 200 - 16 19 0
CUBS          002 000 012 -  5  8 1
```

NATIONAL LEAGUE through Saturday, August 16, 1924

Pittsburgh	74	39	.655	—
Cincinnati	68	47	.591	7
Brooklyn	68	47	.591	7
New York	62	52	.544	12.5
St. Louis	56	57	.496	18
Chicago	54	59	.478	20
PHILLIES	44	71	.383	31
Boston	30	84	.263	44.5

LIVE WITH SHOE POLISH OR DIE

August 17, 1924

The Black Phils might have been welcome to play at Cubs Park the last two days, but the big hotels in town still wouldn't put them up. Which is why we were holed up at the Esquire in the Bronzeville section of South Chicago when word got to us this morning that Al Capone wasn't happy.

Benny showed up at my room in two minutes, sweating like a death row prisoner. We'd already messed with Capone twice this year, the last time almost getting us killed out on Lake Michigan, and if Capone knew we had anything to do with the Charleston Boys rubbing out his favorite ball team, there'd be hell to pay and we'd be the first ones cashed in.

Lucky for us, Rube Foster had another one of his famous plans. "My shoeshine buddy Nips over on Wabash stocked me up with enough brown Kiwi to Negro-fy Jefferson Davis, so Benny darlin', all you gotta do is stay in a seat five miles away from that monster mobster heel." I hated the idea of wearing a disguise until Rube reminded me that Capone was away on some special heel business and missed the first two games or we might already be dead.

The Kiwi polish was sticky and smelled awful, but Roy did a great job putting it on my face and neck and hands, so by the time I ran out to the third base coaching box in the top of the 1st, I almost believed my name was Cool Papa Spanelli.

The other Big Rube Idea was to let up on the Cubs today to keep from riots starting or baseball shutting us down or Capone pulling out his gun. So Charleston started Judy Johnson at third and Rev Cannady at second instead of Jud Wilson and Tubby Scales, and he also gave bashers Turkey Stearnes and Mule Suttles the day off.

We got a run off Elmer Jacobs anyway right off the bat when Heathcote kicked around a leadoff single from Bell and Oscar scored him with a fly. I looked over at slimy Capone in his front row seat and saw him fold his arms and bark at the goons sitting next to him.

Cannonball Redding was firing for us, but he wasn't as fast as the last time I'd seen him and four Cub singles in the 1st scored two and got Capone out of his seat clapping. I was relieved for the first time in three days. Would we have a real game?

Umm...nope. Bullet Joe Rogan led our 2nd with a single. Johnson got one, too, and after Cannady grounded them over, Jacobs flubbed a weak dribbler by Biz Mackey to tie the game 2-2. Cannonball then blasted one high over the left bleachers for three runs, another dead quiet crowd and the sight of Al Capone tearing his program in half and tossing it on the field. When Charleston walked and Dobie Moore homered, it was 7-2 and a third straight Chicago massacre was off and running.

The boos were louder than I'd ever heard. The sweltery heat was starting to melt the polish off my face and down the back of my jersey, and I tried to keep my shoulders hunched so Capone wouldn't notice. After we made it 9-2 in the 6th, I did see him whisper to some big ugly men and disappear down a grandstand tunnel, which was even more scary because we couldn't see what he was up to.

The Cubs came back with a run to help their pride a smidgen, but Rogan, Johnson and Mackey got us two right back in the 9th with three doubles off Wheeler, and we ended up outscoring them in the sweep 42-9 and hitting ten home runs. Ye gads. These characters can't play lousy even if they try.

Big shiny cars with their engines running were parked outside our club house door like we figured they'd be, so it was the Black Phils' turn to dress up. They snuck out a side service door with a cleanup crew's push brooms, me right in the middle of the line. We got onto a bus back to Bronzeville and then the train station without the mobsters seeing us, and Mackey had booze bottles for all of us in the first five minutes.

Now all we have to do is start a series in St. Louis tomorrow, where there's supposed to be more racists in the stands than anywhere. The players were pretty quiet on the train, wondering what was going to happen there, and Rube didn't even leave the station with us, telling Oscar he was doing the short drive separately by car with Benny and Roy.

My guess is that they're up to something. Again.

```
BLACK PHILS   160 002 002 - 11 14 1
CUBS          200 000 100 - 3 11 4
```

A WHISKER AWAY FROM A DONNYBROOK
August 18, 1924

Our train compartments got real quiet as we pulled into Union Station this morning. Biz Mackey was joking with a few other players, but mostly we were all just getting grips on our bags, thinking how the people of St. Louis would welcome us after the three-day pasting we gave the Cubs.

The humidness here hit us like a brick wall the second we walked outside, and we saw a few pickup trucks with creepy muscled guys rolling by. We moved fast to the curb, hopped in taxicabs and scooted over to the Ville section in northwest St. Louis. Benny and Rube were waiting for me, Oscar, and Cy at Roy's house, where him and his great wife Lucille had agreed to put us up and cook.

If Roy was a saint then Lucille was Mary herself. This woman served a pork roast for early lunch that just about dove off its bone, along with fresh greens and potatoes and the best lemonade we ever had. All with her three little boys to feed, too. Some people are just put on earth to remind us of home, I guess.

At the table we talked about the weird situation we were in, and what to do about it. Cardinals president Sam Breadon had wired Rube with his worries about possible fan violence at Sportsman's Park if we whacked his team around like we did the Cubs, even though the St. Louis fans were "giddy with sinful delight" over us beating up their arch rivals.

Rube's idea of the day was for Oscar to start almost all right-handed hitters in the lineup because Cards starter Jesse Haines had big trouble facing lefties, and for our pitcher Big Bill Foster—Rube's half brother—to "go easy on 'em" to keep the home fans excited. Oscar wasn't nuts about the plan, and didn't think Big Bill would go along. "Don't you fret, darlin'," said Rube, "The boy's nineteen years younger than me and he's gonna listen."

Well, either Judy Johnson didn't listen or he just didn't care, because he murdered Haines' first pitch into left for a single. The colored pavilion in right field was so stuffed there were fans on top of its roof, and with Judy's hit the whole thing shook like it was going to fall apart. It was strange, because the entire rest of the park was plumb quiet, and it got quieter when Oscar ripped a double to send Judy to third. Charleston was the only regular lefty we had in the lineup, which he figured he could get away with because he was the player-manager, but the Cards didn't seem happy about any of this. Nobody likes to have someone help them win because that's a pride-killer, and after we took a 1-0 lead on a deep Tubby fly, St. Louis went to town on Big Bill.

Taylor Douthit spit in his hands and gapped a double right off. Jack Smith did the same thing in the other direction and the game was tied after two Cards batters. Big Bill had thrown his lazy curves like his older half brother told him to, but he'd had enough of that and bonked Ray Blades on the hip with the next pitch. Ray glared out at him, the white crowd unleashed bloody screams, but the umpire got in Blades' face and calmed him down. The ump forgot about the next two batters, though, because Hornsby and Bottomley both hit killer singles and the Cards had a 3-1 lead!

Our dugout was nothing but a pit of angry snakes, and Cy and me couldn't even get a word in. Some of the players thought us falling behind was a good thing to keep the crowd at bay, but Oscar and Big Bill were embarrassed and let everyone know until half the bench was shouting at each other. Big Bill, who happens to be a switcher, went up to the left side of the plate with a man on and clubbed a Haines pitch into the right corner for a scoring double.

Blades singled in a run right back to put them up 4-2, but that just got out innards boiling again. Oscar led with a single, and after Scales and Beckwith made outs, Mule Suttles doubled, Dobie Moore tripled, and the game was tied 4-4.

That's when the first empty pop bottle flew past Suttles' head in left field. Mule turned and looked at the stands, where two colored-hating idiots were standing and cursing and holding up rope nooses. Mule looked like he was going to jump in the stands and beat them to death with his mitt but he didn't have time to because Cooney hit a ball out to him which he had to flag down and catch.

The scoring stopped for the next two and a half innings, the right side of the park cheering, the left side snarling, and then Bullet Joe Rogan walked with one out in the Black Phillie 6th. Rev Cannady, playing first base instead of Jud Wilson, then poked a deep fly that just made it over the left fence to give us a 6-4 lead. Two fans jumped out of the stands, knocked me down in the coach box and tried to tackle Rev as he got close to home plate but Cy ran over from first and held them off.

Policemen arrested the fans, but the pop bottle olympics started up again when we took the field and didn't let up. Hornsby crushed a homer in the 7th to make it 6-5 and shut the white fans up for a time, but when Big Bill rapped into a double play in the top of the 8th to probably kill our next rally, someone stood up behind our dugout and yelled, "Nice hit, Sambo!" when he jogged back in.

This wired our bench like a bolt of summer lightning. Judy Johnson singled. So did Oscar. Tubby Scales hit a ball that I think is still going. Beckwith and Suttles singled and Hi Bell took over for the beaten-up Haines.

Moore doubled off him and we were up 10-5 and trash was falling from the sky. It took fifteen minutes to clean up the place and then the Cards got two runs back with three singles and a double. Dark green thunderstorm clouds circled the park and I was wishing for them to split open.

Then Big Bill had to go and drop down a bunt with a man on in the 9th. Judy Johnson singled and Johnny Stuart's next pitch almost hit Oscar in the head. Charleston got up and yelled something at Stuart and both teams began jawing. A half-eaten sausage roll knocked my hat off. We wouldn't get out of town alive, I was sure of it.

And then the most incredible thing happened: The St. Louis manager saved the day. Branch Rickey, an ex-player and smart religious fellow who served in the 1st Gas Regiment during the War, used to be the Cards' president and now runs the field team, walked out to Charleston in his spotless white uniform and shook his hand. Then he went over to Judy Johnson on first base and shook his hand. Then he went over to our dugout and shook the hand of every colored player on the bench before going back to his dugout.

Nobody knew what to make of this. But it was clear that he approved of the coloreds being here and made the dumber fans in the crowd feel even dumber, and that the game needed to be finished or he might even pull his players off and forfeit the game.

So Big Bill got through all nine innings without being shot. Our "weak" right-handed lineup still got 18 hits and won by four runs. But all of us were too shaken to celebrate much as we took our separate taxis back to the Ville. We sat and played cards most of the night, waiting to hear breaking glass or shotgun blasts or something even uglier like those 1917 riots here pass through the neighborhood, but it was just plain quiet.

Someone oughta give that Rickey guy a bigger baseball job sometime.

```
BLACK PHILS   112 002 041 - 11 18 1
CARDINALS     310 000 120 -  7 15 1
```

SECOND STRINGERS MY FOOT
August 19, 1924

When I woke up on my back porch cot this morning, Rube, Oscar, Roy and Benny were already gone. I thought maybe they all got arrested for peace disturbing, or that a mob came and took them away without waking me up.

Then Lucille stuck her head outside with a mixing spoon in her hand and said they went to the ballpark early to meet the new players and do I want some flapjacks? New players?? In no time I was all washed and dressed and gulping down breakfast and running out the door.

Crazy Rube had yet another scheme in his cuffs, and this time it was to use a second stringer team of colored players who he'd gotten together outside of town two days ago just in case things got scary at Sportsman's Park which they sure have. He was even using a roster of just 21 guys instead of the 28 to show what a good sport he was. He also made the first-stringers love him by sending everyone but Oscar to the horse racing track with a whole bunch of cash to enjoy their day off.

I'm not sure how upset or insulted the Cards were about this, but they had to feel like they had a better chance. Anyway, here's the lineup Oscar was going to manage (and not play for) on the field. Another band of characters to get to know!

CF Rap Dixon
RF Charles Blackwell
LF Frog Redus
C Oscar Heavy Johnson
1B Ben Taylor
2B Martin Dihigo
3B Tank Carr
SS Dick Lundy
SP Roosevelt Davis

Alan Sothoron was throwing for St. Louis, and he can be tough, but these new Black Phillies were happy to be showing their stuff and probably wouldn't even be afraid of facing Dazzy Vance or catching a case of Eppa Rixey.

The park was even more packed than yesterday, and I noticed a lot more colored fans sitting on the pavilion roof and on anything that could pass for a fence outside of the park. There was even a couple of them halfway up the flagpole.

And I don't have to tell you that Dixon and Blackwell singled to start the game and put the park right back in the hot kettle. Dixon has small feet, skinny legs and big shoulders and even though he's from Georgia they cal him "Rap" after the Rappanhock River in Virginia for some reason. Anyway, him and Blackwell are as fast as Oscar and Cool Papa Bell and they danced around on the bases for a minute until Sothoron bore down and got Redus, Johnson and Taylor in a row to give us nothing.

Roosevelt Davis throws a spitball and an emery-ball, and when the Cards couldn't score off him in the first two innings they were barking at him from the dugout. The home plate ump went out to look at the ball because he kind of had to, and I could hear Davis all the way from our bench. "I throw the kind of ball any big leaguer can hit. If they can't do that then they don't belong here."

Great. Something else to get our team riled up. There went Blackwell, singling with one out in the 1st. Redus walked, Heavy Johnson, who was one of those black "buffalo soldiers" during the War and plays for the K.C. Monarchs, singled right under Sothoron's legs and up the middle for the first run. Taylor singled, Dihigo was out on a force, and then Tank Carr, who if he isn't built like one he's built like the other, cold-cocked a pitch completely over the right pavilion to send it into a frenzy and give the Black Phils a 5-0 lead. Second-stringers my foot!

After Frog cracked one in the gap with Rap aboard in the 4th and hopped all the way to third with a triple, it was 6-0, half the crowd was ready to riot again, and Branch Rickey just sat there in the shade of his dugout like he'd rather be taking a nap.

But then his players woke up. Max Flack walked, Howard Freigau doubled into the corner and one out later Specs Toporcer tripled in two and scored on a grounder to cut the lead in half. Lefty Jesse Fowler and his 1.48 earned run average took the Redbird hill, and the fill-in Black Phils walked three times to start the inning. Fats Jenkins pinch-hit a sacrifice fly, a wild pitch and second scoring fly from Dihigo gave us two runs back without a hit, and it was back to a 5-run lead.

The Cards smelled blood, though. Hornsby got into the act with a scoring triple in the 8th off reliever Brown, spitballer Phil Cockrell came on and Bottomley got Rajah home with a fly and it was 8-5. Freigau doubled with two outs but Phil got Gonzalez on a pinch grounder to end the trouble.

Hornsby singled with two outs in the 9th to put two Cards on and make Bottomley the tying run. Sportsman's Park was a crazy house all over again, but Sunny Jim's fly was caught under a garbage shower in deep right by Blackwell and we'd won another one even playing the irregulars.

Rickey came over to Oscar and Cy and Rube afterwards and had a new suggestion no one had even thought of. "Why not mix your colored Phillies with some of your best white ones tomorrow?" It seems that a fair amount of the real Phillies had come to town separately to watch from the stands. Cy kind of liked the idea but wasn't sure Wrightstone and Harper would go along, and Rickey said, "Well, then they're probably not your best men."

He had a point there...

BLACK PHILS   005 102 000 - 8 13 0
CARDINALS   000 030 020 - 5 10 1

THE SORT OF GREAT WHITE HOPE
August 20, 1924

Well, no one expected this.

Practically the whole colored population of Missouri, Kansas and Arkansas turned out today to watch their favorites play the last game with the Cards, while at the same time most local whites decided to stay home. Meaning a half hour before first pitch the right pavilion was bulging at the seams and the streets around Sportsman's Park were flooded with out-of-town Negroes, so team owner Breadon did the only smart thing and opened up the grandstand sections to all colors. Something that has never happened here.

The other historic thing was that Jimmie Wilson became the first white man to play on a team with all coloreds in a major league game. Oscar picked Cy and Holke and Huck Betts too, not even bothering with our biggest racist jerks Wrightstone and Harper, but Wilson got to start behind the plate. Cy recommended Jimmie to Charleston because he was young and durable thanks to his strong legs from a good soccer career he ended just last year, and he also knew he would be tough enough mentally to handle the name-calling he might hear from the mostly-colored crowd.

Lefty Bill Sherdel started for St. Louis and whizzed the first pitch right past Lyons' ear. Our speedy centerfielder shrugged it off and ripped the next ball down the opposite line for a leadoff triple. I've decided it's never a good thing to anger a colored star. Dick Lundy got him in with a deep fly and with Wilson in the on-deck circle with two outs and Heavy Johnson at the plate, the razzing started.

"Hey Gingerbread, what you doin' out there?"

"You ain't tan enough to swing with us, cracker-head!"

"Always knew you were a cotton-picker, Wilson!"

That last one came from the Cards' dugout, probably from Hornsby because Rickey was too intimidated to shut him up. Wilson kept cool, instructed to not fight back no matter what because he needed to set an example for future whites playing with blacks. But it still seemed to bother him when he crouched behind the dish to handle Bill "Plunk" Drake's first inning. They couldn't seem to get together on the right pitches, and Flack and Hornsby both walked before Bottomley ended the scoreless inning with a deep fly. Hornsby even hit Wilson's rump with the side of his shoe as he stepped into the box and Jimmie had to crouch there and take it.

Wilson grounded out his first time up but in the top of the 3rd, I heard him cheer from our bench when Ghost Marcelle led off with a vicious double for us. After Lyons singled him to third, Lundy got him in with his second scoring fly and it was 2-0. Wilson flied out on his second at bat, which got the stands laughing and yelling at him all the more, but Oscar met him halfway to the dugout and put an arm around him like Rickey might've to let the crowd know he was accepted and everything.

The strategy sure loosened up our dugout, because we went nuts on Sherdel in the 5th. With two outs and Newt Allen on first, Lyons singled, Lundy doubled them both in for all four of our runs batted in, Rap Dixon tripled, Heavy walked and Tank Carr singled to make it 6-0! Wilson walked to the plate, trying to block out the volleys of "white boy" catcalls, and just about screwed himself into the ground swinging at strike three.

"Enough of this bunk," muttered Charleston, and put Cy into the game in center and Holke at first base to give him some white company. Drake meanwhile bored down even harder on the Cards hitters and didn't even allow them a hit through the first six innings. Heavy Johnson singled with two gone in our 7th, and then Holke silenced the colored crowd with a line double to send Heavy to third. Wilson just about ran to the dish, all excited, and singled sharply for two more runs! Even the colored people in the stands had to cheer his courage.

Hornsby didn't, though, and butchered Drake's first pitch in the last of the 7th for a deep double. A Hafey single and two walks brought in one run before Drake got Toporcer on a fly with the bases loaded. After we got three more in the 8th off Eddie Dyer, Oscar got a little cocky and put real Phillie Huck Betts in the game. This guy was probably rusty from not pitching for a week, but the colored crowd really gave it to him and he just couldn't take the abuse. He gave up three walks and three singles and three runs before Charleston finally yanked him for Martin Dihigo, who played second base for us just yesterday.

Martin singled in an extra run for us in the 9th but the crowd was more than happy to see the local white team get crushed again by their racial brothers. It was on to Cincinnati now, a team with maybe the best pitching in the league and a lot of Over-the-Rhine Boys in the stands no doubt itching for a fight. All I know is that I'm going to need a vacation from this tense craziness real soon.

SORT-OF BLACK PHILS   101 040 231 - 12 17 1
CARDINALS   000 000 130 - 4 5 1

BACK INTO THE MIST
August 21, 1924

I learned a bunch of stuff today. All of us did. But I'll get to the life lesson junk later.

Let's start with the all-night train party we had out of St. Louis. The first-string colored players were back from their two days at the horse and dog tracks, some flush with dollar bills like Cannonball Redding and some broke as hobos like Turkey Stearnes. The plain fact was that the Black Phillies who were supposed to be worse trounced the Cards in the last two games and were invited along to Cincy, meaning there were about 49 Negro players stuffed into our three train cars and almost no room for any of them to sleep.

Not that we could've anyway, because Cannonball had a huge dice game going halfway across the Mississippi and Oscar's club of girlfriends who got seats behind our dugout yesterday were parading through the cars and Biz Mackey had a phonograph cranked up and the hollering and hooting and dancing and Louis Armstrong trumpet and thick cigar clouds from Smokey Joe's Havana made it hard to breathe, let alone sleep.

Charleston hadn't told his players who was going to play against the Reds, mainly to keep them all juiced up and ready to go, but we all knew Carl Mays and Eppa Rixey were set to face us and those guys wouldn't be afraid of nine Babe Ruths.

We pulled into Cincinnati mid-morning, climbed onto two special buses Rube had rented for us, and headed right to Redland Field. No one had eaten breakfast but boxes of sticky muffins from the station were passed around and the jokes were flying just as fast.

And then we got to the ballpark, where two dozen cops holding billy clubs and pistols blocked the players' entrance gate.

Rube Foster stood waiting for us right in front of them, looking more sad than a man could possibly look. "Black Phillies gotta close up shop, darlins," he said, his voice all chokie, "Rutledge wired me from New York and I have to agree with the man."

"What are you talking about??" screamed Benny.

"We're just too damn good, that's what I'm talking about. And if we lay the same kind of lumber on the Reds and Pirates, the whole pennant race could turn into a joke. Much as I like showin' up these folks, you can't say it's all that fair."

We were all stunned or shocked. Everyone knew Judge Landis was still in his coma and figured this fun might go on forever. The rest of the white Phillies were standing just inside the gate in their street clothes, waiting and watching, and I caught Heinie Sand's eye as he shrugged his shoulders at me. Oscar stepped up to Rube and puffed up his chest with all the dignity he could muster in the moment.

"Least you could do is get us good seats for the game today."

"Can't do that, boy" It was August Herrmann, the owner of the Reds, also standing inside the gate, "We have sold out games in this town and no colored section to put you anyway."

Oscar looked like he was ready to bust, but Mule Suttles poked him in the side and said, "Forget it Oscar. Let's just find us a good alley." Benny and me looked at each other but it was clear there was nothing we could do. That's right: I was a batboy again.

So Jimmy Ring took our ball, back after a nice little vacation with his 5-15 record, and went up against Carl Mays and his 17-6. The Reds fans were all buzzing in the stands, expecting to see the colored stars they'd heard so much about, and the German Over-the-Rhine Boys were as quiet as could be out in the right bleachers. We managed a few hits in the first five innings but basically rolled over and died while the Reds were busy scoring one in the 1st and two in the 4th on the usual Edd Roush triple.

I was kind of in a fog and had to remind myself how to arrange the bats because it had been so long. When Harper and Holke singled with two outs in our 6th I got a little touch of excitement, but this was still Carl Mays, after all.

Then big Cy Williams walked up there, his face all tense. I had a funny feeling about the at-bat but before I could even think about it Cy belted the ball right down the line for a double and our first run. Mays got shaky and threw a wild one that scored Holke and made it 3-2. I think Mays must've known how lucky he was not to be facing the coloreds, but what it did was soften him too much against us, because Mokan, Ford and Ring all doubled in a row with one gone in the 7th and we were ahead 4-3!

And we didn't stop. Holke and Cy singled to start the 8th, and after a ground out, Bressler dropped a fly in left for another run. Mays then did what he's famous for and put a fastball in Mokan's back. Mokan dropped his bat, ran to the mound and swung at Carl's head and the battle was on! Mays was the only one who got kicked out, which got the fans throwing more garbage than we'd seen in St. Louis, and poor Jakie May got smacked around too for a Ford single and second Jimmy Ring double.

Jimmy couldn't even be touched after that, and the White Phillies had picked up where their colored brothers had left off.

Benny and me looked around for Oscar and Biz and whoever outside the field later, but couldn't find them. We went back to the train station on a hunch and sure enough, there they all were about to board for Chicago, Rube's home and the place they could all get connections to wherever they came from. We shook hands with as many players as we could and even embraced a few, and it was hard to talk without crying a little.

"You two and your friend Roy and that Butterboat feller, you all deserve medals," said Oscar. That was good to hear, because from my point we deserved kicks in the behind for starting a project that was so bound to fail.

"Frogs can't get tasty flies unless they come out of their holes," said Rube, his eyes fighting back wetness, "Maybe some day we can all try this again, darlins." And with that he boarded the train after letting every last one of the colored players board first. Heavy mist was rolling in off the Ohio River with the sunset, and me and Benny stood there next to the track and watched until the train hissed and rolled and clacked and finally vanished straight into it.

PHL 000 002 240 - 8 14 0
CIN 100 200 000 - 3 8 2

LESSON LEARNED, ACTION TAKEN
August 22, 1924

Benny wouldn't get out of bed all morning, and when he finally did he just sat there in our hotel room and drank seltzer water. "It isn't fair. We had a chance to catch the Bucs with those guys." I reminded him that even after winning seven straight we're still over 25 games out of first place near the end of August but he didn't wanna hear it. He said he felt the same way he did after rehearsing for a school play for three weeks and then doing the acting—in other words, everything inside him had drained out.

I gave up on Benny and went down to have breakfast with Heinie Sand. He was still pretty sparky over yesterday's game but even though he was happy to be playing again he was just as sad to see the Black Phillies leave.

"I can't imagine what this must be like for them Negroes. I didn't know any myself growing up in San Francisco, but I sure know how tough it is to make the bigs and when you got all this race pressure on top of that it's hard to believe they can even focus on hitting a baseball." I said him that maybe because the ball is white it helps them, and he just laughed and munched on a bacon strip. "All I know is that I wanna keep our win streak going no matter what. If a guy is purple or green and can play up a storm he deserves a square chance, and I'm gonna do my best as sort of a tribute to them."

After yesterday's surprise win against Mays, we had even tougher chances today with Rixey going, and through six innings he was up to his old Redland Field tricks, shutting us down on just two singles. Carlson was doing his usual Houdini act for us, but Ike Caveney's 2-run homer in the 2nd was the only real damage they did off him.

Then Babe Pinelli booted Cy's grounder to start the 7th. After Wilson lined out, Johnny Mokan banged one high and deep to left. Bressler ran up the little hill in front of the fence but a wind gust carried the ball right over the top and the game was tied! Rixey was rattled and threw away Parkinson's dribble for a two-base error and our dugout was cooking again. Heinie took his bat from me with the most determined look I'd ever seen on his face and whacked the first pitch into the corner for a scoring double and a 3-2 lead!

Carlson gave Bressler a double to begin their 8th, and after Steineder relieved Pinelli got him home with a scoring fly. The Reds defense has the most errors in the league, though, and with two gone and two on in the top of the 9th, Caveney muffed another one and we took a 4-3 lead.

But Steineder was off his game, and singles in a row by Critz, Bubbles Hargrave and Walker tied it again and we went extras. Jakie May took over for the still-angry Rixey and Mokan led with a single off him in the 11th. After Parkinson whiffed, Heinie the Terror went back up to the dish and this time shot a ball into the right corner, scooted all the way around to third for a run-scoring triple!

Cincy wouldn't die, though, and loaded the sacks with one out against Huck Betts, who I thought had recovered from getting hammered by the Cards the other day when pitching for the Black Phils. Well, he recovered all at once, as Bressler bounced into a short-to-home-to-first double play with the infield playing up and we had eight in a row!

Heinie got tossed in the shower with his uniform on and had at least three players fighting over who was going to buy him tonight's steak. Benny even came to dinner with us, all jazzed up because we now had fifty wins on the season. "Wait'll we get to Pittsburgh after this!" is all he kept saying, and thankfully, no one was listening.

PHL 000 000 301 01 - 5 9 1
CIN 020 000 011 00 - 4 15 4

A LICKETY-SPLIT FAREWELL
August 23, 1924

CINCINNATI—One more game. One more game played in this sweltering city of hills and the Ohio River, of Carl Headhunter Mays and Eppa Rixey (I could say his name all day), of German speakeasies and crazy Over-the-Rhine Boys and a young fraulein named Ute I hope doesn't live here anymore.

Elected to get us out of town happy was Joe Oecshger, who went home to Chicago while the Black Phillies had his job and did nothing but sit by the lake and read fiction books for over a week, so he was good and rested. The Reds were in a real nasty mood after dropping the first two to us, and it seemed pretty clear that they let up a bit after finding out they didn't have to play those colored monsters.

Proving this in the 1st inning was their biggest star Edd Roush, who dropped Wrightstone's easy fly after Cy got us on the board with a scoring double, and it was 2-0 Phils right out of the gate. Oeschie was pitching like he was still in his beach seat, scattering a single, double and plunked batter through the first five innings. The crowd was getting as restless and angry as it's possible for an Ohio crowd to get, and after Wilson and Mokan doubled and their Cuban starter Luque botched a grounder to give us a 4-0 lead, the entire right bleacher section, filled with Over-the Rhine Boys, stood up together and razzed the field so loud that a flock of pigeons took off from under the grandstand roof and probably headed for Texas.

We all had grins on our faces when our boys took the field for the last of the 6th, but the bleacher cries were like electric shocks under the Reds players' rumps. Chick Shorten batted for Luque and doubled. Walker and Daubert singled. Bressler walked. Lefty Clarence Mitchell took the ball to get rid of Roush and Edd got rid of him with a mash of a triple over Cy's head and a sudden tie game. Steinder took over, Pinelli singled, and Red-lands Field was a crazy-house as they took the lead without making an out!

Ray got out of the inning, but then Jakie May took the hill for Cincy and had worse luck than Luque could've dreamed of. Heinie walked to start the 7th, and Daubert muffed Holke's grounder to put two aboard. After a shallow Cy fly, Butch Henline hit for Wrightstone and got plunked. Jimmie Wilson, his head still swelled up after his history-making game with the coloreds in St. Louis, then ripped Jakie's first pitch high and deep and out of the park in left and Redlands Field was a funeral parlor all over again. A grand slam!! Wilson even took off my cap to mussy my hair when he crossed home plate. Daubert booted the very next pitch hit by Mokan and the sausage wrappers and pop bottles started flying.

Steinder pitched the last three innings lightning-quick to keep our out-fielders from getting skulled, gave up no hits, and we were in and out of the showers and racing off to the train station even quicker. Benny and me kept our heads down so the batches of Over-the-Rhine idiots snooping around the train platforms wouldn't see us, and then the big rolling poker party headed off to Pittsburgh, where we even get a Sunday off tomorrow.

Lying up in my berth later with a head full of illegal gin and rocking back and forth I suddenly remembered we'd won nine games in a row, the last three with whites only. If that ain't a miracle than I don't know what is.

PHL 200 002 400 01 - 8 10 1
CIN 000 005 000 00 - 5 7 4

LOSING OUR FORTUNES AT FORBES
August 25, 1924

Benny couldn't wait for us to get to Forbes Field. "Nine in a row, pal. And Bucs are gonna make ten." After checking to be sure he wasn't high on reefer, I pretended to agree to keep him in a good mood, and hurried into the visiting club house to dress up in my batboy gear.

All the players were excited, because playing the league leaders always sharpens you like a pencil, and Johnny Couch who can sometimes be great was throwing for us against Wilbur Cooper, who is 13-9 despite pitching awful much of the time.

I heard some grumblings during the batting practice from Pirates who felt let down by not being able to face our colored brothers again—after all, they were the only NL team to beat the Black Phils—but all that did was get me excited because the Reds had felt the same way and then gone out and dropped three in a row to us.

The big problem here, though, was that slugging backstop Earl Smith was back in their lineup after a long injury, so beating these guys would be even tougher. But after Hod Ford singled with one out, a ball squirted past rusty-looking Smith and got him to second. Holke then got him in with a single and we had a 1-0 lead.

The amazing Cuyler doubled to lead their 2nd, and Wright got him home to tie the game, but the inning ending when Rabbit Maranville doubled and Cy smoked him at home plate with a perfect throw. A Max Carey single and steal and Moore single put them up 2-1 in the 3rd, but then Lady Luck gave us another big kiss. Holke singled to start the 4th, and when Cy poked one out to center, Carey lost it in the sun for a three-base error!

After a Jimmie Wilson single we had a 3-2 lead, and that's when Couch laid down for no one. Four innings went by with the Bucs only getting one single (by Cuyler, of course), and when Mokan bombed a ball over the left fence in the 8th we had a miracle two-run lead.

But Pittsburgh is where 1924 miracles have been dying all year, and we all should've known better. With two on and two out in their 8th and the unstoppable Cuyler up, an easy grounder got under Ford's glove for an error to load the bases, and Smith made it 4-3 with a single. We loaded the bases with two gone in the 9th, but Art Stone relieved Cooper to face Cy, who popped weakly to right and strand everybody. And you don't gotta be a baseball genius to know what that means.

Yup, with one out in the last of the 9th, the Rabbit ripped a ball that chewed up the grass between Cy and Mokan for a huge triple. Johnny Gooch, who played catcher while Smith was out and batted about .440, pinch-hit for Stone and popped an easy scoring fly to Mokan and the tie game.

This brought in secret Buc weapon Babe Adams, the stingiest relief man around, and he stingied us for no hits in three innings until Kiki Cuyler added to his legend by clubbing a two-out homer off Betts in the last of the 12th to end our win streak and turn our club house into a funeral parlor.

I wished they'd beaten us 16-2 like they usually do, but what the heck. At least we'll be home in a few days.

PHI 100 200 010 000 - 4 12 1
PIT 011 000 011 001 - 5 12 2

THE FIRST DAY OF THE END OF THE PENNANT RACE
August 26, 1924

After the Bucs ambushed us in the 9th yesterday and squeaked out another late win (making them 15-2 against us and 13-4 in extra innings vs. the league), they were mouthing off to writers again about how lousy a team we were and that the Black Phillies really bowed out because they were afraid to face them again. This drove Art Fletcher crazy. He was so mad afterwards he wouldn't come out of the shower and Cy had to do all our talking to the reporters.

Today with Jimmy Ring going against Johnny Morrison, we figured we at least had a fair chance, but the first two innings proved that this is a Pirate year through and through, and nothing Fletcher tries with our bunch is going to work.

Need a little evidence? After Carey and Grimm went out in the Buc 1st, Eddie Moore doubled and up came Cuyler, haunter of our dreams. After winning the game yesterday with a deep blast, Fletcher got cute and walked him on purpose, setting off the home crowd and bringing up Earl Smith.

Why did anyone think that would work? Smith cold-cocked the first Ring pitch into the right corner to score both runs. The Phils got angry enough to get them right back when Cy doubled leading the 2nd and two singles, a walk and passed ball followed, but these Pirates eat challenges for breakfast, lunch and dinner. Wright singled, Rabbit walked, Morrison bunted them over, and Fletcher pulled in the infield for Carey, who cracked one right past Ford for a 2-run single. After a Moore walk, Art said the hell with it and pitched to Cuyler this time—who of course singled for run number five.

The score stayed 5-2 them for the next four and a half innings, Morrison showing why he's 12-4 by shutting down every scoring chance easily. In the 7th the Bucs got another run on a Traynor single and Wright bounced one out to Heinie, who booted the double play chance to make it 7-2 and send Fletcher screaming into the club house tunnel.

Cy took over but he was just as disgusted and wouldn't even take Ring out when Carey led with a homer in the 8th and four straight Pirates singled. Fletcher was nowhere to be found later, and when I asked Cy where he went he took me aside and dropped his voice.

"Western Union. He's sending a telegram to Rube Foster in Chicago."

Oh boy. I knew what that meant. But wouldn't that get us in trouble with Judge Landis?

"Worth the consequences if you ask me," said Cy, "Damn Bucs want some competition for a day? Guess we might as well oblige 'em."

PHI 020 000 010 - 3 9 1
PIT 230 000 25x - 12 16 0

AN ALL-DAY BATTLE INTO THE WET AND DARK
August 27, 1924

I was tossing and turning all night, and it wasn't because of the near-by factory smoke coming in my Schenley Hotel window. Fletcher wanted Rube to bring the colored stars to Pittsburgh for the last game of the trip and put the dang Bucs in their place. To me and Benny it was a great idea, but also a completely nerve-cracking one, which is probably why my friend was down at Muzzy's Pool Hall most of the night distracting himself. If the Black Phillies even showed up who knew what the white ones would do, or how the Pirate fans would feel, or if Judge Landis would kick our team out of the league!

Cy was the only real quiet player at breakfast, so I knew he hadn't told any of the others what was going on, and Fletcher wasn't there because he was at the train station waiting for Rube. That crazy kitchen girl Gretchen who I almost got into trouble with on my last time through here was staying far away from my table, but I was so twisted up over the upcoming game I almost asked if I could hide out in her river cabin the whole day and make possum stew or something.

But no, I am a professional batboy and emergency third base coach after all, and whatever players ended up taking the field were going to need their bats. So I got off the trolley at Forbes and South Bouquet, walked through the side gate and into the visiting club house ready for anything.

And anything's what I got. Rube was in there with a team of his best stars, going forehead-to-forehead with George Harper and Fletcher between. "You HAD your playin' time already, boy!" is all Harper kept saying, and Rube came back with "Then how come you invited us back? Maybe 'cause you lillies beat these Pirates twice all year." To which Wrightstone butted in with his goony face all red, "WE wasn't the ones who sent the invitation, and you haven't beaten 'em ether!" The other players milled around but none of them jumped in until Cy finally separated the mess and yelled at the room.

"No one's taking your job, George! That goes for all of you! We just don't want to leave Pittsburgh knowing they got their 80th win against us, that's all. And what's wrong with seeing them get their teeth knocked out for one day? Forget what color these guys are, they got our big winning streak going, didn't they? Seems to me we owe 'em a little encore."

Harper, who'd already dressed for the game, ripped his uniform off, marched over to a trash barrel and stuffed it inside rather than give it to one of the coloreds. Wrightstone did the same thing, but the other players felt dumb with Oscar Charleston and Mule Suttles standing there looking at them none too happy, and handed over their uniforms.

The Forbes crowd went wild in a good way when the Black Phillies took their field. They'd been reading in the papers about how the Pirates were hoping to play and beat them again, and sure enough, every Buc in the home dugout had a big smirk when they saw Smokey Joe Williams lead the pack onto the field. Bullet Joe had started for us last time instead of the smokey one, and the Pirates cuffed him around for 13 hits. We all knew

Smokey meant business because he had a bigger Cuban cigar in his mouth than usual before he left the dugout.

The game started on the later side to fit all the Pirate and colored fans into the park, and there were folks standing everywhere. The air was real humid and green-black clouds seemed to be getting together on the horizon. Ray Kremer was going for the Bucs and even though Torriente walked to start the game and Mule got him to third with a single, Charleston fanned to help Kremer get out of the jam and set off the crowd. Turkey Stearnes singled off him to begin the 2nd, went nowhere, but Smokey Joe was all-game-faced and got the first six Pirates without a hitch, whiffing Traynor too.

Then Wright booted Torriente's grounder on the hard Forbes infield to begin the 3rd. Pop Lloyd and Oscar both skied out, but Mule crushed one high off the left wall that just missed going out and Torriente ran in all the way from first, giving me a pretty nice breeze in my third base coach box when he went past. Wright made up for the boot with a lead single off Smokey in the last of the 3rd but he was left high and dry. Smokey bounced into a double play to kill a little rally in the top of the 4th, and then the bottom of the 4th happened.

It started kind of quiet with an infield single from Carey. Max danced around off the bag more than he usually does, which I figured was his way of making fun of the colored style. Smokey threw over there a bunch of times, which got the crowd all angry and lost him his focus. Yup, there went Eddie Moore whacking a single into left and bringing up the dreaded Cuyler. Kiki helped us out with a roller out to Dobie Moore, but the shortstop tossed it wide to Pop for an error and the bases were loaded!

One thing's been clear all season with this Buc team: make one mistake and they'll bash your brains into oatmeal. Mama? Serve it up! Big and tough Earl Smith walked to the plate, spit on his hands and put the first pitch high and long over the brick wall in right for a grand slammer! The Forbesians went crazy (except for the colored fans), Smokey Joe hung his head with a hand on his hip and didn't even watch Smith roll around the bases. He walked Traynor, but then got the next three guys and re-lit his cigar when he got in the dugout and just sat there with his legs crossed, like he'd just been out for a night stroll.

Kremer, meanwhile had gotten even tougher. He put us down in the 5th and 6th with only a Turkey single in the way. Smokey got the side 1-2-3 in the same innings, back to his old self, but he knew he couldn't stay in the game if we weren't scoring. So Cool Papa Bell batted for him with one out in the top of the 7th and ripped a single. Torriente got him over to third with another one, which was when I whispered in Cool Papa's ear to tag up on a deep fly. Bell brushed me off like I was a bug and said, "Son? I'm comin' in on a sneeze." Lloyd then popped one halfway out to Cuyler in left and Cool Papa was across the plate in a dust cloud before I could even turn my head.

Cannonball Redding took over for Smokey and got Kremer to bunt-pop into a double play with Wright on first, killing their 7th. Then Mule clubbed his second double to start the 8th. Jud Wilson knocked him home with a single to make it 4-3. The stands got nervous. The dark clouds were closer now and had erased the sun. With Turkey at the plate, Smith let a ball dribble off his mitt and Wilson went to third. Stearnes grounded out to hold him there but Dobie picked out a fastball and cracked it into center to tie the game! Whoa, boy.

Redding threw two more scoreless innings, giving up two singles in each one but getting out of the jams, and on we went into extra innings. Not one person had left the park, also because the exit tunnels were so jammed with standers that no one could move down them if they wanted to. A few drops of rain were falling and rumbles and lightning flashes were kicking in.

Arnie Stone, who took over for Kremer, got the first two Black Phils in the 10th but then Turkey worked himself a walk. Willie Wells batted for Dobie and destroyed a ball into the left gap between Cuyler and Carey. I windmilled my arm, jumped around in the coach box and yelled at Turkey, but he didn't need any help from me. The problem was that Kiki had already picked up the ball and uncorked it toward home. Turkey almost ran into me rounding third, started sliding on his belly four feet from the plate but Smith was waiting there like a good-sized tree, the ball waiting in his hand and Turkey ramming into his gut couldn't knock the thing loose. OUT! ! No one could believe we were still tied.

Redding gave up two more singles in his 10th, one to Cuyler of course, but he got Smith on a deep fly to send us to the 11th. Beckwith hit for Cannonball in the 11th and whiffed, and Bullet Joe Rogan came on to pitch. Traynor, Wright and Rabbit couldn't touch him, and we went to the 12th.

It was almost too dark to play all of a sudden, and the umpires had a meeting to talk about it. But the crowd started yelling and they kept the action going, which was definitely the best plan. Tubby Scales agreed, as he hit for Lloyd and creamed a triple to begin the 12th. Up came Oscar, who was zero-for-five with two whiffs and in no mood to be the game's goat. Stone threw him a big curve and he whacked it high and deep to center. Carey caught the ball and Tubby skipped home clapping his hands. Mule celebrated the lead with a second triple, but Stone got a couple of grounders to end the inning.

It was up to Bullet Joe to save this thing. He got pinch-hitter Gooch and Carey, but then Rev Cannady at third let Grimm's grounder play him and the Bucs had a man on first. Eddie Moore was up, with Cuyler on deck. If everyone in the place wasn't screaming, they sure were inside themselves. Moore worked the count up, then sent a hot grounder out to Willie Wells at short, who stepped on the second bag for the force. It was never close to being easy, but we'd beaten the Big Bad Bucs!

The Pirate fans were so stunned by what they'd seen they forgot to throw things on the field, and we were off it and into the dugout before they could breathe again. The thunderstorm exploded over the park right then, too, and by the time it ended about a half hour later, the Black Phillies and dark clouds were gone forever, and there we were boarding our train back to Philly, ready to roll out the rest of our sorry season with a victory twinkle in our eyes.

```
BLACK PHILS   001 000 120 001 - 5 13 2
PIRATES       000 400 000 000 - 4 10 1
```

THERE'S NO PLACE LIKE NUTTY HOME
August 28, 1924

Ah yes, back in my own lumpy bed. Back to waking up to Mama's bacon and egg smells and an extra bowl of her maple oatmeal and geez I better write to Rachel soon if I know what's good for me. Back to Benny showing up at my door too early and the nickel streetcar ride to hot, smelly and nutty Baker Bowl, which was packed today for a weird Thursday double-header against the worst team in baseball.

With the number to kick the Phillies out of the pennant race down to three, I was looking forward to putting off that sad business with a nice long day running our smoking bats back and forth to the dugout while various Phils took them to the Braves' heads.

No deal. After seeing our colored replacements finish off the Bucs in extra innings yesterday, the white players were still in dreamland, and hit like a bunch of corpses against Mr. Larry Benton of Boston, who at game time had a 5-15 record and earned run average of 7.42. Formerly Luckless Lawrence walked seven Phillie hitters, all at the bottom of our lineup, and not a single one could score.

Meantime Hal Carlson got hurt after doing his typical escape tricks the first two innings, and Steineder had to take over for the next five. Casey Stengel singled in a run off him in the 3rd put he threw darn good until the 8th inning came around. A Cunningham walk and singles from McInnis and Sperber brought on Glazner, who quickly gave the Braves two more runs they didn't even need.

The 3-hit shutout got our club house all heated again between games and this time even yours truly made a speech. "C'mon guys," I piped up, "Didn't we just win three in a row in Cincy? How can we let these stinky jerks push us around? There's brats in knee socks at my school who swing harder than you!" Everyone was laughing at me under their breath up to that point, but then the brat line made everything quiet. I quickly apologized and took those words back, but Cy came over and patted my arm.

"We all hear what you're saying, kid. Just be ready to hit for me in the bottom of the 9th if we need you."

That shut me up good, and I thanked God he was kidding. Even though I did spend a bit more time looking at our smaller bats before Game 2.

Dutch Stryker, who's even worse than Benton, was going for Boston, while the only pitcher who's so bad he should be in prison for impersonating one, Clarence Mitchell, went for us. Three singles gave them a run in the 2nd, but after Wilson got plunked with a ball in our 2nd, Hod Ford said enough of this malarkey and belted one into the packed bleachers in left to give us the lead, and our first runs for a few days.

Then it was time for Clarence the Clown. McInnis doubled with one gone in the 3rd. Mann singled, Felix singled. Cotton Tierney hit a two-out, three-run homer and it was 5-2 Braves. Steineder couldn't be used again, so after four Brave singles began the 4th, Art Fletcher walked out to the hill with his giant butterfly net and scooped Clarence out of the game for Glazner. Whitey wasn't much better, and it was 9-2 them when Betts took over with two gone in the 5th.

I was suddenly hating my batboy job. The score board showed the Pirates beating up on the dying Reds to no one's surprise, and if we lost this second game we'd be finished for the year. I couldn't give another speech or even enjoy watching the game because it stunk like a dead mule and I was too busy hauling bats around anyway. All I had to look forward to was another club house of doom later and someone smashing something and everyone looking for a good illegal place to drink.

Which is when Betts tripled in a run for us. Old Huck, the only sort-of-reliable relief man we'd had all year and used more than an eskimo's snowshoes, had just knocked in our third run of the game for the sheer heck of it. From that point on, Betts didn't say a word, just pitched his brain off and gave the Braves nothing but three singles the rest of the way.

What he gave us was hope. It also helped that Stryker went out with a gimp leg and manager Bancroft stuck Lou North in, a pitcher even worse than Stryker. Cy looked a little insulted by that, and after Gus Felix dropped Heinie's fly for a 3-base error to start our 8th, he tripled Sand home, and two outs later, Wilson bombed one out and it was 9-6 just like that!

North was still in there to begin the 9th, and after Ford walked and Henline hit a pinch-double, Skinny Graham, the best reliever on either team, came on. But Skinny didn't have a chance against the angry Phils. Harper singled right away, and Mann booted a ball in right to make it 9-8. Holke bunted the runners over, and here was Cy walking up again. Skinny threw him a couple low ones, then missed high and Cy shot it on a line into right for a 2-run single and got every Brave walking off the diamond and every Phillie player and fan jumping out of their skulls. What a win!

We felt like the governor had taken nooses off our necks, and Benny bought ice cold cherry fizzers for the whole room down at Mort's later. Which is exactly why you never, ever leave a ballpark early. Living for another pitch, another at-bat, another inning and another day is the sweet and sticky blood that squirts through baseball's veins.

BOS 001 000 021 - 4 10 0
PHL 000 000 000 - 0 3 0

BOS 014 310 000 - 9 18 2
PHL 020 010 034 - 10 10 1

THAT JOB STUNK ANYWAY

August 29, 1924

Rachel beat me to it, and her letter was short and not all that sweet:

Dear Vinny:
Where in God's name are you? I thought we were engaged!

I crumpled the page up on our front stoop, getting a weird look from the postman. Didn't she know I'd been traveling with the team for two weeks? What did she think I was up to?

Benny gabbed my ear off on the streetcar about how many runs we were going to score off Joe Genewich and his 3-16 record, but I wasn't even pretending to half listen. I'd been trying to talk to Rachel's father about our wedding plan for a long time, but my batboy job and colored exhibition game business got in the way every time. On the next Phillies trip to Brooklyn I had to take care of things.

Joe Oeschger got elected to start our next win-or-die game, but he was a creaky wheel from the second batter, when he botched Stuffy McInnis' little bouncer to put a man on first. After the second out, Stengel, Bancroft, Gibson and Padgett all singled, Tierney walked, and it was 4-0 in favor of the lousy Braves. We got a run back in the last of the 1st, and then three singles a walk and passed ball in the 3rd tied the score and got the dugout all electrified when we saw the Reds were up 4-0 on the Pirates across the state.

Oeschie just couldn't keep himself together, though. A Padgett single with two outs in the 5th put them up by one, and then in the 6th, his arm turned into spaghetti. A walk, two singles and a double began things, and after one out Tierney knocked home two more with a single and five Boston runs were across. Glazner took over to mop the bloody floor but we all knew our crazy pennant dream was over.

And that was when I'd had enough. It was another in a string of brutally hot days, and after Cy singled in our 6th to put two aboard, Wrightstone picked the worst time to start yapping at me because I'd handed him "the wrong stick". After arguing for a few seconds I just went back in the dark dugout, brought out the same one and he never knew the difference.

Or so I thought. With the score 11-5 Braves in the last of the 9th he started for home plate to start our last rites, then turned back and shook his bat in my face.

"Ever since you showed up and helped those colored boys take our jobs, we haven't had one piece of luck." When I tried to yell back he told me to shut up, so I yelled even louder.

"So do something about it, you dope! Hit a six-run homer and tie the game!" He raised his bat like he was going to club me with it and I snatched it out of his paw, ran over to a rail next to our dugout and smashed the bat in half, threw both pieces in his direction. Fletcher, every player on the field, in both dugouts and every fan in the stands was staring at me in shock but I didn't give a crumb. I ripped off my hat and uniform, dropped

them in the dirt and walked down the left field line and right out the exit
gate in my long johns.

I think the first time I looked up again was when I reached the Western
Union office and grabbed a telegram form. The guy behind the counter took
one look at me and said, "You better put some pants on there, son." I didn't
say a word, just stood there and wrote out my message:

DEAR RACHEL:
    ROBINS SCHEDULED FOR DOUBLE-HEADER HERE ON LABOR DAY.
BRING FATHER AND I'LL BUY HIM LUNCH BECAUSE DON'T THINK I'LL
BE WORKING.—VINNY

"Son?" the guy said again, "Your pants?"
"Never mind that. Where's the nearest flower delivery place?"

BOS 400 010 510 - 11 16 1
PHL 103 000 102 - 7 15 2

RELAXING IN THE SUN WITH JOHNNY COUCH
August 30, 1924

Mama wasn't all that upset about me walking off my job, because she
never thought a "honky tonk ball yard" was a good place for a young adult
person like me to be spending most every day in. She wanted me to have
a more regular profession like a banker or butcher, and over our eggs this
morning started asking me to look up her Uncle Salvatore at the Reading
Terminal Hog Exchange again. I felt too rotten over myself to even think
about work just yet, and told her that. Besides, I was too nervous waiting
for a telegram back from Rachel about whether she could come down on
Labor Day or not.

Benny sure didn't smooth out my mood any, showing up at the door
just in the time for Mama's last plate of sunnysides. "One more with the
Braves, Vin. C'mon, they need you there."

"Yeah, but I don't need that crappy job or hearing any more crud from
racist jerks."

"Hey, Cy Williams asked me to come here and talk you back into it."
Mama's eyes lit up at the sound of his name. She hadn't gone out with him
for a while.

"He's a grownup. He can get over it."

"Okay, but you're my best friend and I need you out in the bleachers
again to just watch a game and yell whatever we want at the players and
chow down those salty sausage rolls and drink the best lemonade in Pennsylvania and not even care who wins." He flashed his biggest smile of bad
teeth at me.

I hawed and hemmed and hawed some more. Then remembered tomorrow was a day off for the Phillies, meaning that would mean...two straight
days without baseball?

* * *

It was Barnes for the Braves, Johnny Couch for us, and the usual goof-ers in the bleachers having a great time. Oscar the Peanut Man gave us two bags for nothing, fat Rollo Briggs was there to bet on pitches with us, and with nothing to do but watch people play baseball it was the most fun I'd had at Baker Bowl since Carlson threw that shutout back in June on Benny's birthday.

"Lew Wendell? Who's he?" Benny was as puzzled as me when the mega-phone man announced the lineups, and then I remembered that for the last game of a season series between two teams, the managers sometimes start their third-string players who've been on the bench all year. Well, with the basement life of these clubs, everyone but Fletcher's pet dog was getting a chance. The Phils sent Andy Woehr out to third (fine with me, because I didn't have to see Wrightstone's ugly face all day), Wendell be-hind the plate, Parkinson to third, Fritz Henrich (?) to right field and first backup catcher Butch Henline out to left field—meaning straight in front of us.

"Hi Butch!" yelled Benny before the first pitch was even thrown, "Long sea no time!"

The Braves had been throwing every one of their bums on the field all year to try and get the team going, so the only new person I didn't know was Herb Thomas in center. Not that it mattered. Two singles and a scor-ing force-out by Casey Stengel in the 1st put them up 1-0. Padgett and mystery Herb singled to open the Boston 2nd, and Bob Smith doinked an-other single in front of Henline, who kicked it for an error and made it 2-0.

"Wrong glove, Butch!" I yelled, "Catcher's mitt stays in the dugout!" Benny jabbed me with a wink and Henline actually looked around for a second, recognizing my voice. The sun was beating down until we had to unbutton our shirts, there was a good chance we'd get beat by a bunch of wahoolies, and you know what? I didn't even care.

Everyone in the bleachers screamed for hits whenever the third-rate Phils went to bat, and it started paying off in the last of the 2nd. The great Lew Wendell reached second on a Smith throwing error. Parkinson and Henrich singled and then Couch did too and we were tied 2-2! Ford singled to begin our 3rd, but after the next two guys went out, Wendell banged one off the bleacher wall in front of us to make it second and third. Parkinson walked and Andy Woehr binkered a ball through the infield for the lead. Barnes was out of his mind on the mound, served up another single to Hen-rich.

We were all on our feet, stomping and shaking the bleachers until I thought the thing would collapse and crush forty or so people. But Johnny Couch did the crushing instead, ripping Barnes' next pitch over the right wall for a grand slam homer!

"Pretzels for the whole row!!" yelled Benny, and boy if he didn't make good on that right away. We didn't score another run after that but we didn't need to, because Couch was laying back on that mound like a fat dad on a Sunday. Boston scratched out a couple more runs in the 5th thanks to two errors, one by Couch himself, but I think it was because he was getting bored. We finished the year 12-10 against the awful Braves, which wasn't great but Boston had to beat someone I guess.

The other fun thing was that Benny made sixty dollars betting on pitches with Rollo, and was already trying to talk me into going out to Atlantic City for the Phillies' day off tomorrow. I told him I was still waiting for Rachel's telegram but he poo-pooped on that idea.

"Doesn't mean they won't deliver it. Anyway, aren't guys supposed to go out for some crazy times right before they get married?"

I hawed and hemmed and hawed some more...

BOS 110 020 000 - 4 9 1
PHL 026 000 00x - 8 12 3

NATIONAL LEAGUE through Saturday, August 30, 1924

Pittsburgh	80	45	.640	—
Brooklyn	73	54	.575	8
Cincinnati	73	55	.570	8.5
New York	68	57	.544	12
Chicago	63	64	.496	18
St. Louis	61	66	.480	20
PHILLIES	54	75	.419	28
Boston	36	92	.281	45.5

THE LAST BOARDWALK SHOW
August 31, 1924

The final Sunday of summer, and what better way to spend a day off from bad Phillies baseball then with one more trip to the New Jersey seashore? Benny and me decided on Atlantic City this time, mainly because we didn't want to run into those gin-drinking putt-putt girls who tried to fleece us back in June, and we were halfway down my stoop with our clothes bags when a taxi rolled up and out stepped guess who, folks?

Rachel Stone of Brooklyn with her father Saul.

Benny and me stared at them like they'd just popped out of the ground, before I shook the heck out of Saul's hand and embraced Rachel until her perfume was up my nose. "What are you...Why didn't you tell me—"

"Don't you like surprises? I thought you did. And my dad is just thrilled to see our boys in that big double-header tomorrow, right Dad?"

Saul was dressed in a suit and bowler like he was headed for the symphony, and sure seemed to be in a great mood. "We plan to murder you fellows, sorry to say."

Benny pushed out a weak smile and it was quiet for a second or two, so I told them we were off to Atlantic City. Rachel naturally brought up our time at Luna Park and it took about five seconds for me to talk myself into inviting them along. They had already checked into a hotel near Ritten-house Square and didn't bring any bathing clothes anyway, so off the four of us went to the train station.

Atlantic City was more packed than a packed factory of sardine cans. The last weekend of the summer always brings out the mobs, and there were circus acts to watch, and knucklebrains on the sand climbing on each other, and pretty girls for Benny to ogle and me to ignore, and more cheap tasty food you could imagine. I held Rachel's hand the whole time and she whispered to me that Saul didn't know about our engagement yet and when was I thinking of asking him? I couldn't exactly answer that because I wasn't prepared for the shock of seeing them today, so stalled her some more.

The bigger problem was that Saul wanted to find a place with a baseball scoreboard the second we hit the boardwalk. The Robins were home for their last game with the Giants, and it was killing Saul that he had to miss it, so "the least we could do is find an electric board!" It wasn't easy to find a good pretzel there when it was that crowded, let alone one of those things, but Benny did remember a newsstand near a Ferriss Wheel and we spent the next fifteen minutes squeezing through people until we found it.

The score after three innings was

NYG 100
BRK 000

"Why??" groaned Saul, fanning himself with his bowler, "That ingrate Bentley is pitching so why can't we hit him?? Get me away from here—"

So we walked down to the water, where Rachel took off her shoes and leggings and gave her white legs a salty bath, and Saul kept his entire suit on and couldn't relax one second. He said he had to find a rest room and disappeared for a good half hour until we went back to the electric board and there he was in more agony, because the score from Ebbets was now

NYG 100 001
BRK 000 001

"I can't bear this!" is all he said over and over, and it made me realize he hates McGraw's team even more than me and Benny do. "Get me away from here!" he yelled, and this time we took him on a little ride on these fake swan boats, which seemed to calm him down until we went into a tun-nel and his loud groan echoed all over the place and almost knocked me out of the boat. "It has to be the ninth inning by now! I need that electric board!"

We didn't even go back there with him, and when he joined us on a bench in front of a few hundred passing people, we could tell from his hound dog expression what had happened. "Doak was terrible. Gave up eleven hits. And on the same day the Pirates won!" Rachel patted his hand, kissed his cheek, and we started back to the train platform.

Hey Vin," said Benny, "How about you and me go to Atlantic City some-time?" I nodded with a sigh, looked over at poor Saul. Guess it was a good thing I didn't bring up marrying his daughter.

PART SIX
September

DAZZY OVER THE RING
September 1, 1924

I had it all figured out. First I'd get me, Rachel and her father great seats behind the Brooklyn dugout with Heinie's help. Then I'd count on Dazzy Vance winning his 20th game of the year against Jimmy Ring, which is kind of like betting on a leopard to handle a bunny. Then I'd get Saul alone in the fifteen or twenty minutes between games with a new cold lemonade and ask him if I could marry his daughter.

I would wait till we go out to dinner later, except like that day here in July when I asked Rachel the question in the first place, second games of double-headers are high-scoring and don't go the way you want them to, and I don't want him in any kind of mood like he was yesterday. I also thought about asking Heinie to "go easy" on the Robins for me, but that's about as illegal as you can get and I wouldn't feel good about myself if poor Heinie had to hunt raccoons with Shoeless Joe Jackson the rest of his life.

Autumn was definitely in town along with the Robins, though. I wasn't even sweating until the third inning. Rachel was wearing her peach-colored dress and hat and had a pretty sweet smile to match them. The stands were packed for the holiday, and during the little flag-marching parade I noticed Grover our old club house man who they must've talked out of retirement, toting bats around again in place of me. Oh well, I had to grow up sometime.

I was a little nervous the first few innings because Ring with his 6-16 record suddenly decided he was going to pitch well, and shut down the first six Brooklyn batters easy. Then Jimmy Johnston singled to open the 3rd, Zack Taylor got him to third with another single, and Dazzy walked to the plate and ripped one over Heinie's head, who jumped high enough to convince me he wasn't laying down. A Bernie Neis single and Ford error on Wheat's grounder made it 3-0, and Vance probably had all he needed.

I went and got Saul a sausage roll, and he asked me if it was "kosher meat". I said I had no idea if Kosher was the hog farmer's name, but that I'd been eating them all year and they were delicious, so who cared? He went for a popcorn bag instead, and I ended up eating my second sausage roll of the game. Rachel hardly ate a thing, being as nervous as me, and her plan was to go the ladies room between the games and leave us alone.

After a Neis scoring fly made it 4-0 Brooklyn, Vance settled down to business, getting 14 Phillies in a row at one point, whiffing six of them. He has a curve that you can't hit with a tree trunk, and sitting that close made it clear why he leads both leagues with 226 strikeouts. Saul was more excited every inning. "A shutout for his 20th win? Just imagine that!" he said a few times, and then the 9th inning rolled around a bit too quick.

Harper walked for starters, and Saul squirmed his behind around on the seat. Oh great. Was he going to lose his brain if Dazzy didn't throw a shutout? Heinie walked up, gave me a little nod from the home plate area and then cracked one into the left field corner. Phils on second and third! Dazzy struck out Holke, and it was Cy's turn. Now he knew I was sitting there but wouldn't look over at all, and I got the idea he wasn't too keen about me walking off the batboy job and probably didn't even want to go out with my mother anymore. He waited on a big Dazzy curve, whacked it deep to Wheat in left and Harper ran in to break the shutout.

I couldn't believe it, but Saul took off his hat and said something dark and yiddish, and even when Wrightstone lined out to end the game and give the Robins the win, he didn't look all that thrilled. Certainly not ready to listen to a giant question from me.

"I'm going to find a powder room, if that's what I can call it here," Rachel said with a wink, and hurried up the aisle. And there I was, three inches away from her father, with probably no better time to do this. So I sipped more of my lemonade, cracked open a peanut or two. Or three. Then wiped my salty, sweaty hands off on my pants and turned to him.

"Umm, Mr. Stone? I need to ask you for something."

"Popcorn? I think I finished the bag but there might be a bit more—"

"No, no. It's about Rachel. I um, love her a lot, you see. And I was wondering—

"You want to kiss her? It's only a natural thing, my boy. When I met her mother I couldn't even speak about doing that until we'd gone out to see half a dozen shows. There was a burlesque playing at the—"

"I 've already kissed her, Mr. Stone. And now I wanna marry her."

He squinted at me with one eye, then the other. And the sun was behind a cloud.

"How old are you?"

"Eighteen at the end of the month. But I'm finished with school, and I'm going to start looking for a real job, and—"

"And you'll become a Jew?"

"Umm...s-sure. I mean, how hard can it be? I'm sure I can find us a Kosher Brothers hog farm somewhere."

He turned away with a wave of his hand, mulling this over. Some of the players were already coming back on the field to warm up.

"Please, sir. I love Rachel more than anything."

"More than baseball? I don't believe that—"

"It's true. Watch this." I stood and turned my back on the field. "Let's go right now. I'll even miss the second game."

Suddenly there was a loud cheer that shot from one end of Baker Bowl to the other. Saul looked around me and saw fans pointing to the scoreboard:

The Cubs had beaten the Pirates 8-3 in their first game.

"Are you crazy??" He grabbed me by the wrist and jerked me back in my chair. "You can marry Rachel and come live with us in Brooklyn if you want, but we are not missing the second game!"

And so I became a soon-to-be-married half-Jewish man. Rachel returned and we hugged, and then both Stones screamed themselves silly for two hours as Jack Fournier got two singles, a homer, drove in five, Dutch Ruether made us look stupid and the Robins put Clarence Mitchell through a meat grinder 18-5 in the second game.

I hate to say it, reader-people, but the outcome meant nothing to me.

Rachel's warm hand was in mine even while the fans around us were booing, throwing things and finally giving up early and going home. We went
and got Mama after, and she was so shocked by the news she didn't even
notice we were celebrating at a restaurant that wasn't Italian.

And did I mention the Bucs lost the other half of their double-header?
Well Saul did, over appetizers, salad, the main course, and dessert.

BRK 003 100 000 - 4 9 0
PHL 000 000 001 - 1 3 2

BRK 402 200 604 - 18 22 0
PHL 100 000 031 - 5 6 2

WOOZY HUZZAHS
September 2, 1924

Rachel and her father took an early train back to New York because
Saul actually had to work for a living, and I was thrilled just to see him get
away from his team before he had a heart problem and the wedding was
called off. Last night at dinner it was decided Rachel and me would hitch
next Saturday night. That seemed a little too quick to organize things and
learn my Jewishness, but the whole thing was going to be at their synagogue, Saul already knew the date was open, and he wanted to get the
thing done so he could follow the end of the pennant race without distrac-
tions. Boy does he ever sound like me.

Mama was on a crying routine this morning because she knew her other
man was leaving and she'd be all alone, but I said maybe she'd meet a new
guy at the wedding if she kept her face dry for a couple hours. She liked
that idea, but was kind of wishing it was an Italian wedding instead.

Benny came by to take me to our next game with Brooklyn but wanted
to stop at Mort's first to "pick something up" that he left there. There was
a big sign on the door that said PRIVATE PARTY TODAY but he opened it
up anyway and shoved me inside.

"Surprise!!!"

Two dozen or so people were waiting for me, the usual Mort's regulars
and a bunch I knew from the neighborhood, and they toasted me with tall
glasses of bubbly red liquid I'd never seen before. Mort came around the
counter, pounded my back and walked me to a table with a giant bowl of
the same drink. "Super Vinny cherry fizzer! In honor of your soon-to-be
betrothicals." He poured me a mug of it and it was down the hatch. It was
spiked with someone's homemade illegal wine and had some kind of kick.

"We didn't know when you were leaving for New York," said Benny, "So
I thought we should take care of this celebration business right away." A
phonograph started up with jazz music, and a few of the saucier girls who
were there took turns dancing me around, and before long I was having the
time of my life. Even Pop Lloyd from the nearby Hilldale Daisies showed
up.

It was sure a decent place to follow our 7th place team. Mort ran over with ticker reports after every inning, and when I wasn't laughing, burping or doing the Charleston I followed the best I could. Back-to-back home run belts by High and Wheat gave Brooklyn a quick 2-0 lead, but then Burleigh "Ol' Stubblebeard" Grimes threw what could've been the worst inning of ball all year, seeing what his team's situation was. Harper tripled, Sand singled, Holke doubled, Cy singled and Wrightstone walked before he even got an out. Wilson hit into a double play but then Mokan reached on a single and error, Grimes kicked another one away and it was 4-2 us.

Wilson homered later after they got a run back to make it 5-3, then it was 5-4 after a High triple, and then Bill Hubbell coughed up the lead in the 8th, giving the Robins three beginning with a High double this time. We got one back on two walks, a bunt and a grounder, so it was 7-6 going to the last of the 9th. The ticker also told us that the Bucs were losing yet again to the Cubs, so this was suddenly a huge game. Mort poured in another batch of Super Vinny fizzer, and the guests who could still stand were bunched around the ticker waiting for every pitch.

Mostly everyone seemed to be pulling for Brooklyn, being Giants and Pirates haters, but when Phillie hero Cy Williams came up with one out against Ehrhardt and the ticker suddenly said WILLIAMS HOME RUN... BRK 7 PHL 7, the place divided itself with cheers and boos. Benny was off in the bathroom getting sick when Brooklyn's Eddie Brown scored what was about to be the winning run in the 10th on a Hubbell wild pitch, but when news came across that Pittsburgh had lost, his face looked less green right away.

Can this be a pennant race yet, we wondered? Brooklyn will be up at Braves Field next Saturday for a double-header, but if the games go late, will Mr. Stone be able to give his daughter away before midnight? Oh, the lives of insane baseball fans...

BRK 201 001 030 1 - 8 16 2
PHL 400 010 011 0 - 7 12 2

BUCCANEERS ESCAPE FROM BRIG AGAIN
DWINDLING LEAD RE-FATTENED WITH PLUCKED CARDINALS
September 3, 1924

By C. Jedediah Butterworth
Base Ball Freescriber

PITTSBURGH—After a memorably foul night in a Chicago hotel room, brought about by a massive consumption of steer at the Berghoff, I contact Master Spanelli once again to return his favor and give him a day's break from National League reporting.

Also, with the Senators idle again and me having quite enough of Comiskey Park for a while, I desire ribald pennant race action, and the Steel City is where it occurs this week. The Cubs are gone, to the gratefulness of the locals, and the lead that was recently nine games has been slimmed to six. The usually-swatting Cardinals have replaced them, and Flint Rhem faces Johnny Morrison in the opener.

Now Morrison has had the Irish luck since April, fashioning his lukewarm talent into a sizzling 12-4 mark, and everything falls right for him again in the early frames at Forbes. The usual devastating and timely injury to the opposition occurs in the 2nd when Sunny Jim Bottomley is hit on the ankle by a pitch and will be out for three of the four games here. St. Louis gets a rash of runners aboard but double play balls by the sterling combo of Wright and Maranville quickly extinguish them.

For his part, Flint Rhem is throwing wonderfully for the visiting nine, and the game is still scoreless going to the last of the 7th. A fat 6-0 lead for Philadelphia over the Robins has been on the score board for some time, and the Forebesian throng is getting restless. The Cardinals have wasted enough chances, say the base ball gods, and it is time to make them pay. Thus, Wright walks and Maranville singles. Thus a bouncer by third-string catcher Walter Schmidt clanks off Cooney's glove at short for an error. Morrison plates the first run with a deep fly, Carey shoots a ball to deep right-center for a triple and the Pirate lead is abruptly 3-0.

Morrison strolls back out to the hill to relax in his 8th inning lawn chair, but he never should have raised his feet, for Cooney makes good on his muff with a searing lead triple. Wattie Holm pinch-bats a single. A wild pitch gets Holm to second, two grounders get him home and it is 3-2.

Then the 9th arrives—oh, the dramatic, gloriously tragic 9th—and the mystifyingly dormant Hornsby erupts with a lead walk. Two outs go by and the denizens rise to their feet, waving hats. But Cooney singles to hush them, catcher Mike Gonzalez doubles in both runners to mute them, and St. Louis has a 4-3 lead!

It is at junctures like this that Pittsburgh has awed and shocked the base ball world for months. No lead, whether big or small, has been safe here in the Buccaneers' maritimes. Even with Cardinal relief expert Jesse Fowler at the wheel, even after Clyde Barnhart bats for Morrison and skies out to begin things, no one is ruling out a fresh uprising.

And like most Pirate ambushes, this one happens with four slashes of a bloody cutlass. Carey doubles, Grimm singles, Moore singles, Captain Kiki Cuyler fires a whistling liner over Douthit's head in center, and Pittsburgh is awash in noise and delirious revelry once more.

Saddened as I am for today's chapter in the pennant race, I am honored to be here and witness the latest local miracle, even though it still has my mind buzzing hours later. At the hotel, a fetching young female table servant named Gretchen slips me a tiny glass of homemade liquor to calm my nerves, and I am more than grateful to her...

STL 000 000 022 - 4 9 1
PIT 000 000 302 - 5 12 1

THE BATTLE OF MIKE AND EMMA'S
September 3, 1924

I was just going to move up to Brooklyn by taking the train, but then I started finding all kinds of boxes of extra things I wanted to bring, and decided I wanted my own clothes chest instead of one of Rachel's girlie ones, so enlisted Benny to drive me up to New York in a rented truck.

We got an old Ford one that lurched along and exploded exhaust out of its pipe every ten miles or so, and it was real slow going. On top of that the Weehawken and Hoboken ferry boats were both closed because of real choppy water on the Hudson River, and autos were backed up for miles, so Benny pulled an old dirty map out of the glove box and we headed north to work our way around.

The map was impossible to read and it was my job to read it, and me and Benny spent so much time arguing directions that by the time we crossed a much narrower part of the river we accidentally took a wrong turn and ended up in Connecticut an hour later. Now I knew how Butterworth got so lost in Vermont.

Benny was being a pig-head by refusing to ask anyone for help, until I finally lost my temper, ripped the damn map up and tossed it out the window. Lucky for us we were running out of gasoline, so Benny was forced to stop at a combination petrol station/pharmacy/store/grill in this small town called Tonimicut, and I got a chance to ask someone for directions.

What I wasn't expecting was to walk into Mike and Emma's Grill and be smack in the middle of a full-scale shouting brawl. One half of the room had people wearing Red Sox hats and waving little pennants, while the other half was in Yankee caps and jerseys and sat under a wall of framed, signed photos of Ruth and Huggins and Bob Meusel. And everyone was grouped around a miniature electric board that followed reports from New York, where Boston and the Yanks were playing their last of four games. It seemed like all good-natured yelling, but I'd never seen such a ruckus in an eatery.

After a waitress lady wrote down the correct directions for us, we decided to sit at the counter for a couple sandwiches and take in the daffiness. Tonimicut was close enough to Massachusetts to be split down the middle between the two groups, and then things got crazier. Seems that Mike, from a family of Yankee fans, had married Emma, from a family of Red Sox fans, and when they opened the grill together the place became a natural baseball earthquake spot. And having Boston hop over New York in the standings two days ago sure didn't help.

"Ruth? You can have that fat ape!" yelled one of Emma's brothers after he hit a 2-run homer in the 1st, his 42nd of the year. "He'll bust a gut and put his team right down the pike, just you watch!" "I'll be watching you bums sink into last place, that's what I'll be watching!" shouted Mike's dad in his carpenter outfit. It was 2-1 New York when doubles by Schang and Shags Horan helped them to four more runs and a 6-1 lead, and the whole room almost tilted in the Yankee fans' direction.

Me and Benny were having the time of our life, like watching a louder, more smelly burlesque show, and it got me a little nervous about me the Phillie fan being about to be married into a serious Brooklyn family. After an Aaron Ward error, single, two walks and a plunked batter gave Boston two runs in the 5th, the other half of the place started bleating again. Benny wanted to get back on the road but I had to stay and see how the drama turned out.

Each team took turns scoring a few more and it was 9-4 Yanks in the 8th when Ruth came up for the last time against Bill Piercy. It was so deafening I couldn't hear my teeth chew my cherry pie. The Babe, already with a double, walk and homer, crashed another homer, his 43rd of the year, fifth in his last four games according to Mike's nephew, and seventh in his last nine. And grapes and handfuls of bread crumbs flew back and forth across the room.

The final was 11-5 for a series split, and we stumbled back outside with our ears shaking. I had no clue the Red Sox and Yanks had such a rivalry going, but I figure once Boston gets their team good again in a couple of years that'll all calm down.

I shared my new marriage nervousness with Benny put he poop-poohed it away. "Y'know, when I went to the restroom there I got a look at Mike and Emma themselves. Leaning over a sink in the kitchen and hugging each other with smirks on their pusses. Hell, if they can make that goofy arrangement work, anyone can."

PIGEONS TO THE RESCUE
September 5, 1924

Mr. Stone took the day off to help me set up the new room in their house for me and Rachel, and believe me it took us the whole day just to get my clothes chest up the stairs. The banister was in the way so we had to take that off first and hammer it back on, and meanwhile Rachel's little brother and sister were running all over the place and half of their relatives were stopping over to meet me.

What this all meant was that Saul should have been going crazy because he was missing news of how Dazzy Vance was pitching up in Boston. The Braves beat his Robins bad yesterday and by the time me and Benny finally got to Brooklyn in the truck he was in such a state I thought he was going to call off the wedding. He tried to teach me a few Jewish words late last night but I was too tired to concentrate and he finally gave up and said I had the rest of my life to work on this big religion change.

Anyway, while I was busy sweeping the new room today and moving furniture around, Mr. Stone kept disappearing and coming back with little smiles on his face, stuffing small pieces of paper into his pants pocket. Around the fifth time he did this I asked what was going on and he motioned me to follow him out a back window and up the fire escape.

He had a huge pigeon coop up on the roof, with about three or four birds inside. They all had names and he introduced each one to me, and then we heard a flapping sound overhead. "Here comes Lucy!" he cried, and the new bird dropped down and landed on his hand with a coo. He petted her and pulled a rolled up piece of paper off one of her legs, where it was tied with a rubber band. He unfolded the paper and grinned.

"We got three in the 5th! Dazzy with a 1-hitter still!" It seems that a friend of his at a betting room across town would send scores by pigeon once in a while if you paid him for the service, and Saul sure had some kind of bird tab going.

Hank DeBerry had just hit a big triple to make it 5-0 Brooklyn. "Do you know what the Pirates are doing? Or my Phillies?" Saul whipped out an ink pen, scribbled the two questions on a new slip of paper, attached it to Lucy's leg and sent her off with a kiss.

We could hear Rachel's mom calling for her husband at that point, so I said I'd stay up there on bird watch while he went back down to help her. Rachel was off with her girlfriends dealing with the dress business, Benny was off finding me a pair of new shoes. so I had the next hour or so to my-self up on the sunny roof. It was a nice view. Even though it was hazy I could see the Brooklyn Bridge and make out the towers in Manhattan past that.

Another pigeon with brown spots on its head and whose name I didn't know came flying in to tell me that Brooklyn had scored two more times in the top of the 7th and someone named Red Lucas was on to pitch for Bos-ton, so I guess the Braves had flat out given up for the day.

Lucy was back by the time Saul reappeared, smelling like barley soup. "PIT 6 STL 1 after five" was on her note, along with "NYG 5 PHIL 0", so we both had reasons to be upset, even though I'd stopped caring about the Phillie season the day I walked off my batboy job.

We all had a big Sabbath evening meal, the house stuffed with two dozen friends and relatives, and I never shook so many hands in my life. I didn't see much of Rachel, but that was okay, I needed time with my thoughts instead. Benny clinked my glass of too-sweet imported wine with his later and said he was going to miss getting in trouble with me.

"Well," I said, "Guess that means we'll have to try a little harder."

TO WHO THIS IS CONCERNING:
September 5, 1924

DEAR SPORTING EDITER:
I HAVE YOUR BUTTERWORTH AS PRISONER. WILL NOT RELEESE HIM UNLESS YOU CUNVINCE PENCILVANIA GOVERNOR TO LET ME KEEP MY RIVER HOUSE OUT SIDE PITTSBURGH. THIS IS NO JOKING.

THE WOMAN WHO KNEW TOO MUCH
September 6, 1924

Benny was sleeping downstairs on one of Saul's couches, so he was the one who answered the door at 3 a.m. when Munsey the publisher of the *New York Sun* showed up to tell us Butterworth had been kidnapped yes-terday. Seems that Cal's pilot friend Smith, who he was sharing a hotel room in Pittsburgh with, got sapped on the head when he was in the bath-room and was able to whisper something to a maid before he passed out.

And then Cal's recently new boss came to us because he was afraid to go to the police about it.

What a mess. Here I was about to get married at sundown later, but there was no way me and Benny could let Cal stay kidnapped out there. Especially because we had a darn good idea who did it. That young and crazy table waitress named Gretchen who nearly kidnapped me a few months back had somehow lured Cal into the same trap of doom. Everything in Munsey's ransom note pointed to it, especially the part about the river cabin, and Gretchen had gone missing from her job when we called the hotel and asked for her.

So the plan was set. I left a note next to Rachel's pillow saying me and Benny had an emergency wedding errand and we'd be back before sunset come hook and crook, and then we grabbed a pre-dawn steam train to Pittsburgh.

There was one more Cardinals game at Forbes Field, and even though we were both tempted to catch it, we knew the wedding would never happen if we took it in. Smith was in the local hospital and wasn't much help being on all these drugs, but he did mention he smelled perfume behind him right before he was knocked out.

We rented a canoe from a place by the river and started paddling down it. I told Benny I'd recognize Gretchen's river cabin, but after an hour downriver we started seeing so many of other ones it was hard to tell them apart.

Then I saw her jalopy of a truck, and her crummy cabin beside it. We pulled right, hid the boat under some low branches and hopped out on the bank. I snuck up to the door and knocked. There was scuffling inside and I heard her creepy voice, "Who's there?" I said I was from the State Housing Board, and had an important paper to sign so she could keep her cabin.

I saw a curtain move, and heard her give a little gasp, and then she opened the door. "Vinny! It's you!" I could see Cal tied to a bed in the background, gagged up and wriggling in his long johns, but Gretchen stared at me with lust in her eyes, like she'd forgotten how I escaped from her and what she'd just done to Butterworth. "I knew you'd return someday..." she whispered, "Now we can wash away together."

"I don't think so, lady. Actually you got a friend of ours in there and I'm getting married later." Her eyes went wild. She stepped out of the cabin with a meat cleaver raised and Benny jumped out of nowhere and knocked her on the head with his canoe paddle. She crumpled to the ground and I jumped inside to untie Butterworth.

"That evil, evil harpy!" he shouted, obviously hungry, starved, and delirious, "How can I repay you?" I said we'd figure that out another time, but right now we had a wedding to get back to.

And so we did, after getting the police out to Gretchen's cabin, and after getting a giant plate of train food into Cal's stomach. We pulled into New York around 5 p.m., got to Brooklyn by six, and walked into the Ambrose Street Synagogue for the wedding the moment before the sun dropped. Everyone in the place turned and looked at the three of us in shock.

"Sorry we were gone so long," I said, "But we had to go over and pick up Cal!"

RACHEL GETTING MARRIED...AND HONEYMOONED
September 7, 1924

What's a hangover like with Jewish wine instead of the regular illegal stuff? A heckuva lot sweeter. Especially when you have this fuzzy memory of guys dancing you around while you're sitting in a chair.

The good thing was that I didn't have to know any yiddish to pull it off. We stood under this canopy thing while the rabbi blabbed away and then I had to smash a glass with my foot which only took three tries because the shoes Benny got me were pretty darn flimsy, and then it was just this big party in the next room forever and ever, and I got to dance with Rachel some even though she was mostly surrounded by girlfriends the whole night. Rachel's relatives were nice except there were too many of them and every one asked me how I spelled my last name. Cal Butterworth was there, but he was still messed up from his kidnapping and mostly just sat in a corner with his plate of food. Watching the bash I'm sure he was missing his family.

So I'm not anybody to brag or give details that are no one's business, but I did finally sleep in the same bed as Rachel and the love business went real good, considering my drunkenness. She had a big smile on her face when the morning light hit it so I guess that's what counts.

And then it was talk of where to go for our honeymoon, which we hadn't even had a chance to think about. Saul wanted us to hurry up in case he had to bring us to the train station or something because the Giants were at Ebbets Field today and he didn't want to be late for the game. Rachel gave me a goofy look when she heard that, I looked at her right back...and the spot for our pre-honeymoon was decided without a word.

Saul talked to his favorite ticket manager at the ballpark and got us seats by ourselves, thank God, that were right behind the Brooklyn dugout. He'd also talked to most every usher, too, because one after another came down to us with free peanuts, sausage rolls, lemonades and a spanking new Robins pennant just for Rachel. We felt like a king and queen.

Mule Watson was going against Bill Doak so you'd think Brooklyn had the advantage, but Watson has been as lucky a bad pitcher all year as Hal Carlson has been for the Phils. On top of that the Giants have been hot as Hades lately, as their four-game demolition of Baker Bowl just proved.

And they were at it again in the 3rd when the first six of them got on base with two singles, a walk, then a single-double-single, the rally not being worse only because Youngs got caught rounding too far off first after his hit. Wheat got the Robins one back with a double, but it was 5-1 New York all the way to the bottom of the 7th, and Rachel and me had plenty of time to talk about real honeymoon places. She brought up Niagara Falls, but seeing a bunch of pouring water seemed like a dumb way to spend a honeymoon to me. I thought we should go to Europe because neither of us had ever been there, but we both knew that was probably too expensive. As something in the middle we decided on French Canada, meaning Montreal and Quebec City. Neither of us knew French but we could take a train there and still eat get great food.

It was around the time we figured that out when Johnny Mitchell cracked a double down the right field line and knocked home two Brooklyn runs. "We're back in it!" yelled Rachel, leaping out of her seat. Someone should have told Doak that, though, because in the 8th he went back to pitching horrible. George Kelly started with his second double (geez, has that guy been hot!), Youngs singled, and after Wilson forced out, Irish Meusel doubled and it was 6-3 and Robinson finally yanked Doak off the hill. Ehrhardt whiffed Snyder to end the mess, and things looked bad.

The Mule got the Robins out in the 8th with just an Andy High single, and the Giants still had their three run lead going to the last of the 9th. Before Dick Loftus came out to bat for Ehrhardt, Rachel turned and gave me a big smooch. "Kiss me back," she said, "'cause we can't have our married life start this way." So I did, and Loftus walked on four pitches. Hmm. So we kissed again. And Neis singled Loftus to third. We grabbed each other's faces this time and Mitchell doubled to make it second and third! Harry Baldwin replaced Watson, and with the infield back, Wheat made it 6-5 with an infield grounder that scored Neis and sent Mitchell to third.

Ebbets Field was crazy and me and Rachel were crazier. I swear, with Fournier up we wanted to start undressing each other but Jack made us not have to by popping a fly deep deep enough to left to score Mitchell with the tying run!

We had nobody decent for relief now so Jim Roberts got sent out there, but the Giants couldn't do a thing with him in the 10th. Brown singled to start our half, Stock bunted him over, and when Ernie Maun came on for a rare relief appearance, me and Rachel gave up the kissing act and just held hands so we wouldn't miss anything. Zack Taylor singled Brown to third, Tommy Griffith hit for Roberts, and we were all on our feet, and here came the pitch and there swung the bat and the ball was lined into right before we could even pray and Brooklyn had won the huge game 7-6!!

There's one more Giants-Robins battle over in McGraw's yard tomorrow, so this French Canada deal might get put off another day.

NYG 005 000 010 0 - 6 11 1
BRK 001 000 203 1 - 7 14 0

THE RUDE AWAKENING
September 8, 1924

Rachel made the mistake of bringing her new Robins pennant over to the Polo Grounds today. The first balled-up pretzel wrapper hit the top of her hat by the 2nd inning and the first shower of peanut shells by the 4th, and then it was time for us to move our seats because I was still in my after-wedding glow and didn't feel like punching anyone's nose.

It was another pitching mismatch, but this time for the Giants. Hugh McQuillan got Wheat to bounce into a double play to end our 1st, and then New York went to work on Art Decatur. Frisch singled, O'Connell got plunked, scorching George Kelly singled and so did Hack Wilson and we were down 2-0 lickety-split.

Then Fournier smashed homer no. 29, best in the league, way out into the right bleachers and Rachel jumped up and yelled and waved her pennant until she had to duck for cover. There's always a couple good handfuls of Brooklyn fans at the Grounds, and most of them make it out alive but it always helps if you're a girl. The peanut shower happened after we tied it up in the 4th on a Brown walk, a bunt and singles from High and Taylor, and we found a more calm area just past the first base grandstand, where I convinced Rachel to roll her pennant up for a while.

It gave us bad luck. Fournier let an easy grounder go through his legs and down the right field line, a play you almost never see, Gowdy reached on a boot by Mitchell and one McQuillan double later we were down for good 4-2. Ruether tried to keep the game close by relieving Decatur in the 8th but all he did was give up two singles and a three-run cannon shot to Travis Jackson, and the hollering of the Giants fans sank us deeper in our seats.

The only good thing was that the Robins ended the season series 13-9 against them, but it didn't make Rachel any happier. She was still blaming me for making her roll up her pennant, and wouldn't talk to me for the first ten minutes after we walked out the grandstand tunnel, and I said this is stupid and it's about time we left on a real honeymoon already. "Uh-uh," she replied, "Your Phillies are playing at Ebbets tomorrow and I can't leave unless it's with a good baseball feeling."

Great. Now I have to root against my own team to get us out of town.

BRK 010 100 000 - 2 8 3
NYG 200 200 03x - 7 9 1

HELLO AND GOODBYE
September 9, 1924

Rachel was so sure her team was going to beat mine today we'd already bought our train tickets to Quebec and had our packed bags stored away in one of the ticket-taker's booths at Ebbets Field. The fact Dazzy Vance was pitching had a lot to do with it.

But baseball's a lot like life, I had to remind her as we found our seats behind third base. Things that look certain hardly ever turn out that way. This may have been the quickest game these teams have played all year, but there were more tense moments packed into it than your average cliff-hanger moving picture. Like these:

--Wheat doubles in the 1st, gets to third on a Cy Williams error but doesn't score.
--Phillies get two on and two out against Dazzy in the 2nd but don't score.
--Zack Taylor scores for Brooklyn with two outs on a Bernie Neis single in the 2nd, then Robins load the bases but Wheat flies out.

--Ford singles in Mokan to tie it in the 4th and Dazzy has to whiff Lew Wendell with two outs and two on.
--High triples with one out in bottom of the 4th but doesn't score.
--Neis triples with two outs in bottom of the 5th but doesn't score.
--Phillies get lead off singles in the 6th and 7th but don't score.
--Robins get two singles in the 6th and 7th but don't score.

Finally, in the last of the 8th, with Rachel chewing her fingernails and me worried about our marriage already, Brown led with a walk, my pal Heinie threw a ball into the East River to put runners on second and third, and none other than Dazzy knocked one into left for a go-ahead single, his third game-winning hit of the year to go with his 22-8 record and 2.06 earned run average. And it was also Brooklyn's 80th win.

"Never a dull game, is there?" Rachel sighed when it was over and we were fetching our bags. By the time we got to Pennsylvania Station we found out the Pirates had lost another double-header, and life suddenly seemed real strange. My first visit to a foreign country was coming up, but without talking about it I'm sure the first thing on our minds was how we'd be able to get baseball scores.

PHL 000 100 000 - 1 5 1
BRK 010 000 01x - 2 10 0

IT'S ALL FRENCH-CANADIAN TO ME
September 12, 1924

To us, I mean. To us. Geez, it's been hard to believe I'm married now, even though I am. The fact we we didn't really go out on regular dates and everything wedding-wise happened so quick sure didn't help.

But now we're up here in Quebec City on our second day, and it might be the closest we ever come to being in France so it's sure a great place to celebrate love. We're in this old castle of a hotel called Chateau Frontenac, which is so gigantic and king-like I keep expecting to see mobs roll up guillotines and pound on the doors. We have an incredible view of the St. Lawrence River, and the food's been delicious even though I can't read the menu and don't know what I'm eating half the time.

That's another thing about Rachel I just learned: she does know French, or at least enough to get us through the day. We visited an old fort and saw the walls that the British soldiers climbed up, and we rode in horse taxis and walked cobblestone streets dodging horse dung until we got blisters on our feet and never once did we get lost looking at our French city map.

And I bet you didn't know there's real baseball up here called the Quebec-Ontario-Vermont League. That's right, they just started a six-team Class B operation, and we caught the last few innings of a game between the Ottawa-Hall Senators and Quebec Bulldogs, who've been in first place for both halves of the season. The two Vermont teams, the Montpelier Goldfish and Rutland Shieks, dropped out for money reasons after the first half, and hardly anyone was at the game today and the field was in awful shape but no one seemed to care. We sure didn't, because after a day without ball we were both missing it bad. We were even able to get the American scores tonight from a French-Canadian version of Mort's, this tavern on a back street called Leclaire's that had jazz music on a gramophone and served fabulous local ale.

Yup, you heard me. They tried to pass the Prohibition thing in Canada too but the Quebec province threw it right out, so there was legal booze to be had all over the place. Rachel picked wine and I went for this stuff called Boswell's, which got the frog legs in my stomach dancing in no time. Tomorrow we'll be taking a train down to Montreal, where I figure the ale will be running like sink water.

It's been great spending so much close time with Rachel. We've tried to just enjoy the moments instead of worrying or even talking about future ones, because that's what honeymoons are for. Actually, marriage should probably be the same way.

IN THE KINGDOM OF MOLSON
September 14, 1924

Montreal is a bigger Quebec City with less horse dung and more English-speaking. After our Frontenac chateau experience it was a shock to be in a regular size hotel off of St. Catherine Street, the road where everything's going on here. There were restaurants and tobacco merchants and lady undergarment shops and big shopping stores and half-naked girlie clubs and more taverns than you could count. Rachel and me even split up for an hour or so to give us a chance to take in what we liked, and then we met up at a supper club called Brasserie Champlain over on St. Denis Street, which we were told has a lot of sporting fans.

Well, that wasn't telling the whole story. There were framed pictures of horse jockeys, local baseball teams, boxers and about 89 different hockey players stuck on the walls. Behind the bar there was even a ticker machine so we could get the American ball scores. We had to sit there anyway because there wasn't a table ready for us yet, so everything worked out.

The bartender, whose name was Jacques, liked Rachel right away because she spoke French to him. He was an expert on Molson Ale, which believe it or not has been around since 1786, and started pouring out one kind after another for us. The Export one was plenty delicious, and it didn't take long for Rachel and the barman to be talking about baseball. Brooklyn was up 3-0 on Cincinnati with Doak pitching and when Jacques discovered Jack Fournier was her favorite player he poured us two free ales right away.

"Jacques Fournier!" he said, "He is from Michigan but is French!" So began our next hour of ale-drinking. Fournier as it turns out was having a great day and ended up with three singles, a double and a walk as Doak shut the Reds down on just two hits. A jazz combo started up around 5 p.m. and very tipsy Rachel pulled me off my stool for a little dancing. Wrong idea. Molson reached the three million gallons of ale production a few years ago and it felt like two of those million were inside me.

The rest of the night was just a big drunk mystery, but I think we were standing on the bar singing a French song at one point and Jacques had his sweaty arms around us. The last night of our trip won't exactly stick in our heads, but at least a few dozen people in Montreal won't forget it.

CIN 000 000 000 -0 2 0
BRK 100 022 11x - 7 17 0

NATIONAL LEAGUE through Sunday, September 14, 1924

Pittsburgh	88	53	.624	—
New York	82	60	.577	6.5
Brooklyn	82	60	.577	6.5
Cincinnati	79	63	.556	9.5
Chicago	73	68	.518	15
St. Louis	68	74	.479	20.5
PHILLIES	55	86	.390	33
Boston	39	102	.277	49

MEN ON A MISSION
September 16, 1924

When me and Rachel got back to Brooklyn yesterday, there was our own bedroom upstairs which Saul had all ready for us,and there was a fabulous homemade dinner of brisket beef waiting to be eaten, and there was a telegram from Benny in Philadelphia sitting on the table for me to read:

BUCS MUST PERISH. THREE GAMES AT BAKER START TOMORROW. OUR LUNGS DESPERATELY NEEDED.

What could Rachel say? She wanted Pittsburgh to lose more than anyone except maybe her father. And after our nice relaxing honeymoon, she agreed that an after-marriage reunion with my best friend for a few days could be a healthy thing, and Mama wouldn't mind hearing about French Canada either. So that was that.

I reminded Benny the second we got on the streetcar today that the Phillies had lost nine games in a row, but he didn't want to hear a drop about it. "The dang Boston Braves beat the Pirates yesterday, Vinny. Wise up!" Still, this wasn't the same Phillies team I batboyed for during the summer, and it was pretty obvious in the 1st inning. After Max Carey led with a single off Hubbell, Schultz let a double go to the wall in right, Wilson kicked a dribbler in front of the plate and the Bucs had two unearned runs right off the bat.

"Oh Kiki!!!" yelled Benny from our bleacher seat as soon as the best player in baseball took left field in front of us, "Now I know why they gave you a bird's name! Because you're a scavenger like the rest of your team! SCAVENGERS!!" Cuyler turned around for one scary moment and Benny dropped behind a fat guy in front of him, which wasn't easy for him to do because there were only about three dozen people in the entire bleachers.

What's made the Pirates a first-place team all year is that they never, ever seem to get rattled, and Benny's scavenger plan did nothing right away. Wright, Maranville and pitcher Cooper all singled to begin the third. Carey walked, Grimm doubled past Schultz again for two more, and after a Moore single it was 6-0 Villains.

Our team looked like they'd rather be getting their teeth pulled out. Cy grounded out four times for the day, and we swung at every piece of junk Cooper threw up there, not walking once the whole game. Cuyler made outs his first two times so Benny started calling him "Crummy Kiki" along with "lucky oaf" and kept jabbing my ribs to get me to yell along with him, but it didn't feel right after I yelled a few times. Crummy Kiki responded with singles his last three trips up to get his average to .376, and the Bucs ended the day with 17 hits and a shutout.

"We need a new idea for tomorrow," is all I said to Benny as we trudged down to Mort's after the game. "They haven't won no stinkin' pennant yet!" is all he would say.

PIT 240 011 000 - 8 17 1
PHI 000 000 000 - 0 6 2

AIN'T NO PIRATE'S LIFE FOR US!
September 17, 1924

"That was an embarrassing embarrassment yesterday," is how Benny greeted me this morning, fresh with a new plan for sinking the unsinkable Pirates' ship at Baker Bowl. "Look. They know they're good, the Phillies know they're good, everyone who's been following this damn game all year knows they're good. What we gotta do this time is make them feel guilty about beating our brains in."

"And how do we do that?"

He smiled and pulled a giant roll of gauze bandage out of his pocket. "Hold out your arm."

So there we were an hour later, an usher I knew walking us down to some great empty seats behind the Pittsburgh dugout, me with my left arm and half of my head completely wrapped in bandages, giving me the look of a shellshocked mustard gas victim. I also had some baking flour rubbed into my face to make me look more pale, and I guess it was working because a half dozen or so Phillie fans moved out of the way to let us pass. Benny was all spruced up and had on fake whiskers so he could pass for my dad, and when one of the old Pirate coaches headed past us, he caught his eye with a wave.

"My son's very first game!" he said with a wink, "Take a little pity on us, okay?" The coach didn't say a word back but kind of nodded so we figured he was telling the players when he went into the dugout.

Which didn't explain why the Bucs got four singles, a passed ball and three runs right out of the gate. Oh, I know. Because stupid useless Jimmy Ring was on the mound again, shooting for his 20th loss, and we'd forgotten to talk to him first. It probably wouldn't have worked anyway because he would've recognized us in a second, but even if he laughed it might've loosened him up and got him pitching better.

Nope, it was Benny's job to yell at Pirates lefty Emil Yde the second he walked to the mound. "Your teammates are heartless cowards, Emil!" he began, "But you don't have to be! Look at my poor kid here! Give us a break, would ya??" Yde wouldn't even turn his head, but it was clear after he whiffed the first batter Schultz that something wasn't right with him. Hod Ford doubled into the corner, Holke walked, and Cy beat out an infield hit. "Thank you, Emil, thank you!!" shouted Benny, "My boy just smiled, did you see that?" Catcher Earl Smith walked to the mound to settle Yde down, probably to tell him to ignore the idiot yelling behind their dugout.

Up stepped Jimmie Wilson, the tiny crowd making a ton of noise, and Jimmie cracked one high and deep to left. Cuyler ran back to the fence and jumped but it was in the seats for a giant slam!! We led 4-3!! I forgot I was supposed to be crippled and jumped out of my seat and Benny had to shove me back in it while he got to hoot and holler.

Holke booted one at first with two outs in the 2nd to let the Bucs tie the game, and then nothing happened until the 4th, when Grimm tripled and Moore singled him in to put us behind 5-4. After Schultz walked with two gone in our 4th, Ford got his third hit, another double, to put men at second and third. Holke came up and had a long, tough at bat. His seventh foul ball came right into our row and I jumped up out of instinct and snagged the thing, but the bandage broke on my left arm in the process and there I was standing there, the crowd around us cheering the catch and every Pirate standing at the top of the dugout staring at me hard. Uh-oh.

Traynor led the 5th with a single. Wright walked. Maranville doubled, Yde singled after lining another foul ball into our section on purpose. Two outs later Moore walked, Cuyler hit Pirates triple no. 122 on the year to give him 138 runs knocked in, Ring was sent to the salt mines and we were losing 10-4. I ripped the entire bandage arrangement off my head and glared at Benny, and he bought me a pretzel and lemonade and patted my back. "It's okay, pal. We don't need no stinkin' ruse. COME ON PHILS!!"

I don't know if the Phils heard him or not, but we woke up all over again in the 5th. Four singles, a walk and third Ford double gave us four runs right back and it was 10-8! On the score board, Brooklyn and New York were also winning, so this could be a fun day after all. Steineder was in for us so we had a chance to hold them, but we forgot who we were facing, I guess. Two outs in the 7th, Moore singled, Cuyler walked and Earl Smith doubled them in and we were down 12-8 just like that. I'm telling you, if the Senators beat these guys in the World Series it'll be a damn miracle.

I stood and yelled at my old friend Heinie Sand in the last of the 9th. He already had two singles and a triple for the day, gave me a nod and then popped one in the seats just for me! It's pretty sad when you mash the Bucs for 10 runs and 15 hits and end up losing—our 11th in a row if anyone's still counting—but the good news is that we only have to play these bloodless rascals one more time.

PIT 310 150 200 - 12 17 0
PHI 400 040 002 - 10 15 1

TAKE THAT, WISE GUYS
September 18, 1924

So I had a long talk with Benny this morning while we ate hot muffins from a wagon on Broad Street. Yelling at the Pirate players wasn't helping one bit, so unless we were going to run on the field and trip or tackle them, it was probably a better idea to just sit in the stands and do some rooting and praying like Phillies fans normally do. What we never imagined was the Bucs tripping themselves up by being braggy jerks.

Yup, manager Bill McKechnie decided our team was so horrible that he could shuffle all his lineup spots like playing cards and beat us anyway. Which is what he did, leading off Cuyler, batting Wright third and Traynor fourth and speedy Max Carey all the way down at seventh. Their pitcher Kremer went along with it, even with him going for his 20th win, but Wright spoiled his plans in the Phillie 1st by tossing away a grounder and helping us get two runs.

Both Kremer and Hal Carlson pitched nothing but zeroes for the next six innings, Carlson doing his usual runner-stranding magic. After another Wright flub in the 7th, Hal tripled off the wall, scored on a Heinie single, and we were up 4-0! Then the Pirates got mad again, and put together a nifty two-run rally in the 8th started by another Cuyler single. Mokan singled in our fifth run, and Betts actually got them out in the 9th when Cuyler rapped into a twin killer.

"We beat the Bucs!" yelled Benny, making much more noise than the other thousand or so people who were there. "Yeah, and we end up 4-18 with them!" I shouted back. Then I gave him a good hug because I was headed back to Brooklyn tonight to start my new life with Rachel.

The strange thing is that the Pirates are also headed to Ebbets Field and their final three with the Robins, so I guess the start of our new life might include a pair of sausage rolls.

PIT 000 000 020 - 2 10 2
PHI 200 000 21x - 5 10 0

WHAT WERE WE THINKING OF?
September 19, 1924

Back in Brooklyn, me and Rachel and Saul jazzed up for the big final Pirates-Robins series of the year, over 25,000 people packed into Ebbets— and Tiny Osborne goes out to the mound and gets skinned alive.

After the Bucs' embarrassing loss to the Phillies yesterday when their manager fielded a cuckoo lineup, why did any of us think Brooklyn even had a chance against them? Carey ripped Tiny's first pitch for a bleeding triple into right center, and then things got bad. Moore singled with one out, the Cuyler single we can set our pocket watches to was right after that. A Traynor single made it 2-0 and the sausage rolls we'd eaten before the game were already bubbling in our guts like rotten lava.

Maranville doubled on the first pitch of the 2nd and Grimm got him in with a single. After Meadows disposed of the Robins again, Cuyler yawned and put one over the fence on the first pitch of the 3rd. Osborne, definitely soiling himself out there, got the next two guys easy but then Wright doubled, Maranville singled, and pitcher Meadows doubled to make it 6-0 in a flash.

Wilbert Robinson walked to the mound to paddle Tiny's fanny and send him to bed, and then the weirdest thing happened. Jim Roberts, a completely terrible pitcher (says Saul) who's hardly been used at all, took over and threw 2-hit shutout ball for four and a third innings! You just never know in this game, you never know. Brooklyn tried to make a game of it with two runs in the 4th and Fournier's scoring single in the 7th, but it was pretty obvious that even if the Robins tied the game the Bucs would take out their cutlasses and draw and quarter somebody else. Oh yeah, and today's three Cuyler hits puts him up to .379.

We were all quiet as mice eating dinner at Rachel's house later, and me and her read fiction books and drank tea later with some opera on the phonograph, because it was tough to find things to talk happy about. Dazzy Vance goes tomorrow against Cooper with Brooklyn's pennant life on the line, and if he fails, at least we'll be forced to get on with our lives and I can shut off that stupid opera.

PGH 213 000 000 - 6 14 2
BRK 000 200 100 - 3 7 1

A MUTED CELEBRATION
SHOCKER AND PENNOCK END AMERICAN LEAGUE PENNANT RACE WITH UNCANNY WHITE-WASHINGS
September 19, 1924

By C. Jedidian Butterworth
Base Ball Freescriber

ST. LOUIS—With a Senator win or Tiger loss poised to finish off all American League drama, it seemed fitting to coax a flight to the Mississippi out of Dean C. Smith. If Washington were to prevail today, readers would choose to be at their side, and the spectacle of Ty Cobb reaching his volcanic peak is one I would choose to avoid at any cost.

So here I am near the banks of the Great River, watching Walter Johnson warm up to face the sinking Brownies. At 22-10, Walter will most likely finish second to Rip Collins in any Pitcher of the Year consideration, but I would not want to step into a batter box against him on a day like this. True to form, he dispatches with the first nine men he faces, but his batting mates cannot break through against Urban Shocker, despite five men getting aboard in the first three innings.

The Train does away with Sisler and Robertson to begin the St. Louis 4th, before Baby Doll Jacobson ignites the crowd with a searing triple between Goslin and Leibold. Ken Williams meekly pops out to end things, and Johnson visibly bears down all the more. Bennett nicks him for a two-out single in the 5th, but after Harry Rice lines out we move to the 6th, still scoreless. The early news from back in Detroit is encouraging, as New York has a 1-0 lead into the 4th, but the Senators want to win this prize with a win.

Yet Shocker has them in a constant bind, allowing one runner to reach base every inning and leaving him there. With one out in the Browns' 6th, Walter finally hiccups. Sisler lashes a single. Robertson gets him to third with another. Baby Doll, his triple still fresh in the Train's mind, seems to rattle him further for Jacobson then knocks a single into left for a 1-0 St. Louis lead!

Johnson smites every Brownie hereafter. but all that does is make the Washington frustrations mount. Ruel walks with two outs in the 7th: stranded. Rice singles with two outs in the 8th: stranded. Harris singles to lead the 9th, but Peckinpaugh flies out, pinch-batter Richbourg bounds into a force, and Ruel fans on three pitches and the Nats have dropped a game they had no business losing.

We writers are allowed access then to the visitor clubhouse, where the glum but anxious players sit around in their half-dressed states and wait for the upstairs ticker machine to wire us further news from Navin Field. Ghastly quiet fills the room for a good half hour, and then a press row boy pops in with a burst of news—

The Yankees have scored five times in the 5th!

The club house explodes with cheers. Manager Harris' coaches and a few of the players try to shake his hand, but Bucky will have none of it yet. "Still four innings to go, men!" he proclaims, and the expectant hush gradually returns.

While the players largely play cards to keep their nerves in check, the reporters are forced to speculate among themselves or discuss possible Senator rotations for the World Series. The Washington scribes are a decidedly animated bunch, including a young fellow named Povich who seems smarter than the rest, and I have just as much trouble standing still as them.

Inning after scoreless inning, the press boy appears to announce the same score. My feet are becoming sore. Finally, the full bottom of the 9th action is sent down and read aloud to us by the apple-cheeked youngster:

"Haney pop out...Heilman single...Manush single...Woodall double play—"

And nothing else is heard. Roars and leaping cleats. Hand shaking and back patting and hugs and even some teary-eyed players. Harris emerges from an office with boxes of cigars and the room resembles an opium den in seconds. Joe Judge has a couple bottles of Canadian whiskey stashed in his equipment bag and those are passed around for frantic swigs.

For my part, I am happy for the first Washington pennant in years, but my heart goes out

to my home fans in Detroit, wondering what in tarnation happened back there today. When I
discover the answer later, I am grateful I journeyed west to share these moments with champions.

WAS 000 000 000 - 0 6 0
STL 000 001 00x - 1 5 0

PUT THE ARSENIC AWAY
September 20, 1924

Dazzy knew what to do. Dazzy always knows what to do. Matter of fact
the few times he's lost games this season it's because the Robins hitters
went to sleep on him. So here's Max Carey stepping into the batter box,
Brooklyn one loss to the Bucs away from heading to the boneyard, and
Dazzy buries a fastball in his right shoulder to knock him out of the game.
Oh, the Pirates leaped off their dugout bench and yelled and screamed
and called Vance something I can't tell you, but the game went on and
Pittsburgh was all shook up, because Grimm bounced the next pitch into a
double play and a rally never happened.

And the plunking changed everything. Cuyler had to move to center
field from left where he's sometimes wobbly anyway, and with two outs in
the last of the 1st and Andy High on second, Fournier smashed one deep to
Kiki's left. It got over his head easily, he fumbled the ball near the fence,
and High scored for a 1-0 Brooklyn lead. Rachel leaped for joy and I got an
early cheek-kiss out of it.

In the 6th, a Brown double, Fournier triple and Wheat single off Cooper
put Brooklyn ahead 4-0. Dazzy belted a home run earlier, his fourth of the
year, to make it 2-0 in the 3rd, but the big story was his pitching. After the
1st inning business he retired TWENTY Pirates in a row and looked good
enough to throw a no-hit, no-run game.

Traynor finally got the first Bucs hit with a one-out single in the 8th.
Wright followed with a hit but Dazzy wiped out the next two guys, and a
Grimm triple and Moore sacrifice pop gave the Pirates their only run in
the 9th. To finish off the glorious day, Vance whiffed Cuyler, who ended up
going 0-for-4 with one butchered outfield play. It may have been his worst
game of the year, and we were honored to see it.

Tomorrow it'll be Morrison against Grimes with the same dire situation
on the line, and Cal Butterworth wired this morning to announce he was
flying in our direction to take in the game, now that the American league
has a champ. That should make an even more fun party, especially if he
likes brisket beef.

PGH 000 000 001 - 1 3 3
BRK 101 002 01x - 5 10 0

GRIMES IS ALL WET, THANK THE LORD
September 21, 1924

By C. Jedediah Butterworth
Base Ball Freescriber

BROOKLYN—After following two contests in distant cities the last few days, it is a pleasure to arrive at Ebbets Field with both pennant participants romping in front of me. It is also grand to reunite with young Master Spanelli, his fetching new bride Rachel, and Rachel's father Saul, a jolly fellow with deep knowledge of the Robins and his pet pigeons.

Famed spitballer Grimes is hurling for the home nine, one loss to the Pirates away from extinction, so the ball park air is charged with fevered anxiety from the outset. And Burleigh's ball is at its wettest. Grimes acts as if he is throwing the gooey sphere on nearly every pitch, so the hitter is never sure when he'll really see it, and the method has Carey, Grimm and Moore out of balance as they make three quick outs.

Morrison has been the surprise winner for Pittsburgh all season, but a walk to High, single by Wheat and scoring fly by Fournier put Brooklyn on top 1-0 in the bottom of the inning. The Ebbets throng then has a groaning party, for short-stop Mitchell flubs two balls in the second around a Glenn Wright double to even the game 1-1. The Robins fire back with a 2-run salvo, though, in the 3rd: Neis doubles, High walks, Wheat doubles and Brown hits the scoring fly.

From there, the Swami of Saliva takes over. Every time a Pirate reaches base, a whiff or double play follows. Three out of the four middle innings begin with a Buccaneer reaching a bag, but all are abandoned on the high base path seas. Our seats along third base are not the closest, but I can still see the pitches breaking seven or eight inches, and the Pirate flailing is apparent for all to see. Grimes strands a pair to finish off the 9th, retiring Maranville and pinch-sticker Barnhart, and the magical digit remains at two heading into Monday.

Over a bountiful Jewish dinner at Rachel's family house later, we discuss the next day's potential, with the blistering hot Cubs invading Ebbets and Pittsburgh hopping across town to the Polo Grounds. To dramatically survive another day is all one can ask for at this point.

PGH 010 000 000 - 1 6 1
BRK 102 001 00x - 4 8 3

CHILLS AND THRILLS WITH MY NEW BENNY
September 22, 1924

This was the ball game day to beat all ball game days. All five boroughs were crackling, what with the Bucs at the Polo Grounds and the on-fire Cubbies at Ebbets and both games completely critical. Pittsburgh's magical digit stood at two, so the race could all be over or half-over or keep on going.

Cal thought we should each pick one of the games to go to but I said heck with that, let's try both. I pulled off the same trick when I was here with Benny back in May, and that was for games that were hardly important. We could start at Ebbets and if things got out of hand, shoot up to Coogan's Bluff on the el train. Isn't that why they invented out-of-town score boards? Anyway, I needed to be with Rachel and her father in case Brooklyn got their faces pounded in, because that's what a husband and son-in-law should do.

Pretty weird season for these Cubs, huh? They're under .500 for most of the first half, then turn into a juggernaut around the time they're eliminated and they just haven't stopped, having just beat the Giants two out of three. Luckily the Robins missed Pete Alexander this time but still got Vic Aldridge in the opener against Bill Doak. Doak can either be shaky or unhittable, and from the start it's the second category. Chicago can't even scratch a hit off him until Hartnett doinks a single leading off the 5th.

Meanwhile, High triples in a 1st inning Robins run, then scores on a passed ball. Four straight singles and a scoring double play grounder in the 4th make it 4-0, and then the crowd roars even louder because a big "3" goes up for the Giants on the score board to wipe out what was a 1-0 Bucs lead! I look at Cal, who's just bought himself a sausage roll covered in mustard and onions and doesn't look like he's ready to move.

"Whaddya think?"

"What do I think about what?"

"About going to the Polo Grounds."

"Now?? I've just purchased my lunch!"

"C'mon, Cal, you're a big reporter, right? This game's in the bag! You wanna miss the Pirates losing?"

Rachel wasn't thrilled about me leaving, mostly for superstition reasons, but she was almost too fixed on the game action in front of her to notice.

"Shake a leg, old man!" I jabbed Butterworth's arm and he grumbled and followed me out, trying to eat his sausage roll at the same time.

By the time our train rumbled over the Manhattan Bridge there were mustard drips and onion pieces on his coat, and he held onto a pole like he thought we were going to end up in the river. I guess it's what happens when you just take taxis and aeroplanes everywhere. We changed over to the 6th Avenue elevated line and headed north. Two newspaper boys with bundles of *Herald Tribunes* under their arms got on and were talking baseball so we asked if they knew the ball scores. "Giants winning, Cubs and Brooklyn all tied up!" he yelled. Butterworth went nuts. "What?? What happened?"

"You got me, mister. I just heard this from a pretzel guy near the park."

So we had to wait all the way up till our stop at 155th Street. What we didn't figure on was how jam-crowded the Polo Grounds was. The Giants were the league champs the last three years, after all, and the Pirates were trying to take their place so every seat and standing spot was filled. There was a smoky cigar haze in the air over the park, and we could even see a bunch of fans watching way up on the bluff.

Butterworth didn't have a press pass for the game so couldn't get us in that way and I hurried him around to a spot under the outfield fence that worked last time. It did this time too, except we were forced to squeeze our way through a crowd to a rope strung across the outfield. Cal was grumpy and uncomfortable but we didn't really have a choice there.

It was 4-2 Giants in the top of the 5th, with Pie Traynor in the box against Art Nehf. We could just make out the Brooklyn score on the raised board behind us, which was now 6-4 Robins after 6th. A guy next to us said he heard from someone else who heard from someone else who heard from a press row kid that Zack Taylor homered off the foul pole to put them ahead.

Then Traynor ripped a single into left that Kelly fielded right in front of us and everyone's shoulders sagged. Max Carey was up, who bats cleanup against lefties and had already doubled in the first Buc run in the 3rd. This time he bombed a pitch high and deep to our left, Kelly raced over, the crowd pulled back on the rope to try and give him more room to catch it but it was way into the crowd and the damn score was tied!

Kremer came back out, trying to get his 20th win that he missed out on last time, but the Giants pounced on him like leopards on a deer. Kelly scorched a doubled, Youngs singled him in, Wilson and Terry walked, Jackson singled in two more, Nehf hit a scoring fly and four New York runs were in! I thought of hurrying back to Brooklyn right then but me and Cal both knew how capable the Pirates were of coming back at any time.

So we stayed put and watched Traynor smack a homer in the top of the 7th to get them closer. Cuyler doubled to begin the 8th, but Nehf bore down and squirmed out of the mess, then after Kelly singled in Heinie Groh for a ninth Giants run, Grimm bounced into a huge double play in the 9th, and Kremer had been beaten again. Everyone would survive another day!

We pushed our way through the cheering exit crowd, back to the el platform, and back onto the train. The stupid Cubs had tied the Brooklyn game again with two in the 8th and it was 6-6 going into extra innings. Most everyone on the train was talking baseball, and at every stop, whoever got on would get grilled for an Ebbets Field score.

Believe it or not, they were in the 12th inning, still tied 6-6 when me and Cal got there. Rachel had chewed most of her fingernails off and Saul sat there with a handkerchief draped over his face like an Arab person. "We've had so many chances to win this game," Rachel moaned, "SO many chances!" There was the bases loaded thing in the 7th when Brown popped out. There was the two Robins on base in both the 10th and 11th. Rube Ehrhardt had already thrown almost five relief innings for us, and wouldn't be available the rest of the series, which was bad news for tomorrow with Decatur starting.

And here were the Robins with two more on base against Rip Wheeler and left there when Taylor and Mitchell make outs. Butch Weis reached on a walk with one out in the Cubs' 13th, but Hollocher hit into a twin killing. Neis then walked with one out in our 13th, High skied to center, and up walked Zack Wheat. Rachel couldn't stand it anymore and jumped up on her seat.

"Attack it, Zack!! Attack it!" Some of the fans around us chuckled because a woman was getting loud, but most were too nervous to react. Wheat's a .370 hitter with a bushel of big hits for Brooklyn all year, but this looked like one of those games that was never going to—

CRACK!!

And there it went!! High and far and higher and farther and completely out of sight to right field and Rachel was jumping on me and hats were flying everywhere and Cal's glasses were steaming up and I think he yelled for the first time in his life and Saul was thanking whoever his God was and Wheat ran across the plate and into a hooting crowd of teammates waiting for him, something I'd never seen before and the Robins were four games out for the first time since forever and ain't this the greatest game ever invented?

```
CHC 000 022 020 000 0 - 6 10 1
BRK 200 202 000 000 2 - 8 12 1

PGH 001 120 100 - 5 9 2
NYG 003 140 01x - 9 11 2
```

A FORMER HERO DISGRACED, A NEW ONE BORN

YOUNGSTER TERRY'S TITANIC BLAST SPELLS DOOM FOR PLUMMETING BUCCANEERS
September 23, 1924

By C. Jedediah Butterworth
Base Ball Freescriber

A full day of dashing about Gotham was too much for this reporter to bear, so it was a pleasure to drop into my comfortable, non-rolling chair in the Polo Grounds press row today.

Pittsburgh had lost three straight games, a marvel in itself, and Lee Meadows was tabbed to finish McGraw's Giants off once and for all. Across town at Ebbets Field, my young protege Spanelli was taking in the second Cubs-Robins game, and hopefully enjoying himself. His father offered to send me scoring missives by carrier pigeon, a daft notion to be sure, and I needed to remind them that the facility here would be keeping us fully abreast of the adjoining action.

Virgil Barnes toed the slab for New York, and while he's been as inconsistent as most of the Giant twirlers, he is capable of a good effort. This was surely one of those. Six Pirates struck singles in the first six innings, yet only one tally was across the dish on a scoring fly by Maranville.

For the Giants, a Travis Jackson single in the 4th knotted the game, and an ill-timed boot by Traynor with the bases loaded and two outs in the the 5th put the home nine ahead 2-1. This came only minutes after Giant right field roamer Youngs snared an Earl Smith home run attempt at the lip of the fence.

It was then that the crowd, forced to root for their arch rivals whether they enjoyed it or not, cheered loudly when it was discovered that Brown had socked a 3-run wallop to erase a 3-0 Chicago lead and put Brooklyn ahead 4-3 after three innings. Was another miracle in the offing?

It didn't appear to be, for Carey, Grimm, and Moore all struck hits off Barnes with one out in the 6th and we were knotted 2-2. Up stepped Cuyler, the King of the National League for certain, yet owner of just one hit in his last 15 times up since his huge opening performance in Brooklyn.

Typewriters and voices muted around me, over twenty thousand fans leaned closer to the field. Barnes wound, threw, and Kiki lifted a harmless truffle of a fly into the waiting glove of Hack Wilson in center. Earl Smith dribbled out and it remained tied.

Then came one of the grander moments of 1924. After O'Connell and Kelly made out to begin the Giant 6th, Youngs reached on a Lee Meadows walk. Wilson doubled him to third, and rookie Bill Terry strode up. The reports on this slugging imp have been promising, but McGraw has been slow to utilize him, and chose this day only because of Meadows' problems with left-side stickers.

Terry proved that on the very first pitch, propelling the ball on a monstrous arc into the throbbing right field bleachers for a 5-2 lead!! Spanelli's account of yesterday's hat-flying with Wheat's winning blow may have been surpassed here. The entire Polo Grounds shook with glee. The heroics by Terry were critical, for George Kelly has reverted to the punchless effort he turned in for the majority of the season. Four out of the five times he batted with men aboard, yet supplied nothing but two whiffs and three groundballs, one a twin-killing.

Barnes ran into difficulty in the 8th, but Jonnard and then Dean entered to save his hide. By the time the game climaxed, a 5-3 Brooklyn win in the nearby borough confirmed the seemingly impossible. A team had actually closed to within three games of first place, the Giants still breathing one behind them, with four games remaining for all. If this scenario repeats itself in tomorrow's finales, not one smidgen of work will be done in this city for days.

PGH 000 100 110 - 3 11 2
NYG 000 110 31x - 6 11 1

DAZZY DUZZN'T
CATASTROPHE AT EBBETS AND POLO GROUNDS NIGHTMARE FINISH OFF THE NATIONAL LEAGUE
September 24, 1924

By C. Jedediah Butterworth and Vincenzo Spanelli
Base Ball Freescribers

All tension has been severed. The races in both leagues are over, and the Pirates of Pittsburgh will face the Senators of Washington in the 1924 World Series. The two climactic National games, like most of them this past week, were maddening spectacles, and our unlikely pair of documentarians met over egg creams at one of Louis Auster's soda fountains in

Brooklyn this evening to discuss what they had just seen...

Spanelli: I should've gone to the Polo Grounds, damn it all. At least I could've watched McGraw lose. Instead I had to deal with Rachel blubbering into my shirt the last two innings.

Butterworth: Trust me when I tell you she will recover from her depression, my son. All true ball fans do when the budding trees come back around.

Spanelli: Yeah, well...it stunk like a dung pile anyway. And I'm not your son.

Butterworth: Shall I begin or should you?

Spanelli: You start. I can't even talk about it.

Butterworth: Fair enough. Honestly, it did seem as if another miracle day might occur early on. The Giants notched a 2nd inning run on Cuyler's dropped fly, while over at Ebbets Brooklyn had that early 1-0 lead—

Spanelli: I know! And Dazzy was pitching! And like I've said before, Dazzy always knows what to do, and eight of them Cubs screwed themselves into the ground whiffing on that curve of his in the first seven—

Butterworth: Would you care to let me finish?

Spanelli: Oh. Right. Sorry Cal...

Butterworth: So then the 4th inning began. And two of the three chief disappointments all season for New York went to work on the home crowd's spirits. I'm talking about shortstop Travis Jackson, who flubbed yet another grounder to keep a two-out Pirate rally going, and pitcher Jack Bentley—

Spanelli: I've seen him before. He's an ingrate.

Butterworth: Um, yes...Who proceeded to give up a 2-run double to Wright and single to Maranville and the Giants trailed just like that.

Spanelli: The Bucs have done that all year, y'know. Smash your whole china collection if you drop one teacup on the floor. Hey, that was kind of metaphorish, wasn't it?

Butterworth: Why yes. And then with Wilbur Cooper inexplicably mystifying enemy hitters again, it was time to bring the 1924 curtain down with the final George Kelly hitting tragedy of the year.

Spanelli: Really? Seems like his damn pants have been on fire.

Butterworth: His bat, perhaps. His bat. But never against Pittsburgh. With one out in the last of the 6th and his team trailing 4-1 after a Max Carey home run, Kelly rapped into a double play with the bases loaded and ended the inning. With two outs and two aboard in the 8th, he grounded into a force.

Spanelli: In the meantime Vance has a 2-0 lead going to the 8th after another Zack Wheat homer, and if anyone can hold a skinny lead it's Dazzy. But no, damn it. Not today. Gabby Hartnett rips a triple to start the 8th, Weis doubles, Hollocher singles and Rachel and her dad are screaming and ready to slice their own necks open and the crowd around us is even more insane, and then Grigsby works a walk with one out, Friberg beats out this cheap single and then the worst thing of all happens. Grantham grounds a double play chance to Wes Stock at third but the ball bounces off his groin or something and the go-ahead Cubs run scores! It was horrible!

Butterworth: Hmm. Eerily similar to some of Rip Collins' recent tragedies—

Spanelli: No, you're wrong. Dazzy just duzzn't!

Butterworth: Master Spanelli! You are beginning to sound like a Brooklyn fan.

Spanelli: No, I'm just a baseball fan. A pennant race fan. Just like you. And I wanted one more day of one.

Butterworth: Yes, but we still have a scintillating race for the best record in the game, haven't we? And a World Series that is bound to excite! And I can guarantee they are dancing in the streets in the western half of your home state this very moment.

Spanelli: Tell that to Rachel and her father. Which reminds me, I need to go over there now and peel them off the floor.

Butterworth: And pass up a second egg cream?

Spanelli: Well...

CHC 000 000 030 - 3 6 1
BRK 001 001 000 - 2 5 1

PGH 000 301 000 - 4 10 1
NYG 010 000 000 - 1 6 1

IS THEIR LIFE AFTER DRAMA?

September 25 & 26, 1924

We may as well have been standing over a grave. That's how quiet lunches and dinners at Rachel's house have been the last two days. Even her little brother and sister knew not to make too much noise while their dad was staring into his bowl of beef barley soup.

"That 8th inning the other day?" he mumbled to anyone who was listening, but probably more to himself, "Dazzy had maybe two innings like that all season. And that's the time he picks for the third one?" I carefully reminded him that the Robins still had to win most of the rest of their games, but Saul wouldn't listen.

"That is the entire point. We could have. All we have left is three at home with the Braves while Pittsburgh gets the Cubs. If we win that last game it is definitely and figuratively possible!"

Rachel was still too sad to even mumble, and she coped with the depressing feelings after dinner by starting to write another novel. I didn't ask what this one was going to be about, but I'm sure there's a character from Pittsburgh who will get murdered pretty early.

Her father has been working on finding me a job at a printer through friends of his, and tomorrow I'm supposed to go and get interviewed, so most of tonight I spent looking through my clothes for something presenting to wear while Rachel scribbled on notepads across the room.

I suppose I'd be as sad as her if the Phillies just missed out on a league pennant, but from watching her and her dad I'm not sure I'm looking forward to actually being in a race. At least Saul had more of an excuse. He had to see Brooklyn lose the World Series only four years ago and four years before that.

"Vinny? I could really go for a cup of tea."

I told Rachel that's nice, why don't you go down and get one, but I knew in two seconds that was the wrong thing to say. She ripped a page out of her writing notebook, crumpled and threw it in my direction.

"If you'd rather stand in front of the mirror then look at me, you can forget taking me to that play tonight."

I said I thought she didn't want to go in the first place but then she said she changed her mind, so I said you're not allowed to just change your mind all the time, and she said she had every right to.

"Is this why we got married? To have stupid fights??" I yelled, and it suddenly got real quiet downstairs.

"I cannot talk to you when you scream at me."

"Fine." And then I was grabbing my coat and tramping out of the house for a nice relaxing walk in the early Autumn air.

Geez, we'd been married for how long now? Two weeks? Her father was more than right before at the dinner table, and it was the same thing I told Butterworth at the egg cream place: Another day of pennant drama can make everything feel better.

So how are we going to make it through the winters?

A GRAND PIRATE PARADE
CITY CELEBRATES FIRST BUCCANEER FLAG SINCE 1909
September 27, 1924

By C. Jedediah Butterworth
Base Ball Freescriber

PITTSBURGH—Returning to the city where I was fiendishly apprehended just three weeks ago is not an easy task, but I have good reason, and the reason is enough to assuage all nerves.

It is a parade for the hometown Pirates, Champions of the National League, valiant liquidators of the Robins, Giants and Reds. Mixing a lethal combination of punctual hitting, tough pitching, on-base speed and impeccable fielding (their 210 double plays turned are 33 more than their nearest competitor) they are more than deserving of the cheers and gifts bestowed upon them here as they roll through leafy Schenley Park in open autos on this gloriously crisp day.

Ahead in the distance is Forbes Field, aflutter with flags, where they will host Chicago in their final home game before accompanying the Cubs to Illinois for the last two skirmishes. They will then either return here or move on to the Nation's Capitol for the start of the World

Series, and that choice will be determined in these final days, as Washington is nipping at the Pirate heels for the best record.

Goodness! Manager McKechnie just received a flower bouquet from the Mayor. Kiki Cuyler, despite his poor bat-showing in New York, still garners a few kisses from young female fans, and a brass band plays on a raised scaffold for the passing, conquering heroes.

The game that follows at Forbes is an out-and-out thriller, matching Tony Kauffman against Emil Yde, and the Bucs prove throughout why they're being called the "Draperies of Steel." Chicago plates a pair in the 1st on four straight two-out singles, but the Pirates swing right back onto the ship with two of their own, helped by a butchered ball at second by Grantham. Yde walks the first three batters in the Cub 4th, and a deep fly and Friberg single make it 4-2 for them, but here come the Pirates again! Smith doubles to open matters, Traynor singles him in, Maranville singles with one retired and the home horde rises as one to cheer on the inevitable explosion.

But this time Kauffman gets Yde on strikes, Carey on a ground ball, and the 4-3 Chicago lead is safely intact.

For the Pittsburgh bench, it must be a relief to look up on the outfield score board, see both Brooklyn and New York winning easily, and not even care. They make brave efforts to take the game the rest of the way, but Cuyler, the power source in the heart of their offensive machine all season, is still in one of his almost non-existent slumps. He now is without a hit in his last three games, his average has "tumbled" to .366, and he offers little today with an 0-for-3 showing after a scoring fly in the 1st.

Yet the Buccaneers are never dull, even in defeat. When Yde loads the bases with Cubs in the top of the 9th, Babe Adams takes over to face Hack Miller. Hack rips one to Wright at short, who fires home to begin a giddily sweet double play. The brutal Hartnett is then walked to re-fill the sacks, and Butch Weis whiffs. A Rabbit double with one out in the Pirate 9th rekindles the crowd, but Kauffman is allowed to bail himself out, and gets Jewel Ens on a fly and Carey on a pop.

The Forbes gathering is disappointed, but only for ten seconds. Then they stand, toss their hats, and cheer their pennant winners as loudly as they can to keep their ears ringing all the way to Chicago.

For my own part, I am still undecided about whether to accompany them and collect thoughts from the Pirate players in the days prior to the championship series. I could also go to Boston and speak to Bucky Harris and his Senators. I stare at the New York Sun press ticket in my hand that will gain me access for the entire World Series, and realize I've been given an extra one. Bonnie could leave the wee ones with her sister, and be my companion.

Or I could bring a friend...

CHC 200 200 000 - 4 9 2
PGH 200 100 000 - 3 8 0

CAL OF DUTY

September 27, 1924

Well, like I warned everybody, I had my job interview at Schneeberger & Sons Printers this morning over in a smelly part of New York called Queens. And either I did really good with my question-answering or they needed people awful bad because I was working in their big press room in about half an hour.

One of the Schneeberger sons did the interviewing, and I hated him in about three seconds because his hair was pasted to his head like black paint and he had these evil schoolteacher eyes that made you wonder when his paddle was coming out. His father owned the printer and knew Rachel's dad, which was why I was sitting there in the first place. When he asked me what I knew about printing I said I was a big book reader, and that didn't exactly make him happy. Nor did me telling him I was a batboy for the Phillies this past summer.

"I see," he snapped, and scratched a dark spot on his nose, "My condolences in that regard. I and most of my cohorts follow McGraw's men, you know."

Wonderful. A snotty Giants fan might be my new boss. I asked how his father came to be friends with Rachel's then. He almost smiled but thought better of it, I guess.

"Brooklyn won the season series by 13-9," he sighed, "And my father is paying off their wager by bringing you on board." He stood and held out a pasty hand. "Congratulations, boy. Follow the signs to the lower press room." It's pretty weird how baseball seems to involve itself in everything in my life, but I guess there's a lot worse things that can do that.

Anyway, about an hour later I was wishing that the Giants had won the year's series. The giant offset printer was incredibly loud, and all the press guys worked with cotton stuffed in their ears and had to talk to each other by yelling everything.

"TAKE YOUR BALLS!!" yelled the first guy who saw me, holding out a handful of cotton balls. I followed him over to what they call a plating area, which was where I'd be helping them lift the plates and get them onto the giant rollers that printed on the giant paper rolls. It was funny that all these people were working on a Saturday, but news never sleeps, and Schneeberger printed about six different local papers. I had no idea the newspaper business was thriving so much.

"NO IDIOT! THIS WAY!" That was from Scottie, the foreman of the room, who was sort of a walking tree trunk with ears and a moustache. And he was the nicest of the bunch. Most of them stared at me like I was a rat that crawled in their lunch and snickered to each other about every mistake I made. They shouldn't have been the ones to talk, though, because I swear not one of them still had five fingers on a hand.

There was a squat guy who kept ducking outside to smoke cigarettes, but sometimes he'd come back in after a long break and he'd have cigarettes to pass out to the other guys. He would also flash number signals every time with his fingers, which got me curious.

"PUDGIE'S A YANKEE FAN!" Scottie yell-told me, "POOR GUY! THEY'RE 3-3 WITH THE ATHLETICS AFTER FIVE! YOU A BALL FAN?" This time I just shook my head. It was rough enough in that room.

So I was sweating after another hour because there was hardly any air, and there was ink on my fingers and my feet hurt and my back hurt more and then Pudgie popped back in screaming at the top of his lungs. "GRAND SLAMMER FOR THE BABE!! IT'S 8-3 NOW!!" His buddies didn't seem to care and I cared even less, but at least it got everyone thinking about baseball instead of how to torture the new kid.

"JOHNSON'S TOO OLD AND ALL THE SENATORS DO IS HIT SINGLES!" yelled Scottie, "BUCS ARE GONNA STRANGLE 'EM!"

"YOU'RE WRONG!" Pudgie shouted back, "NATS HAVE GREAT PITCHING AND THE BEST FIELDING!"

"NOT LATELY" yelled somebody else, and before you knew it the bets were flying around the room. Some guy I didn't recognize came in right then and handed me a sealed envelope.

"WHAT'S THIS??"

"WESTERN UNION!"

Oh geez, not Benny again. I tore the thing open:

MASTER SPANELLI:
COULD USE PROTEGE FOR WORLD SERIES. INTRIGUED? SUN PAPER TO PAY EXPENSES.
—C. J. BUTTERWORTH

I stared at the telegram in shock, then glee. Scottie tried to peek at it. "WHAZZIT SAY?"

"IT SAYS THIS—" Then I put my lips together, gave each and every one of my former Schneeberger workmates the loudest raspberry ever heard, and walked out the exit.

DR. BUTTERWORTH'S SERIES PROGNOSIS
September 28, 1924

By C. Jedediah Butterworth
Base Ball Freescriber

Because it will be another day before we learn which ball park I will be meeting Master Spanelli in for the World Series, I decided this would be an ample opportunity to briefly discuss the warring attributes of the two participants. In short, my fearful predictions.

FIRST BASE: Charlie Grimm (Pgh.) vs. Joe Judge (Was.)
These are the two best fielding first-sackers in the sport. Judge is a far superlative hitter, but Grimm has had his lion's share of important strikes. Still...Washington advantage.

SECOND BASE: Rabbit Maranville (Pgh.) vs. Bucky Harris (Was.)

The Senator skipper has been a sterling leader, and has driven in the second-most winning RBIs on the team after Goslin, but Maranville is his hitting and fielding match, and not averse to swatting the occasional back-breaking triple from his eighth slot in the lineup. Draw.

SHORT-STOP: Glenn Wright (Pgh.) vs. Roger Peckinpaugh (Was.)

Both men can muff balls, but both have extraordinary range and start numerous twin-killings. Both are also stronger against left-hand pitching, so with Pittsburgh starting two left-handers and Mogridge the only one for the Senators...Slight Washington advantage.

THIRD BASE: Pie Traynor (Pgh) vs. Ossie Bluege (Was.)

No contest in this corner. Fielding is even and excellent between them, but Pie is by far the better batsman...Pittsburgh advantage.

LEFT FIELD: Kiki Cuyler (Pgh.) vs. Goose Goslin (Was.)

The most valuable man in each league, and patrolling the same outfield meadow! Goslin (.328, 14, 143, 21 GWRBIs) owned the first half of the season, Cuyler (.364, 15, 140, 17 GWRBIs) the second, but Kiki is a much better flycatcher and has 31 stolen bases in 37 tries to boot...Pittsburgh advantage.

CENTER FIELD: Max Carey (Pgh.) vs. Nemo Leibold (Was.)

Carey takes this competition for his superlative speed (50-6 stealing bases) and better hitting-punch, though Leibold makes fewer errors and can get on base nearly as well...Pittsburgh advantage.

RIGHT FIELD: Eddie Moore/Clyde Barnhart (Pgh.) vs. Sam Rice (Was.)

Moore has a sizzling bat but Barnhart is weaker against portsiders. Rice does more things well, though, and if he notches one more run batted in his last two games in Boston he will finish with 100, against zero home runs...Washington advantage.

CATCHER: Earl Smith/Johnnie Gooch (Pgh.) vs. Muddy Ruel/Bennie Tate (Was.)

Smith is the most powerful and dangerous at the backstop position, but Ruel is always on base and will be instrumental in keeping Cuyler and Carey from robbing the basepath store...Washington advantage.

STARTING PITCHING: Ray Kremer, Lee Meadows, Johnny Morrison, Emil Yde (Pgh.) vs. Walter Johnson, George Mogridge, Curly Ogden, Tom Zachary.

All of these twirlers are capable of pitching suffocating games. All are also capable of being shelled, though the Big Train certainly the least likely, and he may start three of the contests. For that reason alone...Washington advantage.

RELIEF PITCHING: Babe Adams, Arnie Stone, Wilbur Cooper (Pgh.) vs. Alan Russell, Firpo Marberry, By Speece (Was.)

Adams is the cream of the crop, and Cooper joins the pack from the rotation. Russell has a rash of saves but has been plain horrible in September, and Marberry is a human heart palpitator....Pittsburgh advantage.

BENCH: The Senators are far wider and deeper, with Doc Prothro, Lance Richbourg and Earl McNeely adept with the stick. Jewel Ens and Gooch, if he isn't starting, lead a much paltrier Pirate brigade...Washington advantage.

MANAGERS: Bill McKechnie (Pgh.) vs. Bucky Harris (Wash.) One of the better battles on hand. Harris is quicker to make substitutions because he has more to draw from, but the Pirates have been getting timely hits all season no matter what order they're put in...Draw.

BALL PARKS: Forbes Field and Griffith Stadium are home run cemeteries, perfectly suited for both teams' gap-shooting attacks. Each club leads its league in triples and is near the bottom in clouts. Pittsburgh must drop its final game in Chicago and Washington must win both of theirs at Fenway to bring the home advantage to the Senators, so at this writing, the Steel City should likely prepare for the first festivities.

By my count, that is 6-4 in advantages for Washington. But nothing has gone the way it has supposed to in 1924, and I am usually a poor soothsayer, so I will lean toward the club with the probable extra home game. Pirates win in six games.

THE END OF THINGS
September 29-30, 1924

There I was on Monday, meaning yesterday, all excited about joining Cal and seeing my first World Series, and we still had no clue where the thing was going to start. The Pirates had decided to mess up everyone's Pittsburgh reservations by starting to lose, and if they could just beat the Cubs in the last game or have Boston pounce on the Nats again, the event would open in their park.

Rachel was sad and a little angry she wasn't coming along of course, but still packed me a bag and promised to put a few sandwiches in. I told her it was Butterworth's special invitation and besides women weren't allowed in most press rows, and certainly not at the World Series. This caused her to go on a ten-minute speech about how females still weren't allowed to do anything except vote, and how that was all going to change someday soon if she had anything to do with it. I was sure she would.

To make her feel better I talked her into going out to Ebbets for the final game of the year against the Braves, a pretty good bet that Brooklyn would make 90 wins. Well, that wasn't the smartest idea. The Braves were out for revenge for some dumb reason and after Doak hit Ray Powell with the very first pitch they racked up eight hits and four runs on him in the first three and a half innings.

"I can't watch this," Rachel cried, "Take me home. I'd rather peel potatoes!" Her father was the brilliant one, giving up the game to actually work for a living. She was obviously still upset about losing the pennant, and even more upset that the Pirates now looked like garbage (They were down 4-0 in Chicago on the score board.) I took her hand, turned her face to mine, and lowered my voice.

"Don't you know why they call this a pastime? Because that's what you do. You pass the time. My lousy Phillies have lost 96 games this year, and that's with colored all-stars taking over for a whole week. How do you think me and Benny got through the whole season?"

"Because you're nuts?"

"No, because we know how to sit and enjoy the sunny afternoons and all the little things that go into watching a baseball game. Look out there now. Fournier's leading off, and he's a great hitter so every Boston infielder gets more tense right before the pitch is thrown. See that? You can use your perifery vision and just catch it. It's also the only game where the defense has the ball. And almost every game I go to, something happens I've never seen before."

For the moment, Rachel wasn't thinking of killing herself. She even smiled. And then Fournier cracked a single off Larry Benton into right. And so did Brown. And Mitchell walked. And Taylor singled. Milt Stock did, too. Bill Doak singled. Bernie Neis tripled. Andy High doubled. Rachel was standing on her seat screaming deliriously, eight Brooklyn runs were home, and our world was all healed up again.

And guess what else? The Cubs blanked the Bucs, Zachary and the Senators eeked out a 3-2 win at Fenway Park, and everything would come down to tomorrow's Washington game in Boston. Pittsburgh had the higher difference between runs scored and given up, meaning that if they lost and finished with the same record as the Bucs, Pittsburgh would get the advantage.

And good old Cal Butterworth was starting our big party early. He wired me to join him up in Boston for the final game, with Walter Johnson pitching, and Rachel was in such a good mood after the Ebbets game she didn't even mind seeing me off a day early.

* * *

Fenway Park was stuffed like a Thanksgiving goose for the last day of the season, and there were even a few pockets of cranks in the stands that had come up from Washington. Cal was in great spirits and had a stool for me set up in the press row, right behind his typewriter spot.

Alex Ferguson and his 18 losses was going for Boston, and he had no chance. After Ruel walked to start the game, Clark flubbed a grounder at third and Judge singled to load the bases. Slumpy Goslin whiffed again, but Sam Rice did the almost-impossible, singling in two to put the Nats ahead and give himself 102 runs batted in with NO homers for the year. Bluege and the Train added run-scoring singles and it was 5-0 just like that.

One run for Johnson sometimes is enough, but just to make sure, the Senators added five more in the third, with Rice, Bluege, Harris, Peckinpaugh, Johnson and Ruel all reaching base before an out was made. It was a rout, folks, and Harris felt so good about things that he put Marberry in for relief after the 5th to make sure Walter had his 24th win and could start getting rested for the World Series. The Red Sox made a little bit of noise but not enough, and even their home fans were on their feet applauding in the 9th when Williams and Clark bounced out to lock up Griffith Stadium for Games One and Two.

After a rough week, Washington finished strong, and as I boarded their train car with Cal and a flock of reporters at South Station, we were starting to wonder how the Pirates would really do against these guys. Tomorrow we will begin to find out.

NATIONAL LEAGUE FINAL

Pittsburgh	92	62	.597	—
Brooklyn	90	64	.584	2
New York	90	64	.584	2
Cincinnati	88	66	.571	4
Chicago	83	71	.539	9
St. Louis	75	79	.487	17
PHILLIES	57	97	.370	35
Boston	41	113	.267	51

AMERICAN LEAGUE FINAL

Washington	93	61	.604	—
Detroit	83	71	.539	10
Chicago	81	73	.526	12
New York	81	73	.526	12
Boston	72	82	.468	21
St. Louis	71	83	.461	22
Cleveland	69	85	.448	24
Philadelphia	66	88	.429	27

PART SEVEN
October

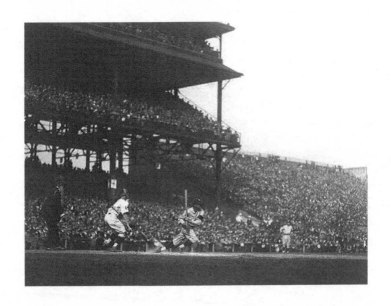

ALL KINDS OF CAPITOL FUN
October 2, 1924

WASHINGTON, D.C.—Ain't that jazzy? I gave myself a location so I can start sounding more like a big time baseball writer, seeing I'm going to be friending around with a bunch of them here the next few days and who knows, maybe Butterworth will let me write about one of the games.

Actually, I've already been here a few days, waiting for Game One of the Series tomorrow, and it's been nothing but dinners and parties. The first bash was the one on the train Tuesday night as the players and us rolled in from Boston. Thousands of Washington fans were waiting at the station, and bands were playing and ladies were so randy they were trying to grab Ossie Bluege. Cal and me the other reporters had to get off at the opposite end of the platform and race up to see all this action, and I almost got my teeth knocked in by the tweed elbow of someone's sport coat for my troubles. I heard later that Charles Dawes the Vice-President showed up, Coolidge saving himself up for Griffith Stadium no doubt, but I never saw the guy.

The next day was sunny and cool and the city looked beautiful and I couldn't believe I lived in Philadelphia and never even got down here. After going to a bunch of different Senators parades with Cal I broke off and visited the Smithsonian Institution Museum, and the brand new Lincoln Memorial, and then walked up every one of the 897 steps and fifty floors of the Washington Monument. They had an elevator but it took almost fifteen minutes to get to the top and I figured I needed the exercise, even though it nearly killed me.

They had all the press people booked at the fancy Hamilton Crowne Plaza Hotel, and there were parties in every ballroom every night. I didn't have the best clothes for them, but Cal rented me a sharp waistcoat and bow tie and passed me off as his "understudy" whatever that means. Stuck in a room with a bunch of men smoking cigars and blabbering about baseball wasn't exactly my glass of fizzer so I broke off again and snuck into a bigger room that had a jazz combo playing and some local dressed-up ladies dancing with eager men. Bucky Harris and Roger Peckinpaugh were there with their wives and it was then that I started to miss Rachel and wished I'd talked Cal into bringing her along somehow. I'm sure she had the perfect flapper outfit somewhere and could dance these women right out the glass window.

GRIPPING FROM START TO FINISH
PIRATES AND SENATORS STAGE UNFORGETTABLE OPENING ACT
October 3, 1924

By C. Jedediah Butterworth
Base Ball Freescriber

WASHINGTON, D.C.—Did we really just witness this? It begins with President Coolidge wishing Walter Johnson luck, and thirteen innings and nearly three hours of utter tension later, the 27,000 at Griffith Stadium and countless more following Game One on electric boards around the nation are rendered speechless.

The parade of bands and dignitaries seems endless before game time, and all it does is swell the suspenseful knot in everyone's throat, for this is a matchup that seems nearly even when jotted down on paper. It is a cool, sunny afternoon in northwest Washington, perfect for sharp play, and the press rows around me are clattering with typewriter keys.

The Big Train begins his twirling day as if he has his namesake to catch at the station, dispatching the first nine Pirates with rapid ease. Kremer is a bit looser with his dexterity, but is able to escape a pair of minor pickles in the first three frames.

The 4th tells a different tale, though. Carey opens with a line single and steals second on Ruel. Grimm singling him plateward, but a ferocious arm-bullet from Nemo Leibold finishes Carey at the plate to ignite the crowd. The Pirates are just sharpening their cutlasses, though. After Moore walks, Cuyler sizzles a ball to deep left-center, scoring the first two runs. When Smith singles on the next pitch it is 3-0 Pittsburgh, and the park falls into a funereal silence.

Judge ends that mood quickly, though, with a booming double to lead off the last of the 4th. A walk to Goslin, Bluege single and pair of well-timed force-outs give the Nats two tallies right back, and the teeming horde is engaged in the contest again.

Three quiet innings follow, Kremer and Johnson matching outs, until Maranville leads the 8th with a double. A Kremer bunt moves him along, and after a Carey walk, Grimm plates the run with a force-out, due to Harris putting the middle infielders back. The 4-2 score seems to depress the locals yet again, and it isn't until Rice singles with one gone in the last of the 9th that they stir back to life. Bluege grounds out, and then Harris has a strange hunch and removes himself for left-swinging Richbourg. Lance waits for a fastball that he fancies, and mashes it deep to center. The ball sails over the head of Carey as Richbourg flies to third with a triple! It is suddenly 4-3!

Here is Peckinpaugh now, bouncing a ball out to Wright to end the game—except Wright boots it and Richbourg scores the tying run! Johnson then stays in the game and doubles, but little Peck has to stop at third. The moment Babe Adams is summoned from the Pirate bullpen, Tate bats for Ruel, pops out, and the game folds into extra chapters.

With daylight on the wane and all nerves on the edge of a blade, Adams and Johnson then do their finest work of the year, each holding the other scoreless for three innings. For the Train it is actually four, and even though he strains to finish each frame out there, Harris is clearly reluctant to go to his wobbly relief corps of Russell, Marberry and Speece.

He doesn't need to. For in the last of the fateful 13th, Goslin begins with a single, his first safety of the Series. Rice and Bluege both sky out, and up comes backup second sacker Tommy Taylor, forced to enter the contest when Bucky shockingly pulled himself from the lineup to produce Richbourg's incredible triple.

Taylor miraculously does the same! Clubbing a ball high and deep to center field! Carey is off with the crack but can't get to the wall in time, the sphere skipping merrily off the top of the barrier and bounding away from Carey! Here comes Goslin, burning around third and into the arms of waiting mates for the game-winning run!

What a spectacle! What a World Series opener! It is hard to see Taylor being swarmed on the field through the cloud of flying straw hats, and by the time I reach the Senator club house with my assistant, it is stuffed to capacity and we are forced to wait for quotes in the outside tunnel.

But there is nothing really that needs to be said. Only remembered.

PGH 000 300 010 000 0 - 4 7 1
WAS 000 200 002 000 1 - 5 10 0
W-Johnson L-Adams GWRBI-Taylor

BABE OUT OF THE WOODS
RELIEF ACE ADAMS SAVES GAME TWO, KNOTS SERIES
October 4, 1924

By C. Jedediah Butterworth
Base Ball Freescriber

WASHINGTON, D.C.—The reporters swarming around batting practice today are like honey-fattened bees, buzzing about every detail of yesterday's scintillating extra-frame victory for the Senators. How could these clubs come close to topping that scenario?

For the Pirates, their goal is to expunge the horror from their minds as soon as possible. And Clyde Barnhart's rope of a single leading off Game Two against Mogridge seems like a fine first step. Grimm bunts Clyde to second, but Traynor whiffs badly and after Carey hustles out an infield hit and steals second, the extraordinary Cuyler lines to Peckinpaugh to end the threat.

Lee Meadows seems on his game for Pittsburgh, though, and gets the Nats with no effort in the 1st. Mogridge retires the first two Bucaneers in the 2nd, then reverts to the foul pitching ways that have plagued him since Labor Day. Gooch singles, as does Meadows, and Barnhart's second shot brings home the first Pirate score.

Goslin and Rice strike singles to begin the Senator 2nd, but go nowhere as Tate, Bluege, and Peckinpaugh all roll out. It is not a comforting omen. With one out in the 3rd, Carey blisters a two-sack hit and Cuyler walks. Wright and Maranville follow with sharp singles, Gooch lifts a scoring fly out to the Goose and it is instantly 4-0 for the visitors!

The bloodletting continues in the 4th. Barnhart collects his third safety, a double, to begin matters, and after a ground out, Traynor singles him to third. Barnhart is forced at home on a Carey grounder to Bluege, but a predictable Cuyler single brings in a run and finishes not-very-gorgeous George for the afternoon. Peckinapugh caps off the inning by kicking away Wright's grounder, it is 6-0, and the aura of doom we felt much of yesterday returns to the Griffith yard.

Meadows finally flinches in the 5th, as Tate singles, Bluege walks, and with two outs Lance Richbourg, rewarded by manager Harris with the leadoff position for his heroic triple in the first game, singles in Tate to get the home nine on the board.

In the 6th it gets even more interesting. Goslin bombs a double with one out, Rice and Tate single and Bluege hits a scoring fly to make it 6-3! As they always seem to do, though, the swaggering Bucs come right back, scoring a run in the 7th on a walk to the Rabbit, stolen base and double by pitcher Meadows himself off Marberry.

My young assistant fetches me a cold pop halfway through the 8th, and I have my head turned to open the bottle when Goslin starts the Senator inning with a line single. Rice doubles and the ball park is alive once more. Tate singles home two and Meadows is sent packing! The crowd cheers his departure, but it's less of a blessing than they think.

Because in strolls Charles Benjamin "Babe" Adams, the toughest relief man in either league. He walks Bluege, sees the score inch to 7-6 when Wright boots another two-out grounder, but then induces Harris to line out with two men aboard.

Russell hurls a scoreless Pittsburgh 9th, and then Babe returns to the hill. Fresh from the 9th inning dramatics yesterday, the thousands of loyalists on hand rise as one to cheer a new rally to life. Judge singles, and it's begun!

Then Goslin raps into an easy double-play, and it is done. The Goose did manage two singles and a key double, but he has been excelling at times like this all season, and his recent failures have not endeared him to Washington base ball society. Rice flies harmlessly out to Moore in right, and this tension-stuffed championship spectacle moves on to the Steel City in a perfectly even state.

PGH 013 200 100 - 7 14 1
WAS 000 012 030 - 6 12 1
W-Meadows L-Mogridge SV-Adams GWRBI-Barnhart

THRILLING ATMOSPHERE, ICKY GAME
October 6, 1924

By Vincenzo Spanelli
Baseball Fan Scribe-at-Large

PITTSBURGH—After two real close sizzler-games in Washington, everyone hauled west on the train yesterday and made their way out to a city this scribe-at-large feels like he's been to twenty times already this season.

But it never looked anything like this. Pirate flags hung everywhere, along with a couple of straw-filled dummies of guys in suits I figured were supposed to be senators hanging from lamp posts by their necks. Anyway, it's the first World Series here in Steelville since 1909 when Wagner was playing, so the whole town's pretty sauced about it.

Ogden was going for the Nats, and he was 19-6 for the year and was probably going to be tough. Morrison for the Pirates was "only" 14-5 but had three shutouts and was even tougher than the other guy at times.

Leibold managed to work a walk in the 1st but a nifty double play started by Grimm wiped that thing right out. A Carey double and Moore single later, the Bucs were up 1-0 and the Forbes crowd was giving me a headache already.

I guess Ogden didn't get a good night's sleep because he had just about no petrol in his tank. A walk and singles from Traynor and Maranville and Grimm got three more runs across in the 2nd and the Pittsburghians were singing and dancing little jigs in the aisles. I kind of wished I was down there singing and jigging instead of trapped up in a stuffy writer box, but oh well, that's what being a paid professional is about.

After that early excitement came five innings of absolute nothing— except for the three more double plays the Pirates turned on the stinky Senators, every one of them started by the Rabbit. Ogden was kept in because he calmed down awful good, but when the 8th rolled around he lost his mind again. Moore walked and Cuyler singled. Smith got one in with a long fly, Traynor walked, Wright singled and Harris finally brought on Russell to put Curly out of his misery.

I was left to drown in mine, though. Pitching was the name of this snoozer, and you know me, I'm used to 11-10 games at the Baker Bowl day every day, so when Morrison gloved a grounder by Peckinpaugh for the final out after Washington scratched out a measly run, I jumped out of that press row like my drawers were burning.

At least Walter Johnson goes again tomorrow for Game Four. Me and my mentor who you're probably used to reading here Cal Butterworth saw him a few times on the train to Pittsburgh, and he was as polite as a ball player can be. You'd never know he could change the shape of your face with just one of his buggywhip heaters.

WAS 000 000 001 - 1 5 0
PGH 110 000 02x - 6 7 0
W-Morrison L-Ogden GWRBI-Moore

SHELL-SHOCKED AND AWED
LATE VOLLEYS OFF JOHNSON SINK SENATOR HOPES
October 7, 1924

By C. Jedediah Butterworth
Base Ball Freesciber

While I did appreciate my young understudy's attempt at sports writing yesterday, he is currently reading up on his journalism techniques with an armful of newspapers at the back of this room. Walter Johnson is going in Game Four with a chance to tie the Series back up, and I need the occasion to be professionally recounted.

PITTSBURGH—Virtually suffocated yesterday by the spectacled wizardry of one Lee Meadows, the Senators are determined to polish their clubs this afternoon against Ray Kremer. Oftentimes just a run or two are enough when the Big Train is chugging on the hill, and manager Harris seems certain they can muster that amount.

Rice launches the attack with a shattering triple to begin the 2nd, but an infield hit that Tate beats out fails to bring the runner in. Bluege is struck to fill the sacks, a Peckinpaugh force keeps everyone at bay, and it is left to the regal Johnson to single into left for two quick runs.

Harris knocks in another one out later, and Walter has a 3-0 cushion!

Pittsburgh puts a small handful of men aboard, but two double plays erase them pronto. The 4th frame alters the dramatics, though. Traynor and Wright open with singles, Kremer moves them ahead with an expert bunt, and the poisonous Max Carey singles them both in to make it 3-2 and awake the teeming crowd. A Judge single and long Goslin double to start the Washington 5th had failed to bring in a run, and in the 6th they manage to leave another pair aboard.

It stings them like a hornet right away. Cuyler doubles with one out in the Pirate 6th, Traynor triples him in, and the game is knotted 3-3. And then the 7th happens, a grisly example of Washington's swatting woes. Carey drops Goslin's fly in center to begin the inning with a 2-base error. Rice singles but Goslin holds up at third. Bluege walks with one out but Peckinpaugh and Johnson both ground out to leave three adrift this time!

It stays tied until the 8th, when Judge's single, Goslin's single and third hit, and Rice's single make it 4-3 for the Nats. Mathews and Ruel replace Goslin and Tate for defense, and Johnson strands two Bucs in the last of the 8th by getting the brutal Traynor on a force-out.

Three more Senator hits sandwiched around a sickening pop double play on a bunt attempt by Peckinpaugh send the suspenseful thriller to the last of the 9th. Sixteen runners all told are abandoned by Washington for the afternoon, a number that may soon be haunting their dreams.

For Wright draws a walk to begin the lower 9th. Johnson bears down to fan Maranville and pinch-batter Gooch, though, and we can almost see him hiding a grin from the press row. One more out and the Series is tied.

Except the one more out is Max Carey, punishing the ball all Series with an 8-for-17 performance, or .471. And he does it again, rifling a ball high off the right wall for a double and tie game! Johnson cannot believe it, nor can this reporter. But we barely have time to contemplate the miracle when Grimm strikes the next pitch into the right gap for another scoring double and the ball game for the Pirates!

The Day They De-Railed the Train is what Pittsburghers will call this incredible game, and with a 3-1 advantage now in the Autumn Classic, it may also be known as Walterloo.

WAS 030 000 010 - 4 16 0
PGH 000 021 002 - 5 12 1
W-Kremer L-Johnson GWRBI-Grimm

DIDN'T SEE THIS OR THAT ONE COMING
October 8, 1924

By Vicenzo Spanelli
Baseball Fan Scribe-at-Large

PITTSBURGH—Can you believe that Butterworth yesterday? What a snot-face! Sticking me in the corner with journalism papers to read like I just peed myself in the fourth grade or something. Mr. Tuggerheinz wouldn't even have done that.

So nuts to him, I thought, as I followed him out of our hotel this morning. I'm sitting with the crazed Pirate fans this time and I'm going to write about the game the way I want and I'll get it to his *New York Sun* guy before he turns HIS in and he can just plain live with it. And if the Bucs win it today I'll probably end up drinking more than I've ever drunk because after all, it is a Pennsylvania team we're talking about, right?

Two lefties, Zachary for the Nats, and Yde for the Pirates, were pitching today, and both have had their crap-parties lately. Yde's actually famous for pitching seven or eight great innings and then melting into a puddle in the 9th.

This time his teammates were doing the melting, and pretty early. With Senators on first and third and two outs, a ball got past Gooch and in came the first run of the game. Then in the 2nd, Ruel hit a ball out to Cuyler who I'm sick of hearing about already and Kiki flubbed it for a two-base error to put men on second and third. Zachary then doubled home two and it was 3-0 Washington and there seemed about as much chance for a big Pittsburgh party as I did of becoming Governor.

Lucky for them, Ossie Bluege was playing third base for the other team. After a Grimm single and Traynor walk, Carey bounced an easy double play ball down to Bluege and he did everything but touch it as the ball ended bouncing off a seat rail behind him for a two-base error. Cuyler hit a sacrifice fly and just like that it was 3-2 and people around me were going ape and banging on their seats.

Around the top of the 4th after Carey dropped a ball I made a note on my pad about how the Bucs seemed to have butter in their gloves, and suddenly a pair of real gloves covered my eyes from behind. A scratchy voice said "Guess who?" in my ears.

"You got me," I said. "I know it ain't you Cal, that's for sure."

Then I smelled perfume. I spun around and looked up at Rachel Stone Spanelli, wearing a sweet light blue dress and matching hat and none other than my best buddy Benny standing behind her. I was so shocked I couldn't even talk.

"Think we were gonna stay home while you had all the fun?" Benny asked.

"I can't believe you're here! How did you ever—"

"Your old principal, that's how," said Rachel.

"You mean Tuggerheinz?"

"He knows the Phillies owner, remember?" said Benny, "Anyway he got left World Series tickets but got sick and couldn't go and left them with your mama—"

"—who sent them to me—"

"—who came down to Philly and scooped me up first—"

"—and now we're here!"

I jumped out of my seat, gave Rachel a hug and kiss and shook Benny's hand and then he took my seat while I went to the other side of home plate and sat with Rachel in theirs.

Meanwhile two more innings went by with no one scoring and the place getting real tense, because the last thing Bucs fans wanted was for their boys to have to go back to Washington.

The Senators begged to differ. Yde got all kinds of shaky all of a sudden, as Bluege singled, and Peckinpaugh and Ruel walked to load the bases. Up came Zachary, like most of the Senator pitchers also a great hitter. Sure enough, he painted the ball down the line an inch from the foul stripe, good for a double and two more runs batted in. Leibold grounded out but then Yde flubbed an easy grounder and a third run ran across.

Gooch tripled one in for the Bucs to keep their fans alive, and after Judge hit a scoring fly in the 8th, Yde knocked in another Pirate run with a two-out single. This finished off Zachary, brought on Firpo Marberry and got the Pittsburghers cuckoo again, but the Firp was up to the task this time. Smith hit for Barnhart and grounded out to leave two on the bases, and after Grimm singled to begin the Buc 9th, Traynor rapped into a killer double play, Carey bounced out, and we were all headed back to Washington!

Were we ever. Rachel and Benny and me were squeezed into the press people's parlor car along with assorted players, wives, writers and operators. Nobody slept because you couldn't. I wouldn't put the train ride in the same fun league as the incredible one we took with Oscar Charleston and Smokey Joe Williams and those Black Phillies back in August, and that's just something else the colored players were better at than us.

It was so packed on the World Series express I don't think I got a word in with Butterworth all night. Which was probably a good thing, because when he sees my name instead of his in the paper tomorrow morning he's gonna blow a valve.

WAS 120 003 010 - 7 7 1
PGH 002 001 010 - 4 10 3
W-Zachary L-Yde SV-Marberry GWRBI-none

HOT PIE AND OTHER LAST DESSERTS
October 10, 1924

The top of the Washington Monument turned out to be a great place to hide from Butterworth. I knew the last thing he wanted to do was waste time on the long elevator ride or climb even twenty of the steps. When we got back to Washington Rachel and me stayed with Benny in a rooming house in the colored section of town, also a great place to avoid Butterworth, and we spent most of yesterday's day off playing cards and reading my Game 5 story in the *New York Sun* over and over.

But today was Game 6, and it might be the end, so we couldn't hide forever. Rachel wanted me to go face him already and put this baby business behind us but I chose to just find a space to stand out in back of the left field stands so I could watch the game and not have to think about it. Rachel wanted a real chair, though, she broke away and went who knows where as soon as we got into the ball park.

Benny was off getting us food when Cal suddenly appeared out of no-where, his face all red like he was going to spout lava out of his ears.

"Thought you could get away with that, didn't you?"

"You mean my game story? You're right, I did!"

"You cost me twenty-five dollars yesterday, son. And now Mr. Munsey won't use either of us!"

"Gee, Cal. I'm sorry about that. I just—"

"You're just an insufferable little snipe, is what you are. If you were my son I'd give you a thrashing right here you would never forget!"

"Good thing I'm not then, huh?"

His cheeks puffed out and he raised a hand and then Benny was there, dropping his sausage rolls and separating us with all the muscle he had.

"C'mon, you two, cut that out! Can't we all just get along better?"

Cal and me looked at him, then at each other. Benny's line did have a nice sound to it. He forced us to shake hands with all these ball fans stand-ing around watching, and then the Senators taking the field and all of them cheering, and then he had another question for us.

"So who's going to write today's game story?"

ONE MORE SHOCK FOR THE ROAD

By Rachel Stone Spanelli
Female Ballscriber

WASHINGTON, D.C.—Before a tumultuous, terminally mad throng bursting every crack in Griffith's ball yard, an unforgettably enthralling spectacle was performed for Game Six of the 1924 World Series this after-noon. When it was complete, nary a fan was without a thumping heart or sliding tear.

The contest matched the same Game Two moundmasters Meadows and Mogridge, but this had no resemblance to that one-sided sleep-inducer. The Senators were fresh off their exciting final triumph in western Penn-sylvania, and eager to get an early advantage to calm down their recently unsteady ball-thrower.

And so they did. Here was Goslin leading the 2nd with a free pass, and Rice singling him along, and Harris singling him back into the home dug-out, a golden run clutched in their hands. In the 3rd it was Pirate right roamer Barnhart helping them out, dropping an easy Tate fly for a two-base gaffe. A single by Judge, double by Goslin and two successive wild heaves by Meadows brought home three runs, and sent the gathering into seizures of joy. Another hideous Pittsburgh misplay by Wright with two outs in the 4th brought Harris in with another run, it was 5-0 for Washing-ton, and Walter Johnson was already sitting comfortably in the shadows, planning his opening pitches for Game Seven.

But this reporter hails from the fair city of Brooklyn, a place of base ball disappointment I am very accustomed to, and something never felt correct or sure about this five-run lead. These Pirates are just too professional and utterly dashing to belly up and die on us, and when seldom-used Jeff Pfeffer took over for Meadows and squirreled out of two straight runner-jams, it seemed very likely a shift in the fates was coming.

And so it did. Heinie Mueller batted for Pfeffer with one out in the Pirate 6th and blistered a double. Barnhart singled him home. Local hopes surfaced again as Grimm bounced an easy double play roller out to Bluege at third. But the Lord saw fit to drop a stray pebble in his path. Ossie reached as the ball abruptly changed course, then kicked it will-nilly, and it was suddenly second and third.

It was here that Harris made a fateful decision, one that may resonate in the sport's history for time evermore. With the lefty-butchering Traynor due at the dish and Mogridge on the verge of collapse, judging from the sweat I could make out glistening on his thick neck, right-hander Marberry was summoned to take his place.

But Pie baked him instantly, clanging a monstrous triple off the left-center wall, bringing home both runners and thrusting the Swashbucklers back into the fray. The Nats got one back on a Judge single in the last of the 6th, but with Mogridge now vacationing, the Washington bullpen was forced to save the game, a not-very-frequent occurrence in these parts of late.

What's more, the Pirates would have been happier getting their teeth extracted than having to face The Big Train in a climactic game.

And they suddenly played that way. Grimm and hot Traynor singled to begin the 8th, bringing in Alan Russell. Carey walked. A single by Wright and walk to pinch-sticker Smith brought home two and made it 6-5. Fans were turning their backs to the field, women were clutching their men or if none were with them, the nearest ones. After Leibold was left on second by the Senators in their 8th, it grew quieter than the Vatican for the top of the 9th. Barnhart led with a walk. Grimm singled him to second. Traynor finally made an out with an easy fly, and when Carey grounded into a force there was just one out left.

How could it not be Kiki Cuyler striding to the plate now? Seriously, how could it not? Russell stared in, the grandstand shadow tickling his big shoulders, likely shut his eyes and whipped in a fastball. Cuyler cracked it into left to tie the game! Cursing and wailing erupted around me. Glenn Wright was next, and took a gentler approach, looping a ball into center that dropped in front of the onrushing Leibold. Wright scampered in before he could even look up and the Pirates had the shocking lead!

And then we were left with Babe Adams, sweeping the debris off Griffith's soiled floor. Rice popped to third. Bluege singled, to at least save him from suicide after his earlier stooge-moment, but not even manager Harris could muster a hit this time, grounding into an easy force for out number two. Peckinapaugh was lifted for young Lance Richbourg, triple-hitting star of Game One, for it is the young and fiery that always produce hope.

But Richbourg bounced right back to Adams, who floated the ball over to Grimm, who threw the ball and his mitt and his hat so high it still hasn't come down and the Pirates charged onto the field and lifted Adams on their shoulders and no one could believe what had just happened.

And yet it did. And we are all richer for having experienced it. For it is the fate of many a tragic ball hero to die on his home battlefield, his brother-in-bats lying about him, staring at the cold autumn sky and already dreaming of spring.

PGH 000 003 022 - 7 10 2
WAS 013 101 000 - 6 14 1
   W-Adams L-Russell GWRBI-Wright

* * *

Well, Rachel let me read a copy of her story as we got back on the train, and I was pretty knocked out by it. I told her it was a good thing she was giving up novel-writing because it seemed she had a better future with this kind of thing, but that sort of insulted her so I apologized right away.

Cal and me and Benny ended up watching the second half of the game from a pretty good spot near the left field pole, and Benny even met a girl ball fan from Philadelphia who he got onto the return train with him. Butterworth was my friend again, because the game was so gripping that by the end we'd even forgot we'd had an argument. All in all, it was an incredible Series, with three of the games decided by one run and not even one homer being hit. He was taking a different train back to Detroit so we gave each other hearty handshakes and wished him the best for next season, even though he wasn't clear what he was going to be doing yet.

I didn't either, but then I thought maybe me and Rachel picking up different baseball writing jobs wasn't the worst idea. "Uh-uh," she said, as the express back to New York started pulling out, "I don't think all the train travel and late nights would be the best thing for me."

"How come?"

She squeezed my hand and looked in my eyes. "Because I'm with child, Vinny."

I stared at her a long second, then looked around the train car. "A child? Where?"

"No, dummy. " She put my hand on her belly. "In here."

I couldn't breathe. I know this sounds real weird, people, but suddenly, at that moment, I just wanted to be back in Mrs. Crackerbee's class, reciting multiplication.

AFTERWORDS

Thanks go out to Tom Baker and Lou Siegel, Tom for his early belief in the concept and coming up with the name Tuggerheinz, Lou for his constant tweaking tips and heartfelt devotion to the Web site. Internet scribes Mike Lynch and Craig Calcaterra provided early encouragement by linking their readers to the site before anyone else, and Scott Simkus deserves a special mention for creating the magical Negro Leagues card set that helped get me through a season largely devoid of a pennant race, and for enduring an online interview with me. Google and their endless archive of fabulous images also deserve thanks.

Last but not least, *1924 and You Are There!* would not have been possible without the love, support, and tolerance of my incredible wife Carmen, who actually designed a desk extension just for my Strat-O-Matic games when we built our new office.

And so, to Vinny, Cal, Rachel, Benny, Mama, the Over-the Rhine Boys and kids outside Navin Field, to Cy, Oscar, Rube, Heinie, the Babe, Kiki, Goose, Walter, and I suppose even Ty...it's not been real.

—J.P.,
Culver City, CA

ABOUT THE AUTHOR

 JEFF POLMAN is a journalist, screenwriter, and baseball blogger. He has written for *The Huffington Post*, *The Hardball Times*, *Seamheads*, and other Web sites. *1924 and You Are There!* is adapted from the first of his four fictional replay blogs, which include *Play That Funky Baseball*, *The Bragging Rights League*, and his latest, *Mysteryball '58*. He is a lifelong Red Sox fan and resides with his wife and son in Culver City, CA.